WRECKAGE
A NOVEL

WRECKAGE

A NOVEL

EMILY BLEEKER

Text copyright © 2015 Emily Bleeker

Published by Lake Union Publishing, Seattle

www.apub.com

Amazon, the Amazon logo, and Lake Union Publishing are trademarks of Amazon.com, Inc., or its affiliates.

ISBN-13: 9781477821930

ISBN-10: 1477821937

Cover design by Shasti O'Leary-Soudant / SOS CREATIVE LLC

Library of Congress Control Number: 2014916226

Printed in the United States of America

To my husband, Joe—You are my best friend, my confidant, and the one person I'd love to be stranded with on a deserted island.

CHAPTER 1

LILLIAN

Present

Sometimes you have to lie. Sometimes it's the only way to protect the ones you love. Lillian replayed the phrase in her head, fiddling with her wedding ring. She'd said it every day for the last eight months. Maybe today she'd believe it. *The only way*, Lillian repeated, spinning the plain gold band around her finger, once for each lie that she'd told. Losing track for the third time in a row, she shoved her hand under her thigh to keep from counting again. If only it were harder to lie, maybe she could stop. But lying was easy. Well, easier than telling the truth.

And no crying, she coached herself firmly. She'd had her fill of crying in front of total strangers. Today she was determined to show the world her strong side, not her ugly-cry face. No one wants to see that. Plus, crying would ruin the makeup coated all over her face. It was more than she'd worn in years, and a nice young lady named Jasmine was smearing on another layer.

When Jasmine pulled out a large pink aerosol can, spraying till Lillian's hair could be labeled a fire hazard, it seemed she was finished. Stepping back to examine the final product, the girl shrugged her shoulders as if to say, *That's as good as it's gonna get.* Not exactly confidence boosting.

As the makeup girl bounced away, Lillian sat quietly, examining her manicured burgundy nails, feeling like she was playing dress-up. A tomboy as a kid and now a mother of two boys, she never thought much of makeovers, but she couldn't deny the allure of pretending to be a whole new person. If she couldn't be the old Lillian and she couldn't stand her new self, then fake Lillian was probably the best option.

The house, like Lillian, had also been transformed in preparation for the film crew. After a week of cleaning on her own, Lillian finally gave up and hired a service that left the two-story colonial immaculate. Of course, it took a pair of production assistants less than five minutes to decide it was all wrong.

They'd burst through the front door just after sunrise. Too nervous to eat breakfast, Lillian watched in silence as one of the high-strung assistants, the one who smelled of coffee and tobacco, ran from room to room collecting every single family picture on display throughout the house. After moving the antique wingback chairs from the study to either side of the Lindens' upright piano in the living room, they strategically placed the pictures across the piano's lid.

Blowing a piece of crackly hair from her eyes, Lillian studied the photos' final positions. The family portrait from the main hall replaced the floral canvas that used to hang above the piano, and the picture of Jerry and the boys from Josh's nightstand nestled against the silver-framed picture of Lillian holding hands with two little boys wearing backpacks.

She looked like a stranger in that photo. How long had it been? Three, maybe four years? That long brown hair tumbling around her face and a real smile lending brightness to her emerald eyes. Her skin back then was creamy as buttermilk, with freckles tossed across her nose like cinnamon. If Lillian met that woman at a PTA meeting, she'd want to have her over for a playdate and ice cream. She looked happy. Two frames over was a picture from the upstairs hall. It was taken several months ago when Jerry realized they hadn't sat for a family portrait together since . . . since she came home. Jerry picked out the final prints because Lillian wanted to pass on it. They turned out horrible. The boys looked uncomfortable in their matching ties and Jerry's arm seemed to hover around Lillian like he couldn't bear to touch her. Now it was going to be on national television. Everyone would see the two Lillians, side by side, before and after. The "after" Lillian cut off her long hair and clipped her bangs away from her face. Her smile was tight, forced, and her eyes were no longer the color of emeralds but the pale green of jade.

Lillian imagined walking over to the piano and shoving every last one of those photos onto the floor. It would only take one sweep of her arm to get them all. They'd crash to the ground in a pile of glass and glossy paper. Biting her top lip, she held back an amused smile. Even visualizing it was so satisfying, but the last thing she wanted to do right now was draw more attention to herself.

To avoid further violent fantasies, Lillian shifted her gaze away from the line of frames filled with smiling faces and focused on searching the piano for dust. The mahogany surface was a magnet for dirt, and the smell of the orange oil she'd rubbed over it still hung in the air. Lillian loved that piano. Just before Josh was born, she'd practically forced Jerry to buy it. He laughed at her since neither of them could play a note, but she had insisted. The piano wasn't for them; it was for the baby growing inside her, for Josh and then Daniel.

Lillian shook her head. No wonder that young mother in the pictures smiled so easily. She didn't know yet that sometimes life makes different choices than you do. Stupid life.

The heavy oak front door banged open, making Lillian jump. A tall, fine-boned woman in a tan suit barged through as if she'd lived there her whole life. Lillian watched her with fascination. She'd recognize that face anywhere: the long, thin nose and high, hollow cheekbones, her blonde hair moving like a helmet of styled straw, and those eyes, so light blue they almost faded away. They all belonged, unmistakably, to Genevieve Randall from *Headline News*. Lillian and Jerry used to watch the news program every Friday night, arguing playfully about the real-life sagas Ms. Randall narrated on the screen. She was even thinner in real life. *Great. The camera really does add ten pounds.* Lillian sucked her stomach roll behind her belt.

The crew snaked a mic through the back of the investigative reporter's coat jacket and shirt, then clipped it discreetly on her lapel. Lillian was impressed at how well Genevieve Randall ignored the hands grasping around inside her blouse. She shuffled through a deck of notecards until they finished. Then, she straightened her suit coat, fluffing the white silk blouse that peeked out through the vee of her lapels. Snatching up a few more papers, she stacked them into a neat pile before resting her ghostly gaze on Lillian.

For a brief moment it felt as though the reporter was staring through her, or more like into her, like she could see all of the secrets lined up inside Lillian's mind. It made Lillian want to wrap her arms around her body to ward off the X-ray eyes.

"Mrs. Linden," Genevieve Randall called from across the room, her voice echoing in the two-story-high entryway. "It's so good to see you in person. Thank you for agreeing to talk to us today." Her red-soled stilettos clacked loudly on the wood floor as she crossed to the second wingback chair, across from Lillian.

How does Genevieve Randall know me? Lillian wondered briefly. Then she remembered. Everyone knew who Lillian Linden was; her face had been all over the TV off and on for the past two and a half years. It was a fact that still took her by surprise.

Genevieve Randall sat down in the chair like a feather falling, immediately assuming the reporter position: back straight, shoulders relaxed, and a flashing smile on her face. "It's such a pleasure to meet you, Mrs. Linden," the reporter said, extending a hand with long, thin fingers.

"Likewise," Lillian whispered, pressing on a nervous smile, shaking the cold hand, hoping her lingering calluses didn't scratch Ms. Randall's baby-soft skin.

"I was excited when my producer green-lighted this project." Ms. Randall folded her hands demurely over a stack of papers in her lap. "I've followed your story from the beginning. I can't wait to hear it from your point of view."

"Well, thank you for coming." Lillian shifted in her seat.

"My pleasure. Now, we'll get started in a few minutes. And please remember, when I'm interviewing you try to feel comfortable. Answer the questions like we're friends sitting down for a cup of coffee. Okay?"

"Remember that list of questions I sent you? I plan on sticking to those, so no surprises. All I need from you is to be as descriptive and accurate as possible in your responses. Does that seem manageable?" She smiled, her teeth whitened so often they bordered on see-through.

"I . . . I'll do my best." Sweat beaded on Lillian's forehead, threatening to drip down and ruin her makeup mask.

"And you *do* understand that this is an exclusive interview? After signing our contract, you can't accept any other offers."

"I understand completely." Lillian chewed on the inside of her cheek. The exclusivity clause in her contract was the only reason she'd agreed to an interview with *Headline News*. That little phrase was her escape hatch out of the media circus that had become her life. If she could get through this one interview, she'd finally be safe.

"Okay. Had to get the legal stuff out of the way." Genevieve glanced around. "Now, where's your husband, Mrs. Linden? Jerry? I was hoping to talk to him once we're finished."

"He's upstairs getting ready." Lillian brought her thumb up to nibble on the nail but stopped when she remembered the shiny polish.

"I told him he didn't have to watch my whole interview. It's easier for both of us that way."

"That's fine. This is about you. Whatever makes you the most comfortable is what I want. How about the kids?" The cap of a chunky red Sharpie clacked against her teeth as she reviewed her notes.

"At the neighbor's house," Lillian said, eyes narrowing. "I thought I made it clear I didn't want them involved." The kids had gone through too much already. No more interviews. She and Jerry agreed on that a long time ago.

Genevieve glanced up. "No, no, I was hoping we could get one family shot at the end. Don't worry, Lillian, no questions."

"Okay, maybe *one* shot." Cameras were fairly commonplace for Josh and Daniel the past few years. They probably wouldn't notice one clicking away in the background.

"All right, I'm almost ready here," Genevieve snapped expectantly to the man with the headphones. "My questions, Ralph."

The young guy with dusty-blond hair and oversize black-rimmed glasses who'd rearranged all Lillian's pictures ran toward the reporter, staring at the ground like a dog dominated by his alpha. She flipped some rumpled pages scrawled with ink into the intern's hand, then resumed going through her stack of cards.

"Run over those notes with Steve before we get this going," Genevieve Randall ordered. The young man slinked away in submission. Lillian was sufficiently intimidated.

After running a sound check with the crew, Ralph helped Lillian check her mic and then called Jasmine in for a last-minute touch-up on both women, though Lillian was sure it was purely for her benefit. Then everything became eerily still with Genevieve the only one in motion. Smoothing her already perfect hair, she said, "Roll tape." The cameras were on.

"Five, four, three, two, one . . . interview with Lillian Linden."

CHAPTER 2

LILY-DAY 1

Fiji

The doors open easily, and the moist heat of Fiji floods in and mingles with the stale air-conditioning from inside the small airport. I take a deep breath. The smell of cooled air escaping into the atmosphere is apparently same in all parts of the world.

"Well, Lillian, look at us, a couple of jet-setters." Margaret slips her age-spotted hand into the crook of my arm, rushing us toward a tiny jet appearing on the horizon. "I wish you would've worn something a little more . . . appropriate for the occasion."

Back at the resort I had thrown on a pair of cutoff jeans and a worn green tank top over my swimsuit two minutes before the limo arrived. I'd barely slipped on my ratty Nikes as the bellhop tossed my bags in the car. No one but Margaret cares what we look like in Fiji. I could walk down the beach naked and the cabana boys would just ask me if I wanted a refill on my cocktail.

We've been in Fiji a week already and I haven't carried my own bag once. Everyone seems to be on strict orders to treat us like celebrities. Between the crazy amounts of food and the compulsory lack of exercise, I might return home twenty pounds heavier.

"Sorry, Margaret, it's all I had clean. No one told me there's a dress code."

"It's not a dress code, it's a sense of self-respect. If you can't do it for yourself, please at least think of me. Would it hurt to put on a touch of makeup or put up your hair?" She flips her own hair as if to illustrate the kind of work one should put into her appearance. "You have such a pretty face, why don't you let others see that?" Dozens of comebacks dance on my tongue but I don't say anything. I never do.

"I have some makeup in my bag. I'll put some on when we sit down if that'll make you feel better." Margaret cringes, glancing at my grungy blue JanSport from college, which is my version of a purse. It totally drives Margaret crazy. I have a closet full of purses she's given me over the nine years Jerry and I have been married, each one an effort to lure me away from the pack. I might use them for special occasions but I never use them around Margaret; it's my super-passive-aggressive way of saying she's not in charge of me.

"Yes, dear, thank you." Shockingly, she doesn't comment on the bag this time. "I think you'll find it makes *you* feel better as well." She pats my arm emphatically and I swallow my words. They go down harder every time.

Margaret now seems born for this lifestyle, not that she's ever lived it. As a young widow of a deputy in rural Iowa, she was a bargain shopper and coupon clipper. But in the past week she's mastered the art of waving toward the luggage and slipping a tip through gently touched fingers.

Today she's dressed in all white, wearing an outfit that looks like it's from 1983. She definitely looks more prepared for a ladies' lunch than a plane trip, but she thinks it's the height of fashion. Aside from the suit, she looks pretty cute. Her hair's teased into a halo of creamy honey, sunglasses resting casually on the bridge of her nose. When she smiles, the delicate wrinkles on her cheeks emphasize the powdery sheen of makeup she carefully applied this morning.

"Now, here we are." She gasps.

Up close, the jet's even less impressive. A red-and-blue racing stripe runs down the side, making the plane look more like a prop in a movie than a machine we're supposed to fly in. It's small, much smaller than I would've guessed a jet would be. I count three windows trailing out toward the tail and no discernible cargo area.

The daily agenda slipped under our door this morning said we'd be on this plane for nearly four and a half hours. Some guy from Carlton Yogurt is supposed to meet us on the plane and escort us to the "private island." Four hours with my mother-in-law and a complete stranger? I might need to grab one of Margaret's sleeping pills to get through the trip.

There are only three stairs to climb to reach the entrance of the tiny gray jet. Margaret marches up the steps first and I don't resist. This has been her vacation from the start, so I go with the flow. It works for both of us; she gets her way most of the time, and, as a trade-off, I don't go insane.

When she called and told us she won a free trip to Fiji from a sweepstakes she'd entered, I didn't believe her. I thought she'd been snookered by a fast-talking salesman. She lives four hours away from us in a retirement community in The Middle of Nowhere, Iowa, and Margaret's the only person in the world who looks forward to getting calls from telemarketers.

I really *do* love Margaret, in my own way, but that doesn't mean she's an easy lady to get along with. Before coming to Fiji I thought of this vacation the way I think of a trip to the gynecologist: necessary but uncomfortable. But Jerry thought I needed a break from my life as a mom and Margaret thought it would be good "bonding"—so here I am.

Thank goodness I listened. Fiji is pure bliss, even with Margaret attached to my hip. I don't know if it's the perfect weather or the intoxicating scent of flowers in the air, but something is different about her, about us. Without Jerry and the boys around, Margaret's "suggestions" on how to be the perfect wife and mother are at a minimum. As a result I'm finding it much easier to enjoy paradise than I originally thought.

Ducking my head through the curved doorway, I turn a little corner and take in the interior of the plane. The first thing I notice are five flawless leather seats, two lined up one behind the other on each side of a small aisle and one more in the rear middle. Margaret squeezes past our flight attendant, who's quietly milling around in the front of the plane, and heads toward the second row of seats. There are TV screens on the back of every seat and enough snacks and drinks for Daniel's whole kindergarten class. Looks like I was wrong. This is traveling in style. I mean, food *and* television? That's my kind of vacation.

I should've trusted Janice, the Carlton rep. She kept telling us that the second half of our trip's supposed to be amazing. She's never actually been to Adiata Beach. Her boss usually goes on both parts of the trip, but he couldn't make it for the first week this year, our week in Fiji. They had a huge drawing in the PR department to see who'd go instead and Janice won. I'm bummed she won't be with us now, but she says her boss is a nice enough guy. There's no way he's going to make me laugh like Janice did; that lady was hilarious. She gave me her e-mail address so we can keep in touch.

"Excuse me, miss, could I have some water, please?" Margaret shouts toward the front of the plane before plopping down in her seat.

"Margaret," I whisper, "I can get it."

"No, dear, this is her job. Let her do it," she says, embarrassingly loud.

A tall sandy-blonde woman strolls down the aisle. Fine lines surrounding her eyes and mouth make her seem as friendly as she sounds.

"Hey there, hon, what can I do for ya?" Her voice is coated in a honeyed Southern drawl.

"You can get me water, bottled if possible? No ice. Just a cup." Margaret pauses to consider something silently. "I hope the water's chilled already?"

"Of course."

"Good. Lillian, tell this nice woman what you want."

"I'm fine, thank you." The last thing I want to do is make the flight attendant's life harder. She has Margaret for that.

"She'll have what I'm having," Margaret says with an air of authority that keeps me from arguing further.

As the flight attendant sways to the front of the plane, I stick my hand in the front zippered pocket of my JanSport, my book pocket. It's the perfect size for any type of novel, though certain types of Russian literature might stretch it beyond usefulness. By the time I get my book out and flip to the first page, the attendant's back.

This lady's either really good at her job or clairvoyant. She gives Margaret extra napkins, a pillow, and a blanket. She'd probably give Margaret prime rib if she asked for it, which thankfully she doesn't. Hands on the chairs to either side, the flight attendant assesses us both.

"If you ladies need anything else, my name's Theresa. Give me a holler."

Margaret nods, too busy untwisting a child safety cap and sorting through a rainbow of pills to respond. She pops two small white circles in her mouth and swallows. That will knock her out for a few hours at least.

"Thank you." I attempt to salvage an iota of politeness. Theresa nods, apparently more amused than offended.

"We should have a smooth flight ahead of us; I'm sure you'll sleep well. Night, honey," Theresa coos to Margaret, then thrusts a frosty water bottle at me. "Here ya go."

"Thanks." I toss it into the open zipper of my backpack for later.

"No problem, hon—that *is* my job, after all." Her eyes twinkle and I know she heard Margaret earlier. "Now sit back and relax. Dave should be here soon and we can get on our way."

"Dave?" The name sounded familiar. "Is that the pilot?"

She shakes her head; stiff wheat-colored strands tickle her face. "No, Dave's the yogurt guy. Don't worry, he's nice, kinda cute too."

"Dave Hall?" I think that was the name Janice told me.

"Yes, ma'am, that's the one."

CHAPTER 3

DAVE

Present

The call came at 5:30 a.m. Dave lay in bed lingering between sleep and consciousness, his eyes snapping open at the first ear-piercing ring. Way. Too. Early. The phone rested on a short black table by his side of the bed.

He glanced at his wife, still sound asleep with her black satin eye mask and earplugs snugly in place. Dave used to think that only people in movies slept that way, and then he met Beth. She had more requirements for a good night's sleep than anyone in *The Princess and the Pea*. It used to annoy him, but he was starting to find it endearing.

The phone rang again. Despite the earplugs, Beth stirred and shoved one of the pillows over her head. Tight golden curls spilled out from underneath. Their bed had more blankets than anyone's in hot, sunny LA. Beth kept the air at sixty-five, thumbing her nose at the environmentalists and freezing her husband in the process. Shaking his head to clear it, Dave grasped for the phone before it rang again.

"Hello," he answered, his voice raspy with sleep.

"Hello, I'm calling for David Hall. Is he available?"

A telemarketer. His thoughts quickly turned stormy. "It's FIVE a.m. and I'm sure I don't want what you're selling. Please take me off your list and never call again," Dave growled.

Before he slammed the receiver down, the voice continued. "Sir, please wait. Lillian Linden told me to call you."

Dave paused, then placed the phone back on his ear. "What did you say?" His heart beat unsteadily in a combination of abating fury and budding curiosity.

"Uh, I'm from *Headline News*. I'm calling with a message from Lillian Linden." The voice was young and very nervous.

Dave turned in his bed and sat up slowly, grasping the phone closer to his ear. Shivering as his bare feet hit the wood floor, he tiptoed deftly to the master bathroom attached to their room. After closing the door with a little click, Dave let his voice rise to full volume.

"Listen, I don't know who you are but I have my number unlisted for a reason. I've given you people all you wanted—interviews, photo ops, appearances. I want you to leave me and my family alone," Dave snarled.

"I don't think you understand, Mr. Hall, I'm calling you with Mrs. Linden's permission. *She* gave me your number."

"Ha, yeah right." Dave snorted. "Lillian gave you my number? Suuure. You know what, kid? You're lower than dirt to bring her into this. Don't you think she's been through enough already? Give me your editor or producer or whoever your boss is, 'cause I'm going to do my best to get you fired."

Silence echoed from the phone. Dave started to think the kid hung up when he heard faint voices in the background, then the rustling of a phone changing hands.

"Hello, is this Mr. Hall? Mr. David Hall?" A man's voice this time, definitely boss-like.

"Yes, and who am I speaking with?" Dave put on his most businesslike voice, the one he used when speaking to management types at work.

"My name is Bill Miller. I'm a producer over here at *Headline News*. I understand you want to speak with me."

"Yes, sir. I don't know who that kid was, but like I told him—I don't do any more interviews or appearances. I've made an effort to return to anonymity and would like to continue down that road. I'd appreciate in the future if you forgot my name and phone number ever existed," he said, gritting his teeth. "Especially at FIVE o'clock in the morning!"

"I'm incredibly sorry, sir." Bill Miller sighed. "Ralph, my production intern, failed to realize that you're in California while we're in *New York* and didn't account for the *time difference*." Bill emphasized the words, probably for pathetic little Ralph's benefit.

"Okay, okay. The time was a misunderstanding, but still, that Ralph kid gave me a line about getting my number from Lillian Linden. I know that's a lie. I don't know how you found my number but I think I've made it extremely clear. I don't want to do any further interviews with the press."

Bill paused awkwardly. "Well, Mr. Hall, I'm sorry to tell you that Mrs. Linden *did* provide us with your telephone number. She agreed to participate in a *Headline News* exclusive dedicated to telling your whole story."

Dave's mouth opened but no words came out. Lillian caved? They hadn't talked in months but this kind of news definitely merited a "heads-up" phone call. Of course, she wouldn't be sharing the "whole story" as Mr. Miller put it. Dave wasn't afraid of that. But offering up an exclusive interview to a notoriously aggressive news show? Beyond confusing.

Dave ran a shaking hand through his bed-head hair, an enormous knot twisting inside him. He wanted more than anything to call her, to hear her billowing laugh and know she's happy. He was dying to hear about the boys, about her new life, about . . . but he knew that was an impossibility. No contact. That was the deal.

"I'm sorry, Mr. Miller, you seem like a nice enough guy but I'm not interested." He tried to sound certain. "I don't want to get back into that spotlight and neither does my family. You'll have to do this one without me."

A low chuckle crackled through the receiver. "You know, she said you'd say that. Almost word for word too. Crazy."

A begrudging smile snuck onto Dave's face. Lily always did have the uncanny ability to predict his thoughts before they'd even entered his mind. It wasn't possible to count how many times he'd jokingly accused her of being psychic. Dave's heart filled with a strange cocktail of happiness and longing. This was why he didn't talk about her, about their time together.

"Well, you can tell her she was right. Good-bye, Mr. Miller."

Miller rushed to interject. "Mr. Hall, please, there's one more thing. Mrs. Linden, she asked me to give you a message when you said no."

Would this conversation never end? "Fine, tell me, but then I'm hanging up."

"She said," Bill Miller cleared his throat, stalling. "Um . . . well . . . She wanted me to say, 'You owe me.'"

Those words struck Dave like a slap in the face. He grasped for the counter to steady himself.

Suddenly he couldn't push the red End button; he couldn't form words to say all the nasty things he'd been compiling in his head. He could only sit there, unable to speak, because what this man said was right. Dave did owe Lillian, more than anyone but the two of them would ever know.

CHAPTER 4

DAVID-DAY 1

Fiji

The weather's perfect. Palm trees sway rhythmically and the glassy blue water winks at me in the sunlight, trying to entice me down to its edge. And here's me, not giving a crap.

I'm wearing the same clothes I put on over twenty-four hours ago, and the fancy brown leather shoes Beth gave me for Christmas last year are pinching my toes with every step on the sticky blacktop. But that's nothing compared to the torture waiting for me on that plane.

I know it annoys Janice and my other coworkers, but I despise Fiji and Adiata Beach. It has nothing to do with the actual cluster of islands in the middle of the South Pacific. It has more to do with being at the beck and call of entitled strangers for two full weeks—usually old people. And once I walk into that cramped little jet, I have to pretend to like these people.

I don't know what it says about Carlton Yogurt that the past five winners of the Dream Trip have been over the age of seventy. At least that ad campaign about "increasing regularity" with special probiotics is working. Note to self: find a new job with a young, hip company like Pixar or Apple. I wouldn't get a trip to Fiji every year but I also wouldn't have to talk about how often old people poop.

I think I've been turned off on the South Pacific for life, because now when I come to Fiji I can't consider anything other than what kind of babysitting I'll have to endure this year. At least this time it's only one week.

That's my mantra: it's only one week, it's only one week. I repeat it with every step up the rickety metal staircase into the jet's cabin. Squinting, I see Theresa come into focus, her hair impeccable despite the heat. I'm sure half a can of Aqua Net's responsible. It's nice to see a familiar face, though, and hers is always such a friendly one.

"Hey there, Dave, good to see you again!" she greets me. "Heard you just joined us, glad you made it for the best part. Private tropical island, all inclusive resort—honey, I wish I knew how to get your job."

I cringe. Thankfully she doesn't notice, too busy taking my carry-on bag and stowing it in a compartment near the cockpit. Turning around, she tilts her head toward the cockpit door, her sweet Southern drawl lowering to a whisper. "Instead I gotta deal with Captain Kent Grabby-Hands up there."

"You and Kent aren't together anymore, I take it?" She didn't seem to mind Kent's roaming hands last year, when they were living together.

She shakes her head. "No, but his hands haven't caught on to that fact." She laughs at her own joke before changing the subject. "So, how's the baby? Any pictures?"

The word "baby" sends needles right through my chest. "No baby, Theresa. Not yet."

Turning around on her stubby blue heels, the corners of her mouth tug down like someone's forcing a frown on her naturally cheerful face. "I'm sorry, Dave. I thought . . . you said you and your wife were trying

for a baby two trips ago, and then last year you said you were going to
do that in-vitro stuff so I assumed . . ."

Why did I ever tell people we were "trying" to have a baby? At first
they made jokes and jabbed me with knowing elbows. Now there's
only pity.

"The in vitro didn't work either. We're trying one last thing and
then . . ." I shrug, not knowing what comes next. If I felt like spilling
every detail of my personal life I'd tell her Beth's in premature menopause and we are using donor eggs. I would say that I want to explore
adoption, but Beth's obsessed with the idea of being pregnant. But I
don't say anything because she won't understand. No one can.

"I'm sorry, Dave, I didn't know," she says, like she's greeting family
and friends at a funeral.

"It's fine." I squeeze the handle of my computer bag once, twice.
"So, I should probably say hi to Captain You Know Who."

She taps her long fuchsia nails on a small door marked Emergency, the plastic making a hollow sound with each clack. "Sure, hon,
you go ahead. I'll take your drink order when you're done."

Thankfully, she turns and walks away without trying to make any
further attempts at an apology. Spending time with strangers might be
exactly what I need. I knock softly on the thin metal door to the cockpit. When no one answers, I swing it open.

"Hey, sweetheart, get me some coffee would ya?" Kent says, without turning around. "Oh, and check where Mr. PR is. We gotta get out
of here in the next ten or we'll be waiting in line for an hour." His bald
spot's doubled since I saw him a year ago and his remaining blond hair
is buzzed short. It's not a good look. That shouldn't make me happy,
but it does.

I clear my throat and he takes in my arrival without a hint of
embarrassment. I don't think Kent knows what embarrassment is.
"Hey there, man, glad you made it. Now go sit down so we can get in
the air, and close the door for me, would ya?"

Conversation over. Why I try to be social with that caveman I'll never know. Shoving the door shut I try to squeeze away the annoyance, crushing the handle on my bag again, and again. Still not working.

Shuffling down the narrow hall toward the cabin, I can't help but smile. I've spent dozens of hours on this plane over the past few years. Now it's familiar, almost homey. All of the little flaws are dear to me, like the hairline crack in the lavatory door, the overhead light in the rear of the plane that's been burned out for two years straight.

Besides those tiny irregularities that only someone familiar with the plane could point out, the interior's nothing special. Five tan leather seats and full-size fold-down tables accessible to each of the front chairs, small screens that make you think a movie will be shown in flight. It won't, but the illusion's perfect for the contest winners. It's like flying in a fancy shoebox and, as much as I hate this whole trip, I'd rather be here than at home.

"You know the drill, hon: Pick any seat you like, fasten your seat belt, and turn off all your gadgets till we're in the air. Let me know if there's anything you need. We have some snacks and refreshments in the front. Otherwise, relax."

"Thanks, Theresa." I'm only half paying attention because I've homed in on the winners. I push my computer bag under the first seat in the front row as Theresa makes her way up to the front of the plane, keeping one eye on the women in the second row. On the left, an older lady with puffy light-brown hair is already snoring. Must be Margaret Linden.

I was given a brief file on each of the women from Janice to help catch up after my late start, so I know a few things about Margaret: she's the winner of the trip, she's elderly (shocker), she lives in Iowa, and she elected to bring her daughter-in-law, Lillian, as her plus one.

Across the aisle, a younger woman leans against the window with the shade pushed fully open. She's holding a book, but it dips beneath the seat in front of her so I can't read the title. I wish I knew what she was reading. It has her so engrossed she doesn't seem to notice how her brown hair tumbles down over her makeup-free face, already tan from a week on the beach. The sun hits her in this perfect way, like she's bathed in artificial lighting for a movie. My mouth goes bone dry—she's beautiful.

Just my luck. I'm really good with old ladies, lots of practice I guess, but attractive women get me all anxious and jittery, and I say incredibly stupid things to them. To think I was just complaining about the elderly.

My pulse pounds at my temples. Hopefully I remembered to toss Tylenol in my bag, or maybe Theresa has some. Rubbing the sides of my head, I try to remember what was in her file: *30-year-old female, Margaret's daughter-in-law, stay-at-home mom.* I hadn't even glanced at her passport photo. Eventually I'll have to talk to her, but not right now. Right now I need meds, stat. I yank at my bag, the pain in my head getting worse the longer I'm leaning over. Finally it pops out and I shuffle my feet to keep from falling over. Could this day get any worse? Plopping the bulging leather bag onto my seat, I unzip the front pocket. If the medicine is going to be anywhere, it'll be here.

My hands rifle through random office clutter, pens, scraps of paper, and a surprising amount of pennies, and I swear under my breath. If I'd just get organized like Beth always tells me to, I wouldn't be in this mess. Damn it. I'm zipping the pocket closed with more force than necessary when I notice bright green eyes staring at me. The "plus one." Her lips pucker like she's holding in a laugh, and she waves like we're old friends meeting again after a long separation, making me panic for a moment. No—I'd remember that smile, or at least I'd remember the way it makes my palms sweat and elbows tingle.

Putting a finger to her lips she points to sleeping Margaret Linden and mouths, "Later."

"Okay," I say, giving a stupid little thumbs up. I'm so bad at this.

When she returns to her novel, I sink into my seat, putting the laptop on my thighs. My head's so full of conflicting thoughts, I jump slightly when the computer chimes on.

I don't know how it's possible to long for home and be glad I'm away from it at the same time, but it is. Part of me craves Beth. I want to find a strand of her hair tangled in the button of my shirt in the middle of the day, or hear the front door open and know by the cadence of her footsteps that she's home. Yet, sitting here, alone with a computer full of e-mails, I'm freer than I have been in months.

I never imagined trying to have a baby could be so stressful. It's something *so* easy that other people do it accidentally, but, apparently, too difficult for us to manage. I rub the bridge of my nose hard, as if I could rub out those memories—the months of arguments, the temperature readings and charts and negative pregnancy tests. I need to forget, because right now there are three little embryos getting all cozy in Beth's uterus. If they all take, we could have triplets. Triplets. I know the idea should scare me but it doesn't.

It's good I'm here, to get some space between us so the air can clear before I get home. After the blood test we can make new plans. If the embryos fail, there's a chance Beth will be willing to give up on her obsession with pregnancy. We could talk about adoption again. After all, the most important thing is to have a child; I'm dying to be a dad. This break might be the best thing that's ever happened to us.

The phone buzzing in my pants pocket makes me jump. Thank goodness I switched it to vibrate on my last flight or Mrs. Linden would've been rudely awakened by my AC/DC ringtone. It's probably Mr. Janus, making sure I made it to the plane on time. Before putting the phone to my ear, I see Theresa peek her head into the cabin and frown.

"Two minutes," she mouths as the phone buzzes again. I nod and push the Talk button.

"Hello?"

"Dave?" Beth answers, her voice gravelly and swollen.

"Hey there. What's up?"

"I needed to hear your voice." She sighs a little, like hearing me talk gave her relief. "Last night was the worst night of my whole life and I've been wishing you were here to help." Her voice catches in her throat and makes me sit up a little straighter.

"What happened, Beth?"

"I'm so sorry, Dave . . . I don't know what's wrong with me. I . . . I started bleeding last night and went to the doctor this morning. He said . . . he said we were losing the embryos." She shoves the words out like unwanted visitors.

I turn toward the window and whisper, "Wha-what do you mean? How in the world did that happen? They said we wouldn't know for another week."

Muffled cries spill out. "I forgot to get my shots."

"What do you mean 'forgot'?" She knew how important those shots were. Her body doesn't make enough hormones to carry our babies. Dr. Hart made that clear.

"I don't know, I forgot. You weren't here to remind me and I've been so busy with work and the shots make me really tired. I just forgot. I told you not to leave. I told you I needed you here."

"How could you *forget* Beth? This isn't like forgetting to feed a dog in the morning, those could have been our babies." *MY babies*, I want to scream, but I hold the words in before they escape. "How many shots did you miss?"

"Three," she whispers.

Three. I don't understand. I've only been gone, what, twenty hours? Not two days, and definitely not three. I was home for two of those "forgotten" injections. I asked her how she felt after each shot, I babied her, made sure she still felt okay. Beth *told* me she visited her nurse friend Stacey every day, that she gave her the shots, that they didn't even hurt. Why did she lie?

I can't breathe. I've never been claustrophobic but this is what it must feel like, like there isn't enough oxygen in the room, like the walls are closing in. Scratching at the top button of my polo, I yank at it, fighting against the one idea I don't want to believe—she did this on purpose. I press my forehead against the cool plastic plane window. The hand holding my phone shakes as I try to calm myself enough to talk.

"Dave, honey, are you there? Please don't be mad at me, please? Come on, baby, talk to me. Please." Her voice grates on my ears.

The plane jerks forward and yanks me back into the present. The doors quietly closed during my conversation. Theresa stands in the passageway between the cockpit and cabin. There's that pitying look again. She points to the cell phone, signaling me to turn it off so we can get in the air.

"I have to go, we're taking off." I'm surprised at the roughness in my voice.

Beth sniffles loudly. "All right. Call me later, okay?"

"Yeah, sure."

"I love you," she whispers.

I can't bring myself to say it back.

CHAPTER 5

LILLIAN

Present

"So tell me, Lillian, why did Margaret choose you to go with her?" Genevieve asked, pushing the story forward.

"She said I deserved a break. We'd never been on a trip together just the two of us so she thought it might be fun." Lillian flipped her hands in conclusion, pretending she'd thought going to Fiji was more important than taking Daniel to his first day of kindergarten.

"The first week in Fiji went off without a hitch?" A well-sculpted eyebrow lifted, inviting detail. Next to the question in Lillian's pamphlet was a note in parentheses that said: *Be descriptive*. She'd practiced with Jerry, telling him all the details of her trip with his mother. When she finished, his eyes filled with tears. He'd never heard the good stories.

"Yeah, the island was beautiful and the people were amazingly kind and friendly. Carlton had someone from their PR department at our service at all times, making sure our vacation was incredible. That first week we went on a helicopter tour of the island, set sail on a sunset cruise, and took scuba diving lessons—or rather I took them while Margaret swam and sunned herself. But really most of the time we spent eating, lounging, and being lazy." An actual smile played on Lillian's face.

"The second week was to be spent where?"

Her smile disappeared and fear and remorse threatened to make her clipped, matter-of-fact voice tremble. "At a private resort in French Polynesia, Adiata something . . . um, Adiata Beach, I think. The company made the arrangements."

"Could you specify what the arrangements were for getting you and your mother-in-law to this island?" Genevieve leaned forward in her seat. She knew this was the important part, the part that would get viewers to tune in.

Swallowing a lump, Lillian swore she could smell the combination of jet fuel and hot asphalt melting in the sun as she answered. "A private jet was chartered for our use."

Then the reporter asked the question she was dreading, the one that would start it all. All the lying.

"What happened on that plane, Lillian?"

Lillian knew what the reporter was hoping for when she took this interview—tears, wailing, and, if she was lucky, some spiritual enlightenment. That's what they all wanted.

"It all started out normal. Margaret took a sleeping pill when we boarded the plane and was sound asleep. Theresa, the flight attendant, took our drink orders, I kept reading, and I think Dave was working. To be honest, it was a quiet trip."

How that word didn't choke on the way out, Lillian would never know. "Honest" wasn't a word that described what Lillian was spinning, but it sounded good. If she was being honest she'd talk about how the three hours confined on that plane suddenly felt like a moment, like a figment of her imagination but also like the last real thing that happened to her. How everything that happened since was like a surreal dream from which she couldn't wake up.

But then again, she never intended to be honest.

Lillian tried to refocus. It wouldn't help her keep on script thinking about what really happened. At this point, she wasn't completely sure herself what the truth was. It was only at night, in the darkness, that she found she couldn't forget. In the dark it would be impossible to listen to Genevieve Randall ask inane questions about the plane, how long before takeoff, what drink she ordered . . . because Lillian knew what was next. It was easier in the daylight.

"Now tell me, Lillian, what was the first sign of distress?"

The hope that flashed in Genevieve's eyes annoyed Lillian. She'd seen it in dozens of interviewers. The worst moment of her life became a reporter's hope for career advancement. The idea smoldered in Lillian's chest, and she took a moment to smooth an invisible crease in her jeans before continuing.

"We were in our seats, about forty-five minutes from reaching the resort, when a loud bang came from the right side of the plane. It felt like someone bumped into us, but I saw nothing but clouds outside the window."

"Hmmm, so what happened next?"

"Theresa, the flight attendant, came out of the galley and told us we'd lost an engine but everything would be fine. She advised us to buckle up and hold on tight and said we'd be there in a little bit."

"That must've been scary," Genevieve said, eyebrows pinched together. If she wasn't Botoxed to her hair roots, her forehead would've wrinkled in faux concern. Each question was more of a wish than a query, and with her head cocked to one side, the reporter looked a bit like a spoiled cocker spaniel begging for a treat.

No treat for you, Pookie, Lillian thought before answering. "I believed Theresa. I mean, I'd never been on any kind of a private jet before and it was her job, so what else was I supposed to think? I put on my seat belt and tried to not worry too much."

Lillian's hand fell into her lap, twitching. It had been months since she'd told the whole elaborate lie, and her brain was working hard to remember all the details in order. The last thing she needed was for Genevieve to notice a discrepancy. The woman was clearly good with details.

"All right then, when did the realization settle in? When did you know you were in real trouble?"

"The plane started to lose altitude and that's when we flew into the storm instead of above it. The turbulence was unbelievable," she murmured. "The captain's voice came over the speaker and told us to brace for impact. I think everything seemed so unreal that I wasn't sure it was actually happening."

"What goes through a person's mind when faced with such a life-threatening situation?"

Lillian stared at her glossy nails, contemplating how much to say, the short dark hair falling over her face making her wish the chestnut strands provided some sort of real protection.

"You think about family, about things left unsaid and undone. Then you think about how to get through it, how to survive."

An annoying smile spasmed on Genevieve's lips. She'd found her first sound bite.

"What was everyone else on the plane doing to prepare for impact? What about your mother-in-law, Margaret?"

"Margaret was shocked awake by the turbulence but still a little dazed. There was an aisle between us, and the noise was unbelievably loud, so we couldn't talk. But until Kent told us to brace for impact I held her hand. I tried to tell her I loved her, I told her we'd be okay. Dave was in front of me. I couldn't see him."

"And then Theresa, what was she doing?"

Theresa. Once, almost three months after returning home, Lillian was on a flight to California when she thought she saw her. The flight attendant had glided up and down the aisle taking drink orders, her wheat-colored hair covering the side of her face.

Lillian had been half asleep on the Valium her psychiatrist prescribed for her first plane trip since the crash. It had been hard to leave Jerry and the boys behind, but he couldn't take off any more time. Jill sat beside her instead.

That's when she had heard Theresa's voice.

"Hey there, hon, what can I get'cha?" The knowing Southern drawl was unmistakable.

"Theresa?" her drugged voice rasped. "Is that you?" In that moment, she almost drowned in a flood of hope and confusion, until the smooth face came into focus.

"No, hon, I'm Jen. But you can call me Theresa if you want to." The flight attendant winked playfully.

"I don't want anything to drink," Lillian slurred. Jill apologized and ordered her some apple juice anyway, and Lillian drifted off to sleep, sure she'd just seen Theresa's ghost.

Lillian shook the hazy memory out of her mind and put on a brave face, preparing for the impending drop on her own personal roller coaster. It was coming, she saw it up ahead, that drop that everyone else seemed to love but her. To Lillian it wasn't invigorating or exciting. It just felt like falling.

"Uh, Theresa was up in the cockpit with Kent, but after the announcement she came back to get buckled in like the rest of us."

Genevieve leaned forward, mock concern on her face. "Lillian, I know this is difficult but please tell me how Theresa died."

CHAPTER 6
LILY-DAY 1

Flight 1261

The flight attendant stands at the front of the plane running through a little spiel about seatbelts and floatation devices but I'm not listening. I'm watching Dave Hall. He leans against the window, staring. I can't see his face. But once, as Theresa mimes putting on an oxygen mask, he rubs his temple and then his face like he's wiping away tears.

Concluding her presentation, Theresa sits down in front of me and buckles her seat belt for takeoff. No one speaks. Dave Hall remains frozen, slouching against the window and staring out into the ocean as we ascend into the sky. The force of takeoff pushes me into the seat and I surrender willingly, taking in one last look at Fiji, the glowing white beaches tracing the rich green center like a strand of pearls. Then there's only water, shimmering sapphire blue.

When we finally level out, I pick up my book again. It's a romance, not my usual, but I only had ten bucks in my pocket and it was the cheapest one there. I'm in the middle of one of those steamy love scenes. Blushing a little, I flip through the chapter, searching for a page free of throbbing body parts.

All I hear in my head, though, are Dave Hall's words on repeat: *Those could have been our babies. How could you forget?* Slapping the cover closed, I sigh and run a hand through the tangled strands of my unbrushed hair. This is going to be a long flight.

A sharp ding sounds. The flight attendant unbuckles and faces our seats.

"Y'all can use your electronics again if you want. Just no phones." She glances at Dave like she wants to say more but instead tiptoes toward the galley.

Time to be distracted, finally. Shoving my backpack out of the way I yank the heavy black laptop bag onto my thighs. Normally I'd never lug a computer with me on a beach vacation but Jerry downloaded some video chat software. I saw the boys on their first day of school and every other day since. It's not the same as being there, but it's definitely a step above the phone.

I dump my silver digital camera out of its bag and hook it up to the computer with a long white cord. I've been e-mailing pictures and stories from our trip for Jerry to read to the kids. I don't get to play the part of adventurer very often in my predictable suburban life, which is fine, but it's also fun to prove to them that I'm more than just a mom.

I think that's why missing Daniel's first day of school has been so hard on me. It's always been this far-off thing, a figurative graduation from my life as a full-time mom. Now that it's actually here I have some decisions to make. Jerry insists that I don't *have* to rush back to work but I'd rather not spend the rest of my days folding laundry and polishing the silver. Jill's been begging me to come back to Stevenson part-time and pick up a few history classes for her, even promising me my old classroom. At least I'd have a better place to put all my Civil War books. But I don't know if I'm ready to be a teacher again. I'd have to deal with teenagers and, even worse, their parents.

Jerry thinks I should go back to college and get the master's I put on the back burner when he started law school, but becoming a student again scares me almost as much as cliff diving. Then again I totally owned that sixty-foot jump on Taveuni Island. What's a little time in grad school compared to that?

Once the pictures start to zip from one electronic device to another, I risk a glance at Dave Hall. He also has a computer on his lap, but he doesn't seem to be watching the glowing blue screen. He's staring at an insignificant spot on the wall in front of him. Why does he look so—broken?

Oh no, I'm feeling the urge to help. I could sit in Theresa's seat. I'd only talk to him for a minute or two. Okay, it probably wouldn't change his life or end world hunger, but if it took that withered-flower look away for even a moment, it would be worth it. Jerry can't stand it when I'm aggressively helpful like this but I can't help it. I was born a fixer and I'll probably die a fixer.

After an extra-long glance at snoozing Margaret, I tiptoe down the aisle toward Theresa's empty seat. My thigh bumps the armrest as I crash into the seat. I muffle a squeal, and when I click the seat belt, Dave Hall glances at me. The surprise on his face says that he expected to find Theresa. Not knowing what else to do, I reach out my hand.

"Hi. My name's Lillian."

He stares at my hand like he's never seen one before. This is a mistake. Before I can fold my hand away, Dave Hall clicks shut his laptop and tucks it under the seat. Then, like he's finally awake after a long night's sleep, he grasps my dangling fingers with a crushing grip. I lean forward, because I'd like to keep my arm in my socket if possible.

"Hi, Mrs. Linden, I'm David Hall." He rushes through the words so fast they begin to slur. "Please call me Dave. I'm here to help your trip be a dream. Anything you need, please feel free to ask." He points his thumb at his chest and actually says, "I'm your man."

"Well, Dave"—I say the name slowly—"I'll be sure to put you on speed-dial in case of emergencies. I just wanted to come up and say hello. I'll let you get back to your work." I would run, but he's still holding my hand.

His face falls and his grip goes limp. "That was kinda cheesy, wasn't it?" Desperation drips from his eyes, into his voice. "I'm very sorry, maybe I should start again."

Apparently I've found a way to make Mr. Hall feel worse. Awesome. I'm *so* not good at this helping people thing.

"Listen," I say, yanking my hand away. "I'll head back to my seat. It was very nice to meet you, Dave."

"Mrs. Linden, please don't go," he calls, putting out a hand to beckon me toward him again. "I'm usually much better at my job." A gold wedding band distracts me, flashing in the light.

It's a lot like Jerry's, the kind you could get at any Sears jewelry department for fifty bucks. Just like Jerry's the years of constant wear faded the previously shiny exterior to a dull finish. I remember when I bought the ring the saleslady said Jerry could bring it in whenever he wanted and have it polished, free of charge. But, as time went by and our marriage was numbered in years instead of days, I came to like the lackluster finish. Every scratch, every ding is another day, another memory of our life together and there's no way I'd ever want that polished away. Why did I have to see that ring? Now I can't run away.

"No, no, please don't feel bad on my account," I say, trying a little bit too hard to make him feel better. "I'll find a spectacular way to embarrass myself before this week's over, and then we'll be even."

He glances at me from the corner of his eye, smiling. "You know, that should've been listed in your file. It would've been a helpful warning."

"My file?" At least he's joking around. "Are you saying you've been spying on me, Mr. PR Guy?"

"No, I'm saying *Carlton Yogurt* has been spying on you. I, on the other hand, am just reading what they gave me. Innocent bystander."

He puts his hands up as if fending off an attack. When he smiles it's like I'm seeing him for the first time. He's probably about as tall as Jerry, pretty average, but seems taller because his nearly black hair curls into a halo on the top of his head, adding an inch or two. His seemingly natural olive complexion is smooth, and dark lashes frame his deep blue eyes.

He's not perfect, though. His nose leans to one side when he smiles and he's definitely carrying a few extra pounds. But he's attractive enough to make me feel a little weird about sneaking up here.

"Innocent bystander my eye." I laugh, swallowing that uneasy feeling. "If you have the pull to be on this trip every year I don't think you're some worker bee." Dave raises a dark eyebrow. "Yeah that's right, I spoke to Janice and she gave me a little file on *you*."

He folds his arms on his armrest, mirroring my pose and making fine sinewy muscles stand out under tan skin. Smirking, he studies me in a way that makes it hard to look at him.

"Well, Lillian," he says, his voice dropping an octave. "I'll show you mine if you show me yours."

All the sound sucks out of the room leaving my ears ringing. Is he flirting with me? It's been so long since a man other than my husband showed some kind of interest in me, I don't remember what it's like and I definitely don't know how to respond. Oh my God, does he think I'm flirting with *him*?

No, no, no! I twist the stone on my wedding ring around my finger three times, working on a way to brush it off, make it a joke. Or do I tell him he's making me uncomfortable, that I'm a married woman? I'm going to be on an island with this man for seven days, so no matter what I do, it's going to end up being awkward.

Then, before I say anything, Dave's face turns red. "I'm sorry, that came out *really* wrong. I didn't mean . . . I mean . . . it sounded like . . . uh . . ." He swipes a hand over his mouth, stunned. "I think I should stop talking now."

I laugh, giddy with relief. "It *did* sound like . . ."

Dave starts to laugh. "For the record, I was *not* hitting on you."

Suddenly the idea seems ridiculous and I can't stop laughing, which escalates quickly until Theresa sticks her head into the cabin, eyebrows raised suspiciously. Our laughs fade into muffled sighs.

"Sorry," I gasp, still out of breath. "I'm in your seat." Tugging at the belt, I let my hair cover my flushed face, embarrassed by the insinuations in her raised eyebrows.

"That's all right, hon, you two seem to be enjoying yourselves," she says with enough innuendo to make me want to shrink and hide in the overhead compartment. "Either of you want a drink?"

I jump at the chance to change the subject. "I'll have anything cold with caffeine in it."

"And you, hon?" She points at Dave, a new sparkle in her eye. "Want a beer?"

"Just water, thanks," Dave says. His troubles have returned, hanging heavily on his slumped shoulders. I'm sure he could use something a lot stronger than water.

Theresa retrieves our drinks at light speed while we pretend not to look at each other. Once we both have plastic cups in our hands, Dave lifts his in my direction.

"To private islands in the middle of paradise," he toasts.

"Cheers," I add, raising my cup to meet his with a light tap.

Dave downs his in one massive gulp and then fiddles with the empty cup. I sip mine slowly, noticing his nails are trimmed short and shiny enough to scream "manicure." This guy is definitely not from Missouri.

"Mrs. Linden," he starts. I study the soda in my cup, hoping he didn't catch me staring.

"Please, call me Lillian. It might get a little confusing with two Mrs. Lindens around." I wait for him to continue but he stares at his cup as if it could speak. "Dave, are you okay?" I whisper.

"Yeah, I'll survive. Seriously, I'm sorry about before, when I was on the phone. I know everyone heard. My wife and I have been trying to . . ."

I put up a palm to stop him. "Dave, you don't have to tell me anything. I didn't come up here to be nosy. I wanted to make sure you were okay."

His mouth closes. Tiny wrinkles ripple through his cheeks in a half smile. "Thank you, Lillian." He glances down at the cup in his hands and I imagine him filling it with the words I stopped him from saying. "I appreciate it. I mean, I should've known. Your file did say something about being a good, helpful person."

Poking his shoulder, I snicker. "You *are* going to show me that file before this week is over." His baritone laugh mingles with mine.

Then we talk as if we've known each other for years. It's not hard to avoid serious topics. I talk about home, Jerry, and the boys and eventually show him every single picture in my wallet. He, in turn, tells me a hilarious story about the '05 Dream Trip winner getting so drunk she tried to seduce him. She also happened to be eighty-two years old. Our conversation flows seamlessly and before I know it the sky is darkening as the sun starts to set, throwing a pink haze on the clouds below us.

"Wow, now *that's* pretty." Dave gazes out his window at the chameleon clouds shifting color and shape down below. Before I can finish admiring the view, there's a loud bang, and the plane lurches to one side. I instinctively duck for cover.

"What in the world was that?"

Lifting my head I see Dave is frozen, peering out of the window. "I . . . I see smoke. I think . . . I think the plane is . . . on fire."

"Dave," I put on my mom voice, "I'm sure everything's fine. Has anyone you've known *ever* been in an airplane crash? No, right? We're going to be okay, I'm sure of it." I sound a little like a preschool teacher explaining to her frightened student that a bumblebee is more afraid of you than you are of it.

But, I'm not sure. Glancing behind me, I check on Margaret. Her head tips toward the aisle, her chest rising and falling regularly. So she can sleep through that crazy bang and turbulence but has to sleep in the master bedroom when she visits 'cause the basement is too noisy? I'm too worried to roll my eyes. Thank God she's wearing her seat belt.

Theresa rushes into the cabin. "I need to tell y'all that we're having a little mechanical problem but luckily we're forty-five minutes away from our destination. Kent thinks everything should be fine. Make sure you all have a seat belt on, and he says we should be peachy." She stops and tips her head to one side. "Hey, is that your laptop, hon?"

She's talking to me. I forgot all about my computer, still sitting on the seat behind me.

"Yeah, it's off, though. I swear I didn't try to use the Internet," I say, suddenly concerned that I somehow caused this.

Theresa laughs. "You did nothing wrong. Just put it under the seat when you get a chance, okay? We might be headed into some . . . turbulence. Nothing serious."

She's almost too calm. Everything doesn't seem anywhere close to "peachy." Something caused an engine to billow smoke and make a noise that shook the whole plane and made my ears ring. What if we don't make it to the airport at all? What if it *is* serious?

Dave doesn't seem satisfied either. "Theresa, what *kind* of mechanical problem are we talking about here?" I can tell he's trying to act calm and collected but the tremor in his voice gives him away.

She shifts from one foot to the other when the plane lurches sideways with a vicious crack.

Theresa smacks into the lavatory door, falling hard on the floor. The lights go black. The plane creaks and groans. There's no way it can take much more of this before it rips into a million pieces.

Just when I've convinced myself we're diving nose-first into the ocean, the plane evens out and lights flicker on. In the stale yellowy light, everything seems eerily normal. Dave's hair is a little disheveled. Theresa is okay, pulling herself to standing.

"I don't care what Kent said, y'all have a right to know," she pants. Balancing expertly on her heels, she places her hands on either side of the fuselage. "We lost one of our engines. We should be able to make it there on one but it'll be hard to keep altitude, so instead of flying above the clouds we'll most likely be in them, or below them." She takes a big breath. "We're flyin' through a storm."

A flash of lightning floods through the windows and the lights flicker. The plane jumps again, pulling my seat belt at my hips, digging the denim waistband of my shorts into my skin. Dave grasps at his armrests till his nails blanch.

Theresa staggers with each lurch. "Theresa, get in your seat." I fumble with the seat belt.

Theresa shakes her head, shouting over the vibrating rolls of turbulence. "Do *not* take off that belt. It's too dangerous!"

Then, gravity is gone. We fly upward, straining against our belts and another flash of lightning streaks through the cabin. When we level out Theresa is lying on the floor, knocked down like before. Hair covers her face, but through it she stares at me, unblinking, her right arm turned sickeningly behind her, so askew, like a twisted marionette. Her head is pushed too far toward her shoulder almost dipping past it to her shoulder blade. She lies there, shockingly still, as if cut from the puppeteer's strings.

"Theresa!" I try to reach her without unbuckling my belt. The plane dips again and groans angrily, refusing to give in to physics.

"Dave!" I shout, hoping he has a plan, or a parachute or superpowers, but his eyes are closed tight, like he's praying. Maybe I should be praying.

"Dave, DAVE!"

Suddenly he snaps to attention, staring at the lifeless body in front of him. "What happened?" Dave asks, dazed.

"Theresa is dead," I shout. "I think she broke her neck."

"Oh my God, oh my God!" Dave yells. "What's going on? How did this happen?"

As if he's been listening, Kent's voice crackles over the speaker. It's a professional, calm voice, like he's reading a script. He wouldn't be so calm if he knew about Theresa lying broken on the floor a few feet away.

"Unfortunately, due to some mechanical problems, we're preparing for an emergency water landing. Please keep your seat belt latched, seat in an upright position, and put on the flotation device located under your seat. Don't try to inflate them until after the water landing. After you've put on the flotation device, please follow Theresa's instructions on assuming the brace position and finding emergency exits." The speakers click off.

We are crashing. Numbly, I wrestle into a neon yellow life preserver, knowing it might never even be used because I'll be blown into a million pieces on impact. I will never see my family again.

What did I say to them that last time we spoke? Did I tell Jerry how much I love him and that he's my absolute best friend? Why did I waste so much time fighting with him about this trip? Oh God, he's going to feel so guilty.

Josh, my first baby. I didn't put him down for a whole month after he came home from the hospital, even when he was sleeping. I used to form myself around his little body in bed each night making a cradle with my legs and arms, watching his tiny chest move up and down with each breath. Now I won't see him grow up. And little Daniel, with the perpetual layer of dirt under his fingernails, the first to laugh at my stupid jokes. Will he even remember me?

Buckling the last strap on my life jacket I'm careful to leave the dangling white cord undisturbed. Then I remember—Margaret. God,

I was so caught up with talking to Dave Hall, I forgot about my sleeping mother-in-law. I try to turn my head but g-forces hold me down, pushing my tears backward into my hair in angry streams. Why am I fighting? Maybe I should say my last prayers, make peace with the inevitability of my destruction. Maybe this is the best way for Margaret too, to die after a full life and a fantastic vacation.

Then rebellion swells inside of me, pushing out all that fear and doubt. I won't give in. I will fight for myself and for Margaret. Tensing my neck, I force my head to turn toward the rear of the plane.

"Margaret! Margaret!" I yell. She's awake but disoriented. "MOM! Over here."

Her eyes roll around aimlessly until finally they meet mine. Her fingers twitch toward me, frozen in place by the same forces I'm fighting. "Lillian! What's happening?"

"We're landing in the ocean. Listen carefully. You need to get your life jacket on. It's under your seat."

"I can't." She wrestles feebly. "I can't . . . please God, please, take me home." She shuts her eyes. "Take me home to Charlie."

"NO, Margaret, NO! You're not giving up. I won't let you. Get the life vest on. Do it. NOW!"

Her face is wet with tears. "I love you. Tell Jerry. Tell the kids."

The world explodes around me. A metallic flash whizzes past my head and crashes into the far side of the plane. Silver slivers fill the air like confetti, all that's left of my camera and a precursor to the much larger destruction to come. The wall of force holding me in place dissolves into nothingness. Theresa told us how to brace for impact but I can't remember.

Something solid hits me in the shoulder, shoving all air out of my lungs. Taking stuttering breaths, I duck lower in my seat, looping my arms behind my thighs.

It's like we're going over giant speed bumps and my arms have a hard time holding on. The second engine, the only running one, whines as it fills with water and eventually falls silent. Then with one final jerk, the plane comes to a stop.

Water seeps into my gym shoes letting me know I'm still alive. I glance around in sweeping semicircles, but all is blackness.

Unclasping the seat belt, I push up to standing, my legs wobbling beneath me. I hold on to my headrest and slosh through the water, already several inches deep. A voice breaks the deafening silence.

"Lillian? Is that you?"

Dave. It sounds like he's still in his seat. I'm not alone. Being alone right now is almost as scary as the idea of being dead.

"Dave, thank God! You have to get out of here. The plane is sinking." Somehow, I sound calm. "Margaret. Did you hear that? We have to get out," I shout into the darkness behind me.

"Wait," Dave calls, "I think I need your help. I . . . I can't get my belt off."

"Okay, hold on." In two steps I crash into him, my hand landing on his face. His forehead is wet and sticky. Blood. Ignoring the metallic odor, I trace my hand down the front of his polo shirt, strangely guilty about getting it dirty. The water is up to my calves when I finally unlatch his seat belt and step back, but he doesn't move. I'm growing impatient. Margaret hasn't made a sound since the crash. I should be helping her right now.

"I can't get up, I'm so dizzy."

"Here." I grab both of his arms and throw them around my neck. "You've gotta get up."

I pull till my muscles burn. Once Dave is finally on his feet, he teeters and then lays his head down on top of mine, crunching my chin into my throat. "Dave, wake up! Come on, please, get up!" I shout, shaking him gently. The plane rocks side to side with each wave, hard rain pounding loudly against its steel body. Eerie blue emergency lights begin to flicker on and off adding confusion instead of clarity.

He coughs. "I'm fine, I'm fine."

"Can you stand on your own? I need to get Margaret."

Lifting his head off mine he steps away, sways but doesn't fall. "I'm okay. Go ahead," he says, leaning against the wall. "Just hurry."

When my eyes adjust to the flashing staccato of the emergency lights, I can make out the outline of chairs behind me but still no Margaret. The water now splashes around my knees.

"Mom, Mom!" I shout. Stumbling forward, I find the top of Margaret's empty headrest and trace down the grooves in the pliable leather until my hand lands on her back. She's nearly submerged, slumped over the armrest.

I kneel down beside her, shivering as the ocean water soaks into my clothes. I can't see her clearly but I hear her breathing. Shoving her up with one hand, I reach for her seat belt with the other but something hard and rectangular is in my way. I push it into the water and yank off her belt, anger propelling me more than fear now.

Margaret's body is like a sack of skin filled with sand. I struggle to gather her in my arms like a sleeping child, one arm under her legs and another behind her shoulders. Squatting low, I push against the seat behind me for leverage and try to stand. She only lifts an inch off of the seat.

Oh God, no. How am I going to get her out? It's not enough that our plane crashed or that I watched Theresa die right in front of me, but now I have to choose between saving my life and attempting to save Margaret's?

I take the anger and use it as fuel. Digging my fingers into her doughy skin, I try lifting her again, my arms shaking from exhaustion, or cold, or anger. She doesn't move at all this time. The convulsions in my arms continue, spreading to my torso and thighs, making me vibrate like when the plane was skipping across the water.

Then, as I'm trying to lift her yet again, pressure registers between my shoulder blades. It's Dave. He's standing above me. "I opened the escape door," he says, his dark polo plastered to his body. "I pulled the lever for the lifeboat, it should be inflating right now. We have to get out fast before the water covers the door."

"I can't . . ." My voice breaks. "I can't lift her. I can't get her out."

"I don't know how much help I'll be but let me try."

Dave crouches down to my level till the water reaches his shoulders. Putting his arms under Margaret, he leans against me with his shoulder and I readjust my feet to get balanced.

Dave Hall's eyes shine in the darkness and when they lock onto mine, full of confidence that we'll succeed, I believe it too. "Are you ready, Lillian?" I nod weakly. "On three, then. One, two, three." With barely any effort we stand up, lifting Margaret as though there's nothing in our arms but a baby. I've stopped shaking.

CHAPTER 7

DAVE

Present

That night on the plane was the first time Dave ever saw death. When he was ten his grandfather died, but his only memories of the funeral were of sitting around on hard chairs while his father talked with lots of people Dave didn't know. Mostly he remembered staying in a hotel with cable and a pool and that his Dad let him stay up with his cousin till almost midnight watching HBO.

A kid in high school was killed by a drunk driver, though. Dave walked past the open casket, glancing briefly at the boy "sleeping" inside. Dave was a sophomore, the kid a senior, but he was more like a child inside the satin-lined coffin, his hands crossed solemnly on his chest. The makeup on his face gave him a waxy appearance, more like a department store mannequin than a human being.

Everyone kept saying how peaceful he seemed; all Dave saw was the outline of gashes down his face carefully camouflaged for an open casket. But what he remembers the most was how quiet he looked, no furrowed brow or cocky grin, nothing.

Then Dave saw Theresa and finally understood that he only knew *of* death. It wasn't until the cacophony of fear—objects flashing past his face, screams echoing in his head—that he was properly introduced to Death and his horrific talents.

As they became better acquainted, Dave learned that Death is the opposite of peace: it's struggle, it's ugly, it's horrific, it's dirty. And ultimately, Death is emptiness. Like the way Theresa's body floated limply in the water as he and Lily pushed past her to safety, carrying Margaret in their arms. The way he knew that whatever made "Theresa" was gone forever.

How could he jam all of that into a succinct answer? His mind went blank, and Genevieve Randall let out a loud, irritated sigh. "CUT!"

The strong scent of expensive perfume wafted past him. Clenching her boney knees together, Genevieve Randall eased herself onto the couch beside him, their legs almost touching. She leaned forward, trying to force him to focus on her.

"David," she crooned, "I'm sorry, did I say something wrong? It seems like you checked out on me."

He blinked a few times trying to clear the fog from his brain. He'd almost forgotten how exhausting these interviews were. Genevieve Randall had been asking Dave questions in the middle of his living room for the past hour, and he was already tempted to tear off his mic and head upstairs for a nap.

"David. Hello?" She waved her hand in front of his face. That name yanked him to reality.

"It's Dave," he corrected. No one ever called him David. No one except Lily.

"I'm sorry, *Dave*, but we have a deadline and it's extremely important we get this interview done, so is there anything I can do to make this better for you? *Dave?*"

Ralph ran up holding a frosty glass in his stubby fingers and shoved it into Dave's hands. Dave mumbled a thanks and took a polite sip. The clinking ice settled when he lowered the cup. Mmm, ice in water. Sometimes he forgot those little things.

"No, I understand," he mumbled tracing his index finger around the rim of the glass. "I'm ready to continue when you are."

"Well, I'm ready *now*," Genevieve sighed. Her warm breath smelled of mint and tobacco.

"So I'll have Jasmine come and touch us up." Her voice shot to the side, causing Jasmine to appear from thin air. "Let's say we'll start rolling tape again in five." She held up a hand's worth of fingers before stomping across the room and out the front door. Maybe a cigarette would take her down a notch.

As Jasmine fussed with her makeup brush, Dave snuck a look at Beth sitting across the room beyond the ring of crew members, sound equipment, and cameras. Their eyes caught and her face flashed with something like concern. Then she glanced away, checking her phone casually. Dave knew what that look meant. They'd gone five months without cameras and reporters and were happier than ever. Beth couldn't understand why he'd agreed to another interview. She hated listening to this story as much as he hated telling it.

Genevieve's voice sliced through his thoughts. "David. I'm sorry, I mean Dave. Are you ready?"

"Yeah, go ahead," Dave said, as casually as possible, readjusting on the fluffy couch, ready to try again. Ralph ran in to retrieve his water and within seconds the questions started again.

"How much time would you approximate passed between the crash and when you and Lillian and Margaret Linden exited the plane?"

"I'm not completely sure. It felt like forever but it couldn't have been more than a minute or two. We pulled out Margaret, and Kent came out on his own soon after. It only took a few more minutes for the plane to completely submerge. If we'd been in there, if we'd all passed out like Margaret or, or were stuck in our seats, we all would've been trapped inside and dragged down to the ocean floor."

"Mmmm, yes, terrifying. But none of that happened did it, because you escaped? How did you escape the sinking plane?"

"I think it was a combination of luck and cooperation. I inflated the lifeboat while Lillian tried to retrieve Margaret. Kent worked on trying to contact help with the radio, but the water was rising too fast and it shorted out before he could get a signal. Then he grabbed the first aid kit on the way out." Now to give Kent his props. "That kit made the difference between life and death a number of times. We wouldn't have survived without it."

Genevieve paused dramatically, staring at her notecards. "What about Theresa Sampson? Did anyone help her out of the plane?"

He thought they'd covered this already. "No, she was already dead. We had to leave her behind."

Ms. Randall opened her mouth wide in exaggerated surprise. "You mean no one went back?"

Dave cocked his head to the side. "No, ma'am. It was clear she was dead."

"Did you check her pulse on the plane? See if she was breathing?"

"No. But you could tell, you know?" Of course she didn't know. How could she know what it was like to look at that empty vessel shattered on the ground?

He was beginning to remember why they decided to start their lies in the first place. Everyone is so judgmental.

"Hmmm, I see." She sneered in an eerily familiar way, just like Kent did when he'd found out about Theresa's fate two and a half years ago. Seeing that look again, the accusations that simmered beneath the surface, made Dave's blood boil. He scowled at Genevieve, hoping she hadn't tried these dramatics on Lily.

"I don't know what you're trying to imply, Ms. Randall, but we did our best in a horrific situation. You, none of you," Dave swept his eyes around the room ignoring the camera's intrusive stare, "have been through what we have." Leaning forward he said forcefully, "I'd appreciate a little deference in the future."

Blinking rapidly, Genevieve twittered innocently, "I'm sorry; I wasn't trying to imply anything. Pure curiosity, David."

She lingered on the name in a way that made something unsettling stir in Dave's gut, a premonition, a sense that Genevieve Randall knew more than he'd ever expected and that she wanted to share her secrets with the world.

At this point he had no choice but to continue the charade. He'd buy his and Lillian's freedom by answering Randall's apparently incomplete list of questions. Or was it actually full of questions he wasn't ready to be asked?

CHAPTER 8

DAVID-DAY 1

Somewhere in the South Pacific

The waves keep shoving me underwater, like bullies in a pool. This will go down as my final mistake—I know it will—but it was the only way. Every time I think through it, I come to the same conclusion. It had to be me.

Lillian crawled into the inflated octagonal lifeboat first, arms extended, ready to pull Mrs. Linden over the slick yellow plastic. Stinging rain pounded down as she pulled and I pushed until the unconscious woman tumbled into the boat. The force of her rescue left me standing in the arch of the plane's doorway as the boat drifted away, attached only by a long rope. I yanked hard at the nylon braid, urging the raft back to the shrinking doorway. Then Lillian started to climb over the rounded edge of the boat.

"Margaret doesn't have a life jacket," she shouted from one of the inflated benches, bouncing up and down with each wave. "Trade places with me. I have to get it."

"NO. Not enough time . . ."

"Too bad." She cut me off.

"Would you let me finish? I meant you going would take too much time. I'll go back. It'll take five minutes, tops."

She hesitated and then flipped into the boat. "Fine, but if the plane starts to go under, you get out . . . Okay? Promise."

"And you cut the rope using one of those knives in the pouch by the tie-off so you don't get dragged under."

Her hands fumbled around the inside of the plastic pouch attached to the side of the boat and held something orange and silver. "I've got it! But you'll be back, right?"

"Right," I yelled to her as I disappeared into the dark fuselage, still lit by the fading emergency flares.

Sloshing through the rising water, avoiding Theresa's floating body, I yanked the life jacket from under Margaret's seat. High-stepping through the water, I stubbed my toe on Lillian's waterlogged backpack. Without thinking, I tossed the heavy bag onto my back, slipping my arms through the straps. By then the water was up to my armpits and I was swimming more than walking. I brushed past Theresa one last time. She was a good woman. No one should have to die like that.

The arched doorway of the plane was filling with rushing water. I pulled on the string hanging down from my life jacket to fill it, took a deep breath, and dove through the exit, eyes and mouth closed tight against the rushing salt water. Pumping my arms and legs desperately, I knew I had to get far enough away from the plane so it didn't suck me under with it.

When my head finally broke through the water, I squinted through the rain, trying to find Lillian, to find the life raft. It was gone.

Spinning around in circles I watched, helpless, as the plane nosedived toward the ocean floor.

◆ ◆ ◆

Now I float. Lillian's backpack is weighing me down, almost canceling out the lift from my life jacket. I'd drop the bag but wrestling it off my shoulders seems overwhelmingly complicated. I'm way too focused on breathing and scanning the waves for the raft.

A crash of thunder pounds across the blackness and vibrates through my whole body. Lightning splashes on the stormy waters in front of me and, for a moment, the sketchy outline of something floating in the water reflects the millisecond of light. It could be nothing, or it could be the raft.

I set my aim by the brief flashes and kick through the water. Panic adds clumsiness, and I can't seem to make my arms and legs move at the same time. Forget swimming, breathing is more important. I can barely get a deep enough breath in between waves to calm the ache in my lungs. Waves slap my face, salt water seeping through the corners of my sealed lips. The quiet darkness beneath me pulls at my feet, each wave holding me under a fraction of a second longer than the one before.

Another wave towers over me like a giant playing with his toys. I duck under the water before the wave hits. As it rolls above me, I float suspended in the ocean. The life jacket tugs me upward before I'm ready to leave the stillness, refusing to let me give up. Breaking through the foamy skin of the water, my cheek grazes the slick wet plastic of the lifeboat.

"HELP!" I scream, trying to outshout the storm. "Lillian! Help me up."

A hand grabs the back of my shirt and pulls me over the edge.

"Here," my voice scratches out, "I got it." I hold up the yellow jacket, then lie breathless on the bottom of the bobbing boat.

"What, did you get lost on your way out?" Kent's gruff voice is almost a comfort. If I had more energy, I'd hug him.

"No, Mrs. Linden needed a life jacket. Thought it was going to be a short trip, till you decided to set sail on me," I mutter, jerking my face out of the inch and a half of water in the bottom of the boat. "I nearly drowned out there, not that I'm complaining or anything," I mumble sarcastically.

Squinting through the rain, I can see Margaret Linden slumped against Lillian on the other side of the boat. She's still unconscious and Lillian looks like she's close to joining her mother-in-law. Kent tosses the life jacket across the boat, hitting Lillian in the chest. Her eyes flutter open.

"You, you're alive!" she yells. "When you didn't come back, I thought . . . I thought we'd never see you again. I thought . . ." Her voice cracks.

I'm alive. The words sink into my saturated skin. I survived a plane crash. I helped save a life, and I got the bag.

"I have something for you," I yell back, scooting carefully across the slick yellow plastic toward Lillian, propelled by the need to show her what I found. Kent plops down on a bench in front of me.

"Where's Theresa?" Water pours down his face and into his mouth. Something like human emotion chips at Kent's granite exterior. "Did you see her in the water? I didn't see you till you slammed into the boat so maybe I can't see her." He scans the water.

Suddenly parched, I open my mouth wide, trying to get some of the fresh water falling from the sky. Why is it so easy to get wet in the rain but so hard to get a drink? As I let a few sweet drops slide down my salt-swollen throat, Kent leans over and gets in my face.

"What's going on? Where is she, Dave?" I don't know what to say. I look to Lillian for help but she's not paying attention. She's covered in blood and holding a bloody cloth against Mrs. Linden's head, and the elderly woman's white suit coat has a dramatic trail of red cascading down its left side.

"Why are you looking at her like that?" Kent growls. "Tell me."

Grappling for the right words, I stare at my wrinkled white fingers so I don't have to see his face. I'll do it quickly, like pulling off a Band-Aid. I think about how the doctor told me my dad was dead after the heart attack. I'll say it like that. "Kent, I don't know how to tell you this but—I'm sorry . . . Theresa is dead."

After a brief pause, Kent snorts. "Okay, asshole, you don't know what you're talking about. She's a better swimmer than any of us. She's gonna be fine." He digs a thick finger into my shoulder.

"She's not out there, Kent!"

"You don't know that." He glares down at me, lips turned up in disgust.

"Yeah, unfortunately I do." I climb onto the bench next to him and speak carefully. "When the plane was going through all the turbulence she didn't have a chance to get seated, and when we were hit by that bolt of lightning and the plane jumped she . . ." My mouth goes dry again. I don't want to say it. I don't want to remember it. "When the lights came on she was on the floor and her eyes were open. She wasn't breathing."

"Are you telling me you left her in there?"

"Kent—she was *dead*," I insist. "We barely carried Mrs. Linden out; we would've died trying to get Theresa's body out too. There was no time."

"No time? You had time to save those two." He pointed at Lillian and Mrs. Linden, huddled together against the rain. "You had plenty of time to get that life jacket and retrieve the soccer mom's backpack but you left Theresa in the plane to drown?" he screams, red-hot fury replacing stubborn confusion. He twists his fingers into my shirt until the collar presses into my windpipe.

"She was already *dead*. There was nothing I could do. Honest, man, nothing."

Kent stands in the tilting raft, faces me, and attempts to lift me into the air. He's a good head shorter than me and at least twenty pounds overweight, but under the potbelly he's strong. I try to break his grasp but I'm weak from swimming; there's no escape as he tilts me toward the foamy abyss. How long will my life jacket keep me afloat? Will sharks find me before or after my heart stops beating?

Then, for no reason, he drops me in the boat. Scrambling onto the bench, I curl into myself, watching his every move. He steps away from me, collapsing on the bench adjacent to mine.

"I'm going in," he says, resolved. "I can't leave her there. I gotta go back."

"You can't get her, Kent. The plane is underwater." He can't leave us. I don't know how to turn on the rescue beacon and the only first aid training I've had is how to open a Band-Aid. He knows this ocean, he flies it every day. I never liked Kent, but we need him.

He rips off his life jacket and pilot's shirt so he's down to his soaked white undershirt, and he hands the pilot's shirt to me. "Give this to my mom if I don't make it," he mumbles.

The shirt sags in my palm. I should get her address right now because Kent is going to die.

"Please, stay in the boat and put your life jacket back on. When the rescue workers come, they'll get her out. I promise. Here, take it. Take your shirt."

"No," he shakes his head, "I can't leave her. I'd rather die."

"Then you *will* die," Lillian yells across the boat, leaning forward. "Just like Theresa, just like Margaret."

The older woman is slouched across Lillian's lap. Dead.

"Whatever, lady. I'm going in and nothing you say is going to stop me."

"It was my fault, you know," Lillian ventures, "Theresa dying. If I hadn't been on that flight she'd probably still be alive." The rain picks up, slowly rinsing off the blood that covers her like paint.

Kent turns away from his search for the invisible plane and glares at Lillian. "What are you talking about?"

"I was in her seat when the turbulence hit. She tried to make it to another open seat, but when the plane jumped, she hit the ceiling. She was dead when the lights came back on. If it wasn't for me, she would've been safely buckled. She'd be here right now." She points to where she sits across from us. I hope she knows what she's doing.

"Why are you telling me this now, huh? What's in it for you? You feel guilty about flirting with Dave here? Want to clear your conscience before we all die?" A snarky smile creeps up, curling his lips, baring his teeth. "Yeah, Theresa told me about how you two were acting like a buncha teenagers."

"I don't know what you're talking about," I interject, attempting some damage control. "We were just chatting. Anyway, she's married."

"Yeah, last time I checked you're married too, Romeo."

I open my mouth to argue but I stop short. Instead of fighting with Kent about minutiae, I need to talk a little sense into Lillian.

"Theresa's death was an accident. You didn't know what was going to happen, none of us did. You can't blame yourself."

Lillian shakes her head. "It's not just Theresa. There's Margaret." She chokes on the name. "I killed her too."

Her words are confident and unwavering. I'm surprised at the hypnotizing effect they have on Kent. He turns away from the ocean, suddenly looking like an old man, and sits on the inflated bench, silent.

"Remember, Dave, when Theresa told me to put my laptop away?" she continues. "When we crashed, somehow it . . ." She stares down at the lifeless form on her lap, fingers tenderly drawing back some stray hairs that had fallen across Margaret's face. She tucks them behind

Margaret's ear, revealing a gaping wound, still oozing crimson. "It hit her head. I found it on her lap when we were helping her out of the plane. If I hadn't been so careless, if I'd stayed put, if I'd cared more about my husband's mother than . . . "

"Stop it." I cut her off. "You didn't *kill* anybody."

"I don't know, Dave, she makes a good argument," Kent snipes. My hand balls reflexively into a fist.

"Shut up, Kent! You're such an idiot, leave her alone."

He sits a little taller, sizing me up for a fight, puffing up like a riled rooster. Lillian reaches out a hand toward us.

"Stop, stop! Dave, please let me finish," she says, as if I'm annoying her. I watch Kent for a half second longer before sitting back, resigned to being an onlooker.

"What I'm trying to say is that I feel responsible for the loss of two lives today. I honestly don't know what I'd do if you were the third. If you go in that water, Kent, you *will* be the third." She points to the choppy waves surrounding us. "I don't expect you to forgive me but stay. Please."

Kent sits swaying with the rise and fall of the storm-tossed raft. Right when I think he's gone catatonic, he turns away from us, taking one last sweep of the water. His massive creased forehead wrinkles. He still loves Theresa and now she's gone forever. I can't imagine what that must be like.

What if that was Beth still in the plane? What if I knew I'd never wake up to her cold feet pressed against my legs again or hear her sigh at one of my puns? What if one brief moment took away everything we'd planned, including our dreams of one day holding a child in our arms?

For a second I forget about how cold and wet I am, and the way my throat feels so raw it might be bleeding, and I make a decision: if he wants to go back for her, I won't try to stop him again.

He asks her one last question. "Are you sure? I mean, are you sure she's dead?" There's a strange calm about him and, like everything else about Kent, like his volatile temper and the way he never really looks you in the eye, it makes me nervous.

Lillian nods. "Yes, unfortunately I am."

He opens his mouth like he's going to start arguing again and then stops, slumping in his seat.

"I'll stay."

A sad smile crosses Lillian's face before she covers it with her hands, sobbing. I want to comfort her like she did for me after Beth's phone call. Okay, if I'm being honest with myself, I want the warmth of a living human being in my arms because I'm more likely to die tonight than live.

I slide around the octagon till I'm close enough to tap her shoulder. I hesitate a moment too long, and a large wave crashes over us, tipping the boat almost vertical. The raft rolls beneath us, and I grab wildly at anything to keep from being flipped out, but there's not much to hold on to. Doubling over, I find only one thing to hold onto—myself.

I stay balled up like that for a long time, after the raft goes still, even after the rain slows and the ocean calms to a choppy lull. I can't let go. Gradually an unsettled sleep overcomes me. I give in gratefully, so physically exhausted that my body starts to shut down involuntarily. My only hope is that even if I have nightmares, they'll be better than my reality.

CHAPTER 9

LILLIAN

Present

Reaching the top of the stairs, Lillian was overcome with exhaustion. She grabbed onto the handrail, catching herself. Her feet pulsed in the stylish but tight green Versace pumps that peeked out under her designer jeans. It seemed impossible to be this tired from sitting and talking for an hour and a half.

Slipping her index finger into the sling-back strap, she pried the shoes off without much difficulty. Jill had picked out the outfit and was probably sitting at home having a good laugh right now. Lillian would have a word with her when this day was over.

Jill claimed the low-cut, emerald-green wraparound top would bring out Lillian's eyes and slim her waist, but instead of making her feel curvy and attractive, it made her self-conscious. It was so low in the front she had to sit up taller in her seat to keep the neckline from sagging and showing off an embarrassing amount of cleavage to the camera.

It was hard to get used to her new bra size. She'd been a steady B cup for the majority of her life, even during pregnancy and nursing, but in the past few months she'd suddenly filled out like a girl going through puberty, and she wasn't just expanding in the chest.

After a year and a half of near starvation, Lillian was never full. It didn't take much, a tiny stir of hunger in her gut, and then *bam*, this overwhelming surge of panic, an animal instinct, took over. Eight months after their rescue, she was holding strong at twenty pounds over her "before" weight and fifty over her "almost died on an island" weight.

Somehow, even as a woman who had always been effortlessly thin, she loved her new, fuller figure. The simple tug of fabric against her waist was a constant promise that she didn't have to be hungry all the time, that she could feel pleasantly full with a quick trip to the pantry.

When she walked out of the hospital with Jerry more than two weeks after the rescue, she leaned into his side, flinching away from the flashes and camera lenses. Jerry didn't pull her in, though. Instead his arms hovered around her thin form, barely touching her skin, as if she was made of glass.

She was sure it was a sign he didn't love her anymore, or that maybe he was disappointed she was still alive. But standing in front of a full-length mirror at the hotel, Lillian finally understood why he kept her at arm's length.

Her body was more than lean; it was skeletal. She traced curious fingers along her hipbones. They jutted out so violently that she was afraid to push too hard for fear of puncturing the skin stretched between them. She let her hands travel up to her stomach. Loose skin laced with silvery stretch marks hung sadly under her shriveled belly button. She pinched the wrinkly skin between her fingers nostalgically, finally glad for the marks that reminded her why she'd fought so hard to stay alive.

Other than those nearly invisible lines, the body in the mirror belonged to a stranger. Or perhaps it was more like a once-familiar landscape ravaged by a terrible natural disaster. As she counted her ribs, visible beneath a thin sheet of skin, tears dripped down her cheekbones, her once-bright eyes nothing more than sunken holes. She suddenly understood Jerry's revulsion, and couldn't blame him for shrinking away from the woman in the mirror. She was repulsed by this stranger as well.

Things were different now. Lillian rubbed her tingling feet, smiling. Lately it felt like they were newlyweds again. Whenever she stood close to him, his fingers would sink gratefully into her smooth, cushioned skin, and when she woke up in the middle of the night, like she always did, she found his body wrapped around her from behind, his head on her pillowy shoulder or arm.

If it took a few extra pounds and a new wardrobe to keep that spark, she didn't mind. Shoving her shoes back on, she pulled the straps over her heels reluctantly. It felt like her feet had gone up a size in the minute she'd had them off. Trying not to wobble, she pushed open the door to her room. Jerry lay on their bed wearing his reading glasses, typing furiously, his light brown hair combed into a neat part. He was dressed in a full suit, the blue pinstriped one reserved for weddings and funerals. The one he wore to her funeral.

He rubbed his socked feet together unconsciously, like Daniel did when he zoned out watching a movie. If it wasn't for the shiny black work computer on his lap and papers sprawled across the entire king-size four-poster bed, she would've tackled him with a bear hug. Instead Lillian crept across the room, feet silent on the loose shag of the chocolate-colored carpet in their bedroom.

"Hey there, how's work?" Lillian whispered, caressing the smooth cherry finish on one of the posts. Jerry glanced up from his computer and took off his reading glasses. A bright smile crept onto his face.

"Hey there, hot stuff, this is a nice surprise. How are things going down there? You holding up?"

"Yeah, we're not even halfway done but one of the camera battery packs malfunctioned, so we took a break."

"Mmmm," he murmured, biting the rubber tip of the temple on his glasses. "I must know, how's the infamous Genevieve Randall? As scary as she looks on TV?"

Jerry wasn't a Genevieve Randall fan. He called her fake and overdone. Lillian thought it was incredibly cute of him.

"Worse, I think she might be a robot."

"Hmmm, good or evil?" Jerry raised his eyebrow playfully.

"Evil, what other kind is there?"

"Touché." He laughed. "So how's the robot treating my wife? Trying to take over your body yet?"

"That's the pod people. Get your sci-fi evil villains straight."

"Sorry, robots aren't pod people, got it." Folding his glasses, he sat up a little straighter. "But seriously, what's she like? Is she any different from the others?"

Shaking her head, Lillian studied an invisible spot on the bedpost, trying to sound casual. "No, she's just like all reporters. She keeps trying to get me emotional, get the 'real story.' You know what I'm talking about."

"Yeah, I know." He closed the laptop and slid it under the bed. "Come here, relax a minute." He scooched over a little, turning on his side and crunching some of the papers in the process, then patted a small space next to him on the bed.

"I don't think I'll fit," Lillian sighed, assessing the size of the bare spot on the bed and remembering her new generous hip size. He patted again, refusing excuses. Kicking off her heels, she raised a dubious eyebrow, which Jerry ignored. He slipped his hand around her waist, fingers holding on tight to a rear belt loop.

"Oh, we'll make you fit." With a quick yank he tugged her into the warm spot he'd just vacated, tucking her legs between his own. He cradled her head neatly beneath his chin, right above his heart.

He smelled like his fancy cologne, the kind she bought him at Macy's when he made partner a year before her trip to Fiji. He only wore it on special occasions like a big day in court or a date night that included more than grabbing a bite at Taco Bell and walking around Walmart looking for storage bins. He wasn't like a lot of men, dousing himself in cologne until any open flame could set him ablaze. No, as with everything else in his life he was measured and conservative, allowing one puff of the spray. Lillian buried her nose in the crease of his neck, inhaling his smell.

"You don't have to do this, you know."

"I know I don't." Lillian paused, considering how to explain it again. "I want to."

Jerry sat still, right arm wrapped all the way around his wife, caressing her free arm. His light strokes sent shivers down her spine. She tipped her head back enough so she could kiss his neck.

Settling down on the bed, she imagined the thoughts tumbling around Jerry's brain. At times like this she wanted to blurt out the whole story, no more secrets between them. But then she'd always come to her senses and remember why she had to hold fast, how everything would change if he knew.

"*Why* do you want to do this all over again? I thought you hated it." She could feel his warm breath in her hair as he pressed his lips against her scalp.

"I want it over, and I think if everyone finally hears the story, the whole story, then they'll leave us alone. And that contract, you said the exclusivity clause is binding. This will be the last interview . . . ever."

He laughed, rubbing his lips across her hair as he shook his head. "Well, yeah, but even that has loopholes. Even though you have a pretty spectacular lawyer, I'm afraid it'll take more than one interview to get those vultures to leave us alone." He paused. "So I'm assuming Dave agreed to an interview?"

Her pulse exploded at *his* name. Lillian didn't like talking about him with Jerry, who claimed the jealousy was gone, the burning, ferocious jealousy that once threatened to claim their marriage like a forest fire. But hearing his name come out of Jerry's mouth still riled her up into a defensive position.

"Apparently he has." She tried to sound uninterested. "One of the Robot's minions told me today. He said they're going to California next week to film his part."

"You didn't talk to him, then?" he probed carefully.

"No, Jerry," she spat. "I haven't spoken to David—" Lillian gritted her teeth. She shouldn't call him that anymore. "I mean Dave, since you asked me to stop. It's been nearly five months." She stumbled over her words. If Jerry knew what a good liar she was he'd know better than to be suspicious of such a sloppy delivery. Lies, good ones at least, are smooth and well thought out. It's the truth that's sloppy. But Jerry didn't know.

Dropping his hand from Lillian's arm, he let it hang limply off the edge of the bed. "Hmmm, okay. The last time I spoke with Beth she told me they were done with interviews so it surprised me, that's all."

"When did you talk to Beth?" She pulled back just enough to see his face. Jerry and Beth met in Fiji in the days after the crash and had been long-distance acquaintances ever since. Lillian didn't realize they were still in touch. It wasn't always safe having Jerry and Beth chat.

"Oh, a few months ago." He waved his hand casually. "She called me at the office with a few little questions about the Carlton settlement. She sounded so happy with Dave home. She said they weren't giving any more interviews because they're trying to get pregnant again and she didn't want the stress to interfere with starting a family." Jerry shrugged. "Maybe it's not an issue anymore. Maybe it worked already."

"Maybe." Lillian tipped a shoulder up, copying Jerry's laissez-faire attitude even though she felt like crying. Jerry put his hand on the broad space between her shoulder blades, gently pulling her onto his chest.

"So, what have you guys covered so far?" He was clearly trying to change the subject. Lillian played along.

"The crash and a little after. We hadn't gotten that far when the battery died. I can tell you one thing, Genevieve Randall was not happy."

"I didn't think robots were capable of emotion."

"Well, this one is capable of annoyance, that's for sure."

Jerry laughed and pumped her for more, "What's up next, then?"

"Um, the next series of questions on my list are all about survival. Have you ever noticed everyone seems to find that part fascinating? Genevieve is going to be a little disappointed, though, because I wasn't as involved in all of that. It was more a Dave and Kent thing. I was the gatherer and the men the hunters—so very sexist of us."

"I think the feminist movement will forgive you this one time."

"We'll see. I'm sure I'll get plenty of letters saying otherwise. Everyone seems to have an opinion on everything, not that I care. Anyway . . ." she faltered, pulling in closer, tucking her hands, suddenly cold, under his body. "Then we're gonna talk about everyone: Margaret, David, Kent, and then . . . Paul."

She whispered the last name, like a secret. Jerry's jaw went taut against the crown of her head. Lillian was glad she wasn't looking at him.

"I'm sure Genevieve Randall will enjoy that thoroughly." He sounded furious but Lillian couldn't tell at whom. "Maybe I'll come down for the last bit, when you get rescued. After the part with, well, you know." The words cut, and even though they were lying in each other's arms, at that moment it felt like they were still thousands of miles apart.

"You know what Jer? Don't come. It's fine. If it's gonna be that big a deal, I wouldn't want to put you out."

"God. You know that part of the story is hard for me. I can't hear it again."

Lillian pushed off of Jerry's chest, bolting upright. "Oh, well, I'm sorry it's hard for you, Jerry, goodness knows we wouldn't want to make *you* uncomfortable. I think you forget it's not some *story* to me. It's my life."

Jerry lifted up on one elbow. "Come on, can you blame me? The way you talk about him. How much you loved him. How can I not be jealous?"

"I don't know. I get you being jealous of David, really I do—he's a plane flight away in California. But Paul? Paul is gone, Jer, what's there to be jealous of?"

Jerry found an excuse to pick at one of the dark blue buttons on his jacket. "Damn right I'm jealous of *David*, that man is clearly in love with you. But I can stand it because at least you picked me over him. When you made it home you could've been with Dave. God knows even to this day he'd leave poor Beth in an instant if you asked him."

"Don't be ridiculous."

"No, you trying to deny it is ridiculous. You don't see what I do so claiming otherwise makes you seem naive." He sounded like he was in a courtroom. His condescension incensed Lillian.

"Me naive? How about 'poor Beth'? How naive can you be? If you knew what I know about that woman, you wouldn't feel so badly for her." She slapped at the cream-colored duvet cover.

"Please, explain. I'm all ears because, you know what? That little display," he pointed at her with a trembling index finger, "sounded more to me like a jealous lover than a concerned friend."

"No, it's nothing." She waved her hands in surrender. "Never mind, please. I don't want to go through this whole Dave thing with you again."

His forehead creased as he searched her face. Lillian could only guess what he hoped to find written there. She held her head up high as if she had nothing to hide. Then she saw that his normally flinty eyes were wet and filled with uncertainty. It wasn't often she saw self-doubt in this naturally self-assured man. The button Jerry was fussing with fell onto the bedspread. He picked it up with the kind of sadness reserved for the loss of something substantial, something more than a mere suit button.

"I guess we're still not ready to talk about him," he said, still staring at the button. "I can deal with it. You picked us. In a way I'm a little sorry for Dave. Don't get me wrong, I still can't stand the guy, but at least we understand each other. I'm envious of the time you two had together and he's envious of the future we have together. I can't blame him. But Paul?" He paused, looking up at her, uncertain. "I don't think there's anything you wouldn't do for him. You'd give up all of this if you could bring him back."

Lillian opened her mouth to deny it but she couldn't. Losing Paul, burying him next to Margaret in the hot, dry sand, was the biggest regret of her life. All the sorrow in the world couldn't explain how she felt about him. She had lain by his grave until Dave had to drag her away. When she lost him, she had been so full of grief she didn't think there'd be room for anything else ever again. Denying that would be like saying he never existed. It would be like losing him all over again.

Jerry wiped a tear off her face with his thumb, cradling her cheek for a moment.

"That's what I thought." He sat up, his forgotten papers crackling beneath him. "It was a tragedy he died. I'm sorry you had to suffer through that, but I wish more than I've wished for almost anything in my life that you'd let him go and remember that your family is still here and we need you." Jerry's voice cracked, eyes filling with tears again. Seeing him break like this knocked out Lillian's fortifications.

"I miss him so much, Jerry. He shouldn't have died. I should've kept him safe. I wish you knew him, that you could understand, and I hate that you don't. And it hurts so badly to talk about it, to go through it over and over again. You know," she said, tracing a finger down his blue silk tie, "sometimes I wish I never told you about him, never told anybody."

Jerry wrapped his large hand around hers until it disappeared.

"Sometimes I do too." He put his arm around her shoulders, pulling her into his chest where she hid her face from Jerry and the memories he didn't want her to carry.

He whispered in her ear. "I'm sorry I brought all this up, Lil. After today you don't have to talk about him anymore if you don't want to. I love you and you're home, that's all that matters." She nodded, her nose rubbing against the starchy fabric of his dress shirt. "I want to make it up to you. Let's go out tonight, just you and me. I'll get a sitter while you finish your interview, okay?"

"That's sweet but I don't want go anywhere tonight, Jer," she said, wiping her nose on the sleeve of her blouse, leaving a dark trail down the expensive green fabric. "Damn it! Not what I need right now."

"Don't worry. We'll fix you up nice and pretty." He pushed away a few stray strands of hair stuck to the wet trails on her face. "But tonight, I'll put the kids to bed and make dinner, maybe a movie? Nothing about planes or natural disasters, I promise."

He gave her that rueful smile, the one Josh used when he trailed mud through the living room and Daniel used when he wanted pizza for dinner instead of chicken casserole. She was utterly vulnerable to its power.

"Now, go get cleaned up before they start shooting again." He patted her hair, frozen in place by numerous hair products. "I'm afraid my shirt may have messed up your makeup." Smears of black mascara and eyeliner were streaked across the front of his shirt along with splotches of powdery foundation.

"Oh no, your favorite shirt." Lillian traced the streaks and smudges, adding another item to the list of things she'd ruined.

"Don't worry, it'll come out." Jerry waved her off. "Even if it doesn't, it's only a shirt."

"Yeah, but . . ." Lillian began to argue when he leaned forward. When his lips met hers, they fit in that exact way they always had, spreading warmth through her chest and to her fingertips, where she felt his heart pounding through the stain in his shirt. Taking her by the shoulders, he flipped her over onto the paper-strewn bed, making her giggle against his pursuing lips. As he traced a hot path down her neck and shoulder, then followed the aggressive plunge of her neckline, she forgot about all the chaotic thoughts moving frantically through her brain and remembered one very important fact—she was home.

CHAPTER 10

LILY-DAY 2

Somewhere in the South Pacific

Warmth seeps through my shirt, rousing me from the fitful sleep I'd fallen into during the night. It all comes flooding in on pulsating waves. Memories of the crash wash over, nearly drowning me, shockingly clear like they were recorded in HD. The violent bucking of the plane, the crunching sound Theresa's body made hitting the ceiling, the onslaught of blood—hot and thick—rushing down Margaret's face, Kent's wild, ferocious eyes. If I focus on one memory too long, the video of memories starts playing over in my mind like I'm living them again.

But I don't want to remember, not like that. It's too painful, too raw. I fast-forward to the endless hours after the crash, a numb, cold, wet blur of rain. I don't remember many specifics, mostly the sound of my teeth chattering through the thunder and the slapping of waves. Much better.

Now, with the sun beating down, I have no idea how much time's passed since our plane crashed. The sun on my skin means I'm alive, but it also means we haven't been rescued. My eyes prick like they're trying to make tears out of whatever is left of my bodily fluids. The sun filtering through my eyelids is a bright yellow that hurts even before I open them. Reason number fifty-seven to keep them closed.

Too bad my mind is running along, tumbling over all the what-ifs and maybes that I'd been holding at bay. I stumble upon one realization that shocks me awake. My lap is empty. Margaret is gone.

Even in those hazy last memories before the blankness of sleep, I was peripherally aware of the comfort of her deadweight on my legs. Now there's a heavy emptiness, like the first time I held Josh and knew that the fullness in my arms matched the vacant spot inside my womb. I have to find her and take her home and bury her next to Charlie.

I force my gritty eyes open, sand raking across my eyeball. No, it's not sand, but the underside of my eyelid rubbing against my eye without the lubrication of tears. Am I that dehydrated already?

It takes a few thousand blinks before I can stand to keep them open. Even then, I'm blinded by the direct sunlight, like a mole emerging from the safety of his underground tunnels. Just when I'm sure I've gone permanently blind, a flood of tears leaks from the corner ducts. I close them again, afraid to let even a millimeter of liquid evaporate before my eyes fully rehydrate. But I have to open them eventually. Keeping my eyes closed doesn't make her alive again, does it?

It's like that weird experiment I learned about in physics class in college, where the cat in the closed box is both dead and alive at the same moment. What did those kooks say? It's not until you look that there's only one outcome or the other. I guess you've got to look eventually or else you'd always end up with a box of dead cat goop.

I open slowly, blinking against the light. I'm in the same general spot I fell asleep in. On the opposite side of the boat, Kent sits with his back to me, still in his lookout spot, probably still searching for signs of Theresa in the endless blue that surrounds us.

The top of his head is bright red, sunburned through his thin blond crew cut, hairline receding noticeably. The white pilot's shirt gapes open showing a tight, thin undershirt tucked neatly into a belted pair of khaki shorts, the tops of his knees the same boiling red as his head. My nose twinges with the familiar pang of sunburn when I bump it while rubbing my eyes.

To my right, Dave is asleep. His head rests on the side of the raft and bounces up and down with every subtle ripple, his face buried deep in his folded, sun-browning arms. Apparently he's one of those people who tans instead of burns, a lucky attribute with the sun high in the sky bearing down on us. His back rises and falls steadily. I'm not as scared with him here.

I roll my head around, shoulder to shoulder and chin to chest. The physical movement is painful but wonderfully distracting. Pausing mid-stretch, I notice a lump of fabric next to Dave. It's Margaret's retro suit coat lying across the bench next to him, far too big and lumpy to be empty.

Creeping along the bench, I feel my arms ache like I had a hard workout at the gym the day before. My shoulder hurts in a different way, a new way, but I can't stop to inspect it. I need to find her. I'll deal with my shoulder when the rescue boat comes.

Her feet stretch out toward Dave, who's still passed out. Her head and shoulders are covered by the coat, one side tinged pink from the blood I'd sopped up the night before. I swallow hard, my throat so dry it feels like the skin is sticking together inside.

I don't want to remember what she looked like last night. The blood, how hot it was against my hand, her skin gaping open, and how the one time I tried to inspect the wound closer—I saw her skull. My empty stomach cramps. I don't know if I want to see what's under the coat.

No, I need to see her one more time. I need to know for sure that she's gone. So much of last night seemed like a nightmare; I need to know it was real. With a trembling hand, I reach forward until my fingertips graze the white fabric, stiff with blood and salt, then I hold it between thumb and forefinger and lift.

First, her sandy hair. It looks soft, like the poofy part of a dandelion. I reach out to touch it but as I pull the coat higher, black streaks of dried blood stick her hair together in thick chunks.

I have to do this fast or I'll never go through with it. Licking my lips, I dig my fingernails into the polyester and, gathering the remnants of my courage, I pull upward in one swift movement. The coat drops onto my lap and I force myself to look.

I expected a gory mess, eyes gaping open, blood, skin, bone . . . but instead there's only a sleeping woman. Someone's bandaged her head and cleaned her face. Her eyes are closed, and in a way she looks peaceful. Using one finger, I trace down the unbandaged side of Margaret's face, running along the smile lines, parentheses around her mouth. In this tiny moment, I love her and grieve like she's my mother.

Something reflective flashes in the sun. A gold strand is nestled in the folds of Margaret's neck, snaking down her collarbone. Margaret always wears Charlie's wedding ring on a long gold chain. Always. I don't care that her skin will be cold and stiff or that I'll have to sink my hand into the crunchy black blood–crusted hair to find the clasp. I want that ring. It's part of Jerry and home.

As I'm looking at the necklace, glued to her skin with blood and perspiration, the serpent-like strand moves up and down ever so slightly. It has to be a trick of the light. Squinting tighter, I see something, the unmistakable movement of a pulse under Margaret's skin.

"Lillian, you're awake." It's Dave. He's sitting upright, his black curls flattened against his head where he was lying. My mouth is too dry to talk. Pointing feebly at the lump of fabric in front of me, I grunt.

Dave smiles sadly, nodding his head. "She's alive."

My eyes burn like I'm going to cry but no tears come, which is probably a good thing.

"Shh, shh, it's okay, it's okay." The raft bounces, then Dave is by my side. When he slips his arm around me it seems so natural to lean into him, let my head burrow into his shoulder, and cry.

He holds me tight, and though he smells like sweat and salt water, I pretend he's Jerry and that everything is going to be all right. Eventually my crying slows and stops but I don't move. I don't want to.

"Did that help?" His hot hand cradles my face, pushing back the curtain of knotted hair.

"Yeah, it did . . . How did you do it?" I want to ask, *Will she live?* but I already know the answer to that one.

"I didn't do anything," Dave snorts, like I've said something funny. "It was right before dawn, the rain finally stopped and I was trying to sleep but I was so cold I couldn't—anyway, I heard someone talking. When I opened my eyes, there she was, white as a ghost, speaking the craziest gibberish I've ever heard in my life. With the dried blood on her face and hair, she looked like something from a movie. Then, like that"—Dave snaps his fingers—"she was out again. I checked her pulse and breathing carefully, and sure enough she was alive—is still alive, I'm guessing."

"Then you bandaged her head?" I tried to turn to look at him straight on, but the nagging pain in my shoulder kept me in place.

"No, that was Kent."

"Kent?"

"Yeah, apparently he's some kind of Eagle Scout or something."

"That's impressive. I was sure you did it."

"Well, I started to, but . . ."

"But he was doing a crap job of it so I stepped in," Kent butts in, raising his eyebrows. "Your boyfriend here was wasting all the rubbing alcohol on grandma, and I knew if anybody was going to make it out of this insanity alive we might need to save some for the rest of us." On the word "boyfriend" Dave stiffens and pulls his arm away.

"Well, whoever it was, thank you." I glance back and forth between both men. "I mean it. I know she's not in great shape, but if she can stay around a little longer, then maybe the rescue boats can help her when they come."

"*Pft*, yeah, *maybe*." Kent rolls his eyes.

"Kent, be human for a few minutes here," Dave warns.

"Oh, darlin', I meant no harm." He's mocking me now. "It's not like I don't want grammy over there to get outta this and go back to her life playing tennis and whatever other shit she fills her time with. I only mean that I wouldn't be holding my breath for some rescue boat to show up and pluck us out of this blue desert.

"Our time is running short," he continues. "It's almost twenty-four hours since we crashed, honey, and let me tell you something." He points a thick, meaty finger directly at me. "Once they find our plane sunk on the bottom of the ocean, they're not gonna be searching for us so hard anymore. I can't blame 'em. We've got no water except the useless salty kind." He spreads his arms out wide, gesturing to the water outside the boat, as though we hadn't noticed we were surrounded by an entire ocean. "We've got no food and we sure as hell got no way to signal our location. The beacon that came with this crap-tastic boat here had a rotted battery, so we're as lost as lost can be." Then, leaning forward and clasping his callused hands in front of him, Kent stares me in the eye. "Baby, you should be sad your mama is still breathing, 'cause she coulda had the easiest way out of this situation."

Well, I'll say this: Kent has this way of telling things right out, brutally honest. It's like a slap in the face—it hurts for a moment, but when the shock wears off your head is clearer.

"Oh my God." I run my hand over the delicate tufts of Margaret's hair sticking out from under the protective coat. He might be right.

"It's good to see someone is finally listening to me around here," Kent mumbles, getting some perverse enjoyment out of my suffering.

"I'm beginning to wish I let you jump in that water, Kent." Dave glares at Kent before slipping a hand into mine, which makes me jump at first. I just met this man but I can't look away. "Okay, it's not looking great for us right now; I can see that, but, Lillian, we have to keep it together. You never know what could happen. Carlton Yogurt is not going to give up that easily. This is a PR nightmare, and that is my professional opinion. Even if they don't find us, we could run into a fishing boat or a shipping lane, or a helicopter might spot us from the sky. There are so many possibilities, but it's going to take some time. We have to be patient and, as impossible as it seems, wait."

"But there's no time left for Margaret. You and I both know she can't live long out here." I point to her lifeless body. "And all I can think about is—*we're next.*"

"You've got to think about good things, Lillian. Think about your children, your life at home, your husband. Oh . . . and here's something," he says, full of good-humored intrigue that doesn't match the seriousness of our situation. He lets go of my hand and stumbles over to his side of the boat.

"This oughta be good." Kent continues his running commentary.

Dave sloshes through the collected sludge of salt water, blood, and seaweed in the bottom of the boat, and back. He sits down next to me again, jostling my left side, causing searing pain to spread through my shoulder.

"When I grabbed the life jacket for Margaret, I also grabbed something else, something of yours." Pausing dramatically he whips out my baby-blue JanSport. The bottom half is soaked through and there's a ring of salt around the top where the water evaporated in the sunlight. Other than that it's the same old bag I've carried for nearly fifteen years. It shouts *home* as clearly as if Dave had yelled it in my ear.

"How in the world did you get this back here?" Reaching out, I caress the smooth, faded fabric tenderly.

"That's a very long and boring story I promise to tell you one day, but first we have to get off this boat. See? Something to look forward to." He gives me a little wink and holds out the bag. "Here, take it."

When I go to grab it, it feels as if a fishing hook is piercing my shoulder blade. I gasp, stopping short of the bag.

"Are you hurt?" Dave lowers the bag slightly, his crooked nose tilting to the left.

"No, no I'm fine. Uh, could you open that for me? I think I might have a bottle of water in there." Dave scans me skeptically, then fumbles with the zipper, pulling hard to get it past a catch in the teeth. His elbow bumps my arm, making me wince. I take two steadying breaths, blowing them out slowly. "The bottle's somewhere in the biggest pocket. I never opened it so it should be full." I risk a look at Kent. "That should give us a better chance, right?"

Kent shrugs but sits up a little straighter, darting glances at the bag as Dave slowly unzips the largest pocket. I try to run through an inventory of what might be in that bag: water, granola bars, Margaret's purse and toiletry bag, my makeup bag, my book, a change of clothes, my water-logged cell phone, a notebook, and a few other odds and ends from home.

Dave peers inside, slipping the zipper open with the side of his hand. His eyebrows raise in surprise. Reaching his arm in deep, he pulls out a sixteen-ounce water bottle.

"Well, whad'ya know?" Kent says in awe. Dave tosses the bottle across the raft where Kent catches it gingerly, as if it's delicate crystal. "Careful! This little bottle here is our life. We can live off of this for the next two days at least if we're really careful about how much we drink. What else is in the mystery bag?"

Dave looks at me again, asking silent permission to rummage through my personal belongings. I nod, the pain in my shoulder making me queasy. Soon they find Margaret's purse and makeup bag, which hold mirrors for signaling planes, a sewing kit, and random medicine bottles, some dating back to the turn of the millennium.

The mood in the raft gradually elevates from near-apocalyptic to semi-optimistic. The guys go through every item and categorize them by use, putting them in various-size used plastic baggies for storage. The distraction it provides is as much of a prize as any of the supplies.

"Lillian, look what I found! I can't believe it's all in one piece, maybe once it's dried out you can read it again." Dave taps my shoulder with the romance paperback, a half-naked couple embracing on the cover.

"Hey, stop it!"

Dave recoils. "What did I do?"

"Nothing, it . . . it's my shoulder." I try to catch my breath enough to speak. "When you touched it like that, it really hurt." If I can keep it from moving again, it'll stop hurting.

Dave crosses his arms, looking at me with pinched eyebrows, a little crease wrinkling between them. I wish he wouldn't worry about me. I don't need his concern—Margaret does.

"Never mind me, I'm fine." I try very hard to sound confident.

"If your voice wasn't shaking so badly, I *might* believe you."

"I . . . it's not . . ." But he's right, my voice is warbling like an opera singer's.

"See?" he says, cocking his head. "Now will you please let me take a look? You might be severely injured and if we're actually stuck out here like *he* thinks, we don't want it to get infected."

"Fine." I've run out of ways to get him to back off, so I turn to let him examine the injury. I bite my lip when he inspects the tender spot by my right shoulder blade.

"There's an awful lot of blood here." He sucks in a breath through his teeth. "Yeah that's what I thought. Lillian, the blood's dried up and your shirt's stuck to the wound. I'm not so sure what to do . . ." He pauses and then calls across the raft. "Kent, give us a hand here."

"I tell ya, we're gonna use this whole first aid kit before the day's over, then what do you plan on doing, huh?" He lumbers across the boat to where Dave and I sit.

After trading places with Dave, Kent's rough fingers explore the bloody patch through my shirt. Clicking the first aid kit open, he searches through the crinkly packs of paper, picks a package, and rips it open with his teeth, spitting the torn-off piece into the ocean. The boat leans sideways as he drops his arm over the edge and splashes his hand in the water.

"What's going on . . ." I can't finish my question, cut off by a hot slice of pain. Kent presses something wet against my shoulder. It's only because I know Dave wouldn't let Kent hurt me that I can stay still, breathing in and out in slow, controlled breaths. He pulls my arm back abruptly, blackness flooding in with the pain.

"You don't have to be so rough," Dave's voice says from somewhere behind me.

"It's called counter-pressure. Unless you want to do this I suggest you shut up."

"No," his voice mellows, "just be careful."

"I have to lift your shirt up." He runs his hand up my bare back, pulling the shirt up slowly. "This is going to hurt," he warns as the fabric pulls on the wound. Then there's more ripping of paper and something rough being pressed against the wound. The sting of alcohol hits all at once, its tangy scent burning in my nostrils, and I whimper a bit.

"I'm sorry, doll, it's very deep." He almost sounds like he cares. "It's gotta be good and clean before I close it up."

"Close it up? How do you plan on doing that?" Dave doesn't sound convinced.

I'm only half-conscious. Another rip and more alcohol, this time Kent rubs hard and it's like sandpaper on the open sore.

"It's too deep to slap a bandage on," Kent explains. "If we don't get it closed it'll get infected and she'll go downhill fast. It's not like we've got ourselves any antibiotics, right?"

"So, how do you plan on closing it up, Kent?" Dave repeats, his impatience building.

"You said there's a sewing kit in that magic bag right? Well, I'm gonna use it for a little sewing project."

"Maybe we should wait till the rescue workers come," Dave argues. "I'm not doubting your abilities but I think they're better trained for this."

"Are you out of your mind or something?" Kent says tossing his last alcohol wipe into the ocean, then sitting up and cracking his neck. "Remember, there aren't going to *be* any magic rescue people, at least not for a long time. If we don't take care of ourselves, all they're going to find is a boat full of bodies."

"It's fine," I say quietly. "Do it now . . . please."

"Are you sure, Lillian? We can wait a little longer if you want." It's Dave, giving me an out. I don't want to wait. I want it to be over.

"Kent—do it *now*."

"That's a smart girl," Kent says, like I'm a horse or dog. Dave doesn't argue anymore, and I try not to listen as Kent preps for the procedure. "Okay, doll, try not to move."

The cool metal needle is sharp. The instant it pierces my ragged skin, I can't help but flinch from the deep, piercing pain.

"Shit! You've got to stay still," he mutters through grinding teeth.

I try to remember the visualization techniques I learned in my birthing classes. Zen, I'll be completely Zen. When Kent's fingers frame the wound, I go deeper inside myself, using all that imagery Nurse Karen taught me during Lamaze. But I ended up with an epidural with both kids, so a lot of good that did me.

On one of my slow exhales, Kent pushes the needle through my skin, faster this time. I can actually feel the thread gliding through. When he sticks the needle through the other side, I lose my cool, twisting away from his tiny tool of torture. A string of curses erupts behind me.

"Look, honey." His voice is shaking almost as much as my body. "If you don't stop moving you're gonna hurt yourself worse. Understand?"

"I'm TRYING!" I shout, sounding so much like Josh it surprises me. Tears of frustration fill my eyes.

"No, no, no . . . don't start crying. Good GOD." He throws up his hands and slaps them down on his legs. "Dave, get over here and be useful for once. Sit in front of her and hold her in place."

Dave rushes over and slips in front of me so we're sitting face-to-face. "You can do this, I know you can." That little worry crease is back. The pain makes me want to yell *You don't even KNOW me!* But instead, I nod.

"Are we ready yet?" Kent growls.

"What's the rush, Kent? You have an appointment to get to? No? Then give us a moment," Dave says with confidence before taking my head and tucking it expertly into the crook of his neck. He rests his head on mine casually, like we've been doing this for years. His day-old stubble scratches my ear.

Tracing down my arms, he takes my hands determinedly, rubbing his thumb up and down the side of my palm. Like he's pushed a button, my whole body falls against him, as if his fingers distributed a dose of morphine.

"Lillian, are you ready?" His voice is as smooth as wave-worn driftwood.

"Uh-huh."

"Go ahead," he tells Kent.

The first stitch flames through my skin like a hot poker, but when I tense up Dave pulls me in closer. "It's okay, you're doing great." Somehow I believe him.

The next stitch is tight but fast, like Kent's getting the hang of sewing through human flesh. I'd be lying if I said that the rest of those evenly placed ties go in easily or that I can't feel the stab of metal gliding through my tender skin, but I can say that in Dave's embrace I learn to endure the pain. It takes eight more stitches: poke through, pull tight, tie, snip, and repeat.

"Done." Kent moves away.

The wound still throbs, and any sudden movement makes me want to scream, but it's better. Definitely better. "Thank you, Kent. I appreciate it."

He waves me off, digging through the bag till he comes up with a prescription bottle.

"Here, take these." He tosses the bottle across the raft and it lands in my lap. The name Margaret Linden and the number 2006 flash up at me. Old antibiotics are probably better than a bacterial infection.

"Let me help you with those." Dave unscrews the top and hands me the open water bottle. I take a tiny sip and toss in the oblong off-white tablets.

"Thanks. You've been amazing today." I hope that the smile I give to Dave says the words I can't find.

"You need to rest." He puts the repacked JanSport above Margaret's head. "Here, try to sleep."

I curl up on the bench, barely aware of my legs being pulled onto his lap, the warmth of his touch making my lids so heavy I can't even try to open them to investigate. Instead I give in, retreating into sleep, pretending I'm home.

CHAPTER 11

DAVE

Present

"How long were you in the boat, Dave?"

"It felt like forever but, from the time we crashed until we found land, it was almost three days," Dave answered succinctly, recrossing his legs so his left foot now rested on his right knee. "To tell the truth, we had some dark moments when I was sure we'd never get off of that boat."

"How did you make it through those days?" Genevieve asked, rubbing her fingertips together like they were covered with a greasy residue. She didn't even sound curious anymore, but Dave was careful to leave his walls up. She wouldn't get in that easily.

"It was mostly luck. When we left the plane, Lillian brought her backpack. In it was a bottle of water and a few other supplies that came in handy. I can't forget the first aid kit that Kent brought with him. Without those two items we wouldn't have made it twenty-four hours."

"And land?" she rushed, skipping whole chunks of questions Dave had prepped for. "When did you see land?"

Dave's answer hitched in his throat briefly, a moment of silence for those torturous, endless hours on the raft that Genevieve Randall brushed away in one sentence. He had to remind himself that less was more. If the reporter wanted to skip all the way to the rescue, Dave shouldn't complain.

"Around noon on the third day," Dave answered finally. "The sun was high in the sky and burning my forehead. We had only a few sips of water left in the bottle and Margaret had fallen into a coma. It seemed completely hopeless at that moment." A long trail of sweat trickled down the back of his neck, as if his body remembered the interminable heat on that boat. "At first I thought it was an illusion. I was weak. We were all at a breaking point. Yet, no one gave in to the temptation to drink the seawater, because Kent said it'd make you go mad. But for a while I was already questioning my sanity. I sat there watching the tiny emerald speck grow slowly in front of me for at least an hour before I said anything to everyone else."

"What were your feelings in that moment?" she probed.

"First was denial, then excitement and hope. We had no way of knowing how big the island was or if it was inhabited, so of course at first we all felt like we'd been rescued and the whole thing was finally over."

Dave remembered the flutter of expectation that batted around in his empty stomach as the waves gently pushed their raft closer and closer to the ever-growing speck. He was the one who was sure they'd floated into salvation. He expected to bob up to land on their little raft and startle sunbathers lying out on the beach. His sun-beaten brain imagined they'd run up to the cabana hut and order everyone a tall, gorgeous glass of lemonade.

"How did you get onto the island without any oars or motors?" Genevieve asked, but not in that skeptical way she asked about Theresa, more robotic and rehearsed.

"Once we realized that it really was land, our joy was soon replaced with frustration. We were lodged in a current pushing us close to but not onto the island. We were moving so slowly, we had plenty of time to plan and organize. First, we tried using our hands as oars in the water but that didn't move us very far off our course. Remember, we were all dehydrated, half-starved, and severely sunburned, so not at our peak performance levels. Then Kent had the idea to get in the water and push the raft by kicking our legs."

"You went in the water?" she interrupted, tilting her head to one side. "Weren't you afraid of sharks and such?" Her honey-colored eyebrows wagged, one a fraction higher than the other, making Dave unsure if nature or plastic surgery was responsible for the incongruity.

"Knowing what I do now, we should've been. But we were so desperate to be off that boat and we thought there might be food and people and communication on that island. I think if we *had* thought of it, we still would've found the risk an acceptable one."

"Please tell me about what it was like when you landed. What was the state of the island and your fellow passengers?"

"The first night was the worst." A chill went through him like the wind whipping his soaked polo. "It was night by the time we reached the shore. We had no fire, no fresh water still, and no food. I mostly remember how dark it was. Lillian cared for Margaret, Kent wandered off immediately, and I slept most of the night in the raft."

The reporter's ears seemed to perk up at the mention of Lillian's mother-in-law. "And Margaret, how long did she last?" How was the end of a woman's life reduced to a single flippant question? He intended to give Margaret the respect she deserved.

"Margaret lost her life within twenty-four hours of landing on the island. There was nothing we could do to help her further. She needed a doctor and a hospital with a fully equipped operating room. I think Lillian let herself hope when we saw the island, but after we landed and realized we were alone, it was clear Margaret wasn't going to live."

"They did an extensive coroner's report on her before her reburial next to her husband in Iowa. Have you had the chance to read it?" He wasn't aware of an autopsy.

"Uh, um . . . No, I hadn't heard." He swallowed with difficulty, hoping to unstick the dry lump in his throat. Why did they even lie about Margaret? To lessen Lillian's guilt? Would people really blame her for leaving that laptop on her seat? Would Jerry? He doubted it. If Dave had been thinking clearer when they made up their story, he would've realized this was a greedy lie, an unnecessary lie, and perhaps a fatal lie. If Genevieve Randall proved they were lying about one thing, she'd know they had something to hide.

She pulled out a manila folder from the pouch beside her chair. "I have it right here." She tugged a few crisp white pages from the envelope, flipping the stapled pages purposefully. "Here it is. It says she died of a massive injury to her forehead, consistent with blunt force trauma." She flipped the papers closed and leaned over them for her next question. "How did that happen?"

"Uh, I don't know. A plane crash maybe?"

The little smile turning up the edge of her mouth worried Dave.

"Of course. Did you treat her for the injury?"

"We tried. It was cleaned and bandaged to the best of our abilities but we couldn't do much without professional help."

"Hmmm, yes I see." She ran her tongue over her thin, barely there lips. "I understand she was hurt in the crash, but the reason I'm curious is: I've watched and read almost every interview the survivors gave, and not one time was Margaret's cause of death mentioned. I was wondering why?"

Listening to the accusations in her tone, Dave put his trembling hands under his thighs to keep her from noticing the spike in his nerves. He had five seconds to decide if he was in real trouble or if he could play it cool, when an idea sprung in his mind fully formed.

"No one took the time to ask us, I guess." He gave the reporter a warm smile, pulling his hands out from behind his legs and running one through his hair. Lillian always said girls liked that, that *she* liked that. "I'm extremely impressed with your thorough investigation, Ms. Randall."

At his compliment she sucked on her smooth teeth, cocked her head so minutely to one side that perhaps no one but Dave detected it, and flipped the report closed. She didn't look down, she didn't take any notes with her uncapped Sharpie, she didn't break eye contact, and Dave felt an icy chill in her frozen eyes cooling the sweat on his neck and raising goose bumps on his bare forearms.

"At least you buried her, unlike poor Theresa," Genevieve mumbled. A statement meant for the editing-room floor, meant to shake Dave off his game because she could do anything she wanted to with this interview. Whatever he said, they'd cut up into small, manageable snips so anything could be insinuated or inferred from his response. He wanted to slam his fist down on the plush cushion next to him. He'd given them that power, handed it right over. It reminded him of how powerless he felt on that raft, drifting along in random currents and weather patterns over which he had no control. Now he was floating along in Genevieve Randall's ocean.

CHAPTER 12

DAVID-DAY 4

An island in the South Pacific

Twenty hours. Twenty. Less than a day. When I was a kindergartener I had the hardest time counting to twenty. My dad would go over the numbers with me every day while I brushed my teeth. One through ten was easy—eleven, twelve, and even up to nineteen—but after that I could never remember twenty. At five years old, twenty was too large to conceptualize. Twenty dollars was a fortune, twenty toys a treasure chest, twenty minutes a lifetime, twenty years eternity.

Today I feel like I'm five years old again—still can't get to twenty. My waterproof watch stops—frozen at exactly 3:45 p.m. Nineteen hours and fifty-five minutes from when we landed on this island. Banged up and cracked down one side of the analog face, it stops keeping time at the exact moment I sit down beside our first fire to eat real food.

It's a simple meal made up of some small coral fish Kent caught, roasted coconut flesh, and a few roots I found foraging. Kent placed large rocks in the middle of the fire that we started using Margaret's reading glasses. After gutting the puny fish with a knife from the raft, he tossed them, butterflied, onto the heated surface. Soon, the air filled with a rich, mouthwatering aroma. I hope Lillian makes it back soon or else I don't know if Kent and I will have enough self-control to share.

Kent paces in front of the fire, poking at the uncooked portions of the fish. I stare at the food like I'm chilling on my couch at home watching the Rose Bowl on my flat-screen TV. Kent grunts something completely lost in the sizzle of fish on rock.

"What?" I snap, looking away from the fire reluctantly, annoyed that Kent would interrupt such an enthralling show.

"Go get the girl. The food's almost ready."

I take in every inch of the pink translucent flesh firming up and turning opaque. Could this be Kent's way to get rid of me long enough to down the meal on his own? No, I'd rather get her than let Kent do it. His tact could fill a teaspoon, and that might be pushing it.

Pushing off the sandy log that abuts the fire's circle, I stomp down to the water where our boat hit land the day before. Squinting down the beach to the point where it curves around to the other side of the island, I see no Lillian. I scan to the trees, to the raft, and back to the water before I realize where she is.

Fueled by hunger and a fear that we'll return to Kent sucking on the empty bones of our sacrificial fish, I sprint down the small beach to the left of our camp. Passing an outcropping of coconut trees, I see her. She's facing the water on a sandy peninsula jutting out into the unfriendly ocean. A breeze laps at the long, wild strands of her hair. She's wearing her cutoffs and bathing suit top, so I can see the angry red gash that crawls up her left shoulder. Kent's stitches are even but sloppy, and even if she avoids infection, the scar will be a nasty one.

She's so alone out there, feet set apart, hands shoved in her pockets, like it's Lillian facing the world. I don't know what she's thinking, I'm afraid to know. I've tried to stay away from her today. I would've stayed away from Kent too, but he's a little harder to evade. It's too hard to be around them, to tally what we've left behind, lost perhaps forever, and understand that whether I like it or not they are all I have left.

When Margaret was still alive, Lillian was different. She had these stubborn embers of hope that warmed us all and wouldn't go out. When Kent took charge of our water supply, doling it out a capful at a time, he told her that Margaret was no longer allowed her ration because it spilled down her face and was, as Kent put it, wasted. She didn't crack. She didn't demand the water back, the water that had been taken out of her bag, that she was kind enough to share with all of us. No—instead she shared her own meager capful with her mother-in-law.

But after we saw the island and determined it wasn't merely a mirage or a hallucination as a result of dehydration, Margaret was almost gone and Lillian started to change.

For a day, we kicked, rested, and waved our arms feebly in the water, until the tide finally caught our little boat. With a few kicks off the ribbon of reef that surrounded the island, we were brought to its sandy shore on the waves as the sun sunk into the ocean.

With the raft safely beached, I jumped in to help Lillian carry Margaret ashore. There we found a banyan tree with roots that arched up as though the tree spent years making a little room for this exact moment. A room only big enough for two, so I retraced my steps to the raft.

Darkness fell rapidly, and once my feet splashed in the black water blanketing the bottom of the boat, a powerful surge of fatigue crashed over me. As soon as I lay down, I was sound asleep. A cool breeze and waves lapping at the beach woke me some hours later. It was dark. No, it was black.

"Lillian? Kent? Are you there?" I called out.

Out of the darkness came a new sound, something like a high-pitched whine, that shook my eardrums. Hope thrummed through me with each wail. An engine? A siren? No. This sound was alive, like some kind of animal.

Every Animal Planet show I'd ever watched flashed through my mind. The episodes I remembered the clearest contained mostly huge snakes, poisonous spiders, and giant rats with glowing eyes.

Burrowing deeper into the slowly deflating bench, I hoped that a two-foot wall of sagging plastic was enough to hide me from whatever was making that sound. "Go to sleep. Go to sleep. Go—to—sleep."

The overwhelming drowsiness that had put me under like anesthesia was gone, and now that sound, that pathetic but haunting sound, had me on high alert. Clouds blotted out the moon and stars, and the palm trees shook in a high wind; I wondered if we were in for another storm. Even the weather had joined the plot against our survival.

"Ahhhh!" I yelled, trying to empty all the steam from my boiling emotions as if through a release valve. "Where *is* everybody?!" All the questions I'd heard Lillian and Kent ask themselves over and over again began to inundate me, lying heavy on my chest, making it hard to breathe. How are we going to get enough food? Enough water? Are they coming for us or did they just give up?

"Dave?" A voice in the distance called my name.

"Is that you, Lillian?" I yelled, my voice still shaky.

"Yes, I'm over here by the rocks. Where are *you*?"

"In the raft, but if you keep talking I'll make my way over to you." I squinted into the darkness, trying to figure out which way to go. "Keep talking and I'll head your way."

I took a step in the direction of her voice. For a few seconds I felt and heard nothing but my feet in the sand and the waves lapping lazily at the shore, until my foot hit something solid, making me yelp.

"Are you at the rocks?" Lillian shouted in response.

"Yup. Keep talking, I'll follow your voice."

"Uh, okay." She paused uncertainly. "What should I say?"

I took a step toward her voice. I'd never make it there before dawn at this rate. I needed questions that required more than a one-word answer.

"Where's Kent?"

"Um, around here somewhere. When we landed he wandered off, and I haven't seen him since."

Nice. Both Kent and I abandoned the two most injured survivors within minutes of hitting dry land. That's chivalry for you. I kept walking, listening to the sound of Lillian shifting her weight a few yards to my left.

"And Margaret, how's she doing? Is she stable?"

"She's dead."

"Dead." I repeated the word. I felt bad that I didn't sound surprised. "I'm sorry, Lillian."

Then she started to cry. I'd heard her cry plenty in the past few days, from pain or fear or guilt, but this sounded different. This was a wail crossed with a scream. I wanted her to stop, but even her breaths were choking, gasping whinnies. That sound, I knew it instantly— Lillian was the injured animal I'd been so afraid of.

Listening to her scared me in a whole new way. It would've been easy to find her then, following the sounds like a rope, but I wanted to run away. I didn't know how to comfort that kind of raw sorrow.

Now I was confronted with a question that scared me more than starving or drowning: If I can't comfort her sorrow, how can I comfort my own?

A salty tear dripped down into the corner of my mouth and I knew: I can't do this alone. I need Lillian and she needs me. Without another thought, I staggered toward her voice, grateful for the dark. The last thing Lillian needed to see was my face, red and swollen from crying. When my foot grazed her leg she let out a choked gasp.

"Dave?"

"No," I joked, lowering my voice, "it's Elvis."

Immediately her hand bumped into my hand, which was wet with tears. "There you are," she whispered, and I couldn't imagine that voice issuing those violent cries. Her fingers intertwined with mine.

"That was like Marco Polo but without the water. It's more fun in a pool." I tried to ignore how nervous her fingers on mine made me.

"I'm sorry, I wasn't much help." The grainy outline of her head developed like a Polaroid.

"Are you kidding me? I'd still be crying like a little girl inside the raft if you hadn't called me over here."

"Come. Sit." Tugging on my hand, she guided me down into an empty spot in the sand. I sat cross-legged beside her.

"How are you doing? You hanging in there?" I asked, feebly, rubbing my thumb across the back of her hand for my comfort as much as hers. She fell against me, putting her head on my shoulder, warming me all over.

"Not really."

"In the morning we can search for food and make a shelter, then figure out our next move. We have more options now that we're on dry land. This is a very good thing." I tried to sound like I knew what I was talking about, pulling her whole arm over my knee and into my lap.

"I can't even think about tomorrow right now." She turned her face into my shoulder. "With Margaret gone, it feels like the sun will never come up, like we're trapped in a hole for eternity."

"That's what I like about you," I teased, "your unending optimism."

"They're not coming." She ignored my joke. "No one's coming."

"No, I guess they're not." No use in lying. She drew in a huge breath and let it out slowly, making the air stir around us.

"Then we'll die on the island."

"Not necessarily."

She shook her head against my wet shoulder. "If no one's coming for us then we're stuck here and like Margaret we'll all die, sooner or later."

"No one lives forever, Lillian." I rub my cheek against her tangled hair. "Not on an island or at home in St. Louis. But we have a lot of living to do in between. We aren't just going to die on this island; we're going to *live* here too."

"But I don't want to live *here* for the rest of my life, Dave. I want to be with my children and Jerry and Margaret and my brothers and my parents and my friends." She shifted suddenly to face me, her warm breath condensing on my face. "Let's say we find a way to live here. Think about it, what kind of life would the next five or ten or twenty or however many years be? Here, on this lump of sand. How can I find happiness here?" Her voice falters and I know this is more than just losing Margaret. She's not going to see her kids again. They'll think she's dead too.

"I know. I want to go home too, and maybe we will. But until then we need to take care of ourselves, and make the best of this situation." I took short breaths between each sentence. "We're going to take care of each other. We *will* make the best of this." This time, I believed myself.

Her eyes, wide and vulnerable, flitted across my face, each of her breaths coming faster than the one before it. Licking her lips with the tip of her tongue, she let out one long, slow blow that tickled the stubble on my chin.

"I guess you're right," she said with an air of surrender. Her head returned to the empty spot on my shoulder and I shifted her weight so she didn't have to put any pressure on her bad arm. "I'm so tired and hungry. I don't know . . . what . . ." She was asleep before finishing her thought. Leaning back into the sand, careful not to wake her, I lay flat, staring up at the sky.

A small patch of clouds broke the weather gods' ruling and parted to let me view a little slice of the sky, the pinprick light of the stars piled one on top of the other. How many solar systems was I watching through that sudden gash in the clouds? I tried to count the stars, as if counting sheep, before the clouds closed and I dozed off.

Kent shook us awake in the peachy morning hours. Overnight, Lillian sunk into a semi-catatonic state, moving like a zombie, carefully avoiding Margaret's stiff body, which had turned a haunting shade of blue in the evening's chill.

Even when Kent shoved a coconut into her hands, the sweet milk sloshing out of the hole he'd cut in it, she did little more than lift it to her lips and sip. Then Kent taught us how to use his knife to break down the nut and bite off the sugary flesh, but she only nodded and nibbled on his offerings.

"That chick is crazy," Kent grumbled, grabbing the empty shells to throw in the ocean.

"Give her a break. Her mother-in-law died less than a day ago. She needs some time to adapt." There's something about that woman that makes me get all protective.

"Yeah, I lost somebody too but you don't see me wigging out." He assessed Lillian, like a teacher grading a science project. "She's not going to make it long. I think she's lost it." Kent tossed each shell individually, sending them spinning like Frisbees as he spoke. "She's not eating, she's not drinking, and she can't contribute to camp. It doesn't mean much to me if she wants to give up, but that's another mouth to feed. I have a strict 'you don't work, you don't eat' policy."

"Oh, so you already have *policies* about being stranded on an island?"

"Don't be a smart-ass." He paused to chew a stray piece of coconut off one of Lillian's untouched shells. "I'm not gonna carry her for very long without something in return."

I stood with my bare feet in the edge of the tide, stunned at Kent's bold proclamation, as though he was king of the island and I was his lowly peon. I began to formulate an argument in my head but gave up. After all I've learned about Kent I should know by now that he's not one to listen to reason.

"I'll try to talk to her."

"M'kay," he said, sucking on a large chunk of coconut, smacking with his mouth open. "Wait." He dug down deep in his cargo shorts pocket. "Here, you should have this."

He pressed a bright piece of orange plastic into my palm, like I was his valet and he was passing me a tip. Unfolding my fingers, I saw the sharp metal tip at the end of the plastic catch the sun. It looked like a beefed-up X-ACTO knife. Kent must have read the confusion on my face because he explained.

"It's a knife . . . from the boat. They had two in there to cut it away from the plane. I thought you should have one, you know, just in case."

A knife, the one I'd told Lillian to use to cut the raft from the plane. She must have put it back in the raft pocket. I was baffled that Kent would give it to me; it's not like we've been buddies post-crash. As I curled my fingers around the glowing handle, I felt fractionally more powerful. Other than the clothes on my back and ruined leather shoes still drying by the fire, it's my first asset. I promised myself I'd learn how to use it to my advantage.

Tucking the tool into my pocket, I noticed Kent watching me with alarm, maybe regretting the decision to give me the knife. I walked away before he tried to get it back.

Kent followed close behind me, wiping his hands on the baggy khaki captain's shorts he'd been trapped into wearing. As intimidating as he can be, those shorts make him look like an overgrown little boy trying to escape Sister Agatha's ruler. He laid out the agenda for the day, taking on the role of leader without waiting for an election. I didn't feel like fighting so I let him play boss, relishing the knife in my pocket resting against my thigh.

First we buried Margaret. As insensitive as it sounded coming from Kent's mouth, he was right, she'd start to decompose in the heat and sun of the day, inviting predators and scavengers to feed. He'd picked the peninsula to be her resting place because of its distance from camp and the jungle. I thought it was fitting to bury Margaret by the ocean—where we all could see her, where we'd be reminded of what we've lost.

It took two hours using fragments of bamboo to dig a hole deep enough so that animals couldn't dig her up. The sand kept cascading back into the pit until I was sure we'd never be done. Finally, we hit wet sand and then the digging was quick. No one talked.

Kent insisted we have a memorial service for both women lost in the crash, but Lillian declined to say anything after we dumped piles of sand over Margaret's stiff body. She clutched a gold chain entwined in her fingers and hugged Margaret's bloodstained coat as if it could bring Margaret back from the dead.

Kent said a few words about Theresa before his voice cracked and he said he was going to hunt. Lillian sat down in the sand beside Margaret's grave and closed her eyes. I don't know if she was sleeping or praying but I didn't think that was a good time to interrupt.

She's still gazing out over the ocean as though she could find her house if she looked hard enough. I know I have to break her out of it or else she'll fade away and leave me alone, here, with him. I can manage life on this rock with her, or maybe even alone, but not without her and *with* Kent.

Now is my chance to have that talk.

As I walk up to her, my palms start sweating. Her stitches look even more raw and tender up close. I want to reach out and put my arm around her and warm her goose-pimpled skin but instead I stand beside her, crossing my arms to ward off the wind. I wait for her to notice me but she doesn't.

"Lillian." She blinks once but still doesn't turn. "Lillian. Kent made dinner. It looks delicious, fish and some other stuff. You should come and eat, there's enough for all of us." I think she shakes her head but it could be the wind in her hair. "Please come, Lillian. We're worried about you. *I'm* worried about you. Please, eat with us." A tear runs down her cheek and traces the sharp outline of her jaw. More follow in rapid-fire succession.

"I know you feel alone but, as selfish as it sounds, I need you right now." I take a step closer. "If I don't have you, I might lose it too."

I let the words hang out there like laundry drying in the wind, and then pretend to look out into the ocean too. Maybe, in all her staring, she's found something more than nothingness to focus on. My stomach grumbles loudly, the few hunks of coconut tumbling around. There's real food back at the fire and the survival part of my brain tells me to leave and claim my share of the food before it's gone. But I can't abandon her again like last night, when Margaret was dying.

"I wish they'd put that in your file," Lillian whispers through a sniff.

"What? That I'm a selfish jerk?" I glance at her sidelong.

"No, I wish they'd told me you were such a good person." She looks up at me and there's a little smile cracking through her mask of sorrow. I can't help but return it, remembering when I'd first said those words on the plane, before the crash.

"I guess we're even." I point down the beach to camp. "Let's eat." The sea breeze pushes us inland. Lillian shivers but I'm not cold. I'm warmed by the light I managed to reignite in Lillian's eyes.

CHAPTER 13

LILLIAN

Present

"We started off digging a hole a short distance from camp," Lillian explained, trying not to laugh at the sour pucker on Genevieve's face. "Everyone used it but after a while it was too gross so we filled it in. When we moved to the lagoon there was a new rule—don't ask, don't tell. As long as it was more than thirty feet from camp or water, you could pick for yourself. That worked a lot better."

"When I asked about personal hygiene," she interrupted, swallowing loudly, "I was asking more about bathing, laundry, soap substitutes . . . that sort of thing."

Apparently it only took a few potty stories to unnerve the unflappable Genevieve Randall. Lillian loved it. She'd tell a hundred more if it made the reporter gag like this one did.

"So you *don't* want to know what we used as toilet paper?" Lillian asked, fluttering her eyelashes innocently. Genevieve pressed her lips together. Maybe it was better that Jerry hadn't come down yet or they'd both be laughing.

"No!" Her voice pitched up with a slight edge of panic. *This woman is clearly not a mother*, Lillian thought. Brief memories of Josh and Daniel's potty-training years flashed through her mind.

They'd been such babies when she'd left on that infamous trip, only five and seven years old, but when she came home they were a solemn seven and nervous nine.

They were waiting for her, surrounded by a flock of cameras and encircled by Jill's arms. At first glance, Jill looked the same as the day before Lillian left, when they'd gone for coffee together. Jill joked around telling Lillian that she should take a picture of the cabana boy in each location and e-mail it to her so she could get the "good parts" of the vacation vicariously.

Everything from her short red hair spiked toward the sky, to her super-stylish dark skinny jeans and loose gauzy purple shirt hanging nearly to her knees, screamed "original." That's what Jill was—original. Lillian always felt very white bread next to Jill's seven-grain, but differences aside, they were best friends.

Three steps forward and Jill came into focus. Her prominent cheekbones stood out dramatically and dark half-circles created smudges under her eyes, barely disguised with makeup. Each arm stuck out from under her loose shirt, scrawny and white like bones, one draped around Josh and the other around Daniel, making Jill look like a giant purple bird protecting peeping chicks. Like they were *her* chicks.

Jill would never try to take her children from her, right? But seeing them like that, intertwined, intimate, Lillian felt like she'd lost them forever.

Jerry squeezed her hand reassuringly. He was watching her again. It seemed like he was always watching her. The weight of his assessment was a heavy load—heavier than the stares of the press and the gawking public.

"Are you ready to see the boys?" Jerry whispered. "Look how excited they are."

Josh had grown four or five inches at least. His sandy-blond hair was long, hanging over his ears and into his eyes, curling up at the ends. If Lillian had been home she would've cut it a long time ago but, she had to admit, it did give him a little bit of a swagger.

His gangly limbs were hidden by a long-sleeved dress shirt, probably purchased specially for this occasion. The vertical green and gray stripes elongated his already impossibly long arms, alerting her that he was a child ready to burst into adolescence. Every part of him seemed to scream, "YOU MISSED THIS." His adult front teeth were fully grown in, too big for his smile. How many times had the tooth fairy come?

How dare she come when I wasn't there? Lillian thought, angry that life went on so easily without her. She suddenly hated the tooth fairy, with her fancy little wings and magic wand. Lillian shook her head to refocus. *Don't be crazy, Lillian. Be normal. Normal.*

She didn't remember how to be normal anymore. Jerry had to assist her with the buttons on her blouse that morning and help fix her lipstick in the car on the way to the airport. During that ride he had tried to fill her in on every second of the boys' lives that she'd missed, like he was the babysitter and she'd just returned home from a night out on the town. Lillian was always the expert on her own children but now she felt like a spectator to their lives.

She glanced over to Jill's other side where little Daniel's face was half covered by the billowing purple shirt. He fit nicely in the curve of Jill's hip, like he was used to finding comfort there. When Jill shifted her arm, the top of Daniel's head popped out and Lillian forgot to be jealous. When she'd left, her kindergartener had hair the color of the sand on her island, so light brown that in the summer the sun bleached the tips blond. But in the past twenty months it'd turned dark and covered his head in a crown of mahogany curls.

Jill tapped him on the shoulder and whispered something that made him look right at Lillian. When their eyes met, she held her breath. He had her emerald eyes, or at least the way they used to be, bright and merry. His little pink lips curled up into a bashful smile. Clutched in his delicate fist was a sign written in multicolored markers and crayons that read WELCOME HOME, MOM! If only that sign was true, that they really could welcome her back into their lives.

The noise around them began to filter in, a crowd, and someone calling her name, drowning out the whoosh of her own heartbeat.

"Lillian, LILLIAN!" She heard it again. She scanned the room for another familiar face in the flood of strangers pushing against the flimsy black ribbon barricade. There was a wall of color, balloons and flowers, blurring in the mass of people and a collage of faces, smiling and calling her name, yelling happy words that didn't make any sense.

Their eyes pushed at her skin, their shouts hurting her ears. A woman shot her hand out beyond the restraints, reaching toward Lillian, tears streaming down her face. What did she want? What did they all want? This was too much all at once. Too many people, too much excitement, too much expectation. She had to escape.

Wiggling her fingers, she tried to force her hand out of Jerry's, thinking semi-logically that running while holding hands would be impossible. She considered the tight metal buckle around her ankle; there was no easy way to slip the stupid shoes off. Why hadn't she worn gym shoes rather than the flimsy sparkling sandals someone put on her this morning in Guam? Even her old Nikes that hadn't made it off the island would be easier to run in. She needed to run.

The plane they'd exited was gone, on its way to Chicago. Even if she could catch a plane, where would she go? She couldn't go back to the island and live there alone; too many memories haunted that place. And there was no way in hell she'd set foot in the hospital room she'd been trapped in for the past two weeks. There *was* one other option. David. He'd know what to do.

The idea of talking to him calmed her like a Valium. Planning it out in her mind, she could get as far as California, walking off the plane and seeing his smile and falling naturally into the safety of his arms. But how could she explain that after dreaming of coming home for so long, now she felt entirely out of place? She could imagine his scowl when she admitted that everyone would've been better off if she'd never been rescued at all. That thought was more painful than everyone staring at her from the crowd. She'd rather stay here than make David hate her more.

Jerry put an arm around her boney shoulder, barely touching her skin. "Those boys missed you so much." His breath smelled of spearmint Life Savers. He always sucked on them during landings and takeoffs to help relieve the pressure in his ears. The memory made Lillian lean into his embrace and smile. "Should I call them over?" he asked, as if he didn't feel the tide pulling them under. She wanted to say no but she nodded anyway, wondering if it was possible to drown on dry land.

Jerry gave the boys a big wave and Lillian leaned against Jerry, so afraid that they'd shake their heads and turn away. Daniel had always been afraid of strangers and Lillian was sure she looked like a total stranger to him now. But as soon as her sons heard their names, they let go of Jill, rushing toward Lillian.

"Mom!" Josh's big boy voice called and it sounded so familiar.

"MOMMY!" Daniel shouted as he ran, his legs blurring beneath him. She braced for impact just before they collided. Daniel hit first, wrapping his arms around her legs, and Josh second, throwing his arms around her waist. The force of their collision blew out all that doubt that had been weighing her down, and instead of falling deeper into the hole she'd been digging for herself, she finally saw a tiny pinprick of light showing her which way to start climbing.

◆ ◆ ◆

No, Genevieve Randall had no children, Lillian was certain. A mom has enough day-to-day familiarity with grossness that she could relate to the hilarity of potty humor. But as entertaining as it was messing with her, Lillian was ready get on with the interview—get it over with.

"Okay, personal hygiene?" Lillian rubbed her hands together, ready to get down to business. "That's easy. We all kept our own hygiene schedules, which spanned from never to once a week."

Genevieve's nose wrinkled up minutely, like she could smell them even now. In the background, Jerry loped down the stairs and settled into an open chair behind Genevieve Randall right in Lillian's line of vision. He'd changed his shirt, this one pinstriped. He caught her eyes and mouthed, "Robot." Lillian covered her mouth and faked a cough to hide her laugh.

"You mean bathing?" she asked hopefully, apparently finding this a more comfortable topic than poop ditches. "In the ocean or in fresh water?"

"Mostly the small freshwater pond we found near the lagoon. It was fed by an underwater spring so the water was surprisingly fresh. We were careful to keep it away from any contaminants." Lillian couldn't resist raising her eyebrows suggestively. "Once a week, on Sundays, I'd take any laundry to the pond and wash it the best I could, then I'd bathe. For a while I used some soaps from Margaret's toiletry bag but after a while I only used them on special occasions, like a holiday."

Is this when they'd show the CGI map of the island? There would be a red dotted line to show the path to and from the lagoon, the freshwater pond, the sandy graveyard peninsula by the old beach.

Or did they go there? Did they send a camera crew to film the remains of their home? The thought made her shiver, as if she was witnessing a cat burglar creeping around her dark house at night, touching all her things, searching lustily for anything of value.

"And the men?"

Lillian shrugged. "I know they washed, well Dave did, I'm not certain about Kent. He always had that manly stench about him. They both spent a lot of time in the water fishing and I think they counted that. We all smelled nasty most of the time."

"I guess you'd know since you all slept together every night." Genevieve raised her eyebrows and Lillian couldn't tell if she was trying to be lewd.

Those nights, dark, silent, sandwiched between the two men, body heat radiating from each side, a hand creeping toward her, darting under the hem of her shirt, tracing up her vertebrae, around her rib cage . . . Lillian blinked slowly, deliberately.

"Yes, every night," she responded.

CHAPTER 14

LILY-DAY 65

An island in the South Pacific

Laundry day. After a week of on-and-off rain, this morning the sun came up in a cloudless sky. It quickly evaporated the rainwater puddles pooled inside large divots in the sand. Finally. I can get my chores done.

The men have been up for a while. I can tell by the height of the fire and chilly bare mats on either side of me. For some reason they've decided to let me sleep in. I'm not complaining, but I doubt there's enough food left in our fruit basket to tide me over till lunchtime.

Dusting dry sand off my feet the best I can, I slide on my dingy gray Nikes. The once-blue Nike swoosh is now a murky black and the laces on my right foot are one hard tug from snapping. Standing in the sand I work out all the kinks in my muscles from where they went numb on our bamboo floor.

Even with the sun, there's still a rainy chill in the air. I pull on Margaret's sports coat and pretend like I don't notice the rusty brown stain crawling down one side. But I do notice. I always notice. I've washed it repeatedly the past six weeks and I'll do it again today. I hate being wrapped in her blood every night just to stay warm.

Slinking around the outskirts of the fire circle, I rummage through the woven bag of fruit I collected during dry days throughout the week. Two green bananas and one overripe mango is all that's left after the locusts I live with had their breakfast. I shrug and toss them in the coat's pockets, saving the meager meal till I'm alone by the freshwater pond where I do my washing. It's a twenty-minute walk from camp but in the stillness of the trees, green hues reflecting off the still water, the food always tastes better when seasoned with a few moments of rare privacy.

That pool's our salvation. Without it, the only source of fresh water would be rain. That sounds like a good idea but rain is much harder to collect than movies would lead you to believe. The first two days on the island were dry. We drank coconut milk and mango juice to stay alive, but we were always thirsty and the fruit juice did a horrible number on our digestive systems. Then Kent showed up with real, clean, cool water. It was like liquid heaven.

We chugged down the first bottle insatiably, not even thinking to ask where it came from or if it was safe. Once the bottle was empty, Dave demanded that Kent show us the source but he refused. That's so him.

The next day we hid and followed Kent halfway around the island through a complicated maze of jungle. Then the trees parted and we saw it: a dark body of water about the size of a hotel pool. Kent drank straight from the pond, filling the bottle when he was done, then marched off into the jungle, presumably to hunt. We waited, probably longer than necessary, until we were sure he was gone. Then Dave and I lost our minds, jumping into the water fully clothed.

At first I drank large mouthfuls, bringing my cupped hands to my mouth as fast as my half-starved body would allow. It was gritty and tasted a little like algae but we decided it must be tolerably clean since we didn't get sick from what we downed the day before. Finally, I gave in and put my face in the water and sucked in the revitalizing liquid straight from the spring. Ever since that day, that pool of heaven is my refuge.

I take off Margaret's jacket and lay it on the ground, flattening it out with the shiny, off-white satin lining facing up. In the rear corner of the shelter is a small pile of laundry Kent and Dave left heaped, at my request, the night before. Dave's shirt, Kent's boxers, a pair of once white, now dark brown socks. I drop the items into the waiting coat, adding the grayish-white bra and underwear I'd been hiding in my back pocket for a day and a half.

Crossing the corners of the jacket, I expertly create a makeshift sack, careful not to dislodge my breakfast. Throwing the sack over my shoulder with the skill of a hobo, I head out toward the beach. Glancing up and down the shore I try to make out the shape of either man, squinting out across the water in case one of the guys is fishing, but I seem to be alone.

Alone. As much as the idea frightened me after the crash, now I have very little time by myself. In fact, the only time I have alone is in my dreams. I'm not even alone in my bed, because I share that with Dave and Kent.

They sleep on either side of me, Dave on my left and Kent on my right. I'm not completely sure how the sleeping order developed, but both men have enough of a dislike for one another that they silently consented to sleep as far away from each other as possible. Some nights, usually during or after a storm, we press together, creating a chain of warmth that can't be surpassed by woven palm fronds or beach grass.

In the middle I never have to worry about being cold, because both men move in close and act as human space heaters. When it's hot they roll in the other direction, letting the refreshing tropical breezes that caress our island cycle through the shelter.

Sleeping together has its downfalls too. The mosquitos are nasty little vampires that never seem to be full. We've cut apart the busted life raft, which was popped by coral on the way into the lagoon, and try to roll sections of it down over our little shack at night to keep the bugs out, but most of the time it's too hot and smelly. Even with the breeze, the smell of two active men sleeping beside me in an enclosed area is overpowering. For a long time I'd fall asleep with my arm across my nose and mouth to keep from gagging.

Kent's the worst. I think he's relishing the opportunity to skip bathing, as though he's a stubborn six-year-old who's too busy playing to take a bath. At least the stench seems to keep the mosquitos away. I guess it's true that over time you can become desensitized to anything, but lately it's more than body odor that's unbearable.

In the darkest part of the night, the fire dies down to embers and the breeze from the ocean crosses the line from refreshing to chilling. We sleep nestled close to each other and I've learned to keep my nose toward Dave, definitely the less smelly of the two men. Dave's an easy person to sleep by. He never encroaches on my space, seeming to anticipate my twists and turns, and when it's cold he's always there with a warm, safe spot to settle against.

That leaves Kent behind me, his deadweight making it impossible to move even an inch in his direction. More and more often I've woken to find him lying uncomfortably near me, his entire body pressed against mine. And now there's this "dreaming" thing.

It started with the intolerable closeness but that's not what woke me up. Over the past few days I've sometimes woken to find his heavy arm draped across my body under the woven mat I made for us. We don't cross that invisible line during sleeping time, it's an unspoken rule—no touching besides the necessary keeping-warm kind.

The first time it happened, he was talking to himself in a strange way, mumbling things I couldn't hear, his acrid breath steaming in my ear, making it clammy. Then his fingers moved, a little at a time, starting at the back of my coat, twisting noiselessly forward. Half-awake, I thought it was a bug or rat, but when his callused fingertips slid beneath my shirt and caressed my bare skin, the world came into hyper-focus.

"Kent, Kent, wake up," I whispered urgently, sure he'd be mortified when he woke and realized what he'd done. His hand went limp and slithered away, almost like he wasn't asleep.

I tried to shake that idea, using every method of thought control I'd ever learned. I couldn't sleep for the rest of that night, worried I might feel that hand moving toward me again or even worse, that I *wouldn't* feel it until he'd gone too far.

Climbing out of the shelter the next morning I was tired and blurry-eyed, and Dave asked if I was feeling all right. I didn't tell him. I didn't ask to switch spots. Part of it was embarrassment, part denial, but mostly I was worried he'd blow this way out of proportion and Dave vs. Kent would always end with Kent in the winner's circle.

For the next two nights I slept in a twilight state, waiting for it to happen again. On the third night, avoiding sleep was impossible. We'd been out nutting all day, climbing trees, tossing coconuts, husking, shelling. Being the lightest, I was always hoisted into the trees. I'd wrap my arms around the slender trunk and climb with my feet flat against the smooth bark. By the end of the day I was sore and exhausted.

The moment my head hit the padded bamboo, I fell into a deep and dreamless sleep, unaware of boards shifting as Dave settled in front of me or Kent behind. I didn't notice a flash of cool air as they slipped under our makeshift covers. I didn't hear Dave's sleepy breathing or Kent's shaking snores. And, at some point during the night, I didn't feel Kent's hand crawl under my shirt, around my ribs, over my bare belly. It wasn't until the sun was about to break over the ocean, right when the sky turned from black to shades of gray, that my exhaustion lifted and I knew. Something was wrong.

His hand made a path across my body that I'll never know, but its resting place was on the front curve of my shoulder, over the collarbone, under my shirt, resting between my breasts. His arm with its thick curly hair lay heavy on my chest, making me want to scream. Wiggling up, inches at a time, I maneuvered out of his grasp, his fingers sliding down my skin like sandpaper. Free, I scampered to the rear wall of our shelter wrapping my arms around my legs, taking short, uneasy breaths. Even with all my clothes on I felt naked and wanted to run away into the jungle so no one could see me. But running was useless; I'd still end up on the other side of the island, surrounded by the same ocean. I could never escape. Cold and defeated, I rested my heavy head on my knees and cried quietly.

If Kent was aware of what happened in the darkness, he didn't let on. The first two nights after Kent's nightmare, or whatever it was, I slept by the fire. I know Dave probably wasn't happy snuggling up to Kent but neither of them said anything about my relocation.

Then the rains moved in and I had to sleep with them again. Most nights I stayed awake, curled in the fetal position, a fierce grip keeping me coiled tight, pressed unusually close to Dave. I'm guessing it's because of the rain that he didn't notice the change, or maybe he just had the decency to not mention it.

A few times, when I'd somehow drifted off, I thought I felt it again— the slinking fingers grasping at the hem of my shirt or the waistband of my shorts, searching for skin. I soon learned if I turned a little farther to my left, or coughed or made any type of human noise, he'd stop.

I want it to stop.

I don't know how much longer I can deal with the torture of sleep deprivation. I'm hoping with some time alone, away from the only humans I've seen for two months, away from the monotony of the waves and the smell of salt and sweat that lingers in our shelter, I can get some clarity.

The bundle is getting heavy and my shoulder starts to ache when I finally reach the double-vee coconut tree that signals it's time to turn onto the nearly invisible path leading to our oasis. Rubbing my fingers across its trunk, I trace the dark-gashed X that marks the way, a simple guide Dave made so we could find the water without Kent's help. Today I need them. The rain caused some of the undergrowth to sprout up in surprising directions, forcing me to stop once or twice to make sure I'm still on the path.

Soon, the trees clear and the ground makes a juicy, squishing sound. I'm suddenly ankle deep in the clear water of the pool, swollen with rain from the past few days. My favorite laundry rock, usually a few inches from the edge of the pond, is surrounded by water. I don't want to get my shoes soaked—they take forever to dry—so I hang my laundry bundle on a nearby branch before slipping off my shoes and wrestling out of my shorts and holey green V-necked T-shirt. Underneath, my sage-and-white tankini strap hangs off one shoulder. It's already losing its elasticity but still covers most of the important parts. I shove the rejected clothes and shoes into the top of my pack, hoist it onto my back, and wade into the cool black water.

The pool's powers of rejuvenation start as I trudge, knee-deep, to my laundry rock. With the last bit of muscle strength left in me, I drop the pack onto the moss-covered rock and sigh, super-tempted to climb up and use the dirty bundle of clothes as a pillow. Some kind of mom work ethic tells me I can rest when my work is done. Lame.

My washing routine is simple—first I wash the clothes, then myself. It doesn't take long to shake out and rinse out the few pieces of clothing, always leaving Margaret's jacket second to last, working on that rusty blood stain, hoping that the pain of her loss will disappear with it. Finally, I swim toward the rocky little alcove that crowns the clearing and stick my hand deep into a crack. A few weeks ago I discovered it, the right size for Margaret's toiletry bag.

Just like the first aid kit saved our lives, Margaret's bag saved my sanity. I found some small metal items like nail clippers and tweezers. There's also a disturbingly large assortment of hotel shampoo, soap, toothpaste and brush, a washcloth, and lotion. I was a little surprised we didn't find a robe in there too.

These tiny bottles make me human again. It's miraculous what a pea-size portion of scented shampoo will do for your spirits. Kent and Dave are fully aware of my stash—and the nail clippers and tweezers are prized practical necessities—-but besides a small bar of soap that Dave keeps stored somewhere around camp, neither of them seems interested in using any of my personal hygiene supplies. That's fine, more for me.

I swim over to the rock and wash my swimsuit, slipping the pieces off slowly, rinsing them in the clear water, and laying them out on the laundry rock to dry. Happily naked, I lather up, spreading bubbles over every inch of my body. I've turned lean and muscular, my abdomen tight and flat, a few off-colored stretch marks the only reminder that my body once produced humans. The hair on my legs and under my arms is growing manishly long. At first it was embarrassing but now the blanket of hair's just as much a part of my new body as my scrawny thighs and jutting hipbones. But I do miss the satin finish of my skin after a shave.

As I scrub, the strong floral scent of the shampoo tickles my nose, and my skin tightens in the air after being scrubbed with the starchy-smelling hotel soap. After working a palm full of shampoo into my hair, I dunk under the water and shake my head around, rinsing the suds from my tangly curls. It feels amazing to be clean.

When my head penetrates the surface of the water, I sigh. This little vacation from camp life is over. Through a slit in the canopy I can see the clouds have settled over the sun. Without the sun, there's a chill to the air, which means there's another storm coming our way. Picking a comb through my hair, I wade up to the rocks and rub the hem of Dave's shirt, almost dry. I'd better pack up quickly and walk back to camp before all my hard work gets ruined by the rain.

I grab my still-wet underwear from the rock and slip it on in the water; the stretchy beige lace at the top still clings comfortably to my waist. Just as I slide the last strap of my bra back on, a crack echoes out of the jungle. It sounds like a stick breaking and it's close, scary close. There are a lot of crawling things on this island that I'll never get used to—snakes, lizards, and rats . . . so many rats. The list ticks through my mind faster than I can keep track.

"Hello? Is anyone there?" My voice bounces back even though I'm whispering.

Tiptoeing out of the water into the silky mud, I move cautiously to the tree line where the mystery sound came from. I don't really want to know what made that sound but I have to. Then, I hear it again, this time I'm certain, something large is moving through the brush. I tuck myself behind a banyan tree. I could climb it but the bark is smooth and the lowest branch a good eight feet up.

There's a loud thump and growl of pain, not quite human but not quite animal either. Something big is heading my way. We haven't found any predators on this island but that doesn't mean they don't exist. Turning on the balls of my feet, I dive into the water and swim to my hidden nook to stash my toiletries and then swim back and pack up the wet clothes, my shoes, and my uneaten breakfast. I throw them over my left shoulder and run barefoot through the trees, toward the beach.

I burst through the last leafy barrier onto the beach and collapse on the sand, dropping everything and gasping for breath.

"What was that?" I whisper on all fours in the sand.

"What was what?" A deep masculine voice echoes.

As I scramble to my feet, Kent comes walking down the beach. He's dressed in his normal uniform—tattered shorts, no shirt, and a spear in his hand. His short blond hair has grown out since the crash but instead of lying flat on his head it spikes out in every direction, making his receding hairline stand out even more prominently.

Oh, it's just Kent. My heart starts to return to its normal rhythm. "I don't know, I was washing the clothes and I heard this noise. It was loud and coming right at me. It sounded like some kind of huge wild animal."

Kent stares at me, his white eyebrows raised skeptically, arms crossed against his bare, furry chest. "And what did this mystery creature look like?"

"I don't know, I didn't stick around to see, but whatever it was, it was big and it was moving fast." It's getting easier to talk now, my breathing almost normal. "Could it be a boar or wild pig or whatever?"

"I don't know, maybe." He shrugs, flipping the spear over his shoulders, hooking his elbows over both ends. "And that's why you're standing on the beach, soaking wet, dressed in your underwear?" He runs his gaze up and down my nearly bare body. "Did Little Red get frightened by the Big Bad Wolf?"

I wrap my arms around my middle, suddenly aware of how close to naked I am. I swim like this all the time but standing here, alone, the way his eyes widen and trace up and down my body, it all makes me want to cover up. The embarrassed heat rushing to my face pushes tears into my eyes. I try to stop them. I don't want him to see me crying, to see me weak.

"Why do you have to be such an ass, Kent? Can't you try to be sympathetic?"

Turning away, I try to hide my face, busying myself picking up the now-sandy laundry pile. One of my mangos rolled down to the water, where it's being kicked around by the waves. Crawling, I scramble after it as though it's the last piece of fruit on the planet, the mango blurring into the foam through my tears. I brush my uneaten breakfast with my fingertips when Kent's hand grabs my bare arm and yanks me to my feet.

"Don't get all hysterical on me, I didn't mean to shatter your fragile feelings."

His grip is tight and his long fingernails dig white crescents into my skin. He pulls me toward him, till his chest hair tickles my forearm. His breath's sour and I gag, glad I didn't eat breakfast after all. I tug against his fingers but they hold me in an iron vise.

"Kent, let me go." He ignores me, yanking me closer.

Pinching a clump of my half-dry curls, Kent wraps a coil around his forefinger, twisting and twisting until it coats his digit like wall-to-wall carpet. Then, letting it spiral off into a perfect curl, he grabs it in his fingertips and rubs it under his nose.

"You smell good," he grunts. "Real good." Dropping the hair, he clamps down on my arms with both hands, pulling my reluctant feet through the sand, pressing his body against mine. His nose traces up my neck as he sniffs again.

I want to run away but I'm frozen like a possum, hoping the predator will pass me by. But when his mouth reaches my ear, his heavy breathing makes me scared.

"I'm not asleep this time, Kent. Let go of me right now or one night while *you* are sleeping you might find a snake in your pants," I growl at him. "And that's not a euphemism."

He releases me, staggering backward, uncharacteristically stunned. "I don't know what you're talking about, *bitch*. Go run home to daddy and tell him about all the monsters in the forest." His hand rests casually on the hilt of his knife, conveniently tucked into the waist of his shorts. "Just don't even think about pointing your finger at me."

I wrap my arms around myself tighter, shivering as he takes one last lingering look up and down my half-naked body before skulking away, muttering under his breath. And I know, then and there, that the predator lurking in the dark corners of this island is no animal at all, it's Kent. When I'm sure he's gone, I don't give myself a chance to think. I grab my things and run from danger for the second time that day—only this danger is real.

Reaching camp minutes later, I run past Dave, breathless. The fire's smoldering, four small fish splayed out on long sticks for lunch. Dropping the pack of ruined laundry in the sand in front of the shelter, I search for the long column of smoke trailing toward the sky. Standing there with my hands extended, I let the smoke caress me, fill my hair and skin, erasing the subtle hint of lilac that followed me back to camp.

CHAPTER 15

DAVE

Present

"Basic survival—how hard is it to live on a deserted island?" Genevieve asked blandly. Her lackluster delivery was a relief. Finally, a safe topic.

"Very difficult, actually. I don't know how mankind made it before cell phones, processed food, and electricity." Dave chuckled low. People loved hearing about how they ate and slept and made a shelter. If they only knew it wasn't hunger that caused their biggest pains, it was their own humanity.

"Tell us about your home, the island. What was it like?" She turned up a corner of her mouth in what Dave decided was meant to be a smile.

"Uh, it was small, only two or three miles in circumference. It had some fruit trees, a lagoon with fish, and in the jungle, a small pond-like area with fresh water bubbling up through a spring in the ground. We were lucky to have fresh water on a small island like that." Dave felt a strange sense of pride describing the place they lived for so long. Telling the truth was much more fun than lying.

"How did you make it a hospitable place? What were your commodities?" Genevieve ticked through her questions at lightning speed but Dave considered the answers carefully, savoring the safety he felt in this part of their conversation.

"We built a shelter using bamboo, thatched palm fronds, and cut-up pieces of the raft for waterproofing. Kent made this complicated water catcher out of some other pieces of the raft that we used as our water supply before we found the spring. We picked snails from the sides of rocks and sometimes if we were lucky caught fish with a spear." The whole lagoon sprawled out in Dave's memory, the exact color of blue, the crest of rocks where they hunted their snails while watching for poisonous sea snakes, the glowing white sand, like a belt topping a never-ending aqua skirt.

"Hmmm," Genevieve responded, skipping whole chunks of questions from Dave's list about how fishing worked and their method of retrieving coconuts. "And the dynamic on the island? Was there a leader?"

Dave held in a sigh. Back to the aggressive questions, back to subversion. "Clearly Kent was the boss," he blurted. "He was used to it from being a pilot and was good at making spur-of-the-moment life-or-death decisions. Lillian and I had no problem following him. It felt natural."

It was hard to say nice things about Kent, even the few that were true, but it was important. That sneaky glint in Genevieve's eyes flared up again.

"Then you and Lillian, what were your roles?"

One. Happy. Family. He'd sell it. Putting on his best smile, the one that made the dimple on his right cheek wink playfully, he answered with forced ease.

"We all did the same kind of work. We foraged and gathered fruit and supplies. We had a standing rule that every time someone left camp they needed to bring at least one piece of firewood back with them. We hunted. Though Kent was the best at that, we all were decent after a while."

Genevieve hummed through pressed lips. "So you didn't mind having Kent, who by your own admission was a sort of gruff and surly character, be your boss?"

"Not really," Dave said quickly. He didn't hesitate, that's something to be proud of at least. "I've been in the business world long enough to know that the person who's best for the job isn't always someone I like. But as long as the job gets done and done well then I couldn't care about personality." Crossing one of his legs casually over the other, he hoped he gave off a relaxed vibe.

Genevieve, in contrast, sat stiffly on the edge of her seat flipping her open Sharpie up and down nervously. "Okay . . ." She drew out the last vowel, glancing through her pile of notecards. "Sleeping arrangements?"

"Clearly, we all slept in the shelter. We wove some palm fronds together to make a mat to sleep on and another one to cover us. Then we slept close together to conserve body heat. On stormy nights, we'd take turns tending the fire through the night so it wouldn't go out."

"And it wasn't strange sleeping with a woman who wasn't your wife?"

"No, it was survival. Some nights Lillian watched the fire, and Kent and I snuggled like little girls."

A ripple of laughs washed over the crew, making Dave's chest puff a fraction. Genevieve Randall was not accustomed to losing control of an interview. Between questions she ground her teeth so much it had to create feedback for the sound guys in the van.

"How about emotionally?" she gasped, clearly dealing with some strong emotions of her own—frustration, anger. "How did you and your fellow survivors deal with being separated from family?"

"It wasn't easy, that's for sure." Dave shifted in his seat. He knew he had to talk about *her* now. "Lillian missed her husband and children desperately. We celebrated their birthdays on the island and all their favorite holidays. She told me she went to sleep each night and woke up each morning with them on her mind."

He had to stop himself from saying more, because he *could* say more about Lillian, a lot more, but he shouldn't know so much about her. He focused on forming a thoughtful answer about Kent.

"Kent mourned Theresa's loss more than any family from home; he never talked about them. I think if Theresa survived the crash, Kent could've stayed on that island forever."

The reporter took an extra breath before responding with another question, one that bit him like a guard dog, warning him he wasn't safe. "And you, Dave, how did you do without your wife?"

Dave glanced over at Beth, her face as still as a china doll. "I missed her more than words can say."

That burning in his stomach began again, like an ulcer, the one he only felt when he was lying. He considered blowing her a kiss but then decided it might be oversell.

Genevieve flipped through a few cards, probably realizing she was way off track. Settling on one, she read the question right from the paper, like a six-year-old in a school play. "Lillian mentioned that you and your fellow survivors had some nicknames for each other, is that true?"

"Yeah, it wasn't anything intentional but when you spend that much time together it tends to happen."

"What was your nickname, Dave?"

"Dave's already a nickname but sometimes they called me by my full name—David."

Genevieve seemed to like that answer. "Is there a story behind it?"

Ignoring the urge to roll his eyes, Dave explained. "They said I was like David, from the Bible. You know, like David and Goliath. When I was hunting or fishing, it was Kent's big joke when I caught anything—like if I caught even the smallest fish, it was equivalent to conquering Goliath."

"Okay, I get it. So Kent was religious? He and Lillian must've had a lot in common, then. *She* came from a home where her father was a minister and her mother a Sunday school teacher. Sounds like they had some common interests."

Trying to keep control he reminded himself that no one told this woman what happened on the island. No one but Lillian could have, and she had even more reasons to stay quiet.

"I'm not sure, Ms. Randall, all I know is that's what he called me," Dave said, knowing that if even one block in the tower of lies was pulled out by this woman, the whole thing would come crashing down.

"Well then, how about Kent? What did you call him?"

"We called Kent 'Scout.' He was proficient at all that survival stuff. Like he figured out how to make a fire using Margaret's reading glasses and taught Lillian and me how to make thatches out of palm fronds and rope out of coconut husks. I mean, literally any necessity he figured out and provided for us."

"Sounds like you were lucky to have him with you," Genevieve pressed, a fine sheen of sarcasm coating her words.

"Very lucky. I wouldn't be sitting here right now without that man." It took a lot of practice to cover up the disgust in his voice when talking about Kent. Making eye contact and smiling plenty helped.

"Uh-huh, I see." She moved on. "Lillian then, please tell us about her name."

Dave glanced at his wife, her face a pale mask of indifference. Sometime he thought Beth was a better liar than the lot of them. It was going to be difficult talking about Lillian here, in his home. Dave made sure not to let his gaze stray for too long before answering the question.

"We sometimes called her Lily," he stated, brief and to the point.

"Is there a story behind that name too?" Her voice dripped with honey, too sweet for good intentions.

"Nope," he said, popping the *p*.

"Did Kent pick that name too?"

"Uh, yeah, sure. He thought Lillian was too stuffy so he called her Lily instead." He leaned back, letting the voluminous white cushions envelop him.

"I'd guess that if Kent had a name for everyone he would've had a name for Paul as well. Right?"

Paul. The name made the vein in his right temple pound angrily. Why did she have to bring him up already? By far Paul was the hardest lie. There's so much to cover up. His feelings toward Paul, Lily's feelings for him, and how bad things became once Paul was gone.

"I'm not sure about that." Dave cleared this throat. "You might want to ask Lillian, she'd be the one with that sort of information."

"You didn't spend much time with Paul, then?"

"When you're all stuck on an island together there's no way to avoid each other," he answered, feeling testy.

"Ah, you wanted to avoid Paul and Lillian, then?" she asked, twisting his words ruthlessly. "Why was that?"

Dave felt riled, like a cobra poked a few too many times, and he was ready to snap at her with dripping fangs. "I didn't avoid anyone," he stated, voice imbued with venom. "*Lily* would be the one to ask about him." He punctuated each phrase with a coiled fist on his knee.

Letting her shoulders drop, Genevieve shuffled the cards in her hand arrogantly, savoring the moment before she spoke again. "I'll have to ask *Lily* about that when I get the chance," she oozed.

CHAPTER 16

DAVID-DAY 81

The Island

Three months ago I never would've believed that soon my daily activities would include holding a spear knee-deep in a cool, placid pool.

Shirtless, with my long khaki pants rolled up to my knees, I feel very primitive, manly, one with the earth. Waking up in our lean-to shelter, making a fire with reading glasses, snuggling with virtual strangers to stay warm at night has become, dare I say, commonplace.

Today Lillian stands high above me on a cluster of rocks that jut out into our little bay. With her sun-browned skin and wild hair blowing behind her, she looks as native as I feel. Her muscles roll athletically under her faded electric-green bathing suit as she tiptoes gracefully through the sharp boulders. Pushing her hair behind her ears, she dips down to pick some shells off the rock's edge, a glint of gold reflecting the noon sun. Margaret's necklace, weighted down with rings, hangs from her neck, tapping her in the face.

Glancing in my direction she waves an empty hand, the other carrying a large leaf filled with her acquisitions. I pretend to scan the water before giving a decisive thumbs-up. I hope she didn't notice me watching her but it's hard not to. Her delicate balancing act is as graceful as a tightrope walker tiptoeing across a wire. And she's hot, so there's that.

Trying to repress a smile, I force myself to focus on fishing. If I let myself get distracted it could mean disaster. Lillian's doing more than searching for crustaceans—she could be saving my life.

When we found this lagoon three days after we landed, it seemed perfect, protected from the waves and the wind by tall black rocks. The lagoon itself is full of large, lazy fish, and the trees drip with coconuts, breadfruit, bananas, and mangos.

Not to mention that from every other beach on the small island, the only place to catch fish is the reef. In normal circumstances I could swim the few hundred yards out and tread water, no problem. I've even had some spearfishing experience after all my trips to Fiji. But, after nearly drowning in the crash, floating in the ocean, pushing the boat through the water using our tiny reserves of energy to be human propellers—no one wanted to risk going out there.

The beach by the lagoon is also in a lousy location for rescuers to see our camp from open waters. Kent set up an SOS on the largest beach on the west side of the island and then on our side, just beyond the rocks. There's a large signal fire that can be lit at a moment's notice with a torch we keep inside the shelter, dry and ready to go. It's a long shot but shifting the letters and piling fresh wood on the signal fire reminds me that there's still some tiny glimmer of hope.

Then there are the sharks. I've lived most of my life in California and been to the beach more times than I can count, but I've only ever seen a shark with a thick plate of aquarium glass between us. So, from a lack of experience and some propaganda from Shark Week, I've always assumed sharks are like the gigantic dead-eyed monsters from the movies, that I was safe as long as I didn't go out too deep in the water. Nature quickly taught me there's more than one type of shark.

When I saw my first shark, I felt no fear. It was almost cute. As I fished, the mini-shark darted around the blue lagoon, drifting out toward the depths of the reef and then back in toward me like it was checking up on my progress. It reminded me of a playful puppy and was about the same size. I started to consider names for my little fishing buddy when I finally made contact with a fish, slicing through its gills in one lucky blow. Elated, I tried to lift the flipping fish from the water when the miniature predator yanked it off my spear, snapping the slender bamboo in half.

The shark shook the yellow cone fish into tiny pieces right in front of me, large chunks of fish flesh falling on my bare feet. The water clouded with blood and fish parts, churning as several other small gray sharks appeared out of nowhere to take part in the feast.

Adrenaline kicked in and I stumbled away cautiously, remembering something from the Discovery Channel about shark feeding frenzies and not wanting my legs to be included in their banquet. I didn't dare turn away from that spot until I finally exited the water, my heart pounding ferociously.

"Sharks! In the water. Don't go in," I panted. Lillian leaped up from her weaving and met me halfway up the beach.

"Shark? Oh, Dave. Did it bite you?" She fluttered her hands around me, searching for bite marks or blood or something.

"What's this about a shark?" Kent ran out of the trees, knife in his hand.

"Not one shark, lots of them. In the lagoon." My breathing evened out.

"Wait." He scratched the peeling bald spot on the top of his head. "You mean those tiny gray things?"

I nodded. "They took the fish right off my spear."

Kent let out a booming laugh. "Aw, shit. You're such a girl. Those things won't hurt you. Next time try to shove a spear through its noggin and then you'll have something to shout about." He pocketed the knife and tromped into the jungle to finish whatever it is he does out there.

"Come. Sit." Lillian guided me to a log that overlooks the ocean. She calls it our fishing log. "Kent caught some rats this morning so let's forget about fishing for a day or two, okay?"

"Okay," I agreed.

It took two days and a large dose of humiliation doled out by Kent to make me willing to enter the water again. I snuck off after sunrise so no one would see if I failed, but as I walked down the beach with a newly sharpened spear over my shoulder, I heard footsteps behind me.

Lillian.

She claimed she needed to pick the rocks again, even though she'd already collected a huge load the day before, leaving us with enough snails for at least one day, if not two. I pretended not to understand that she was coming with me out of concern rather than necessity. It took a lot of inner dialogue to feel flattered that she cared about my safety rather than emasculated by her desire to protect me.

As always, Lillian ended up being invaluable. From her perch on the rocks she quickly realized she could spot large schools of fish in the crystal water, as well as the ominous dark shadows of predators. As a result she convinced us, even Kent, that fishing should be done in teams, rotating every day with posts on the rocks and in the water.

◆ ◆ ◆

Today's my favorite day in the rotation. Lillian and I work very well as a team. When she's on the rocks I know I'm safe. Of course,

Kent's efficient and we get more food collected when he's holding the spear, but I don't trust him one little bit. When Kent's the lookout, I find myself scanning the water, unsure if he'd tell me if Jaws himself was heading my way. When Lillian's fishing with him, I try to stay close to the beach, not willing to leave her safety completely in his neglectful hands.

Lillian yelps up on the rocks. She's standing on her tiptoes waving frantically. Squinting tightly, I watch her hands. If she sees a shark, she'll put her hands together fingers extended pointing toward the sky. If she sees a large grouping of fish, she'll hold her hands parallel to each other, flipping them from fingertips to wrists. I hope for fish but watch for large dark shadows in the water around me.

Before I can recheck the warning, I'm surrounded by a school of yellow tuna. The tuna are huge. Sporting a bony fin on their spines, they look almost as fierce as the sharks, but at least these guys don't have teeth.

It's rare to find tuna this close to the island but Kent's been telling us for weeks that certain types almost throw themselves ashore during monsoon season. I don't have time to be annoyed that he was right.

Holding the spear high, I'm ready for attack. Two things I've learned from my crash course in spearfishing are—strike fast and strike often.

The fish surround me, the featherlight flick of their tail fins tickling my knees, and I stab at the water with rapid-fire movements. The spear makes a sloshing sound, slipping in and out of the water, making no splash.

When Lillian finally reaches me, the water creeping up her bathing suit top, I have a glittering yellow tuna flipping on the end of the spear. Its weight bends the reed relentlessly.

"That was amazing!" she gasps, out of breath from her run from the rocks. "You were like a ninja with that thing. Kent's gonna die when he sees this."

I'm smiling so big it hurts my cheeks. "I'm as surprised as anyone. I think I might have a little amnesia, because everything before your freak-out on the rocks is a little hazy."

Nearly jumping through the water, she grabs my arm holding the spear. "Let's get out of the water, Bourne Identity. You did just kill some fish and you know what sharks like to eat."

"You worry too much." I try to be confident, hating that she thinks I'm a wuss, but when she turns away, I quickly scan the water with a hint of panic. Whew, no fins.

When we reach the shore, she flops down on the beach. Sand clings to her wet, bronze legs where they stick out from her cutoff shorts. I toss the still-twitching fish to the ground and then hop down next to her, winded but happy.

"Mmmm, I can almost taste that fish now. Fillets for us all— perfect." She shakes large drops of water out of her tied-back hair.

"I caught it, I should get first dibs. Who says there'll be any left once I'm done with it."

"Well, I saved you from the sharks so I should get something in payment. We can let Kent eat all the snails I collected." Her eyebrows rise in that way they always do when she plays along with one of my games.

"Yeah, good idea, he'd *love* that." I grab a smooth white shell tossing in the tide by my feet and rub it between my fingers silently. "I know—you tell him about the snails and it's a deal. He'd so kill me if I tried to keep him from food. Especially fresh fish."

"I'll tell him." Her eyes flash like steel. "I'm not afraid of that man. You know I've never even heard him use my real name. He calls me 'babe' or 'hon' all the time?" She wrinkles her nose like the names give off an offensive odor.

I turn onto my side so I can look right at her. Her face peers out from the crook of her elbow, squinting against the afternoon sun. "I think it's because of your name. He kind of hates it."

"My *name*? He told you this?"

"He may have mentioned something."

She laughs, digging her fingers deeper into the mane of hair, green eyes picking up some of the blue from the ocean. Somehow she's still as beautiful as the first time I saw her sitting on that plane. I run my hands through my own thick curls. I didn't get the haircut I wanted before leaving California and now it's catching up with me. Between the curly black poof on my head and thick rough beard on my face I feel like Sasquatch.

"It doesn't really fit you. Lillian. In my family you would've been Lily."

"For real? Lily? How're you so sure?" Thankfully I'm over my initial nervousness around her but there are still times when we're alone and really talking I find it hard to look at her without my heart pounding. I concentrate on the sand, hoping my pulse will slow down.

"Believe it or not, my dad was a florist. As a kid I spent the majority of my spare time in his shop, The Enchanted Florist." My eyes roll instinctively; I've always hated that name. "Lilies, any kind, were his favorite flower. He would've called you Lily, I'm sure of it."

"I kind of like that." She taps her teeth thoughtfully. "Hmm, Lily. I'd love to meet your dad one day, when we get home. He could teach me about arranging flowers and I'd even let him call me Lily." We do this a lot, talk about going home, make plans like it's really going to happen.

"I'd love for you to meet my dad. He's the best man I've ever known. But he passed away a few years ago."

"Oh, I'm so sorry, Dave. I didn't mean to . . ."

"No, no, it's all right, I'm fine." I brush the niggling grief away. It's behind locked doors where it can't hurt. I certainly won't let it loose out here, where it would distract and ravage me. "It's been five years. We were very, very close. My mom left us when I was three, so it was only the two of us my whole life." I sit up and draw a circle in the undisturbed sand in front of me. "I'm glad he didn't live long enough to worry about me back home."

"It's nice you were that close to your dad. I'm not close to either of my parents. My dad's a minister, and I know he loves me but I'm sure he's not proud of me. Everything I've done in my life is good but just not good enough." She digs her toes into the sand, flecks of pink nail polish still clinging to a few of her toenails.

"What, do you have a secret past full of drug convictions and traffic tickets?"

"Noooo." She giggles. "Daddy wanted me to marry Mike Henshaw, the junior pastor in our home church, and be a minister's wife. I tried, I really did, but we didn't work together." She looks out into the water, any sign of humor erased from her face.

"I'm sure poor Mike was disappointed."

"I don't think so. He ended up marrying a girl he met on a mission trip a year after Jerry and I walked down the aisle and now has six kids and his own church in Tennessee. I couldn't make him that happy. Dad thought I was being selfish."

"I don't think you're selfish. I think your dad wanted you to be someone you're not, as if you were a defective piece of furniture from Ikea." I stop short when my voice wavers with anger.

"I guess." She bites the inside of her cheek. "Whatever it is, I've come to terms with it and I don't beat myself up about what he thinks anymore. Once we had Josh and Daniel, things were better. Now they can obsess about the boys."

"You need to introduce me to your parents. Then they'll be thanking their lucky stars for a daughter like you."

"Ha, ha. You're totally wrong." She cocks her head to the side, sizing me up. "My parents would like you. You're funny, you're educated, and you have the best quality of all—you're religiously unaffiliated. Daddy would scoop you up like a spoonful of homemade ice cream."

"Wow, that sounds . . . fun?"

"I should warn you, though; he *will* call you David just like he calls Josh 'Joshua.' It's his thing. He likes the biblical names, for obvious reasons."

"So, David? Like David and Goliath?" I wrinkle my nose.

She nodded. "Yeah, that David. But he didn't just kill a giant. He went on to be one of Israel's greatest kings and father to another famous king—Solomon. My Dad says Jesus's line goes back to David as prophesied in the Old Testament." She lowers her voice like she's passing on a secret. "He's kinda a big deal."

"Well, in that case, I think you and Kent should call me 'your majesty' from now on."

"Yeah, you wish." She slaps my arm lightly.

"I definitely like the sound of it. King David. KING David." I try to make my voice deep and booming, royal-like. Lillian scrunches her face. "Your dad would like it even if you don't."

"No, I think he'd call it 'irreverent and sacrilegious,'" she drawls in imitation. "But, David," she sighs, "I like that name on you." Her lips pucker and I imagine touching them. *God, Dave, control yourself.*

"If you get to call me David then I get to call you Lily."

"I think . . . I like it," she says, pulling her hair off of her shoulders. "Now we have our island identities, our secret identities. It's not like we can be the same people we were before, so why not mark that in some significant way?"

"That's a great idea, let's do it. Lily," I say, putting out my hand in front of her. We shake twice before letting go.

"Well then, *David*, now that we have that settled, maybe you can teach me how to gut a fish?" Up on her knees, she looks like a kid on her birthday, dying to dig into her presents.

"Sure, if you really want to know." I hope she wants to know, so I can have a few more minutes of my day melt away in conversation with her.

"Of course I do." She stands up, wiping her hands on her legs. "Do you have your knife?"

"Yeah, I do. We can clean it over there by the rock." My hand darts to my right hip pocket, checking for the lump that I know will be there. I never leave my knife behind, never. There's something else there, something I've been meaning to talk to her about. "That reminds me of something I wanted to give you—come back and sit down." I clutch her fingertips.

Lily's eyebrows rise with curiosity and she sits again, this time her legs crossed Indian style. That nervous flutter has returned. I hope I can keep my breakfast of snails and coconut milk down. Reaching into my pocket, I pull out a small package, wrapped in palm frond pieces that overlap into an arrow that points right at Lily. It seems smaller than I remember, no longer than my hand, palm to fingertips, and about the width of two fingers.

"Here." I hold it out. The sun's behind her now and I squint to see her face.

"Oh, what's this for?" I drop it into her palm with a plunk that echoes in my bones.

"I guess you can call it an early Christmas present. I was going to wait but . . ." I can't find the right words. "Open it."

Her fingers fumble with the shoelace bow holding the tightly wrapped leaves together. She unravels it so fast, as if she's following the insane pace of my heart. Then it lies in her hands: stone, wood, and cloth made over long hours by my hands—for her.

"A knife? Where? . . . How? . . . Did you make this?"

"No, I bought it at Ace Hardware—of *course* I made it. Do . . . do you like it?"

Her fingers creep around the hilt, thumb running up and down the twisted fabric covering the heavy wooden handle. She inspects the three-inch blade.

"I do like it. I love it. It's amazing. I can't believe you made this. Does it work? Can I use it on the fish?" She points the short blade at the now-dead tuna.

"Yeah, it works." I have to dodge away from the blade. "Be careful waving that thing around, it's sharp. I've been sharpening it for a week now."

"So that's what you've been working on when you'd disappear for hours at a time. Aren't you clever? Kent's going to be so jealous." Her feet patter out a dance. Why does she have to be so happy? This is the part of the conversation I've been dreading.

"Lillian . . . Lily." She smiles at our joke name, but I can't smile. "I don't want you to let Kent know about this knife. I want you to . . . to keep it a secret."

"But, why not? I thought you gave it to me to use around camp. What good is it if I can only use it in secret? It's my secret knife? I don't get it."

This is harder than I thought it'd be. During the hours I spent chipping the stone and carving the wooden handle, I pondered thousands of ways to say this to her.

"Kent's dangerous; he can't be trusted." I say it fast. She opens her mouth, perhaps to protest, but I grab her gently, one hand on each shoulder. "You need this knife for more than just completing chores. You need it for protection."

"Protection?" She glares at the knife like it's burning her hand. "Protect me from what? Are you insinuating you made this knife for me to use against Kent?"

My right hand moves to her face, my fingertips curling into the downy hair at the base of her neck. "Listen, neither of us is entirely safe with him but you're the most vulnerable."

"Why?" she scoffs, pulling away. "Because I'm a woman?"

"No. I mean yes, I mean, in a way," I stumble.

"Thanks for your concern but I'm sure I can take care of myself. What do you think he's going to do—get me in a holdup? Assault me with his overwhelming misogyny?" She holds the weapon out like she's going to give it back and puts more space between us. I can't read the dark cloud that's settled on her face.

"No, it's because of the way he looks at you, Lily. He watches you like a predator with his prey. He thinks he can do anything on this island and get away with it. I'm starting to think he can. Bottom line is—you're not safe with him and it's only a matter of time before . . ."

"Before what, Dave?" Her voice trembles and I can't tell if she's angry or frightened. Taking her hand, the one holding the knife, I bend her fingers over the hilt, holding them in place like that will make them stick.

"Before he takes it beyond looking. Be aware, be careful, because if anything happens to you, I don't know what I'll do."

The thought of Kent touching her burns me from the inside out. She must feel it in my fingertips because she pulls away, knife still clutched in her hand. She's shaking.

"Don't do anything stupid, Dave. Don't try to cross him. He's not a twelve-year-old Boy Scout playing pretend." Her voice quivers and her stone mask of bravery cracks momentarily, and I see she's vulnerable, breakable. "I'll keep the knife if it makes you feel better, but promise me you won't try to handle him on your own. I'll only keep it if you promise."

The vein in her neck pounds insanely fast. God, no. She's covering something up, something bad, something she doesn't want me to know. I want to ask but I don't.

"I have no immediate plans for attack but I worry about you. I hope I'm overreacting but I want you to be careful anyway. Okay?"

"Okay." She nods in agreement before returning the knife to its primitive sheath and taking a shaky breath. "Enough with serious stuff.

Can you teach me about filleting the fish now, before it spoils in the sun?"

"Sure." I turn up the side of my mouth, hoping I can fake a smile.

She jumps up, knife in hand, and runs toward the shimmering yellow-silver tuna that looks more like a small beached whale than a fish. She bends down and attempts to pick up the monster, calling me over. Her laughter, as always, sounds like the wind tickling wind chimes.

When I'm with Lily I forget how much I miss home. Even when I dream about my old life I can't seem to imagine it without her there. I know she doesn't feel the same way, she'd trade me for Jerry in a heartbeat, but I couldn't survive on this island without her. How could I live if she were gone?

A horrible ache fills the space in my chest and part of me is glad I didn't ask what happened between her and Kent, what he did to make her shake like that. I know I could get her to tell me, and if she did . . . I might have to kill him.

CHAPTER 17

LILLIAN

Present

"We saved up our best fruit for a week before that first Christmas. Then in the morning Dave and Kent went fishing so we'd have a big meal later in the day to celebrate. We made presents for each other out of what we found around the island and opened them after dinner that night. We also had decorations. We picked flowers and wove garlands. It was nothing like Christmas at home but we made a valiant effort." Lillian spoke slowly. It was one of her favorite memories.

"Do you remember what gifts you exchanged?" As always with the good memories, Genevieve seemed bored, as if she could think of at least ten things that she could be using this wasted time on.

"I made hats for the guys out of some palm fronds. They sunburned easily, especially Kent with his light hair. I thought that'd be useful. Kent gave me a multicolored shell that I later made into a necklace. Dave gave me my own fishing spear. I had to borrow his or Kent's until then because I was horrible at sharpening one for myself. I guess they were tired of sharing."

"It must have been a hard day, though, without family, so far from home." Genevieve pushed.

"Yes, it was." Lillian had to force herself to keep from answering, "Yeah. Duh!"

"Have you asked your family how they spent that first Christmas without you? What were they doing while you were decorating with ficus and sharpening spears half a world away?"

"They spent it at home with my parents."

Genevieve nodded like she knew better than Lillian what happened while she was away. "Your funeral was around Christmastime, if I remember correctly."

Lillian's nostrils flared and she considered ripping the mic off and walking outside. It felt hot and stuffy. Maybe she'd forgotten to turn on the air. "That's what I've been told."

"The search was called off only a week after the plane was located. You and your fellow passengers were declared dead soon after. Why was your funeral so delayed?"

Staring at Jerry over Genevieve's narrow shoulder, she didn't know how to explain. Jill said Jerry refused to give up, spending their life savings renting helicopters and chartering boats. Apparently Beth was right there with him, pitching in with funds, legwork, and just as much hope as Jerry. It wasn't until her dad showed up that Jerry even thought of going home without Lillian and Margaret sitting beside him. But Pastor Rob was good in emergency situations. Her brother, Noah, always joked that he must have taken a class on crisis management during his years in seminary.

Jerry gave in and flew home with Pastor Rob, but put off having any kind of services. Days turned into weeks and then months. Finally, Lillian's mom and Jill stepped in and planned a memorial in Wildwood for Lillian, and then one for Margaret in Fairfield, Iowa. They had two headstones placed in the family plot in Fairfield. Margaret's snuggled up right next to her husband and Lillian's sat next to an empty patch of grass that would hold Jerry's remains one day. She saw it when they went to Margaret's burial. The epitaph said: "Loving wife, mother, and friend. Lost too soon." Lillian called to have it removed the next day.

"Hope." Lillian held her husband's eye for a beat before focusing on Genevieve again. "I don't think Jerry had lost hope yet. I personally think something inside of him always knew I was out there, alive."

"That first Christmas—what was your family doing?"

"I only know what I was told." Lillian leaned over the stiff upholstery of her armchair. "My parents stayed in Missouri for Christmas, decorating the house and the tree."

Genevieve scowled. "So they went from having a funeral for their daughter to throwing a big Christmas celebration?"

"You make it sound so heartless," Lillian snapped. "Christmas is my favorite holiday; they wanted to make it special. To help my children regain some normalcy." She could never find a way to thank her parents for doing all the things Jerry couldn't because of his grief, buying and wrapping the majority of the boys' presents, making the cookies, reading the stories, remembering to open the Advent calendar, and taking the kids to Christmas Eve services.

Genevieve nodded about forty-seven times like she really, really agreed with Lillian. "So it was hard on the boys?"

Lillian didn't want to talk about this anymore. She could talk about the island and the crash all day but when it came to her kids, she was done. Waving her hands in front of her like she was shooing a fly, she decided to put an end to the emotional manipulation Genevieve Randall was trying to pull. "It was a tough Christmas for them but you know kids. When Santa comes, no one can keep a sad face."

Lillian was glad that as Genevieve asked her flippant questions about decorations and presents the camera was on her face and not

Jerry's. She knew how to put on the mask of apathy, a move Jerry never mastered. She knew how to steady her voice and crinkle her eyes with her fake smiles. She knew how to affect carelessness so no one could see her grief. It was her greatest talent, the most remarkable thing she'd learned being stranded on a tropical island—more impressive than spearfishing and fruit gathering or weaving blankets from palm fronds. She knew how to lie.

"Did you celebrate any other holidays? How about New Year's? Palm hats and coconut husk party favors?"

New Year's. If Christmas was Jerry's low point then that first New Year's was Lillian's. Her own pit, the one she was still so trapped in she couldn't even see the pin of light at the top any longer, was dug that day. But instead of flinching and without blinking back even one rebellious tear she answered.

"No, it was like every other day."

CHAPTER 18
LILY-DAY 112

The Island

Floating faceup in the blue-black water, I let the little streams of sunlight cascading through the canopy tickle my eyelids, performing a dance of colors that my mind makes music to. Arms spread wide I bask in my imagined masterpiece, working hard to push down the memories of home that have been creeping out since Christmas.

◆ ◆ ◆

A week ago, on Christmas Day, I gave myself a gift—a day full of recollection. Until now I've been careful to keep away from those thoughts, finding them less painful to avoid than to relive. But on that Christmas morning, I gave in.

I told stories to David and Kent about my boys, some of them twice. I told them about Josh teaching Daniel his ABC's by writing them in permanent marker across our brand-new flat-screen TV. I told them about Josh's phase where he'd only wear things that were orange and how inexplicably proud I was when Daniel told his preschool teacher that green beans were his favorite food.

I told them about my first Christmas with Jerry and how, even though we had no money, we made each other special gifts and how I still used the little wooden vanity he made me that year to put on my makeup in the mornings. I drove them crazy with stories until Kent curled up in the shelter to get away and I finally picked up on David's forced polite smile.

Even when they were done listening, I wasn't done thinking. I ran through whole days of my life from home from sunup to sundown. Some were from the baby days, where I nursed for hours and became a master swaddler. Others were from the hazy days of chores piled on top of each other and little boys turned wild with boredom.

My favorites—the days I reviewed slowly, savoring like a well-loved novel—were the lazy days when Jerry was home with the family. At times Margaret was there, or my parents. I was surprised, after a few hours of practice, how focused I could get the images and how clear the details. It was like being transported home every time I closed my eyes.

What I couldn't foresee was how my gift, the gift of remembering, would turn on me like a Christmas puppy with rabies. In the week after Christmas Day I tried to turn the "home" channel off and the "survival" one back on, but it wasn't easy. The images, feelings, and smells inundated me in any quiet moment, and around here most moments are quiet.

I almost didn't come to my special spot today because of the silence that haunts it, but I'm glad I did. It's as if the waters of the pool are washing away the residue of pain that the memories left behind as they boiled off into the atmosphere, and I'm starting to feel clean again.

Reluctantly, I meander toward the cluster of rocks where I spread out the clean laundry to dry. Grabbing my shorts, I'm relieved to find them still wet. David's expecting me back for the second half of his New Year's festivities, but I'm still worn out after last night.

Kent refused to acknowledge our party, sleeping like a stone in the shelter while we sat by the fire singing silly camp songs and telling ghost stories. The highlight of the night for me was the hour before what we approximated was midnight. We spent that time comparing plotlines from various Lifetime movies in a competition to determine who'd seen the worst. It was a close race but David eked out the win with his dramatic retelling of *My Son, My Lover, My Friend*. I haven't laughed that hard in months.

We ended up dozing off on opposite sides of the fire. I've slept there every night since my run-in with Kent on the beach. David usually sleeps in the shelter but bunking together last night was so fun, reminding me of the few sleepovers my parents allowed me to attend during my teen years.

But instead of sleeping until noon as I would've done at sixteen, I woke before dawn, once the fire had smoldered down to embers and the chill in the air was unmistakable. It was a habit I'd adopted from my time in the shelter, from the time I had to keep guard against Kent's hands. A habit I can't kick, even when Kent is far away from me.

Christmas was hard on all of us but it had a strange effect on Kent. Christmas night he disappeared into the trees and didn't come back for two whole days. I told David we should check on him in case he'd fallen in a hole or drowned while fishing, but David didn't seem concerned. In fact, he was almost chipper at our unexpected vacation from Kent's continual criticisms. It's not like I missed Kent but I feel safer when I can see him, predict his next move.

David was right, though, Kent was fine. Two days later he sauntered out of the jungle in the middle of the night and plopped down behind me smelling of fish and body odor. I cursed myself for being dumb enough to think I could sleep in the shelter while he was gone, but this time when he tried to touch me I didn't pretend to be asleep. I bolted down to the beach and spent the night by the fishing log, shivering in the damp sand. Kent hasn't said a word to me since that night, but I can feel him watching me.

◆ ◆ ◆

I climb on one of the empty boulders in the little patch of sunshine the clothes are baking in. When the sun hits my skin, I can't help but let out a little moan of pleasure—this is my island version of a spa day. The water evaporates off my body, and my paper-thin bra and underwear are dry within a few minutes of sunbathing. Relaxing back on a flat slab of rock, I'm lulled by the sounds of the jungle, and my mind fills with nothingness so I can drift off to sleep.

A little tickle on my cheek brings me back to reality. I'm well over the freak-out reflex all girls are born with when faced with close encounters of the creepy kind, but this time it's different. Sensation pads up my face, making my fingers itch to push whatever is climbing on me away.

Swatting at the phantom creature, I crunch my eyes closed tighter, hoping it'll eventually go away. I must've done something right because even after I relax my arms and settle into the cracks in the rock that seem to fit my body the best, the tickling is gone.

Then a hand clamps over my mouth.

My eyes fly open. Kent is standing over me, hand pushing hard against my mouth so I can't breathe, crushing my skull against the rock. I grab his arm, trying to rip it off my mouth. His flesh tears beneath my fingernails but he doesn't flinch. His forearm's as immovable as a tree trunk. My front teeth cut into the inside of my lips like they're razorblades and my mouth begins to fill with blood. The dirty metallic taste gags me as it slips down my throat. Kicking, my legs flail from side to side, missing his body entirely.

My lungs are burning, and darkness starts to fill me like water overflowing the brim of a cup. It happens fast; my body stills and my lungs stop trying to suck in breath. There's no room for pain or remorse as I sink below the surface of consciousness. In the inky darkness of my mind, there's a nothingness that's both terrifying and refreshing. It tells me I don't have to care anymore, that it's okay to let go and drift away in its billowing velvety current. The temptation to give in is overwhelming, like gravity pulling me down irresistibly. Then, as I start slipping over that dark precipice one finger at a time, the hand is gone and I can breathe again.

Light develops through painful pinpricks, making me want to go back to that safe black place. Before I can think, or put together the fractured memories that develop like film, the blood in my mouth drips down my throat and I have to sit up to avoid choking. I sputter, and blood-thickened spittle dribbles down my chin. I wipe it away with the back of my hand. Someone's after me. *Kent* is after me.

I squint and everything is fuzzy. I search the pool and surrounding jungle but he's gone. I climb backward to the edge of the rock and tumble the three feet down to the muddy ground. The impact makes my stomach retch. Rolling onto my hands and knees, I vomit a lumpy mixture of blood and fruit, stomach acid burning my throat. My head hurts and I still can't see straight.

A twig breaks in the trees behind me, and I clutch at the ground with mud-caked fingers, trying to crawl away before Kent can come and get me. The mud is like quicksand and the more I fight to get to its edge, the deeper I sink. Breathing heavily, I pull my hands out with a loud sucking sound and plop them down a few inches away. Instead of going forward I'm being drawn down, buried alive. My pounding heart sends blood, warm and disgusting, pouring out of the cuts in my mouth.

"Where do you think you're going?" Kent's voice growls behind me in a mix of amusement and annoyance. His feet slosh through the mud casually, like a parent after a wayward toddler. He's coming closer. I open my mouth to scream but all that comes out is a pathetic gurgle.

He chuckles. I don't look back.

Get to the trees and then run. The thick safety of the jungle is only a few feet away but it might as well be a mile. The harder I try to get away the slower I move.

He's next to me, his bare feet immersed in the muddy silt. Brown slashes crawl up his legs, drying quickly, tangled in the thick coating of hair on his calves. "Why are you running away, sweetheart? You don't have to be afraid of little old me," he mocks. "Come on, hon, get up, we need to get you washed off."

I try to find his face but his fingers tangle in my mud-caked hair. Tugging, he urges me up onto my knees. I don't want to follow his orders but I have no choice. My legs flop uselessly beneath me.

Stand, I scream to them in my mind. *Please, let me stand!* He yanks my head back till I can hear the follicles popping as he rips out a chunk of hair, the light blue glass of his eyes sharp as needles.

"You'd better behave yourself, missy. I don't see this turning out any way but bad if you try to be cute."

"Kent, what . . . what do you want?" I stutter, still half-submerged in the mud.

"What do I want?" he laughs deep in his chest. "I want you to get on your feet right this second, that's what I want."

He tosses a chunk of my hair into the mud and grabs another section, much larger this time and forces me to my feet.

"You know what else I want?" He pulls me up to his face, his breath sour on my cheek, and I have to resist vomiting on him. "I want Theresa back. I want her to be the one sleeping in that disgusting shack. But I can't have that, can I? Why not, *Lily*? Huh?" He pauses like he expects me to answer. "Because of you, that's why not. Because you were too busy flirting with the PR guy to get back to your seat. Now, you traipse around here, half-naked, playing house with that dummy, Dave, and you've got the nerve to act all high and mighty and too good for *me*." His voice builds till a clutch of birds fly away in fear, and spit dribbles from the corner of his mouth. Then, with one punctuating tug, he smiles. "I don't think so. I'm done with your games. Now get in the water or I'll put you in the water."

The next sequence is a blur. I'm not sure how I get from the shore to being waist-deep in the pool but suddenly I'm there, and he's still beside me, his hand in my hair, guiding me like a puppeteer.

"Here, wash with this."

He shoves a small, smooth bottle in my hand. Shampoo from Margaret's bag. White freesia blossoms bloom across the label. With trembling fingers I unscrew the cap. It slips out of my hand and into the water with a plop. Reaching for it, only my hand moves as he holds me up by my scalp.

"Let it go," he growls. "Wash. NOW."

As I rub my muddy, bloody hands together the soap seeps through my fingers like pudding. I wash. Face, arms, body, legs. He snatches the bottle from my hand and pours the remaining liquid into my hair—roughly rubbing it into a bubble-less froth stinging the raw parts of my scalp. Then he pushes me down toward the water.

"Please don't, please, please," I beg, pushing feebly against the water, sure that he's about to drown me.

"What? You afraid of a little water? You seem to like it enough when you play in it every week—flitting around naked when you tell us you are out here working. Now you don't want to take a little dip? Can't make up your mind about anything, can you? Well, that's over now. I'll decide for you. Go *in* the water." He pushes me down further, my face just above the surface. "Go on—rinse off."

He shoves me into the dark water. It stings, flooding my nose and mouth. Choking, I try to get to the surface. Wild bubbles of precious air shoot out of me as my first and possibly last scream falls dead in the water. *No air. NO AIR!*

Using every ounce of strength I have left, I plant my feet in the gooey mud below and lift up against his iron hand. My head breaks through the skin of the water. Air floods into my lungs. Coughing spastically, I spray gigantic streams of pond water out of my mouth. Kent stands there, arms crossed over his bare chest, waiting. When my body finally stops convulsing, he holds me away from him like he's inspecting a pair of dirty socks.

"That's a little better," he mumbles, and begins to guide me toward shallow water.

"Now there's a good girl," he croons. A few feet from the outcropping, he shoves me away from him. My toes ram up against sharp stones skirting the base of the rough, gray boulders. "Get out of the water and take everything off. Now."

I know why he wants me naked and I know what'll happen once I am, but the pounding in my face and head reminds me he's capable of even worse. Shaking, I climb the boulder, forcing myself to breathe slowly and push down the returning nausea as my mouth fills with blood again. I'm sure he can see my hands tremble every time I lift them to find another handhold on the rock. It kills me that he knows how terrified I am but I can't make them stop. Reaching the top of the rock, I pull myself up, the sharp corners of the stone cutting into my palms.

"Stand up," he spits. A nasty smile of expectation creeps across his mud-splattered face.

Knees wobbly, I rise to full height. He's watching my body, scanning every inch as though I were already naked. I feel dirtier now than when I was covered in mud.

"The top first," he orders, and the tremor in my hands returns as I twist my arm around to grasp the latch on my bra. Looping my pointer finger under the strap and my thumb over, I pinch the two sides together, ready for the hook and eye to release, just like I've done every day since I was a preteen. It doesn't budge.

"Is there a problem?" Kent asks, tapping the knife against his thigh. He isn't expecting a response, just action. Twisting harder I wait for the tiny pop that'll take that fierce glint out of his gaze, the one that says he wants to hurt me.

"I can't . . . I can't get it off." I feel like a little lost child, alone and scared and wanting her mommy.

"Once again, I have to do everything myself. Get over here," he growls, reaching the rock's edge. Listening will keep him from beating me further but it won't save me. Scanning over his head, I start to calculate how far it is to the deeper part of the pool, where I could dive down and disappear. When Kent's right hand shoots out to grab my ankle, I curl up on my toes, tensing my calves, and I jump. But, instead of landing ten yards away in water that's six or seven feet deep, I belly flop into the three feet of water directly to the left of Kent and sink immediately to the bottom. Thick sandy dirt pushes my hair away from my face and traces paths along my bare skin. Submerged, kicking off the pliable ground with my feet, I race for my life toward the blackest depths of the pool.

The first stroke is swift and sure. I move effortlessly through the water, like I'm flying instead of swimming. Exhilaration fills my chest and I start to believe I can do it. I can escape!

Then his hand is on my ankle. He pulls me through the water while I wave my arms in the dark, hoping to find anything to hold on to, anything that'll stop my backward progress toward land and pain and horrible things I can't even imagine. But there's nothing.

He pulls me out of the water, tossing me on the shore. I throw up water again until it feels like my stomach's turned inside out. As I writhe on the ground, Kent watches, gratified.

"Enough with the games." He flings one leg over my body, straddling me as I lay prone on the ground. His thick, callused fingers grab my hands and yank them behind my back. A satiny ribbon of material tightens around my wrists till my shoulders burn.

"That's better," he mutters, then drops me face-first into the mud, the grit oozing into my mouth and grinding between my teeth. Fingering the golden chain around my neck, he seems to count the rings: Margaret's ring and Charlie's and more recently—mine. After losing so much weight I put it on there to keep it safe. Nothing is safe right now. "You won't be needing these anymore, will you? What'll your husband think when he finds out what a little slut you are?"

He yanks hard, and the gold cuts into my throat a second before snapping like fishing wire. The rings plop into the mud next to my face and I watch them, those last emblems of my former life, quickly engulfed by brown sludge.

It's easier to watch their loss than to think about what he's going to do, what's coming next. I want to watch him so I'd at least know when he was about to cross that line that'd change everything forever. I make another wish, a better wish, that I'd listened to David and kept the knife close, that it was lying heavy in my hand right now, but it's twenty feet away in the back pocket of my jean shorts, laid out on the rocks to dry with all our other laundry.

In the distance, a bird cries out. It sounds afraid like me. At least I'm not alone. The bird's voice reminds me of the last verse of a song my mom used to sing to me as a little girl when I'd have a nightmare. She learned it as a child living with her missionary parents in Australia. I still sing it to my boys. The words run through my mind and I can't keep them inside. Instead, I sing.

"Kookaburra sits on a rusty nail." The old words trip out of my mouth, not making much of a tune. When I sing I can't feel the cold knife on my skin as he cuts through my bra straps. "Gets a boo-boo in . . . his . . . tail." I can't hear his cruel chuckle as he shoves it off into the mud. "Cry . . . Kookaburra . . . cry . . . Kookaburra . . ." Or feel his hands trace the curve of my back. "Oh, how life . . . can . . . be."

It's almost time, I sense it. I want to sing again so part of me will be free but I can't even perform that one act of rebellion.

Then, as he slips his blade under the fabric on my hip, something breaks through the tree line, screaming.

"KENT!" a furious voice yells.

My heart leaps with hope and fear—it's David.

CHAPTER 19

DAVE

Present

"Let's be candid here, Dave, you and Kent weren't exactly best friends?"

"What makes you say that?" It was hard for him to pretend he didn't hate that man with every ounce of his body.

"Well, call me crazy but there always seems to be this sarcastic undertone to your stories about 'Scout,' if that's what you really called him. It sounds like he single-handedly kept you alive those first few months and there's not a whole lot of appreciation for those services," she said, raising her eyebrows accusingly. Was he that transparent?

"He wasn't exactly the easiest guy to be around. He knew a lot, don't get me wrong, but he wasn't what I'd call warm and fluffy either."

"That's not what I've heard," Genevieve pushed. "His family says he had a love for life and he was a fun guy to be around because of his positive outlook. They also say he and Theresa were very much in love and they were on the verge of getting engaged."

Dave knew that was the last thing Theresa wanted; she'd broken up with Kent a few weeks before their disastrous flight. And Kent's family, that bunch of loons? After meeting his family, Dave wasn't as surprised by the way Kent turned out. After the rescue and their time in the hospital recovering, they all returned to the States, where the castaways were inundated with interview requests. Morning shows in particular loved them. Heck, everyone loved them. Letters and e-mails poured in from around the world and the survivors were instant celebrities. But a few people, two to be specific, were not fans—Joan and Jim Carter, Kent's parents.

"Of course his family would know him differently than I did. We were in a life-or-death situation, barely scraping by. I'm sure he was a great son. I never questioned that," Dave said, always working to appease anyone who had anything to do with Kent, especially his parents.

It took Janice from Carlton to give him the lowdown. She said that after the crash, when the black box was recovered, the airline and Carlton Yogurt used Kent as a convenient fall guy. They said the crash was due to human error, Kent's human error. As a result, his family didn't get the ten-million-dollar settlement Lillian's and Dave's families were awarded. The Carters were livid.

It turned into a massive court battle between the family and the airline, and Janice said it had been a messy and emotional case. Apparently Kent was cited for flying under the influence in '99 and had his pilot's license suspended for a year in the States. That's when he moved to the South Pacific and hired on with the tiny airline called Kanaku, which specialized in private jet charter services. It all looked very bad and at the end of the case, Kent's family lost and the judge basically called their still-missing son a murderer.

It wasn't until Dave had been home a week that the anonymous phone calls started. They'd always come just as Dave and Beth were getting ready for bed: three or four rings, and then silence on the answering machine before they'd hang up. Dave changed their number four times in one month.

Dave was standing in his kitchen one night, making a late night snack after Beth had gone to bed. While spreading out the last bit of mustard on a piece of bread, the phone rang shrilly. Dave jumped, dropping the bread face down on the counter. The phone rang again. No time to clean up the mess. He wiped his hands on the hand towel hanging by the sink, and ran for the phone, hoping it didn't wake Beth. He glanced at the caller ID, sure it would say "Unlisted" but knowing that really meant "Lily." But, when he lifted the phone off of the charger, the LED screen read "Cellular Caller" and a number he'd seen many times—too many times.

This is getting ridiculous, Dave thought. Hitting the Talk button violently, he attempted to control his voice as irritation shifted into fury. "WHAT do you want?"

A shocked silence returned, only breathing and a TV on in the background.

"I don't know who you are but you'd better speak up now because tomorrow I'm getting this number blocked on my phone so this is your chance. I know you're there—I can hear you."

"Why do you keep lying about my son?" a smoke-scratched female voice answered.

"I'm sorry, ma'am, do I know you? Do I know your son?" Why was he trying to talk rationally to the crazy person who had been stalking him? He halfway expected she'd hang up.

"Oh, you know my son," she sneered. "He's the man who saved your life. The one who you pretend wasn't there."

"Kent?" he asked, the idea slapping him hard in the face.

"Yes, Kent. Kent Carter." Her voice grew sharp. "Do you know what you've done to him? To his reputation? All you have to say is he wasn't drinking, that it wasn't his fault, and then they'd all know the truth. I think you owe him that at least."

"I thought we made it very clear Kent was a great help to us, that he was the difference between life and death, over and over again. What else do you want me to say?"

A gravelly sigh, and then she spoke like she was talking to a toddler. "What I said before, that he wasn't drinking. If you said that, everything would be different."

Dave shook his head even though she couldn't see it. "But, like I've told the press, I don't know if he was drinking. I didn't see any alcohol or smell any on his breath but that's all I know. Lillian knows even less because she didn't meet him until after the crash."

"Have any lawyers called you? What did you tell them?" she snapped.

Lawyers. Dave understood immediately. If he told them Kent hadn't been drinking, they'd all get their precious settlement.

"No lawyers have called me, Mrs. Carter, and if they do, I'll tell them the truth too. That's all I can do."

"You little son of a bitch," she shot at him. So that's where Kent inherited his charm and class. "I guess I shouldn't have expected anything else from a lowlife like you, should I? One day people will know the truth about my Kent and then you'll be sorry."

"I'm already sorry about Kent, Mrs. Carter," he sighed. "I wish your family the best. It's late; I must let you go."

"Whatever," she muttered, and the phone went dead.

Dave let the phone fall to the cold stone of the quartz countertop, employing every ounce of self-control inside to keep from yelling the string of profanities running through his mind. He slammed his hands on the counter, and the phone danced in front of him from the force of his blow. Picking it up, he raised the phone over his head to hurl it across the room but stopped short. He held the phone in front of him and punched in a familiar number at lightning speed, the one that made him warm and numb from the inside out.

"Hello?"

"Hey, Lily, how was your day?" Dave leaned against the wall and let himself slide to the floor, pulling his legs close, happy to hear her voice again.

"It was great. We went to the park and had a picnic," she began to narrate without missing a beat. "Daniel finally learned how to do the monkey bars on his own. He came home with giant blisters on his palms but was so proud of himself he didn't even care." Her voice had a richness he only heard when she talked about her kids. "How 'bout you? Good day?" she asked. Dave could hear her nibbling on a fingernail.

"It was fine." He inhaled, trying to stay calm. "Until five minutes ago."

"Oh no," she said knowingly. "Fight with Beth again?"

"No," he sighed. Shit, how many fights had he called her about? He had to stop telling her those things, especially since Lily never complained about Jerry, not once. Shaking it off, he continued. "I got a crazy phone call."

"Really? Just one? Was it the guy who says we were abducted by aliens and that's where we've been the past two years? Did he ask you for the alien's cell phone number again?"

"I wish. That sounds way more entertaining than the woman who just called me." He paused, reluctant to tell her about the call. "It was Kent's mom."

"What was that like?" Her voice trembled. Dave longed to reach out and rub her shoulders.

"It was . . . interesting. She wants us to say Kent wasn't drunk the day of the crash. I think it's so she can get the settlement, but we'd have to testify."

"What did you tell her? You didn't say we'd do it, did you? I don't want to do it, David." He'd do anything she wanted when she said his name like that. He felt invincible.

"Shhh, Lily, shhhh. You don't have to. I'm not going to. If they have the guts to subpoena us, then we'll say what they want."

"But if it's under oath we HAVE to tell the truth," she shouted. How she didn't wake up her whole household, he'd never know.

"You don't have to say anything that'll incriminate you," he reminded her. "Not that they'll ask. Not that they'll call us to testify. Wow, we're blowing this phone call out of proportion aren't we?"

Lily didn't seem to agree. "Maybe." She paused leaving a cavernous gap in the conversation. "Maybe I should tell Jerry everything. He's a lawyer. He could help us."

Jerry. That'd ruin everything.

"Have you thought this through all the way, Lily? You'd have to tell him more than just the Kent part. Wasn't Jerry the whole reason we started this ridiculous lie?"

"I don't know," Lily whispered. "He's a lot softer now but I think things would be bad if he knew the truth. Really bad. I don't want to tell him. I wish I *could* tell him. Before all this, we didn't keep secrets but now . . . I feel like I'm always lying to him."

"That's because you *are* lying to him." He was running out of nice words on this topic, always finding it difficult to control himself when they talked about Jerry. "Okay, how about this? I'll tell him. That way he'll know everything about Margaret and Kent. Hmmm, wouldn't he be interested in the truth about Paul? I'd love to tell him all about that little episode. Go wake him up and put him on. No, wait, I wanna see his face. I think I should fly out."

"You wouldn't do that."

"I think I would. I doubt he'd be as accepting as you think, and then I could have a place in your life that merits more significance than a secret phone call at one a.m."

Silence. "You're right," she admitted. "He can't know, he can never know. Don't get any ideas, David, because if you ever tell him, I'll never speak to you again, never."

The finality in that phrase ripped through his chest like a knife. "I wasn't serious," he backtracked. "I . . . I don't know what I'd do if I couldn't hear your voice."

"You shouldn't say those things to me, David."

"I know. I'm sorry." Dave rushed to make things better. "Don't worry, we'll make this work just like we did with all the interviews," he reassured her. "And we shouldn't tell Jerry."

"Yeah, I know."

Dave had a feeling this wasn't the last time they'd have that conversation. One day, she might call his bluff.

"Let's not worry about Joan Carter for now. I think she'll sustain herself on that little phone call for a while. And I'll block her number first thing in the morning. Anyway, they don't want the truth about Kent to come out. It wouldn't take much to show them how little they really know about their son."

"I hope it doesn't come to that," Lillian groaned. "I don't want to think about this anymore. Tell me one of your stories, David. Make me fall asleep."

He leaned his head back and let his lids shut. "Close your eyes. Think about the waves, hear them rolling in, crashing on the shore, the sweet smell of flowers and sea spray mixing together and surrounding you, and the cool night air on your skin . . ." Dave spoke memories till Lily's breathing was steady and he was sure she'd fallen asleep.

He never asked how she made it from her hiding place in the spare bedroom closet into her bed without raising Jerry's suspicions, or how he didn't notice the hours on the phone bill that they'd spent on the phone every night. If Lily had been his wife it'd drive him mad with jealousy. But she wasn't his wife. She was his friend and would never be anything more than that.

"Was there a reason you didn't like him?" Genevieve prodded. "What did he do that upset you?"

Dave, with all those dangerous feelings rising inside, resisted clenching his jaw, knowing it'd show up on camera. Instead, he put on another smile and tried to work some of his old-time PR mojo.

"I can't say I knew Kent very well before the crash, but all people respond to trauma differently. He was very distraught by Theresa's death and I know that made him less sociable. It's true he helped us, and maybe even saved us. Even though we weren't best friends, it doesn't mean we hated each other either."

"No"—Genevieve's eyebrows bobbed up and down, her forehead attempting to wrinkle—"but it's clear you aren't telling us everything about him. Why not be honest?"

He wanted to tell her exactly why he hated Kent. The way he stood over Lily, knife squeezed in his fat paw, legs straddling her as though she were an animal he'd caught on the hunt rather than the most interesting, caring, and clever person Dave had ever met. Because he put that emptiness in Lily's eyes that's never completely disappeared.

"You want honest? Okay. We were not friends. I don't think anyone could call that man a friend. No matter what his family says, he was a son of a bitch before the crash, and the island and isolation didn't improve his personality. He never once spoke to me with any type of kindness and when he was with Lillian he . . . he . . ." Genevieve Randall leaned forward, enjoying Dave's answer more than he'd intended. He stopped immediately, reset his shoulders, took a deep breath, and lightened his tone. "As I said, we had our differences, but we had a mutual respect and that's what kept us going."

"Okay . . . so one more Kent question." Her smile was sickeningly sweet. "What would you say, Dave, if I told you Kent's family informed us he was an incredibly good swimmer?"

"I'd completely agree," Dave nodded. "But, Ms. Randall, no one can outswim a shark."

CHAPTER 20

DAVID-DAY 113

The Island

As the sun rises, pushing above the watery horizon, I plunge my hands into the shallow pool of water gathered in a low spot close to our beach. Grabbing a wet handful of sand, I rub it furiously between my nearly raw hands, in between my fingers and up my wrists, wishing it were something stronger, something more like bleach.

Bleach, that's what I need. I want to make everything clean again, get the whitest whites like the commercial says. I want to erase the memories from yesterday, clean them out like a stain from a shirt. What was it Lady Macbeth said? "Out, damned spot!" I want to cast out forever what I saw when I burst through those trees yesterday afternoon.

"Dave, turn around and leave," Kent ordered, as though I'd listen to his every command like a trained monkey. Maybe he forgot that I hate him or that he gave me a knife. Most likely he didn't find me a threat. I didn't leave.

"Get off her, Kent." I pulled my knife out of the front pocket of my khakis and flipped the homemade sheath off its tip. Confidence surged through me as I remembered how long I'd spent sharpening it only two nights ago. "I swear if you hurt her, I'm gonna . . ."

"What?" he mocked, barely glancing my way. "You think you can do anything to me, kid? You must have delusions of grandeur or something. If you're as smart as you think, walk away. Let someone else have a go at the girl."

I wanted him to shut up almost as much as I wanted him away from Lily. Taking two long steps forward, I rushed at Kent.

"Seriously? You want to do this? Effing fine." He stepped away from Lily. She twitched in the mud. *Run, Lily, RUN.*

"Don't even think about moving," he warned her. "You can try to run away, girly, but this is an island. I know it better than either of you." He shifted the knife between the two of us. "I'll find you no matter where you hide."

"Lily—don't listen to him," I yelled, staring Kent down. "You should go. Now."

"Yeah, *Lily*, why don't you leave?" he taunted, slouching toward me like a big cat homing in on its prey. "Then you won't have to watch me kill your boyfriend."

Lily rolled onto her side in the mud. Her face was starting to swell, nose possibly broken. My fingers wrapped tighter around my knife.

"David, I want you to leave," she muttered through swollen lips.

"That's never going to happen."

She got up on her knees, breathing labored, green eyes glowing through the frame of black muck quickly drying on her face.

"Please leave, David. This isn't worth your life."

"Lily, shh!" I ordered, taking another step toward Kent, making mental notes. Water to my right, jungle to my left, crazy homicidal maniac in front of me. It wasn't looking good.

Lily spoke again, now standing. "Kent, stop." She spit a reddish-brown mixture of saliva, blood, and mud. "I'll go with you if you promise to leave him alone."

"Stop it," I growled at her.

"That's a nice offer, sweetheart, but I'm a little busy. Don't worry." He chuckled, baring his teeth. "I'll get to you later. I like the chase."

"Run!" I shouted to Lily as Kent sprang toward me, knife held high, pointed at my chest.

In a slightly delayed reaction, I pushed off the soft ground on the balls of my feet, my own knife grasped so tightly in my hand it would've hurt if I hadn't been so pumped up with anger. Kent's thick upper body slammed against my turned right shoulder, hard knuckles pounding my jaw.

Swinging both fists, I tried to land my first blow. Kent, playing dirty as always, kneed me fiercely. As I doubled over, he slapped the knife out of my hand. It flew into the underbrush as bright stars of pain exploded through my groin.

Before I knew it, he had me on my back, stocky thighs crushing my torso. I threw my hands up in front of my face defensively, blocking his rock-hard fists. Unable to reach my face, he hit me in more strategic places like my ears, and a lucky blow or two on my neck.

"You couldn't let me have my turn, could you?" Kent growled, wrapping his fingers around my throat. I opened my mouth to yell at him but my windpipe began to collapse under the pressure of his thumbs.

This is it. My limbs sunk uselessly to the ground and rings of black invaded my vision. *I'm going to die now.* It wasn't peaceful, no light at the end of a tunnel or any of that crap. Only fear and regret for all the things I'd left undone.

My last thoughts, my very last ones, were of Lily—her face on the plane all lit up from the setting sun, the caring warmth in her eyes when she came to sit by me, her stern bravery as Kent stitched her shoulder on the raft, her naked grief after losing Margaret, the knowing smile that danced across her lips when she was making a joke. And the last thought that entered my mind, a realization I'd never let myself fully accept: I love her.

Then I died.

The pain was gone and instead of fighting in the shallows of the dingy pond, I was floating in a great still pool, blinking against a yellow light streaming through the canopy of trees. Small forms skipped on the shore. They looked like children. Two girls and a little boy playing—no, dancing, like fairy sprites—their little giggles rippling through the air like ribbons. A subtle blue mist filled the clearing and swirled with every jump from the kids on shore, like their gauzy white clothes were trailing behind them.

Dazed, I sat up and looked around, finding the water only a few inches deep. Trees surrounded the pool. They weren't palm trees like on our island, they were giant redwoods like the ones my dad took me to when I was a little boy. I scanned the shore, unconsciously expecting to see him waiting for me in the trees. I wasn't cold or in pain and I knew I should be calm and happy, but I wasn't. A thought tugged at the edge of my consciousness, like a forgotten word that's harder to recall the longer you think about it. I couldn't be here, in the forest mist; I had to be somewhere else, I had to be . . .

As suddenly as I was transported to the forest glen, I was pulled by my feet through the water of the pool in one giant whoosh. I was back. Kent was still on me, but his hands were gone from around my neck. Instead, he lay flat on top of me, with his usual perfume of body odor and fish guts. As the haze of death lifted from my brain, I tried to shove him off. He didn't try to stop me.

"Lily! Lily!" I rasped, my throat throbbing where Kent's thumbs almost crushed it. After a few good pushes, I slid out from Kent's unconscious body. Left leg numb, I gimped my way to the tree line, standing so quickly my head spun. My vision was still a little fuzzy from the fight, and tiny grains of mud scratched against my eyes when I blinked.

Hiding in the thick underbrush, I scoured the pool for Lily. I searched the trees flanking the other side of the pool, thinking she'd be close to keep an eye on what was happening but far enough away to easily escape. She wasn't there. Dread building, I flicked my eyes in the opposite direction, counting the seconds I had till Kent woke and we'd have to run.

"Where are you, Lily?" I whispered.

Then I found her, crouched behind the laundry-covered rocks, face in her hands. I glanced quickly at Kent, and left the safety of the trees, careful to give him a wide berth. Then I ran haltingly to the rocks.

She was so tiny pushed up against that boulder, her body folded in on itself. I locked my sights on her so she didn't fade into the dirt and rocks. She's so thin, the bones of her arms sticking out in unnatural ways. Why hadn't I noticed before?

Reaching her hiding place, I fell to my knees in front of her, splashing mud everywhere. My arms ached to hold her and tell her everything was going to be all right, that I wouldn't let anyone hurt her again. But when I reached out to touch her knee, she flinched.

Wrenching her hands away from her face, I saw terror spelled out in the trails of tears etched through the dirt on her cheeks and the blood coagulated in the corners of her mouth. It took her a full two seconds to understand who I was. When she did, her lower lip trembled and new tears formed in her red-rimmed eyes.

"You're okay," she whispered, surprised. "I thought . . . I thought you were dead."

"I thought I was too," I said, lightly.

"Shhh." She reached a shaking hand out and placed it on my lips to silence me. "I can't hear you say that. You're alive. You're alive!" I grabbed her hand, kissing her fingertips, ignoring the blood covering them.

"Are you okay, Lily? Did he . . ." I searched for words that wouldn't make me want to kill Kent. "Was I too late?"

Lily pulled her hand away as though I'd bitten it.

"No." She shivered. "Almost."

I reached for her again, but hesitated. The only thing covering her legs and torso was mud, her underwear stained the same blackish brown. I could only imagine what happened to the bra she pressed against her chest, broken straps flopping over each shoulder. I reached over the rock and grabbed the first piece of nearly dry laundry I touched and pulled it down to her. Thankfully, it was my threadbare blue polo and not something that belonged to Kent.

"Here, lean forward." She tipped toward me, leaning against her bloody knees. I slipped the moist shirt over her head. When my knuckles grazed the back of her skull she pulled away and I saw the dark clumps of dirt and blood clotting in her hair. I guided her arms through the sleeves, taking count of all the places she was bruised or broken. Her palms, knees, and elbows were blackish red with blobs of thickening blood, her face swelling and bleeding on one side like it'd been crushed by a rock. Even her toes were bleeding, one of the nails missing entirely. Oh, my Lily. What did he do to you? I couldn't count anymore.

I let the shirt fall loose around her sides and reached for the collar, careful to keep our skin from touching, refusing to contribute to her pain. After I buttoned the two buttons, I hung on an extra second, the only way I could touch her without hurting her.

When I finally let go of the fabric, Lily's hands shot up from out of the mud and wrapped around my wrist. "Thank you for coming for me, David. Thank you." She wove her fingers through mine, their trembling making me feel my failure more fully.

"I'm sorry, Lily, this never should've happened. I'll never let it happen again." I hadn't checked Kent in a while and it made me prickle all over like someone was watching me. I tried to peek over the rock, but Lily held on with an iron grasp. "I have to stand up, Lily." I started to panic. "I want to keep you safe. Please let me keep you safe."

She still didn't let go. "He's not there, he's gone."

"Huh?" I peeled her fingers off, every muscle in my body flexing, ready for another fight. I crept up the side of the rock and scanned the pool, already planning defensive measures. But Kent still lay in the dirt, passed out. Tiny drops of relief cooled my nerves. We still had time to plan our escape.

I crouched down quickly. "He's still out cold. I know you're hurt and frightened but we have to get out of here before he wakes up. Can you stand?"

"He's gone," Lily curled up into herself. "He's gone, he's gone," she repeated.

"No, Lily, he's still there. We have to go!" I pulled her arm again, ready to pick her up and carry her.

When I yanked her hand off her face, she glared up at me. "David, would you listen to me? He's not coming back, we don't have to run. He's gone!" she shouted. "He's gone because I killed him. I used the knife you made for me and when he was on you I . . ."

"What? What do you mean?" The words swirled around like a blizzard and I had a hard time focusing on their meaning.

She took a shaky breath like she always did when trying not to freak out. Pulling her knees in tighter, she picked at the frayed hem of my shirt.

"When he attacked you, I ran and grabbed my knife from the laundry pile. I swear"—she held up her hand like she was in court—"I was only going to threaten him but he ignored me. He didn't flinch, he just kept choking you. Your face was blue, David. Then you stopped fighting and I got scared." She grabbed something solid out of the mud and held it up. The knife. I'd held that piece of rock in my hands for hours as I chipped and scratched, turning it into a weapon. It was covered in blood.

"You stabbed him?"

"Yes," she mumbled, staring at the ground like she couldn't look at me. "I stabbed him." She hid behind a curtain of dirty hair.

I settled down next to her, leaning sideways till our arms bumped. When she didn't move away, I walked my fingers toward hers. She turned her palm up and I laced our fingers together. With a little squeeze, she unknowingly dulled the pain from my aching head and throat. She must've felt the same, because she curled against my shoulder.

We sat like that without saying a word until my legs started to cramp. I listened to the birds and the wind and a part of me listened for a man rising from the dead. I don't know what she was thinking. I couldn't bring myself to ask her. Instead, I counted her breaths and thanked God she'd been spared. Soon, her breathing went from steady to ragged.

"Shhh, it's okay." I leaned my head on top of hers, avoiding the raw patches. "You're safe. I won't let anyone hurt you ever again. I promise."

"I killed him," she repeated, dazed. "I really killed him."

"You saved my life, Lily. You had no other choice."

"I took his life. I could have stopped myself but I didn't. When I saw him choking you on the ground, I *decided* to kill him. When I picked up that knife I . . . I knew what I was going to do. That's pre-meditation. I'm a murderer."

"He didn't stop when he had the chance, did he? You were defending yourself, you were defending me. I'd be dead without you."

She hesitated, as if searching for a rebuttal. "Do you think I'll go to jail?" she asked.

She was losing it. "Jail?" I tried not to laugh. "What, is the Professor going to call nine-one-one on his coconut phone?" I checked to see if I'd made her smile.

"That's not funny right now, David." She pulled my arm into her lap. "I mean, if we get out of here, they'll dig him up so his family can take him home. They'll know he was stabbed, over and over again, in the back. I've seen *Datelines* with less evidence result in a guilty verdict. That could be me. I could leave this prison only to be put in another one."

"No way. I was there, I saw what he was doing to you and to me. I can tell them." I was trying to calm her but the way she laid it all out I was starting to see her point. What *would* happen if we were rescued? What if they saw Kent's body?

"Then you'd be called my accomplice." She squeezed my hand, her dirt-crusted fingernails shifting up and down against my knuckles. "Anyway, you were passed out when I did it. Your testimony wouldn't help much. I know I must sound paranoid but I'm starting to understand that bad things, horrible things even, can happen to anyone."

"Do you want me to check, Lily? Do you want me to be sure?"

She nodded. We have to face it sooner or later. If he was dead, we couldn't leave him there, at the edge of the pool. That was our source of life, fresh water, and if we hadn't tainted it already with all the fighting we surely would if we let Kent rot there.

Then again, if he wasn't dead . . . the thought made the acidic taste of hatred climb in my throat. What would we do then? I guess we'd have to care for him. It was the last thing I wanted to do but Lily would never allow me to let him die intentionally.

I reluctantly untangled my fingers from hers. The sweat from our hands mixed with the mud on our palms, making my hand sticky and cool when I pulled away and stood up. The full force of gravity slammed me like it was turned up by five or ten thousand pounds of pressure, and it took a few clumsy steps before I could stand up straight.

Kent was still facedown in the mud. It took only a few steps to see the blood, red as food coloring, staining the back of his white pilot shirt. I counted gashes in the fabric . . . one, two, three, four . . . maybe five. If each rip corresponded to a stab wound, then Lily was right: Kent was dead.

If Lily was right . . . I could finish that sentence in so many ways. If Lily was right, I'd have to turn his lifeless body over, I'd have to touch his neck or wrist to search for a pulse, I'd have to look into his empty eyes and know that my struggling beneath him was the last thing Kent saw in his entire life. If Lily was right, I'd have to get rid of him so no one would ever know what happened.

Lily was right. Kent's skin was already cold when I flipped him over, and it didn't take a doctor to see the blood running down his chin from internal bleeding. Something about the way his eyes were frozen open reminded me of Theresa when she went. I'd always thought eyes closed peacefully at the moment of death. Margaret went that way. But people suffering these violent deaths seemed different, like they were forever stuck in the emotion of their demise.

One at a time I closed his eyes, the slimy wet eyelids slipping shut effortlessly. It made it easier to look at him. Sitting on my heels, I took a breath and closed my eyes, hoping that along with oxygen I'd inhale inspiration and some idea of what to do now that I couldn't turn back. Even in death Kent was causing problems. Yet when I opened my eyes, I saw the glint of orange plastic just a few yards away from Kent's body. The knife he had given me, that he had rid me of, appeared as if in answer to my silent plea.

Lily sat in the same place I'd left her, pushed into the rocks, head resting on her knees. As I approached, she looked up, painfully hopeful.

"He's dead, isn't he?"

"Yes, he is."

"I knew it, I knew it, I knew it," she chanted.

"Don't lose it now, Lily. I'll take care of it." I knelt down in front of her as though I were begging her to stop her rapid slip into shock. "No one will ever know."

"How?" She asked the one question I didn't want to answer.

"Don't worry about it. I'll do it all. Let's get you to the shelter, warm you up by the fire, get these clothes dry, and I'll make it so you never have to think about this day ever again." She started to protest but seemed to run out of steam before she could get any momentum.

I helped Lily limp to camp, the clothes slung over my aching shoulder. I ignored my pain, knowing Lily must be in so much more. We didn't speak as we walked or as I stoked the dying embers of the fire once we finally arrived at our beach. Neither of us dared break that solemn silence between us, even when I took her into the ocean to bathe, and she cried because the salt burned in her wounds.

Then I held her, held her tight to my chest as she cried and cried until the sun burned high in the sky and she dozed off into a fitful sleep. I loved her weight in my arms. It was like I'd always been an unbalanced scale that was finally correctly calibrated.

I watched her sleep and when the pounding in my head turned into a dull pulsing, I lay her down gently, like putting a baby to bed. By then I had a plan. If it worked, all incriminating evidence would be erased forever.

I returned to the clearing where Kent's body lay, knife in my pocket and chased away a group of rats by pounding my feet as I approached his stiff body. I lifted one of his heavy bare legs. This wasn't going to be easy.

I dragged him by his feet through the jungle, stopping off and on to rest. He seemed like concrete, and I wasn't sure I could make it. After about an hour, I considered dumping him in the trees, letting the bugs and animals get at him. But I promised her, I promised I'd take care of it.

When I finally made it out of the trees, the sun was dipping into the ocean and I was covered in trails of sweat. Kent was worse, much worse, off, his arms marked with deep, oozing gashes. A black train of blood snaked behind us.

When I reached the rocks, I shoved my arms under his and dragged him quickly up to the edge of the cliff. Breathing heavily, I took out my knife. It was still coated in crusty mud from where I'd dug it out of the bushes by the pool. Kent gave me that knife not knowing that one day I'd use it on him.

First, I cut off his clothes one layer at a time till his body lay sprawled naked on the rock face. The knife in my hand felt hungry for something more than clothing. Some part of me wished I'd had the satisfaction of killing Kent or at least I'd been awake to see his face as Lily landed her first blow. I thought this would be hard. I was wrong.

The sun was almost down and I knew it was time. I pressed the knife through Kent's cold flesh and slashed it, following the thick blue vein on his forearm. The blade made an eerie tearing sound and gelatinous blood seeped out of the long, thin cut. I grabbed his other wrist, sliced deep, only pausing for a second to cover his face with the now-crimson pilot's shirt when I did his neck.

I guess I expected the blood to flow like a faucet but he'd been dead too long, so it just oozed. I remembered how when Kent caught a sea bird or the occasional rodent, he'd cut their throats and string them up. Lily hated the mess; it brought bugs and rats and smelled horrible when it didn't rain every day. But now I needed blood and I could only hope a very important cleanup crew would be waiting in the wings.

Shoving him forward till he bent at the waist over the cliff, I sat on his calves and feet. Gravity did the rest, pulling his blood greedily into the churning ocean below. Sunset was supposed to be the time they feed, sunset and sunrise. I knew they were out there. I could only wait for them to show their pointy fins announcing their ominous arrival.

When the light was almost gone, dark shadows flitted in the water, an occasional fin breaking through the waves. Perfect. I climbed off Kent's legs and gave one last push. Gravity helped one more time and yanked his body down into the ocean, where the predators that smelled his blood waited to devour his flesh and pull him out into open water where his bones would be lost forever. The thought gave me such a rush of relief it almost made me ashamed. Almost.

By the time the stars developed in the night sky, sharks thrashed in the water below. It was louder than I'd expected but it played in my ears like music. I didn't watch. My sudden macabre streak didn't extend that far into the darkness, but I did lie on the cold rocks, still wet from the mist of high tide, and listen. It didn't take long for the splashing to drift off, either getting less frequent or farther away.

Then all was still. I rolled over and stared into the heavens. Was it possible to get used to such amazing beauty? Maybe it was. I was starting to think I could get used to anything.

Kent was dead. Lily stabbed him and I mutilated and disposed of his body. I waited for guilt to overwhelm me but it never did. Instead I fell asleep, safe for the first time since our nightmare began.

Wrapped in that blanket of safety, I drifted into a dreamless sleep where I stayed until the sun broke over the horizon and I felt the stiffness a new day had brought. When my eyes adjusted to the light, a bloody scene lay in front of me. The rocks were deep red with clotted blood, the same as on my hands and clothes. Scrambling to the edge of the rocks, I looked over, unsure what I'd do if his body still floated there. When nothing but crystalline water and waves greeted me I thought, *We are free.*

◆ ◆ ◆

Standing, I hold my hands up to the light to inspect them. Clean enough. The pool I've been washing in is a deep orangey red so I quickly kick a bunch of sand over it. I don't want Lily to stumble into it once she starts her day. A light rain pats my shoulders and for once I'm happy a storm's rolling in. The rain will wash away Kent's blood better than I ever could. The fewer reminders of yesterday, the better.

Heading up the beach to camp, I ball up Kent's shredded clothes, dropping them in the fire as I pass. Damp, they smoke at first, but soon catch fire. Glancing back only once, I see Kent's embroidered pilot's emblem smolder into ash. Then, I bound off into the shelter to check on Lily. Kent is the past. She's my future. I refuse to look back ever again.

CHAPTER 21

LILLIAN

Present

"Could you tell me about the day Kent died?" Genevieve asked.

Lillian was ready for this question. As the story spilled out she mentally kept track of all the "intentional inaccuracies."

"It was close to our one-year island anniversary (LIE). Kent wanted to go fishing on the reef that morning (LIE) and was up before any of us. Usually we'd fish in pairs but that day he went off on his own (LIE). Dave was cutting fruit and I was in the shelter with Paul (LIE, LIE, LIE). We heard a scream (LIE). It was like nothing I'd heard before but it lasted only a minute and then it was gone. Dave and I ran to the big rock we used for crustaceans (LIE), the one that jutted into the bay and looked out over the water. We didn't see anything. We called his name, walked the beaches and then the whole island but it was like he'd just disappeared (LIE). I guess we'll never know what really happened (LIE) but we think he was attacked by sharks (TRUE)."

Her hands lay spread wide against her leg, ten lies in sixty seconds. That had to be a record of some kind.

"How did you deal with that loss, Lillian? It must have been . . . crushing."

"Oh yes, I cried for days, until my eyes and head ached. I didn't know how we'd survive without him."

Lillian watched Genevieve Randall as the words settled and felt a small jolt of electricity when the reporter frowned. She'd pulled it off, again.

One of the things that surprised Lillian the most about lying was the rush. She didn't know if it was because she'd always been a good girl or if she had something seriously wrong with her moral compass, but every successful lie made her feel invincible—for a moment at least. It didn't last, though, the excitement. It was more like a night of drinking: fun for the night but leaving you with a big hangover and hazy moments of remorse the next morning.

The only people she regretted lying to were her family, especially her boys. She tried to tell herself that they were too young and wouldn't understand anyway, but every time they asked about how Margaret died or about Paul she felt like a fraud. What right did she have to teach these children right and wrong when she crossed those blurred lines daily?

Her strategy was avoidance. The busier she could make their lives, the fewer opportunities for dwelling on the past. So Lillian attempted to make that first summer home spectacular. They went to the pool and the park, searched the shelves at the library for the newest Captain Underpants book, and played every game that the boys wanted in their backyard—from baseball to two-hand-touch/tackle football.

One of their summer projects was to change Josh and Daniel's bedroom from a little boy's nursery to a big kid's room. They made a weekend of it. Friday night, they picked out the colors at Home Depot, then taped the ceilings and baseboards while snacking on pizza.

Saturday they painted and painted and painted until tiny midnight blue paint speckles covered their hands, faces, and hair. Even Daniel didn't tire of the hard work. Taking turns picking their favorite songs from Josh's iPod, it felt more like a dance party than a home-improvement project.

That night they camped out in the basement, watching movies and snuggling on the couch bed. It was as close to heaven as Lillian had felt in a long time.

Sunday, after making a quick run to church, they came home for a lunch of chicken tacos and sweet corn before running upstairs to finish the job. They worked fast, pulling off tape, sticking on sports team decals, and throwing away the large plastic sheets that'd protected their furniture and carpet during the project. When the room was complete, Lillian called the boys to stand in the doorway and survey their hard work.

"It looks great, guys!" Lillian squeezed their shoulders simultaneously. Daniel's soft shoulder welcomed her touch, like her fingers and his skin were meant for each other. He cuddled into her, burying his face in Lillian's side like he'd done a few weeks earlier with Jill. Lillian smiled.

On her other side, the thin muscles under Josh's skin reminded Lillian he was more grown than little, and she squeezed him a bit tighter. Soon he'd remember that moms aren't cool and hanging out with family for the weekend isn't a preferred activity.

"It's awesome," Daniel whispered. "Can I call Emma to come over and see it? Aunt Jill made me promise we'd invite them when we were done."

"Of course!" Okay, maybe she sounded a bit too chipper. She didn't exactly love the kids calling Jill their "aunt" but Lillian was working on overcoming her one-sided rivalry with her best friend. Plus, over the past eighteen months the boys bonded with Jill's daughters, Emma and Jane. Daniel's position on girls being "icky" had clearly evolved. He and six-year-old Emma were now inseparable and Josh and Jane had settled into a quiet friendship, spending most of their time writing the next installment in their comic book series: *The Adventures of J&J*. Lillian read all fifteen installments and immediately declared it a literary masterpiece.

"Why don't you go give them a call? We can make sandwiches. Ask Aunt Jill if she has any chips she can bring over, would ya?" Lillian called after the seven-year-old, already skipping down the hallway. "What about you, bud," she asked Josh, "What do you think about your room?"

Flipping his hair back with his left hand in a way that was becoming habit, Josh scanned the room with his dark brown eyes. "Yeah, it's great. Thanks, Mom." He wrapped his left arm around Lillian's waist and hugged her gently. He lingered there for a second before letting his arm fall and then nervously flipping his hair back again.

"Mom, can I ask you a question?" His voice trembled when he said her name and she still knew that meant he was trying not to cry.

"What's up, baby? You know you can ask me anything." She turned to face him. Sure enough, little reserves of tears clung to his lower eyelids. This time she pushed back his hair to see his face.

"Are you going to leave us again?" A miniature tear fell onto his cheek.

Her heart skipped a beat. "Why in the world would you ask that, Josh?"

He pulled away. "You were gone for a long time and you were with that man, Dave. Sammy at school said that 'cause you were with him and Daddy was here that you wouldn't want to be married anymore. His parents got divorced last year and now he takes the bus on Mondays, Tuesdays, and Wednesdays and walks on Thursdays and Fridays. He said his parents started by fighting a lot and then they didn't sleep in the same room anymore and then his daddy moved out with his girlfriend."

Lillian had never met Sammy but she had an immediate desire to find him, point her finger in his face, and say, "Mind your own business, kid!" Unfortunately, this wasn't McDonald's PlayPlace, where she could gently urge some stranger's child to stop wailing on her toddler with his Happy Meal toy. Instead, Josh was going on ten and she couldn't fight his battles for him anymore.

The tinge of truth in what Josh said made her feel worse than ever. It's one thing to lie to an adult, but to your own children? Most nights she fell asleep on the couch or in the spare room after spending hours on the phone with David. Jerry hadn't said anything about her absence and she thanked God for that, not knowing what she'd say if he confronted her with phone bills or hurt feelings.

Apparently the kids had started to notice. What would've been tiny disagreements two years ago, like how Jerry'd stopped putting the toilet paper onto the actual roll or the first time her hair clogged the drain in the shower, turned into huge arguments that had to be taken into the other room away from their boys. The words "I wish you hadn't come back" or "I don't want to be with you anymore" had never been spoken, but they were always there, threatening to break the silence and change their lives.

As her son's worried face peered up at her, Lillian placed both of her hands on his thin shoulders, and looked her son directly in the eyes. "I'll always be here for you, Josh, always. I won't let anything take me away from you and your brother again. When I was on that island, the *only* thing that kept me going was the thought of you two." Josh nibbled at his bottom lip thoughtfully. "You know you can talk to me about anything, right?" Lillian urged him. "Is there something else you need to say, sweetie?"

"The reason I'm worried is, well . . ." As Lillian used her fingers to dry Josh's face, he flinched away from her callused fingertips. "Mommy, stop, listen. Daddy had a girlfriend." He paused, watching Lillian as though he thought she'd scream or faint at the revelation. When she said nothing, Josh continued. "We met her one time and I didn't like her. Daddy said it was okay to like someone new because you were gone forever and you'd want us to be happy. But I didn't want to and I didn't want him to and now look at how things turned out. You weren't gone forever and it wasn't okay to like her."

Lillian let the words sink in. Jerry was completely up front with the fact he'd dated a few times but he'd never mentioned a girlfriend, especially not serious enough to entail a visit with the kids. She wanted to be jealous, any wife in this situation would be. She should want to know what this woman looked like or how old she was. It should kill her knowing that in some romantic situation Jerry might've kissed her or even more. She wished she could transfer the jealousy she felt for Jill to the secret date, but Lillian didn't have the right to judge Jerry since she was completely unwilling to receive his judgments in return.

"Joshua, you're such a tenderhearted little boy." She pulled him in for a hug and he let her. His head now reached her shoulder rather than her chest but he still smelled the same, laundry detergent, soap, and the faint bite of little boy sweat. "Your daddy didn't do anything wrong. He didn't know I was alive. It would've been silly for him to wait forever. Remember the judge your daddy went to see a year ago? He signed a paper that said I was dead. You had a funeral for me and Grandma. He wasn't cheating on me, baby. I completely understand and I'm not mad at all. I'm proud that you were brave enough to tell me and that you love me enough to be worried about me."

"I can't lose you again, Mommy," Josh whispered into her shoulder, letting out a tiny sob.

"Don't worry, honey, I won't let anything come between me and my babies," she said as she rubbed small circles between his shoulders. She meant it.

She thought about that conversation a lot lately. That's why she said yes to this god-awful interview and suffered through manipulative questions and innuendos. She wanted to tell the story one last time and tell it right, and then leave it all behind her: the crash, the island, Kent, David, and even Paul. If it meant lying to Genevieve Randall and all of America, it was a fair trade. So as hard as it was when Genevieve asked Lillian how she felt about Kent's death, she screwed her face into a look of sheer grief, pushed a few tears into her eyes, and responded, "Devastated."

CHAPTER 22

LILY-DAY 156

The Island

It's Sunday again and it's six weeks and two days since I killed Kent. Forty-four days since I plunged a knife into his back—slashing through his skin, stabbing between his ribs—and felt the sickening ricochet of the stone off his vertebrae. I still can't decide if it was the worst thing I've ever done in my life . . . or the bravest.

David seems to have his own opinions. For the past few weeks, he's been sleeping by the fire and I'm lucky if he strings three words together when he talks to me. Sleeping alone in that shelter is a harsh punishment. Sometimes I'm sure I totally deserve it, and the ghosts that haunt the dark shadowy corners keep me awake at night.

Stepping out into the sunlight, I see that David stoked the fire and a freshly caught fish is sizzling on the cooking stone. My stomach rumbles at the savory smell, but as hungry as I am I want to get to the lagoon before David returns. I'd rather starve than eat with him in silence.

Thankfully, preparations for my scheduled Sunday bath take little to no thought anymore. My pack, Margaret's old suit jacket, is a dingy gray and no longer turns white when washed in the ocean. At least the bloodstain doesn't show anymore.

I walk over to the hollowed-out coconut tree stump at the corner of our jungle camp. It's the closest stump to the ocean and easy to identify. Flipping up the thin piece of limestone that covers the rough opening, I grab Margaret's ratty old makeup bag and use my toes to slip the stone over the hole.

Wandering down the beach, I head for my favorite spot in the lagoon. Bathing in salt water is difficult and I never come out completely clean—especially my hair, which is always stiff and coated in a white film of salt—but I still can't go back to the freshwater pool in the jungle.

◆ ◆ ◆

One time, right after Kent died, I tried. I thought since he was gone the fear that tainted that place would be erased by his blood. But as my feet sunk into the moist dirt around the pool, I knew it was a mistake.

"He's not coming, he's not coming, he's dead," I reminded myself. Once I reached the place where he'd grabbed me and the spot where he held me down with my face in the mud until I couldn't breathe, it all came back. How I had to lie there, helpless, unable to get the knife that David had made for me. How close I'd come to surrendering.

I couldn't stay. My heart thumped in my eyes and ears. I staggered away, dropping Margaret's bag of watered-down shampoo and nubs of hotel soap. Margaret's necklace and wedding ring rolled out with a clunk. I couldn't stop and pick it up, not without remembering how it cut my neck when Kent ripped it off and tossed it in the mud.

Instead, I ran through the trees and down the snaking footpath toward the ocean. The hanging branches and vines slapped at my arms and face, pulling at my hair like girls in a schoolyard fight. When I tore into camp, tender crimson scratches covered every inch of exposed skin, beading up with unspilled blood.

David was there, and when I fell into the sand, he took me in his arms and carried me to the shelter. Without letting go he used his teeth to tear open the last alcohol wipe from the first aid kit, cleaning my wounds so tenderly the sterilizing liquid didn't even sting. When the swab was dark red and my breathing returned to normal, he didn't let me go. He held me for hours that day. It's the last time I fell asleep in his arms, the only place I feel safe anymore.

When I woke, the sun was down and I was alone in the shelter. The flickering fire outside threw off enough light for me to spot David, asleep on the ground. His sun-browned torso lay uncovered, sweat gleaming on his back from being so close to the flames. His black hair was so long, the loose curls reaching down his shoulders, and a few strands covered his face. I could tell by the steady rise and fall of his back he was sound asleep.

I missed his body next to mine. Once Kent was gone, I slept on David's chest, his heartbeat my lullaby. But that night, when I reached out to wake him, my hand grazed something cool on the edge of bamboo floor. The makeup bag. Lying on top of the bag was the delicate gold chain that held Margaret and Charlie's wedding rings. How did he find it? It didn't even matter that my ring was still missing. I slipped the chain over my head, an ugly knot where Kent had snapped it. The metal was cool against my chest.

David always seemed to know what I needed. I felt selfish for wanting to wake him. Instead, I grabbed the bag and wrapped it in my arms like a child with his favorite teddy bear. I lay down, bag still clutched to my chest, and fell asleep watching him, letting the warmth from the fire fill the space he usually occupied.

He never returned to the shelter after that day. I still don't know why and David is unwilling to discuss it, so now we play the avoidance game. When we do speak, it's only about food or the weather.

As I step out of my tattered old cutoffs I try to shake feelings of abandonment off with them. Whatever reason he's staying away, I have no other choice than to let him. Pulling the green cotton tee over my head, I unwind the string that holds my hair in place and shake the dirty curls down my back. I hike up the remains of my beige underwear, hanging even lower than the week before. I never thought I could lose my appetite but I guess becoming a murderer will do that to you. Shoving the shirt and shorts into my makeshift laundry bag, I wade out into the ocean. The water's heavenly, as always. It's the way Josh and Daniel used to like their bathwater, warm but not hot.

Nope. Not thinking about that today. I put the pack of clothes on a large rock settled in the middle of the shallow lagoon. The water here comes up to my waist and is perfect for laundry.

After washing the pile of clothes and setting them out to dry, I dunk beneath the water and slide out of my bra and underwear, hanging them on the rock to be washed after I bathe. Then, unzipping the black makeup bag, I fumble through half a dozen tiny refilled bottles of watery shampoo, pulling out my favorite gardenia scent, the one Margaret swiped from the Marriott by our house before leaving on our trip. She'd already used most of it by the time we left Fiji, but it's the last scent I remember of her and I save this one for the most special or most desperate times. The last time I used it was Christmas Day, when David made me that coral necklace and Kent was still alive.

I massage my scalp, the scabs finally all gone and little rough tufts of new hair growing in like sproutlets in spring. The tiny drop of shampoo I spilled into my palm barely suds up but it still smells amazing. I let the delicate scent tickle my nose and imagine that I'm in a hotel room, with wonderfully ugly pictures filling the walls and the beds covered in stiff floral bedspreads.

Just as I'm about to rinse off, the familiar feeling of someone watching sends a chill through me, goose bumps coursing up my arms. Crouching low in the water, I use one arm to cover myself and the other to grab the hanging undergarments. I know the only other person on the island is David, but somehow I'm searching the beach for a stranger.

I pull on the sagging underwear and toss the tied together bra straps over my shoulders. So what if they don't get washed this week? Leaving the other items that need to be washed, I push my way through the tide toward the beach. I don't know where my courage is coming from. Mostly it's a desperate desire to never be taken by surprise again.

"Hello? Who's there?" I shout, my voice quivering in an annoyingly weak way. "David, is that you?"

When I step onto the hot beach, a man's figure breaks the tree line. A scream claws its way up my throat until my brain registers that it's David.

"Oh, you scared me!" I laugh nervously. "Do you have more laundry?"

David shakes his head in slow motion, working very hard to not make eye contact. "No, um . . . I wanted to tell you to be safe out there. I was fishing earlier and the undertow is very strong today."

"All right, I'll do my best." Nothing's changed. Cocking my head to the side, I try to look into his eyes. Usually, if I look long enough, I understand him better. A single inky curl hangs across his forehead, and those eyes, so deep blue I can get lost in them.

"Your hair's down," he mumbles, like he's just waking up. Reaching out with one finger, he outlines a cluster of curls. I've missed his touch. The heat pulsing from his palm pulls me in and I nuzzle my cheek against his fiery hot hand. He takes a shaky breath making my heart race loudly.

"I've missed you so much," I say, closing my eyes. A tear squeezes out and runs down my cheek. David's thumb traces the salty wet trail. I open my eyes, expecting to see that giant wall I've been throwing myself against for weeks. All I see is David . . . and something else, something new. There's a glimmer that makes my pulse pound and skin tingle.

Using his fingertips, he follows my jaw, leaving a prickling trail behind them. He wipes his thumb across my lower lip, which tastes salty from my tear. Beyond thinking, I lean forward, lips parting hungrily.

His eyes dart between my mouth and my eyes, gauging my expressions, reading my desire. It's impossible to think about anything but his mouth on mine, how he'd pull me into his arms and we'd melt together, forgetting about everything but the two of us. My body wants it, my heart wants it, and I hope David wants it too. Reaching, I run my hand across his bearded cheek, down his neck, pulling him toward me. Then he freezes. Letting his hand fall from my face, he pushes me backward toward the water and away from his arms.

"I'd better go," he says, clearing his throat. Shame and disgust are written on his face, and then, turning on his heel, he's gone.

What was that? My feet slap against the water-soaked sand as I rush into the ocean, diving as soon as the water's deep enough.

The waves crash above me as I coast under the water like I belong here. Even when the momentum of my dive runs out, I stay under until my lungs burn. I like this burn. It's a different kind than before on the beach with David, less consuming, more cleansing. If I stay down here long enough will it burn him out of me? Then maybe I won't need him anymore. I hate how much I need him.

I can hold my breath for a long time but when the undertow starts tugging me out toward the reef, I head for the surface. Wiping salt from my eyes, I wish I could rub out David just as easily.

I hastily finish my bath and then clean my extra set of clothes, beating them against the rough stone and rubbing sand on any dark spots. Rummaging around on the top of the rock I pull down the last dirty item, David's old khakis. I can wiggle my entire hand through a hole in his right knee. He has an ongoing debate with himself on whether he should simply rip off the bottom half. One day it's just going to fall off and that'll be the end of that. Dunking the ragged material under the water, I wash them quickly and then lay them out on the rock with the rest of the laundry. I'm finished but I don't want to return to camp, so I lie back in the water and float, staring up at the sky.

A storm's rolling in from the west; it's in the air. Dark storm clouds crowd the horizon, slowly encroaching on the tranquil blue above me. For an extremely brief moment I let myself think about Jerry and the boys, how during the summer thunderstorms Jer would sit on our deck under the awning watching the rain fall, how our kids were the only ones in the neighborhood who slept *better* during thunderstorms.

That familiar gnawing ache of separation spreads through my chest and I remind myself not to hope. For all I know Jerry's dating again, the boys calling her mom, looking for *her* kisses on scraped knees, and I'm no more than a picture relegated to the top of the piano and the children's nightstand. I squeeze my eyes shut, trying to force those thoughts away, the ravaging thoughts that haunt me. It takes a deep roll of thunder that vibrates my bones to make the thoughts scatter like rats into the dark corners of my subconscious. The storm's almost here. I have to get back.

Out of breath and arms shaking, I arrive at the shelter in relatively good time just as the rain moves in with staggered heavy drops. Thankfully, the fire's still burning. Tossing the sopping wet pack into our shelter, I grab the fire cover we made when the rains started to come through. Some days the lean-to structure made of sticks and leaves and bits of life raft is enough to prevent the fire going out during a storm and other times it isn't. Making a new fire is difficult and we've done our best to avoid it, especially now that Kent's gone. Kent. Even thinking his name hurts, especially in those bald parts of my head where the scabs used to be. I push him out of my mind and quickly hang the clothes off the rods of bamboo lining the front of our roof so they can dry some before the monsoon explodes from the sky. Otherwise, we'll be stuck with damp, stinky clothes until the storm breaks and I'll have to wash them all over again.

I shake sand out of my jean shorts and throw on damp clothes before pulling down the cracked yellow sheeting scavenged from the raft. Two of the four sides are long enough to reach the bamboo floor so I can tie them down. The other two flap uselessly in the wind. The rain explodes just as I curl up in the corner where the back wall and a piece of raft meet, keeping me fractionally dry. Where's David? I hate that he'd rather tough out a rainstorm with no shelter than stay dry in the same room with me.

When the wind hits, I rush to pull down the semi-dry clothing, laying them flat inside the shelter. When all the clothes are safe, I climb under the woven palm-frond blanket. The temperature's fallen at least ten degrees and the fire's dwindling. Without the warmth of Margaret's suit coat, still wet and lying out with the other laundry, my teeth start chattering. I should be used to this, lying here, cold and alone. My body seems to remember those times too, shaking from the inside out. What did I do that first night on the island, sitting in the sand with Margaret's corpse on my lap? Back then I thought of better times, of home and family. I pinch my eyes closed, as if to keep out the wind and keep in the memories.

I'm surprised at the face looking back at me. Today, it's not Jerry's face, it's David's. David teaching me to fish and laughing on the plane with me before the crash, how white and straight his teeth looked and how fresh his skin smelled when he held me while Kent stitched my shoulder. It doesn't take long for images to bombard me like the coming rainstorm. Those were my good times, when he smiled and we were friends, before I killed a man to save his life and he abandoned me so inexplicably.

A crash of damp air floods beneath the blanket, interrupting my memories. I reach out to yank the woven cover down but I'm shivering so hard I can barely unfold my fingers. Then David's warm hands are on me, rubbing my arms.

"Lily, are you all right?" I'm too cold to speak so I nod, jerkily. "You're frozen," he whispers. "Where's your coat?"

"Over th-th-there," I stutter. "It's w-w-wet."

He slips his arms around me and I press my torso against his, needing his body heat more than air. He isn't wearing a shirt and the overgrown hair on his chest tickles my face. I pull in tighter, pressing my frozen toes against his feet, still warm from the sand. My right leg slips naturally in between his, locking us together. He smells like wind and salt.

It's so good to be held again, to listen to the beat of his heart with my head on his chest and to feel the way our skin melds together in the spots where flesh meets flesh. I let out a little sigh and wrap my arms around his rib cage, thinking about nothing more than how I can get closer to the velvety heat pulsing from his body. Soon, all my muscles relax.

"Better?"

"Mmmm," I mumble. "So much better. You're the best. Thank you, David." Wiggling up a little to speak, I nuzzle into his neck, his beard soft as fleece against my cheek. I could stay here all day.

David seems to have a different idea. As soon as the word "better" leaves my lips he starts untangling our limbs, pushing me away toward the wall of the shelter.

"What're you doing?" I cry. "You can't go yet, that was so warm." Childishly I hold on. The more insistently he pushes, the tighter my arms coil around him. I don't want to be alone anymore.

"I . . . I need to go get some food for lunch. You'll be hungry after all that shivering." He tenses up against me, like a pillow turning into a rock. It's so obvious; he's making an excuse to leave because he can't stand being around me.

"I'm not hungry," I say through gritted teeth, digging my fingers into his shoulders. "I don't want you to leave yet."

"Well, that's nice for you but *I* want to leave." He takes his left hand off my shoulder where he'd been pushing me away, grabs the wrist on my right hand and pries it off his arm. One quick roll to the left and he's gone, leaving an overwhelming coldness in the empty space beside me.

"Is it possible you hate me that much?" I stand up, letting the palm frond blanket fall away, shaking again, this time from anger. "Do I disgust you so much you can't even sleep in the same room with me? You once told me you couldn't survive alone but that's exactly what you're sentencing me to—a life on this island of complete solitude. How dare you do that to me! You have every right to hate me for what I made you do to get rid of Kent but . . ."

"Hate you?" David says. He sits halfway out of the shelter staring into the ocean, his hair filling with rainwater. "I don't hate you."

"Well, you don't *like* me, that's for sure. All you do is run away and I'm tired of running after you."

"Then stop," he says, popping his *p*. "Stop coming after me, Lily. It'll be better for everyone."

"I thought we were best friends," I say, inching forward. "I thought we meant something to each other. Look at everything we've been through. Don't you miss me at all, David?" I put my icicle hand on his shoulder. He flinches away.

"Things change, Lillian. After Kent, after he . . ." David shakes his head and rain rushes down his nose, cricked to one side. It splashes all over, sending water running down my arms. "I can't do it anymore, it's not worth the risk." He puts his hands onto the split bamboo floor ready to push off into the rain. Before he can get away again, I grab his hand.

"Can't you forgive me? I should've gone with him. Then he'd be alive and you wouldn't hate me." He turns so fast the rain in his hair flies into a halo of moisture.

"Don't you *ever* say that again." His fingers squeeze mine till they ache. "You can't even think you should've gone with that man."

"But I killed him and I made you do things, horrible things, to cover it up."

"No, he *made* you kill him." His finger slides under my chin, lifting my face to his. "I'm glad he's dead, I'm glad I gave you that knife, I'm glad it was sharp, and I'm glad we killed him."

"*I* killed him."

"No." David shook his head and let his hand cradle my face like on the beach earlier. "Kent killed himself. You shouldn't feel guilty. I know I don't." The words come out so easily, leaving me with more questions than answers.

"Then why do you hate me?" I whisper, biting my bottom lip.

"Drop it, Lillian."

"I'm not going to let it go until you tell me what the problem is. Why can't you look me in the eye?" I slip my arm around his broad shoulders. "You know you can tell me anything."

"You aren't going to give up are you?" His body slumps.

"You should know the answer to that by now." I want him to smile but instead he stares at the ocean.

"I'm afraid, okay?" he says slowly. "I'm afraid I'm turning into Kent."

"That's ridiculous. You're nothing like Kent."

"You don't know me, Lily. You don't know what goes on inside my head." He taps at his temple.

"I can't read your mind, but I know you." I push my hand into his overgrown hair, stroking the base of his neck. "You're a good man, a very good man."

"If only I was as good as you imagine me to be. If you only knew . . ."

"Knew *what*, David? Seriously, what could be that bad?"

He turns toward me, grabbing my shoulders roughly. "That I want you, okay? More than I've ever wanted anything in my life. When you sleep next to me, I can't sleep because all I think about is how I want to kiss you over every inch of your skin. And when I sit next to you on the beach, I wish you were mine. That I'd stay on this island forever if it meant that I'd never have to give you back."

Searching my face frantically, he shoves me away, burying his face in his hands. Those words churn in my head, making me dizzy. I've been on this island too long. It's made me forget about love and romance and physical desire. What Kent felt wasn't any of those things. He wanted to control me, to dominate me, but David? No, he'd never behave like Kent.

"David, don't run away from me again." I push my fingers up the nape of his neck, twisting a dark curl around my finger. "This morning on the beach, you could've kissed me. I would've let you." I flatten my palm against his back, filling the space between his shoulder blades. "You walked away. Kent never would've done that. Why did you walk away?"

He glances at me. "I couldn't do that to you, after what he did. I . . . I love you too much for that."

I lean forward and pull his face toward mine, gently pressing my lips against his. They give more than I expected and are sweet with rainwater. The warmth we shared cuddling is a tiny lit match compared to the bonfire that fills me through his kiss. I pull back and look at him, my lips tingling and happy. His eyes are still closed, like he's lost in a dream. Licking my lips, I lean in to kiss him again. He pulls away just before we meet.

"Don't do this, Lily, please."

"Didn't you like it?"

"Of course I did, more than I should. Listen, you don't have to pretend with me. I won't hurt you, I'll stay away. You don't have to do this." He pats my hand and my arm hair stands on end.

"I know I don't have to but I *want* to." I really want to. How long have I felt this way without realizing it? "It's not because I'm afraid or I want to keep peace but because . . . I think I love you too."

He stares at me. "Are you sure, Lily? I need you to be sure."

"I don't know how it took me so long to realize it, but yes. I love you and"—a hot blush fills my cheeks—"I want you too."

He closes the space between us, tucking a damp strand behind my ear; his eyes explore my face as he measures my responses. His lips turn up when I raise my eyebrows, tired of waiting. Letting his hands slip around my face, it takes only a hint of pressure for him to pull me forward. I flick my tongue over my lips, still salty from my swim.

His mouth meets mine gently at first, exploring, like he's sure I'll change my mind any second. But I won't change my mind. Now that I've tasted him, his singular essence of smoke and salt and rain, I can't stop. Wrapping my arms around his neck, I pull him in hard, turning my head to the side so our noses don't mash. Under my palms his shoulders relax and his mouth follows suit. Letting out a low groan, his kiss grows urgent and hungry. I'm just as hungry. Any space between our bodies is too much.

As the kiss deepens, our hands roam freely. His hands slide under the hem of my shirt, up my back. I urge him into the shelter, rolling over the damp laundry. There's desire and passion, but there's this tenderness that makes any particle of reluctance dissolve. I forget where I should be and even where I am. Instead I let myself get lost in his arms and burn with the knowledge that even if we never leave this place, as long as he loves me, I'll never be alone again.

CHAPTER 23

DAVE

Present

"I'm going to skip ahead for a moment because I'm curious about something." Genevieve Randall and "curious," two things Dave didn't like hearing in the same sentence. "After Kent died how long were you and Lillian alone on the island before you were rescued?"

Dave had to think. The sequence of deaths went Theresa, Margaret, Paul, Kent. Yes. That's right.

"Three months," he said and Genevieve nodded. Dave assumed that meant he'd remembered correctly.

"What was that like, being alone together? How was it without Kent there?"

Blissful. Heavenly. In actuality they'd spent more than a year on the island without Kent. Alone and with some distance from the trauma of the crash, Dave got to know Lily in a whole new way that was more than physical. He found out that she was a Civil War buff and some nights she'd diagram whole battles in the sand. He accused her of embellishing them for entertainment value because he'd never found history so interesting before. Dave still couldn't look at a five-dollar bill without remembering her dramatic interpretation of the Gettysburg Address.

And they laughed together, a lot. She giggled at puns but would get nearly hysterical at any type of potty humor. Some of their conversations could easily have come from a couple of twelve-year-olds snickering at the lunch table.

But Dave knew plenty about sorrow and hunger on that island, especially in the last weeks before they were rescued. All he needed to do now was think about the hopelessness of those days. Then he'd be convincing.

"Life was very difficult without Kent," he sighed. "We didn't have the skills to keep up with our food needs. Lillian got very sick and there was nothing I could do about it."

"She was dehydrated and near starvation, right?"

Dave nodded. There was no laughter then, only fear that she would die and he'd have to watch it.

"Why weren't you sick, Dave?" Genevieve Randall asked slowly, evenly.

Dave coughed, his throat suddenly tight. He didn't like the insinuation in her words. Could she be suggesting that he let Lily waste away so he could have a few more bites of food?

"After Lillian got sick, she couldn't keep food down very well. I'm still not sure if they ever found out what she had. You'll have to ask her and Jerry. We've only seen each other a handful of times since the hospital and even then it was very brief."

"Why?" Genevieve Randall puckered her lips before asking her next question. "Why is there this distance between you and Lillian Linden? Are you estranged?"

Dave paused, his mind rushing through possible responses. He was going to have to ad-lib this one. Their careful story hadn't ever gone past the rescue.

"We aren't estranged," he responded. "We live thousands of miles apart and have our own lives and families." Dave poked a finger into his knee. "Remember, Lillian and I didn't know each other before sharing that plane. We helped each other through some difficult circumstances but as far as I'm concerned, it's normal to return to our 'real' lives."

Beth didn't seem to notice his lie. She was too busy nibbling on her pinky nail, scrolling through her smartphone, her blonde curls covering most of her face. Dave imagined her most recent tweet: "Watching Genevieve Randall interrogate my husband. Growing more suspicious :) LOL."

◆ ◆ ◆

Surprisingly, his wife *wasn't* suspicious, or if she was, she didn't let on. In general she was a lot of other things: bored, annoyed, distracted. It should make Dave happy, or at least relieved, that she wasn't trying to break it all down or look for inconsistencies. But instead she made him feel a tiny bit foolish, like he was blowing the crash into the ocean, survival on an island, and firsthand experience of death out of proportion.

Beth hadn't always been so apathetic. When he'd first come home, she was full of curiosity, wanting to know every little detail, every moment she missed. She'd lie in bed at night quizzing him on what he'd been doing on a certain day or try to figure out if they'd ever been thinking about each other at the exact same moment in time, as if it made a difference.

In Guam, she spent endless hours by his side as he was pumped full of IV fluids and antibiotics. Back then it was Dave who had to feign interest. Lily was only one room over, in serious condition, still unconscious and completely unaware of their rescue. For Dave it was hard to think past that room, to listen to anything more than the steady beep of her heart monitor through the wall.

In the hospital, Dave wished he was the one holding her hand. Instead, he was listening to Beth prattle away. It had been a year and a half since he had to pretend to be enthralled with one of her stories and frankly he was out of practice. No matter how well he placed his comments or how flawlessly he timed a raise of his eyebrows, he knew she wasn't convinced.

It only took two weeks of Beth's forced understanding and Dave's inability to BS for things to come to a head. Since returning from the South Pacific neither of them had said more than the common scripts most married people repeat to each other every morning: "How did you sleep?" "Did you hear those dogs barking this morning?" and "Pass the toothpaste."

During the television interviews they were a loving, reunited couple but at home they shared an emptiness between them that speech couldn't fill. One Sunday morning, they sat at the table for breakfast and the familiar blanket of silence settled over them.

Dave shoveled in the bulging egg and cheese sandwich he'd made for himself, his pathetic attempt to copy the Egg McMuffin at home. He'd visited the fast-food restaurant every morning for the past week. Dave would never admit it in an interview but since getting home he couldn't resist a drive-thru window. Besides, all of Dave's pants were four sizes too big now, so if he gained a few pounds in the process at least he wouldn't need to buy a new wardrobe.

So after a few phone interviews, he spent much of his Saturday planning out this home attempt at the famous sandwich, finding it provided him with much-needed distraction.

Taking another bite, Dave chewed slowly, considered the mix of flavors, and noted that perhaps he needed real Canadian bacon rather than deli ham. Without notice, Beth spoke, breaking their implicit truce.

"Are you happy to be home, Dave?" Beth asked, poking nervously at the soggy bran cereal floating in her bowl.

"Huh?" A lump of melted cheese dripped onto his plate. Beth placed her spoon on the table like she was putting a baby down for a nap, but it still clanked loudly on the tinted glass breakfast table.

"Do you even want to be here?" Beth said, her hands balled in front of her.

"What do you mean? Of course I want to be here. Okay, I'd rather be at McDonald's at this precise moment but my arteries need a little break," he joked, tossing the half-eaten sandwich onto his plate.

Beth didn't laugh. "I'm serious, Dave, do you want to be here? Are you even happy to be home?" she demanded, her voice wavering but her light blue eyes remaining still and clear.

"Of course I am," he said, cocking his head to the side. Fooling her was supposed to be easy. She never seemed to take an interest in his feelings before. "What's going on, babe? What has you so anxious?"

Pushing her bowl forward, Beth slumped in her chair, making little blonde curls dance around her face. She was still beautiful.

"You, Dave. You have me so anxious," she said, letting out a massive sigh and rubbing her eyes, ignoring the makeup she'd just applied during her complicated morning routine. "I don't know if you can even tell but you're different now."

She looked at him with big, round, needy eyes, making Dave feel guilty and angry in the same instant, without knowing which emotion preceded the other. It was the anger he couldn't hold back.

"I *am* different, Beth," he spat. "I just spent almost two years living away from home, in a state of near-starvation. I had to search every day for food to keep us alive, worry that a storm would come and blow our meager existence away. Any scratch or cut had the potential to kill us, not to mention the rats, snakes, fish, sharks, and countless other creatures. Living like that"—he pounded a finger on the polished table, making the utensils jingle—"in constant fear and desperation, tends to change a person."

Beth looked at him skeptically from under hooded eyelids. "Then why does it seem like you want to go back? Why don't you want to be with *me*?" She whined the accusation and something in her tone gave Dave flashbacks to the five years they'd lived together before the crash.

That was the Beth he knew so well, always thinking about herself. Perhaps he *had* changed, because three years ago he would've apologized, patted her hand, and tried to make everything better. But that day he pushed away from the table.

"Not everything is about you, Beth."

"*That's* what I'm talking about," she said, tossing her hand in Dave's direction as if she were throwing the accusation in his face. "I'm NOT worrying about myself, *David*, I'm concerned about you, I'm angry, and as much as I hate to admit it I'm freaking jealous!"

"I don't think I've ever seen you concerned for anyone but yourself, Beth." Power surged through him as he spoke words he'd always thought about his wife but never had the courage to say. "And don't you EVER call me David again."

Beth's face, usually set in steel, crumpled under the force of his voice. She concentrated on picking at the fringe on the edge of the mustard-yellow place mat, slowly smoothing each tassel into little symmetric triangles splayed out on the table.

"Do you know why I waited for you?" she whispered. "All this time, why I waited?"

"No." He wasn't even curious but she was going to tell him anyway, because Beth always did what she wanted.

"When the call came that your plane had gone down, I was devastated. First I lost the babies, and then you were suddenly gone. They found your plane two days later and it was empty, except for that flight attendant—"

"Theresa," he interrupted. He was tired of people forgetting about Theresa.

"Fine, Theresa. So the divers, they also found that the lifeboat was gone and that's when I knew. I knew you must be alive out there." She shuffled her fingers over the thin mustard strands, jumbling them back into their previous chaos. "They searched for one week, combing the South Pacific. I flew to Fiji to be close, so I could be there when they found you. Then a major storm came through, and after having to call off the search for two days in a row they canceled it completely. Jerry and I were beside ourselves."

Dave flinched at the mention of Lillian's husband. He'd heard enough Jerry stories from Lily, he didn't need to hear more from his own wife.

"I just knew. I knew that you were out there somewhere. So as dumb as it sounds . . . uh . . . I went to a psychic." She stared up at him, seeming so immature in her eagerness.

Dave raised his eyebrows.

"He told me you were still alive. He told me we'd find you. He said we'd be a family again."

"And you believed him?" Dave asked flatly.

Beth bit her lip and shrugged her petite shoulders. "He knew . . . he knew about the babies."

They hadn't talked about this yet. Dave still wasn't ready. He grabbed his plate and, taking long strides, tossed it in the sink. Then he stood there a moment, clutching the cold quartz counter for support, the aftertaste of cheap American cheese in his mouth. He couldn't face Beth; if he did he'd say something he couldn't take back.

She stumbled on, desperate. "He said we'd have another chance to have a baby, you and me, together." Her voice came from directly behind him and he knew if he turned around they'd be close enough to touch. He didn't want to touch her.

"I don't want to have a baby with you," he hissed, intending his voice to be void of emotion, betrayed when it cracked at the end.

"It's not what you think. I didn't do it on purpose."

"Yeah I know, you *forgot*," he mocked.

"No, I didn't forget," she murmured.

"What? You're going to admit you did something wrong for the first time in your life?" Dave said, feigning shock.

"I . . . I was stupid and stubborn. I thought I could do it myself, that I didn't need the medicine. It was easier to think that than to come to terms with the fact I could never have a baby of my own, never look at a child and think, *Are those my eyes?*" She put her hand on his shoulder. "It was the biggest mistake I've made in my whole life and I'm so sorry."

She sounded sorry but Dave could never tell with Beth if she was acting or sincere. He wanted to tell her to leave him alone, to never touch him again, but he needed so many things right now. And the gentleness in her touch, the warmth of her hand on his skin, it made him remember all the things he'd lost. He wanted something to fill up that chasm that gaped inside him. Instead of shaking her off, he let her stay, and the silence between them was as comforting as any reassuring words.

"I'm sorry I failed you. You deserve better, I know you do," she whispered into his back. "Please, please," she begged, "give me another chance. You've changed, I know that, but I've changed too. Can't you see?"

She kissed his back, following the lines of his broad shoulder blades, her breath penetrating the thin white cotton of his undershirt. Her small hands slipped beneath the fabric, climbing up his chest, tracing over his work-hardened body, making his heart beat fast.

Her familiar touch felt good, and when she pressed her body up against his, instinct took over. No more thinking, no more talking.

She turned him around and pulled his face to hers. Her eager lips crashed into his, reminding him of a hunger he'd kept pushed down, locked away, for so long. He gave in, letting his lips respond eagerly to hers, pulling her in closer, holding on with a tight, forceful grip on her shoulders. As they crumpled to the cold tile floor, enmeshed in each other's arms, Dave kept his eyes closed tight, imagining waves crashing in the background and hot sand burning his skin.

◆ ◆ ◆

"That's a good place to stop; let's take a little break," Genevieve Randall ordered over Dave's head to the cameramen. The room let out a collective sigh. They'd barely started talking about Paul, but Genevieve didn't seem happy with the direction the interview was going. "Let's see"—she glanced at her watch—"everyone take twenty and we'll come back to this." Dave assumed by "this" she meant the next group of questions on the list but that still didn't give him much of an idea of what lay ahead.

When Genevieve Randall stood up, her skirt rustled as it shimmied down her thighs. She paused in front of Dave, her pale eyes flashing.

"Dave, you should take a little break and stretch those long legs of yours; it's going to be a busy afternoon," she cooed. "There's some food over there." She pointed to the formal dining room, where the table had been filled with trays of sandwiches, Danishes, and three industrial-size coffee dispensers. "Something sweet to give you a little energy, keep you . . . sharp," she hinted, and Dave felt as if he had been warned.

He ignored her as best he could, staring at the floor until her clacking heels were muffled by the Brazilian wool carpet in Dave's home office, where the crew had set up headquarters early that morning. Still a bit shaky, he rubbed his hands one more time on the leg of his slacks, hoping there wouldn't be a hole there by the end of the day.

"Dave, you okay?" Beth's voice reached out across the room. Still seated, Beth leaned forward, concern written on her smooth face.

"Yeah," he said gravely. Dave cleared his throat and tried again. "Yeah, I'm fine."

Shoving off the couch, he stumbled across the floor, legs wobbly as though he'd been drinking vodka rather than water. He tossed himself into one of the dining room chairs flanking Beth, and though he'd been sitting all morning, sitting there felt relaxing.

"You don't look fine," Beth said, surveying his face. "Do you want to stop? I hate it when you do this to yourself."

"Nah, I'm great. Nothing new, just same old stuff." Dave patted his wife's smooth hand resting on the armchair beside him.

"But she's asking things no one's asked before and you seemed pretty thrown by it. Like asking about Theresa," she probed, "I've never seen you get so tongue-tied in an interview."

"No," he rushed on, refusing to hesitate, "I'm getting tired and a little frustrated with the stupid questions. They're totally pointless and none of them are on the list. I don't see what she's getting at."

"Me either," Beth whispered. He needed to change the subject.

"How are *you two* feeling? Now, that's a much more important question than any of the ones I've been asked today." He smiled gently at his wife. "Any kicks from my little soccer player in there?" Dave's hand moved to Beth's swollen abdomen, barely protruding above the waist of her skinny jeans.

"He was jumping around when I had some orange juice earlier. He must be sleeping now," she said, arching her back so her belly pooched fully into his palm. It was pliant and firm at the same time, like a ball expanding inside her. It was a feeling he'd never find ordinary.

"I always seem to miss it," Dave said, truly disappointed.

"You'll have plenty of time, I just started to feel him a couple of weeks ago. All the things online say it could take everyone else up to a month."

"A *month?*" Dave frowned playfully. "I don't think I can wait that long. I'm gonna have to have a chat with that boy tonight and let him know his daddy is expecting at least one good swift kick before the week's over. That's an order or no ice cream after dinner." Dave feigned a stern fatherly voice. He leaned in closer, putting his ear on the swelling stomach, as if the baby would have some sort of response. Beth's belly jiggled when she laughed.

"Oh no, not already. I'm not going to put up with any disagreements! Now you two need to hug and make up, come on, hug it out," Beth insisted.

Dave loved this new, lighter side of Beth. He still wasn't sure what happened to change her so drastically while he was away and he didn't care what it was. Beth had dropped her clubbing friends and finally seemed to understand the world didn't revolve around her. It took a few months but by the time she came to him with a positive pregnancy test, he'd finally learned how to trust her again. Now, he couldn't imagine Beth doing anything to harm their unborn child.

Dave took both his hands and wrapped them around Beth's belly, his son growing inside. He hadn't met him yet and he loved him. Then Dave felt a tiny tap on his palm, a nudge like someone asking to pass in a crowded room.

"Beth? Was that a kick?"

"Yeah it was, but I can't believe you could feel that," she gasped. Without even thinking what he must look like Dave leaned in toward Beth's stomach, his face right over where he felt the flutter.

"Hey there, baby, I'm your daddy. I love you and I promise: I'll never let anything happen to you." Sitting up slowly, he looked at his wife, her eyes misty. He slipped his arm under the curtain of curly blonde hair and pulled her in tight. She wiggled her head up under his chin. Dave sighed, content because for the first extended period of time that day he hadn't been thinking about Lily.

CHAPTER 24

DAVID-DAY 201

The Island

I wake with a start to see the empty spot beside me. Lily's gone. As I toss off the thin blanket, fear ripples through me. It takes a full minute to steady myself. She's here, right in front of me by the fire, poking some cooking fish. She hasn't noticed me watching her, so I enjoy the view.

Her hair's tied back, but those little curly pieces around her face and at the nape of her neck have wrestled free. My fingertips itch to guide them behind her ear. Eventually they'll escape again, giving me another reason to touch her. Her torso tucks in perfectly at the waist and I want to put my hands around it, touch her freckled skin, the swell of her hips, the curve of her spine. God I love her.

The past weeks have been surreal but heavenly. Ever since that cold afternoon in the shelter, where Lily and I finally realized what our friendship had evolved into, we've been inseparable.

It still stuns me a little when she reaches over and holds my hand or brushes a butterfly wing kiss past my ear to whisper, "I love you." It didn't seem possible that this place, this island that seemed so close to a prison when we first landed, could now be the one place I wouldn't mind staying the rest of my life.

She looks over to me as though she's heard my thoughts and smiles that smile that melts my heart. "You're awake!"

She bounds across the sand and dives into the shelter next to me. Sand clings to her hands and rubs against my skin as she puts her arms around my neck, kissing me slowly, deliberately. Though passion has its moments, it's these kisses that mean the most.

"Mmmmm, I love you," I mumble against her lips as they slow.

"Always?" she asks, in the little script we've started saying to each other every day.

"Always," I respond before she pulls away, wiping her hands on her knees.

"We have a busy day ahead." She's up to something.

"Oh, we do?" I raise my eyebrows. It slays me the way she's always thinking of activities to do together, like we're a real couple on vacation.

"Yes. We're hiking to the other side of the island today. Our trees are getting overpicked and I think the fish have sent out a warning call in our lagoon, so we might have better luck elsewhere." She passes a coconut shell filled with slices of underripe mango and the meat of a few small fish. I wrinkle my nose. The small ones always taste funny.

"Sounds like a wonderful day," I say, shoveling in the food. The emptiness in my stomach wins out over the anticipated nastiness of the tiny coral fish.

"I know, not exactly gourmet." Lily rubs my bicep and instantly the food tastes better. As I take my last bite, her hand slows and I see that pensive "looking at the ocean" face gloss over her normal cheerfulness. When she looks like that, something has reminded her of home.

"Lily, you okay?" I ask, putting my hand on her tan thigh.

A smile flits over her face as she laces her fingers through mine. "Yeah, I just remembered something, that's all."

I turn her hand up and trace the lines on her palm, wishing I was a fortune-teller and could divine how this would all turn out. "Wanna talk about it? Someone once told me I'm a good listener or something like that."

"Ha, I said you're a good *person*, let's not get greedy." She has a bad habit of falling back on humor when she doesn't want to discuss something. It's more of a giveaway than the blankness on her face. "I guess you *are* a good listener too, but I don't think you'd want to hear about this."

"I want to hear about anything you're thinking. Seriously." I tap her palm with my index finger and wait for her to work it out in her head. I've found it's the only way she's comfortable enough to tell her secrets out loud.

"If the calendar tree is right, I think today's Jerry's birthday," she whispers, closing her hand, trapping my fingertips inside.

It's strange to hear Jerry's name. We haven't spoken about our spouses since the day we admitted we love each other. But I haven't forgotten about him or what I'm doing to him by loving his wife.

"Do you want to celebrate?" I ask, trying not to hesitate. "Like we do with the boys?"

In October we made a cake out of sand and shells and spelled out Daniel's name. We didn't eat it of course, but we did sing, and Lily blew out six little sticks with tears running down her face. We're already planning Josh's birthday next month. But I don't know how I'll feel if she wants to do this for Jerry. I'd have to help her and pretend to be okay with it. I can't act jealous without being an incredible hypocrite.

"No, of course not." She shakes her head, leaning against my shoulder. "It's so strange to think about what they might be doing. We've been gone almost seven months. I wonder if they still think about us."

"I think so," I say, holding her hand a little tighter. "Then again, I can't imagine someone *not* thinking about you." She bumps my shoulder in a playful way. "I'm not so sure I'll be missed, though. I take that back, Janice might think about me every so often, but that's probably because she was next in line for my job and we left her a PR nightmare. Plus, my desk was a mess."

Lily laughs. She'd told me how annoyed Janice was that she didn't get to go to Adiata Beach, envious I was coming for the last week of the trip. How would things have turned out if she'd been on that plane instead of me?

"David, I'm sure Beth thinks about you," she says a little too shortly. I think I sense a hint of her own jealousy and it makes me smile.

"She didn't think about me a lot *before* this so I don't think she'll miss me that much. Now she can work all day and night, sleep with the air at sixty, and use my insurance payout to go out every night with friends. She's probably pretty happy right now." I don't try to hide my bitterness.

A swift punch lands squarely in my bicep. "Stop it. That's unfair." Lily's mouth turns down into a pout when I give her a side-glance.

"You can't judge, Lily, you don't know her." It's painful to feel anything but love toward Lily, but something hard and black inside me is riled by her criticism.

"So, tell me about her. Tell me about Beth."

I toss my coconut shell bowl toward the fire and miss. This conversation has me off my game. I don't want to talk about Beth. I've avoided thinking about her for seven months and I've told myself I'd be happy never thinking about her again. I shove my feet deep into the cool sand outside our shelter, distracting myself.

"Listen," she says, cutting to the chase, "It's clear you two didn't end well, I know that. I heard the phone call and I saw the pain on your face. That's what made me come talk to you and changed everything. I've never asked what happened, never. But things are different now."

Her hand runs up my bare back; tiny grains of sand rub between her palm and my shoulder blades. I lean into her touch, which still sends heat to every corner of my body. "Our relationship has changed. I need to know about this woman whose husband I'm in love with."

Turning on a dime, I put my hand on her face, my fingers settling into the warm cluster of curls at the nape of her neck. I needed to hear that she loves me.

"I love you too," I whisper, pulling her toward me. I kiss her leisurely, her mouth welcoming. It fits perfectly against mine and she pulls me in gratefully, like she needs me more than air. I'll never tire of kissing her.

Just as my pulse reaches its peak, I wrench away reluctantly. I owe her some answers. Pressing my forehead against hers, I wait for my breath to slow.

"I never felt like this with Beth," I tell her. "She doesn't have your humor. She definitely doesn't have your heart." I place a light kiss on her head and wipe away some wild strands of hair clinging to the side of her face, tracing her cheek and the sharp outline of her jaw as I talk. "She was beautiful, the first beautiful woman to show any interest in me. We met at Carlton, actually. She was in marketing and I was just starting out in PR. When our team would go out for drinks the two of us were always the last to leave. We dated off and on for two years before I got up the nerve to ask her to marry me. It took another year to plan the wedding." I sat back, wishing I hadn't started talking about Beth. There's a reason I've avoided her all these months but Lily is enthralled, so I keep going. "Our marriage was rough. It felt like I was the only one willing to make compromises. Beth switched jobs a few years ago to be marketing manager for a software company. She works even more, but often I think that she's staying late just to avoid another one of our fights."

Lily's lips press together pensively and I can't stop thinking about kissing them again. "What about the phone call, David? I think it's time."

"Okay," I nod, and she rewards me with a quick peck before the whole story spills out. "Do you remember how I freaked out after . . . our first time . . . together?" Blood rushes to my cheeks at the reference.

"Yes." She smiles knowingly. "You were worried that you got me pregnant."

"But then you told me about your IUD and how it keeps you safe and all that. To tell the truth, I felt so dumb, like a teenager who missed that day in sex ed, but there's a reason I didn't know about that stuff. Well, Beth and I found out soon enough we didn't have to think about contraception. We couldn't have kids."

She rocks back, away from me, settling onto the floor, the bamboo squeaking irritably. "So, you tried and it didn't work?"

"Yes, we tried. And tried and tried and tried some more."

Lily scrunches up her face, pretending to shudder. "Okay, I think that's enough about the 'trying.'"

"Jealous much?" I ask, wiggling my eyebrows.

"Whatever. Come on, finish the story."

"I finally persuaded her to see a specialist and we went through lots of tests and stuff. We found out that Beth couldn't have babies. She went through menopause like twenty years too early."

"Oh, that's hard. It must've killed her," she says, and then makes this sympathetic sigh, which makes me angry at Beth all over again.

"I don't know, at first she was pretty ambivalent about having a baby, until we couldn't get pregnant. Then, it seemed all she wanted was to be pregnant. To show that she could. To be normal, like everyone else." I shook my head. "After her diagnosis I wanted to look into adoption but she refused, meeting in secret with her doctor to procure an egg donor, and then told me if I didn't want to be the biological father, that was fine, but she wanted to experience pregnancy with or without my DNA.

"I guess she just assumed because I was willing to adopt I wouldn't care that she wanted me to have a baby with an anonymous donor who was most likely some college kid needing to pay her bills. I mean, I'm clearly not a prude." I give her a sidelong glance and she smiles knowingly. "But I've never even had a one-night stand. Having a baby with a stranger was rough for me to wrap my brain around."

"So, you did it, then? The IVF with donor eggs?" She pulls her knees tighter, resting her cheek on top. Not one thing about her seems judgmental. Another thing I love about her.

"Yup. That's why I wasn't on the trip that first week. I was with Beth." I have to stop for a moment and press my fingertips against my eyelids. I don't like talking about this, at all. "She had to take this hormone, to make it all work, to stay pregnant. She'd go to her friend's house to get the shots because her friend's a nurse. They made Beth tired and irritable. She was so angry I was leaving her for the week." Lowering my hands, I wait till the black shrinks away and I can check Lily again. She's listening so intently.

"How about the phone call? What did she say?"

I have to tell her everything. "They put in three embryos. Beth was supposed to keep getting the shots, then go in for a blood test two weeks later. I took the red-eye to Fiji on day five of the two-week wait. That call on the plane was on day six." I have to swallow three or four times before I can continue. She rubs my shoulder supportively but doesn't stop me. She wants to know. "She'd stopped taking the shots. She lied to me, went to Starbucks or something instead of her friend Stacey's house for the one thing our babies needed that she couldn't provide." My throat stiffens up and gets all scratchy, and before I'm aware of what's happening, tears roll down my face.

"But, why? Why didn't she take the shots?"

"I don't know," I cry out, frustrated that she doesn't seem to be following. "She said she forgot but . . ." I can't breathe. "Why would someone do that, Lily? Why?"

"I have no idea." She kisses my cheeks, and I fall gratefully onto her shoulder. "Oh, David, I'm so sorry."

"I don't know why this still hurts so badly," I fumble out between breaths.

"I think it's because you're mourning, David. You can't rob yourself of this, it's the only way you can get to the point where you can forgive her."

"Forgive her?" I sit up straight. "How can I ever forgive her? She didn't just take away those embryos; she took away my dream of being a father." Anger heats my face and sweat drips down the back of my neck. "Those little seeds could have been children and she let them wither and die like unwatered plants. In the process she chucked my dreams like they were garbage. No"—I shake my head—"not garbage. Beth doesn't litter." Lily tries to pull me close again but I push her away.

"I'm not saying you need to forgive her right now." She crosses muscled brown arms, surveying me. "I'm saying you might want to one day. I have to believe if Kent's family knew what really happened in the jungle or if Jerry knew how hard we worked to save Margaret or how alone I was and how much I need you," she pauses, nibbling at her cuticle, "they could forgive me."

"That's different, Lily. You never did anything intentional."

She presses her lips together. "Fine. If you don't want to think about forgiveness then think about it this way. What if that phone call hadn't happened? How hard would this be for you?" She rolls her head around, referencing the beach, the shelter, and us.

I never thought of that. What if I believed Beth was sitting at home, pregnant? Would it still be so easy to not think about home? Would it be so easy to love Lily? To bury Margaret? To dispose of Kent? To live every day never knowing if I'd ever meet my children? I shudder, a breeze cooling the sweat trails crisscrossing my back.

"I'd be crawling out of my skin, wanting to get home to them. I'd try to find any way off here . . ." I pause, catching sight of Lily's face. "Is that how this is for you?"

"At first," she admits, picking at a split in our bamboo floor. "But when I realized how I felt about you, it made it a lot easier."

I roll things over in my mind like a magician flipping a coin over his knuckles. "You're right. I need to let this thing with Beth go. I need to move on because now I have something worth moving on to."

Her hand stops its nervous picking and crawls across the space between us. I can't wait, so I reach across and grab it. When our hands touch, somehow I'm thankful for that awful phone call that feels like years ago, because now I only have one person I want to think about.

◆ ◆ ◆

We get a later start on our hike than planned, but neither of us minds. We follow the shore around to a long stretch of beach on the other side of the island. We call it Bizarro Beach because of its plethora of fruit, its lazy unwary fish, and the horrible infestation of sand fleas that keeps us from moving our camp here.

Fishing on this side is easier. Lily came up with a new method where she weaves some palm fronds together between two bamboo stalks and we sit or stand in the water till fish swim over our net. Then we lift the contraption quickly, trapping the fish inside.

After catching upward of twenty palm-size fish, I gut them, cut off their heads, and then wrap them in seaweed to smoke over the fire. As the smoke does its work, we pick fruit till our baskets are full and then sit out of the sun and enjoy some of the overripe mangos that would fall apart during the rough trip home. Sand fleas nip at my ankles as we sit on a log. I let the orange juice drip down my face and hands. The stringy flesh sticks between my teeth and I don't think I've ever tasted something so good.

"This is so delicious," Lily mumbles, her mouth full, drops of orange juice staining the top of her worn bathing suit. We're well beyond caring about stains anymore. After slurping all that's left of her mango off a large oval pit, she tosses it into the ocean. Standing, she rubs her hands on her bare thighs before taking off in a sprint toward the water. "Race you!"

"No fair, I'm not done!" I shout, shoving the last quarter of the mango in my mouth before sprinting after her. She's clearly not trying very hard to beat me because I catch up in no time and scoop her up in my arms. High-stepping through the waves, we crash down together, the salt water rushing up my nose and into my mouth mixing with the sweet mango juice in a strange cocktail. Ocean water used to make me gag but it's become so familiar now it's almost comforting.

Lily surfaces next to me and before she can say a word I fling my arms around her and lean down to kiss her. After inhaling the saltwater, her mouth is sweet and I pull her into me, my fingers crawling under the hem of her bathing suit top, finding the flesh of her lower back. When she moans and runs her hands down my chest and around my waist, I can't imagine what I've done to find such happiness.

CHAPTER 25

LILLIAN

Present

"Paul." Lillian said the name reverently. "He was beautiful."

Over Genevieve's shoulder, Jerry sat, arms crossed firmly across his chest, golden cuff links glittering off the artificial light pumped into the room. Why did she throw that fit when Jerry said he didn't want to come down and listen to the interview? If it was hard to evade suspicion about the crash and Margaret and even Kent, they were a blip on the radar when she thought about how much she had to hide about Paul. Now she had to do it while Jerry was watching.

"You didn't know about Paul when you first landed on the island, did you?" The reporter continued to dig.

"No, it took a few weeks before I suspected anything, maybe longer. I think Dave and Kent had suspicions before I did."

"What were your first thoughts?" Genevieve Randall led, flipping a chunk of hair away from her face, giving the camera a better view of her "curious" face.

"Disbelief and fear mostly. It wasn't till I saw some sort of physical evidence that I even considered the possibility."

"Why didn't you tell anyone about him after you were rescued? It took, what, a week for you to release that information to the press?"

"The press." Lillian cringed at the sound. Why did *the press* feel so entitled to know every single detail of her life? Now it's suddenly suspicious that she didn't talk about Paul to reporters until after she was out of her semi-comatose state? The doctors knew, Jerry knew, even Beth knew about Paul, but just because the press didn't know, it was a big deal.

"From what I've been told, it was decided he should be kept a secret until we could contact all family involved," Lillian responded with the prepared line, rubbing the buffed finish of her thumbnail with her pointer finger. "When it comes down to it, it wasn't my choice. I wasn't in a good place medically to be making any major decisions."

That was the truth. She still had no waking memory of the rescue. She lost nearly five days. The last thing she remembered was lying in their shelter; she wanted Dave to stop waking her up by dripping water on her lips and face. All she wanted to do was sleep and the sun hurt her eyes.

The next time she woke up, it was so quiet and dark at first she thought she'd been buried alive. Then she saw Dave, sitting in a maroon chair with worn wooden arms. He was wearing a pistachio-colored hospital gown that hung off him like a tent, his eyes red rimmed like he'd been crying. Lillian's own eyes burned and when her hand went up to rub them she felt an odd tug at her skin. Holding it up in the dark she could easily make out the tubes taped to the back of her hand.

"David," she tried to say, but her voice was raspy and strange to her ears. Her throat felt like it was filled with sand. Dave turned his head at her growly sounds.

"Lily, oh my God! Lily, you're awake." He seemed to wipe at his face but she couldn't be sure in the dark. Taking in the hazy details of the room, it all started to sink in.

"Water," she mouthed, and Dave leaped to his feet, pulling an IV stand behind him. Walking over to a small counter sticking out of the wall, he lifted a plastic pitcher and poured so much water into a tiny plastic cup, it spilled all over.

Carrying the cup across the room, his hand shook, the cup dripping a trail of water on the shiny gray tile floor. He slid one hand behind Lillian's head and leaned her forward to drink. The water slipped down her throat. It had a strange metallic taste but Lillian didn't care. It was water—clean, fresh water.

Gulping down the last drop, she tested her voice again, clearing her throat repetitively. Dave sat down after pulling his chair as close to the bed as physically possible. He kept glancing up at something across the room that Lillian couldn't see.

"Where are we?" she whispered, finally certain of her ability to speak.

"Guam. We've been here three days."

"What? I mean, how?" While she could talk, it still hurt, but they didn't need many words to communicate. She was sure he'd understand. Dave wrapped his fingers around Lillian's limp hand, exhaling.

"You were so sick. Just when I thought I'd lost you, I heard something. I ran out to the beach, leaving you for the first time in days. It was a helicopter. Turns out some Italian billionaire owns our island and is trying to sell it. The helicopter was filled with a realtor and potential client. It was about to cross out of sight to the other side of our island and I ran to the beach and jumped around like a crazy person. They didn't see me at first, so I went down to the fishing log and set it on fire. It was so dried out and old, it only took one branch from the fire to make it go up in flames."

Lillian's eyes went wide. They'd stayed up many nights talking on that log, not to mention all the memories of Paul that went along with the hunk of dead wood. To know it wasn't just gone but that David had destroyed it, made her hand with the IV throb.

"I know, I know, I shouldn't have burned it but I was desperate. What was I supposed to do? Let you die?" Tears pooled in his eyes, and the green lights on her monitoring machines reflected off their glittering surface.

"Shhh." She wanted to comfort him but it was too hard to move. Dave used his free hand to dry his face again.

"After they saw me, they left. I thought I'd ruined our chances, that I'd failed you. I crawled inside and lay down next to you, putting my hand over your heart to make sure it was still beating. I fell asleep counting your heartbeats. Around noon the helicopter woke me. They used a ladder to drop down two rescue workers. They didn't even ask who we were; they threw a blanket around me and started to work on you. It was only a matter of seconds till you were in a plastic stretcher, strapped down and hoisted into the helicopter. They pulled me up behind you."

He rubbed the bleached hair on her arms, his familiar calluses scratching her skin. Rescued. She'd finally accepted this day would never come. Now it had and she was scared to death.

"Do they know?" It was getting easier to talk. Swallowing, she tried again. "Do they know who we are?"

Dave gave a humorless smile. It was only then she noticed his beard was gone. His face was clean-shaven and his skin white where the facial hair had been. It was strange to see him without it, like going back in time to the day they stepped onto the plane in Fiji.

"I told them on the helicopter. They were so surprised. I wish you could've seen their faces." His smile was the same, even without the beard, but it made a crinkle in his cheek she'd never noticed before. "I guess we're kind of famous or something. When the plane went down there was some serious press in the States and now everyone wants to talk to us." Dave pushed a long strand of hair behind Lillian's ear. It felt so natural but also so out of place in this new setting.

"Our families, uh, have you talked to anyone?" Her boys, she'd see them again. Then she remembered Jerry and how much she had to tell him. She wasn't ready for the pain on his face when she explained about Margaret dying and what happened with Kent. She'd have to tell him all about what she did with Dave and most of all—Paul.

"Beth and Jerry are here. They showed up within a day of our rescue. Jerry hasn't left your side. In fact, this is the first time I've found you alone. I think the nurses forced him to take a break, something about his mental health." He glanced at the wall again and Lillian realized it was a clock. David was worried about Jerry coming back.

"How's Beth?" Lillian asked, avoiding the topic of Jerry and all the baggage that came with it.

"Oh, she seems very much the same. She's sleeping in the extra bed in my room right now." An unmistakable longing tinted the black-blue of his irises. "I haven't told them anything about us, or Paul. I thought that's what you'd want."

The weight on her chest suddenly dissolved. "Thank you."

Seeing her tears, Dave released her hand and sat back in his chair. He waited quietly as the heart monitor beeped relentlessly in the background and she rubbed her face with a sheet.

"We aren't going to tell them, are we?" he asked, a distinct chill to his voice.

"You think we should?" she asked, incredulously. "You want to tell Beth about us or about Kent?"

"I'll never tell anyone about Kent," he said, the chill thawing a little. "I made you a promise and I'll never break it. But think about it, Lily, they're going to find out. When they dig up Margaret, they *will* find Paul, and then what will you say?" Dave picked at the flimsy wood veneer armrest. Lillian's head thumped against the curved metal frame of the bed.

"I'll tell them about Paul," she whispered, staring at a spot on the wall, biting her dry bottom lip.

"But not about us, is that what you're trying to say?" His finger-nails clicked against the armrest and the muscles in his jaw clenched and unclenched under the thin layer of smooth, hairless skin.

"It might be easier for everyone. It seems like Beth and Jerry waited for us. How are we supposed to tell them about what we did?"

"Because I thought we were in love." He apparently forgot his attempt at coolness and dragged his chair so close to the side of the bed his knees pressed against the frame. "I thought before everything that happened with Paul we were happy together." When he pulled her hand to his closely shaven cheek, it felt like satin and Lillian had a fleet-ing desire to kiss it. He continued, sounding desperate. "You couldn't have been faking that whole time. You loved me. I'm sure." His cheeks flushed red through his tan skin. It was hard for Lillian to see him upset.

"I did, David. I do." Dave smiled and kissed the palm of her hand. The tightness in her throat threatened to suffocate her but she knew what she had to say. "I'll always care about you, but you and I both know we can't be together anymore." He paused mid-kiss, peering at her over the horizon of her palm, his grip slipping away.

"I get it. You're going home to play house. You think that'll fill the hole that's inside you since you lost Paul." He shook his head. "Mark my words, you won't find the answers to your prayers under that roof. You'll spend all your time pretending, and then you'll remember the only real thing you ever had was on that island, with me."

She shrunk away. "You don't understand. You don't have children. It's different. I can't abandon them as soon as they have me back. I have to *try*, for their sake if nothing else." Reality was seeping in and turning her beautiful Technicolor dreams into a bleached-out black-and-white photo.

"That's not fair." He crossed his arms and tipped his chair back, two rear legs creaking with annoyance. "I might not know what it's like to have children but I know what it's like to lose a child, and you're not going to lose your kids. You've risen from the dead. They'll be ecstatic for that reason alone."

"I can't toss Jerry out and the ten, well, almost twelve years now, we've been married because of something that happened half a world away. I won't give up on my family that easily."

Dave rubbed the bridge of his nose as he shook his head. "I can't believe you're doing this, Lily. I never would've guessed you could turn your back on me. What if he doesn't want you anymore when you tell him the truth? Will you come running back to me then?" He glowered at her, hands clasped together like he was praying.

"I'm not going to tell him," she said, plain and simple. Her mind was made up, it had been for a long time. It was the only way she could allow herself to be with David on the island without feeling like she was betraying Jerry and her children. She'd told herself that when the time came, she'd choose home.

"Excuse me?" He let the chair drop with a crack, and Lillian imagined the sound was his heart breaking. "You're not going to tell him? How'll that work?"

"We'll come up with a story, a good story, and we'll tell that instead."

"Why in heaven's name would I do that?" Dave laughed. His voice was getting loud and Lillian worried soon a nurse would investigate.

"I was hoping you'd do it because you cared about me. Because you love me."

He sat very still. Lillian didn't know if it was a good thing or a bad thing he hadn't said "no" right away. He had to understand. It was hard for her too, but she couldn't think only of herself. As much as she wanted to slide over to the other side of the bed and pull David in, to wrap her arms around his hard, lean waist and kiss the hollow of his neck, right next to his collarbone, she couldn't. On the island it didn't feel like cheating. But lying there in a hospital bed in the real world, which had suddenly snapped into place around her like a trap, it did.

"Fine. If you insist, I'll do it," he grumbled. "I'll lie, but you have to promise me that if things aren't all lollipops and rainbows back in Jerryland you'll reconsider what we have . . . or had. I know we could be happy, I know it." He sounded so sure, and for one second she could see their alternate future in his eyes. Walking hand in hand on the beach in California, the boys running through the waves, a blonde head with tiny pigtails bobbing up and down on Dave's shoulders. Then he blinked and Lillian knew it was only a dream.

"I promise, David. This isn't good-bye. We've been through too much together to walk out of this place in opposite directions. Plus, we need to get our story straight. If we're as famous as those paramedics claimed, people are going to try to pull out all our secrets and put them out before the world. We have to stop them."

Dave nodded without changing expression. He shoved away from Lillian's bedside, his chair letting out a tattling screech. The next twenty minutes felt like a business meeting as Dave and Lillian figured out what stories and lies they were going to tell for the rest of their lives.

Almost nine months later and they were still telling them. As Lillian told her tale about Paul it came out smooth as spun silk. She had to pat herself on the back a little; it was working.

"How long was Paul with you?" Genevieve was so into it. It wasn't hard to tell Genevieve Randall had been biding her time, waiting for Paul. Everyone loved Paul, even though Dave and Lillian were the only people who had ever known him. Usually it hurt to talk about having and then losing Paul, but today it felt good. Sometimes it didn't feel like he'd even existed, so talking about him, especially after not talking about him so long, resurrected her feelings.

"Three short but wonderful months," Lillian sighed.

"When did you know?" Her mouth turned up at the corner and Lillian was sure Genevieve was actually interested in her answer.

"I was on the beach, eating a green banana . . ."

CHAPTER 26

LILY-DAY 301

The Island

I loathe green bananas. They taste like grass and crush into uneven clumps as I chew. Usually I toss them into the fire for a few minutes till the skins char a little, making the insides soften just enough to make them bearable. But this morning the fire's too low and I'm too hungry to wait.

Sometimes I forget how wonderful food used to be. Chocolate, steak, doughnuts, pizza, fresh green beans, hamburgers, ice cream— all things I may never taste again. I've learned that memories of taste disappear faster than the other senses. The words "yummy" and "delicious" seem so pedestrian and unequal to the way I miss eating things other than fish and rats and snails and fruit at various stages of ripeness.

I shove the last bite of banana in my mouth, still starving. Peanut butter, yes, that would've tasted amazing slathered all over that sorry excuse of a banana. I toss the empty peel into the smoldering ashes before crossing over to our woodpile and grabbing a few dry pieces of kindling from the bottom. I should get the fire nice and hot so when David gets back with some fish they'll cook quickly. I hope he gets lucky and finds a fish with some meat on its bones. We need to go on a trip to Bizarro Beach because I'm tired of the small fish that taste like seaweed.

Once the fire's blazing again I step back, sweat trickling down both sides of my face. That banana isn't sitting well. I was going to do some weaving this morning but between the heat and the nausea, I look at the lapping blue waves longingly. A quick dip won't hurt, right?

David hates it when I swim alone. Even though the story we've created about Kent's death is a lie, we've practiced it so much it almost feels like he did drown mysteriously. I think David is also ridiculously worried that after having a taste of human blood the sharks would be more aggressive toward us. I told him he's seen too many movies.

I take the time to kick off my shorts and toss my shirt into the shelter, to save myself a chill later. I'm wearing my bathing suit today and it's starting to fit again. I lost so much weight in the weeks after Kent died I could see the outline of my hipbones through my skin. I'm much happier now.

I hold on to the waistband of my bathing suit as I hop into the waves. I don't dive into the water today; instead I slowly submerge myself once the water's up to my armpits, still thinking about David.

When we first realized we were in love, things were super-intense. Many late nights filled with passion like I've never known. It's not like I was some innocent schoolgirl but whether it's from the pent-up tension that burned between us or just that our chemistry is incredibly compatible, we make good use of our free time, if you know what I mean.

I float in the water; the salt makes me buoyant like I'm flying. That content feeling I've only recently become acquainted with fills me. For a full minute I forget how hungry I am and how my children are living and breathing without me a world away.

I'm most surprised at the lack of guilt I feel about my relationship with David. It's come so easily and is clearly more than physical. This isn't some passionate affair that'll burn out after a quick flash; it's more like marriage, our love growing deeper and more meaningful over time. Sometimes I think it's something even greater than marriage. I never spent every moment of every day with Jerry, not for ten months in a row at least. Back in St. Louis I remember a few mornings when Jerry walked out the door to work after a long holiday at home and I'd let out a little sigh of relief. I think most husbands and wives would admit to needing some time away from their spouse but I've never craved that with David. In fact, I miss him the second he walks out of my sight.

He's been gone an hour now and it's killing me. Ever since Kent, whenever I'm alone, I feel like someone's watching me. Deep down I know it's irrational but after what he did to me, I'm glad codependency is my main psychological scar.

Ugh, I'd better get back to the beach and dry off before David comes home and freaks out. Flipping onto my stomach, I take my time swimming to shore. Crawling onto the beach, water slides off of me in streams, and I long for one of our giant beach towels from home. I kept them in the hall closet, bottom shelf. They were softer than some blankets and always smelled a little of chlorine no matter how many times I washed them. Instead I squeeze the water out of my hair between two fingers and . . .

Oh! My stomach flips angrily like someone kicked me in the gut. Still wet, I fall to my knees and something in my belly rolls uncomfortably, like a boa constrictor slithering through my intestines. This is more than a bad banana. This is—I don't know what this is.

"Lily!" I hear David before I see him. "What's wrong? Are you hurt?" He rushes to my side, sliding through the sand on his knees, making it spray over me like a shower.

"I don't know. I feel strange. Something's wrong." My hands are over my stomach, holding tight, trying to make that rolling feeling go away.

David pulls me up by my arm. "Let's get you into the shade."

"I've been so hungry lately; I've been eating like crazy. Maybe I wasn't careful enough?" We're diligent with food safety, knowing there are more ways to die out here than from sharks and snakes. I could've pulled the fish off the fire too soon one meal and swallowed more than fish for lunch.

"You think it's a parasite?" David's eyebrows pinch in the middle, making three lines where they met. I reach up to smooth them away as he lies me down inside the shelter.

"Let's not jump to conclusions, love. It could be gas, as embarrassing as that may be."

David rubs his hands together, shedding a coating of sand. "Let me check you out. Pretend I know what I'm doing."

He smiles gravely like a doctor, taking his hands and working them along the bottom of my rib cage. When he runs them down my sides I can't help but giggle. He knows that's my most vulnerable spot in tickle fights. He lingers there a little longer than necessary, an incorrigible flirt. Then he moves in toward my belly button and the humor on his face vanishes. He leans in closer as though he can see through my skin with X-ray vision. Then it happens, that unexpected bounce inside of me, and his hands jump back, his mouth hanging open.

"Oh crap, I felt that." His hands go up to his face and he flicks his thumbnail over his incisors, making a clicking sound that has now become synonymous with him thinking. "I don't know what to do. Would a parasite move like that? How do we get rid of it?"

"Don't they come out on their own? I thought I heard somewhere that you can starve one out, but I don't think that's an option for us. We should check you too since we eat the same food. Have you been feeling any different? Fatigue? Nausea? Increased hunger? A swelling in your abdomen?" I questioned, finding it funny that these symptoms fit so many medical afflictions: anemia, diabetes, pregnancy . . . pregnancy.

"No," David answered thoughtfully, "I don't think I've felt different lately. Honestly, I've felt amazing but I thought that had more to do with you than anything medical." He must've noticed my face because he stopped mid-laugh. "What? Is it back? Are you in pain?"

"It's definitely not painful," I answered, stalling as I thought through everything. No wonder all this was so familiar, the nausea, the weight gain, the fluttery movements in my abdomen. How could I be so stupid? Sitting up I grab his hand and place it on my belly, just below my belly button. "David," I say slowly, knowing that everything will change if what I suspect is true, "I think I'm pregnant."

He pulls his hand away, roughly, more roughly than I'm used to with him. The look on his face is beyond shock, it's bordering on fury.

"That's not funny," he says through gritted teeth. "Don't make a joke. A parasite is serious and I can't do anything to help you."

"I'm not kidding. I've done this before. I would've realized it sooner but I haven't had regular cycles since getting here, I think it was all the weight loss. But when we got together I put on a few pounds. That must've triggered it again." I reclaim his hand but lace my fingers between his instead of putting them back on my belly.

"But you said we were safe, your IUD and all that?" The words rush out.

"It does work. It did work, for five whole years. I had a new one put in a month before I left, a different kind than before, but they're supposed to be completely effective." I shouldn't have to defend myself, as though I would've lied about my birth-control decisions. "The doctor said there could be some side effects, I didn't know making a baby would be one of them."

David is freaking out. David, who kept his cool in the face of a murderous psychopath, is now losing it because of a tiny person growing inside me. But I'm getting flustered along with him now that the reality of my self-diagnosis is settling in. A baby? Here? What're we going to do?

"What have I done?" David questions himself. He yanks his hand away and covers his mouth like he's going to vomit. "I'm sorry, so sorry, Lily."

"Don't apologize," I order, feeling increasingly irritable. "We did this together. *We* couldn't have known."

"But it's so dangerous. You could . . . you could . . ." He can't finish his sentence.

"Women have been having babies for thousands and thousands of years. More children were born on this planet *not* in a hospital than in one. Besides"—I'm trying so hard to speak calmly—

"I've done this twice. That worked out well, right?"

David has retreated to the opposite side of the shelter, as though putting distance between us now will undo the past five months we've spent together. He folds himself in half, his knees pulled tight against his chest.

"Do you honestly think this could turn out all right?" he asks, his voice trembling with hope, or maybe fear. "Do you think you can have a baby, here, and survive?"

I'm not sure he wants my honest opinion, so I tell him what he wants to hear, what I want to believe. "Yes, David, I do. That means you're going to be a father."

"A father," he whispers as though savoring the word. "But what about . . ."

"We aren't going to worry now," I order. I can't go over a list of things that could go wrong with this pregnancy. "I have to be at least four months into this, maybe closer to five. We have a few months to plan so right now, let's just pretend we're safe and you just found out you're having a baby."

"I'm sorry, Lily," he says, his voice stronger. "I didn't mean to come off like that, like I don't want a child with you. If we were home, if we were safe like you said, there would be nothing I'd rather hear than you were carrying my child." I can see the mantle of fatherhood resting on his shoulders. It makes him sit up and unfold his legs with resolve. "We're going to do this. I'll do whatever I can to take care of you and the baby. Our baby."

"The first thing you can do is get over here and kiss me." I extend my hand. I need to touch him; he calms me, and right now my heart and mind are racing.

"I can do that." David leaps toward me. When he leans over to kiss me, his right hand cradles my face as though it's the most precious item on the planet, his left hand rests on my belly. I'm impressed at how easily he loves this unborn child. I can't wrap my brain around it, and the fetus is growing inside *my* body. A baby. I always wanted a third, always tried to get Jerry on board with the idea but he was never a fan of the plan. Said a family of four is optimal for vacations and dining out. I always thought those were odd reasons to limit our family but I never thought it would happen this way. This is not Jerry's baby.

I try to forget my worries in the welcoming embrace of David's celebratory kiss. My lips move against his automatically. Yet it isn't desire that stirs inside me this time, it's fear. I focus on David, trying to pull myself away from the spiral of doubt that threatens to pull me down.

CHAPTER 27

DAVE

Present

"We'd been on the island a few months. It was just after the New Year, if I remember correctly, when she figured it out." Dave felt strong after spending the break with Beth and the baby. Feeling his little kicks reminded him of Paul, but in a good way.

Unlike talking with Genevieve. She made him remember in a very painful way, a way he wouldn't wish on his worst enemy. Like how every time she said Paul's name, Dave saw his face, his sweet, tiny, perfect little face. The face he'd never see again. The face he'd failed.

"When she told you and Kent, what did you think? What was your reaction?" Genevieve leaned forward, notes crunched on her lap between her legs and her flat stomach. She apparently didn't need notes for this part of the interview.

"We were shocked, of course, and scared. Kent was mad at first—worried about another mouth to feed—but as her belly grew and little Paul made himself known with kicks and nudges, even Kent softened up."

"How did Lillian fare on the island, pregnant?"

"It was very difficult, as you could expect. We worked incredibly hard to get her food and water but it was impossible to get enough calories in there for her and the baby. She lost weight—*more* weight, I should say. We all lost weight after the crash but the bigger her belly grew, the more withered the rest of her became."

That was so hard for Dave to watch. To this day, Lillian had no idea how emaciated she became as she grew that little boy, one blessing of having no mirrors. But Dave remembered all too well.

She was still frail the last time he saw her, when she was in California for the Carlton awards dinner with her friend, or should he say bodyguard. He'd picked them both up at LAX, waiting painfully right outside of the security line.

Someone must've tipped off the press, because several rogue cameras flanked him a few feet away on either side. After three months at home, Dave was starting to find cameras commonplace. He'd been working on ignoring them sitting outside his house and gym, but when he saw Lily standing on the moving walkway, they were the only reason he didn't break through the invisible security line and scoop her up in his achingly empty arms. Instead, he waited.

He counted the noiseless footsteps from when she turned the corner to when she recognized him. Would happiness to see him be written in bold capital letters or delicate curvy wisps? But, large dark sunglasses covered her easy-to-read eyes and her face was empty, completely vacant of any emotion.

Dave told himself she didn't see him, that her smile would break through as soon as his face registered through the tinted glass, but it didn't. His heart sank as she walked, zombielike, toward him, leaning on the tall redhead's arm. Lily's friend was willowy and full of life, working a sad kind of contrast to the wilted and drooping Lily. It made Dave angry. He wanted to pull the two apart, rip off the glasses, and ask her who was responsible for the sadness that trailed after her like smoke. Instead he shook Jill's hand mutely.

"Dave, it's nice to meet you. I'm Jill Spears." The handshake was brief and hastily withdrawn.

Dave nodded. "I've heard a lot about you. I'm glad we can finally meet." He spoke the social script, eyes never leaving Lillian's flaccid face.

"Yes. Same here." She didn't even attempt to smile, readjusting the carry-on slipping off her shoulder. "Listen, Lillian's a little under the weather. Her doctor prescribed some anti-anxiety meds for the plane trip and they haven't worn off yet." She eyed the clicking cameras. "I think we should make our way to the car as quickly as possible. We didn't check anything."

"All right. Why don't you let me take your bags?" He had grabbed the rolling suitcase from her hand and one of the heavy duffels from her shoulder when Jill leaned into him, whispering.

"Take Lillian, quick. She's getting a little tippy." She handed over Lillian's arm, which sagged like a wet towel. Dave almost fell over with the shock of her weight in his hands.

"The car's this way." Dave coaxed Lillian through the clicking cameras, smiling and waving the whole way, and then out to the parking garage, where his car was waiting.

He guided Lily. No, not Lily. The woman dressed in a gray cotton T-shirt and wide-legged jeans held no resemblance to *his* Lily. This woman must be the Lillian he'd heard so much about.

As Jill droned on about kids and home, Dave thanked the universe Jerry hadn't come. It would have been impossible to put on a good face for him, impossible to keep out the accusations that danced through his thoughts. Instead, he nodded at Jill's stories and smiled in the spots he knew he should until he'd settled Lillian into the backseat, clicked the seat belt around her, and put the car into drive.

"Now, how's she *really* doing?" Dave asked, merging into LA rush-hour traffic, checking for the third time over the seat to see if Lillian was still sleeping. Jill raised her arm up into the air and jangled the shiny silver bracelets down toward her elbow.

"If I'm being honest?" Jill rubbed her lips together nervously. "Not well. Don't get me wrong, she's beside herself with happiness to be back with her family, but there's a lot different about her."

"She's been through a lot," he whispered. The memory of what they'd both been through, together, was now like a constant dull toothache.

"Yes. I'm worried about her, though. She's still so sad. She misses her baby. She loved him so much."

Dave glared at the green Ford Escort in front of them. "She *still* loves him. That kind of love never goes away. You all need to cut her some slack and give her lots more time. She had a hard time when Margaret died, but after a while it was easier to bear."

"It's not only that." She ran her fingers through her stiff, red peaks and Dave could hear the crackle of hair product. "The boys fill up most of her day and she's seeing a good therapist, but something's standing in the way of her rebonding with Jerry, and it's not Paul and his death."

Jill paused, scowling at Dave's unturned face. Her gaze was hard and Dave found it awkward to be talking like this, about Lily, with a person he didn't even know. But he wanted to know what "difficulties" she was talking about.

"Okay, I'll bite, what is it?"

"It's you," she said bluntly.

Dave couldn't have been more surprised if Jill had said Osama Bin Laden. He knew he'd sensed a bubbling tension emitting from the aggressive fortysomething Jill Spears, but he'd let himself believe she was being overprotective because of Lillian's present drugged-up condition. Clearly, he was wrong.

"Me? That's the most ridiculous thing I've ever heard." He darted quick glances at Jill's face to see if she was joking.

"Come on, don't play innocent with me. Just so you know, I've been a high school dean for twelve years and I know when someone's lying to me."

"Jill, I don't know what you're talking about," Dave said, panicking. The traffic picked the most uncomfortable time to slow to a crawl. He had nowhere to look but at his accuser.

"True or false—when Lillian has a bad day, she calls you?"

"True," he answered. If he didn't lie then she couldn't call him on it. If she wanted truth, he'd give her as much as possible.

"Good. I'm glad you're not trying to BS me, Dave." She took a moment to shift her body toward him, ready for more interrogation.

"True or false? When *you* have a bad day, *you* call Lillian."

Dave sighed. "True. What's the problem with that? We spent almost two years together, every minute of those years. You can't expect us not to be close anymore."

"Shhhh, this isn't a discussion. I have another question." Jill pulled her legs up, Indian-style, her flowing skirt draped over them casually. Leaning forward, elbow on her knee, she posed the next question. "True or false? You're in love with Lillian."

"Oh, come on." Dave smacked the steering wheel.

"True or false?" she pressed, leaning back against the locked door, arms crossed firmly, making Dave feel sorry for generations of high school students in suburban St. Louis.

"It's not that easy, Jill. Yes, of course I love her," he stuttered out the words nervously, worried saying them out loud would mean more than it should. "But I'm sure you love her too."

"Uh-uh. Not the same. She's my best friend and we've been best friends for most of our adult lives." Jill turned away for the first time since their conversation and started glancing over at Lillian, whose head rested limply against the car window. "Lillian has always been there for me. She was in the delivery room when my children were born, she was there to hold my hand when my Mom passed away and when my husband was diagnosed with cancer. She took care of my kids, brought dinners, and even brushed my hair when both my hands were in casts after a car accident." Worry mellowed the fierceness in her light eyes as she answered. "Yes, I love her, *but* I'm not trying to take a place in her life already held by someone else. I'm not trying to insert myself into a family that needs to be finding strength from within." Jill's long fingernails poked at the spotty exposed skin above the sagging collar of her shirt. "It's easy to see you're in love with her, but she doesn't *need* you. She needs her family right now."

"Jill," he said in a cool, measured voice, "loving someone and being *in* love with someone are two different things. I want her to be happy as much as you do, but I'm not willing to stop talking to her when I *know* our conversations help her." Clearly Lily needed him. Look at the state she was in without him. "Would you ask me to do that? To abandon her? When her number pops up on my phone, are you telling me I should ignore it and let her suffer alone? Because if you *are* saying that, then you're not as good of a friend as you apparently think you are." Gassing it, he switched lanes without using the signal, making Jill hang on tighter to the armrest. Dave smiled a little inside.

"I don't know," she sighed, cracking her index fingers loudly with her thumbs. "Something has to change. I'm concerned."

"Why doesn't *Jerry* do something? He is her husband." Dave regretted the edge in his voice as soon as he said it.

"Mmmm, he's tried." She nibbled nervously at her fingernails, no accusations this time. "She's so shut down, it does no good. What would you do if it were your wife? If she came back like Lillian?" she asked as if she cared what he thought.

"I don't know—stop pushing so hard maybe? Give her some time and some space? I think he could try to be a little understanding." He listed the items, then gripped the wheel with two hands, staring at the scratched-up blue Astro in front of him. "I can tell you one thing I wouldn't do, I wouldn't send somebody to do my dirty work for me. If Jerry wants me to stop calling Lily, he can talk to me like a man."

Jill let her hands drop into her lap, making the shiny bracelets dance against each other. "He didn't send me," she said unconvincingly, staring out the window. "You could stop, you know. It'd be better for everyone."

"I can't stop. I won't." He glared at her for two seconds before he had to merge onto the off-ramp that lead to the hotel. "Not while she still needs me."

There must have been something final in his declaration, because she nodded and leaned her head against the car window, her red spikes flattening with a crinkle. Dave clicked on the radio to his favorite station and turned it down low, letting the quiet melodies fill the awkward silence between them.

When they finally reached the hotel, Dave parked by the loading docks hoping to avoid further photographs of medicated Lillian. As soon as he threw the car into park, Jill jumped out, asking for the trunk to be popped. Dave pushed the button and slowly pulled the keys from the ignition. Time to wake Lillian.

Jill was taking her time pulling the carry-ons from the trunk as Dave opened the passenger-side rear door. Lily's silver ballet flats lay abandoned on the floor of the car, her feet tucked easily under her. Long jeans almost engulfed her feet in a sea of denim, leaving the dainty maroon toenails twinkling in the late afternoon sunlight.

Her hair, cut to her shoulders and straightened, was very unfamiliar, and he wasn't sure he'd recognize her walking down the street in her new clothes and hairdo. Leaning into the car and closing the door behind him, Dave sat beside the sleeping woman and patted her leg.

"Lillian, we're here. Time to get up." Lillian stirred, eyelids fluttering, before dozing off. Dave tried again, scooting closer, resting a hand on her shoulder. "Lily, sweetheart, you need to wake up. You can sleep when we get you inside. I promise."

He swept her hair away from her face. She wore a fine sheen of powder and her eyelashes were darker than he remembered, but besides that, her face was still the one he saw in his dreams and nightmares. Lillian blinked and then opened her eyes.

"David," she sighed, "it *is* you." Sitting up with difficulty, she traced the line of his arm, over his light blue T-shirt, and around his neck, locking him in an embrace. Dave reluctantly wrapped his arms around her, trying not to notice that she still fit perfectly there.

"Yep, remember, I picked you up from the airport? You're visiting California? We have the ball tomorrow night. Part of that whole multimillion-dollar settlement thing." He needed to remind her; he needed her to draw her lines of defense, realizing that her reluctance was the only thing that kept him safe the past three months. The scar above her right eyebrow puckered.

"I've missed you so much," she slurred. "Why did you leave me alone? I'm so alone, David. Why did you leave me?"

"I didn't leave you, Lillian. We're home now. You're with your family. It's what you wanted, remember?"

Smacking her lips, she ran her tongue along her teeth as if she'd been given novocaine rather than a mood stabilizer. Dave was growing worried that whatever she'd taken, it'd been too much.

"I remember. I just miss you," she repeated, laying her head on Dave's shoulder.

"I miss you too. Come on, let's get you to bed." He coaxed her to the edge of the car's rear seat and then pulled her to standing, her arms around his neck.

Keeping his hands on her shoulders, Dave waited as she steadied herself. Once he was sure of her balance he started to pull away, when

Lillian dug her fingers into the back of his neck, holding him close. Dave froze. He should rip her hands off and reclaim some distance between them but also enjoyed the heat that spread from her flaming hands through his whole body.

"David," she said the name again. Her special name for him. It was his favorite and least favorite sound in the whole world. "You still love me, right?"

Dave cringed. Jill stood frowning behind Lillian, bags draped over her shoulders. He could lie, he *should* lie, but holding her in his arms, he gave her the only answer he could.

"Of course I do, Lily."

"No," she said, shaking her head like a spoiled toddler. "Say it right."

He didn't want to say it that way. It was too sacred to be tossed around casually, especially in front of Jill. Lillian's grip tightened. More than anything Dave wanted to escape. He gave in.

"Always, Lily."

Lillian smiled and leaned forward to kiss him lightly on the lips. "Always," she whispered against his mouth. Her lips were smooth and welcoming, like walking into their small island shelter after a day spent hunting. He wanted to lean into them, to pull her body in until he could feel her heartbeat through her shirt, to toss her in the car and run far away from here. But Jill was watching.

Dave stood, forcing Lillian away calmly, his face burning and heart beating crazy fast with conflicting desires. Jill sighed behind them as she turned away and walked toward the hotel's entrance.

He didn't see Lillian again until she walked into the banquet hall the next evening. The bluish-silver sequins of her dress overlapped and reflected even the dim lights from the empty, darkened room. One shimmering strap wrapped up around her right shoulder, leaving the left one bare. Her skin, still stained chestnut from the months in the sun, glowed like it had its own light source. She turned slightly to whisper something in her friend's ear, and Dave caught a peek of the low-dipping back that showcased her flawless waist and shoulders, the jagged white scar on her shoulder snaking out from under one of her straps like it was one of their secrets. She couldn't make it easy on him, could she?

Finally noticing him, she smiled, and he held his breath for a second before smiling back. It was that prickly nervousness he used to get around her, the one that made his palms sweat and words as difficult to get out as pulled taffy. He hadn't felt that way in a very long time.

He used to be such a phony. That's why he was great at public relations: he always knew the right face to show the right people, but it was never *his* face. Then, during a press conference after their rescue, one of the reporters asked a skin-and-bones Lillian if she wore clothes on the island or just went naked. Dave forgot to put on his PR-guy smile, to keep calm and even. Instead he grabbed the mic and told the tabloid reporter to go to hell.

Phony Dave was gone, a convenient casualty of the crash. He used to think it was because he'd matured during his time away, but seeing Lillian, polished head to toe like a flawless diamond, Dave finally understood. She was the one person in the world that knew the real Dave Hall. She knew his darkest thoughts and actions and loved him anyway. He didn't need to pretend anymore; Lillian and that island taught him who he really was.

"Dave!" Lillian waved and made her way through empty chairs encircling tables set with delicate white china and forks and spoons spreading out on either side. "It's so good to see a familiar face." Jill raced behind her wearing a beaded electric-blue dress that hung off her like a 1920s flapper. The boxy dress was clearly meant to be a fashion statement, but to Dave it made the best friend/bodyguard even more manly looking. Her hair didn't help either, all cropped and spiky.

"We have to sit up here," Dave shouted, tipping his head toward a long table at the front of the ballroom. It reminded him of a reception hall for a wedding, but supersized. The walls were ornately decorated with gold filigree and hundreds of paintings of men and women in white wigs. Even Beth would've found the place overkill.

"You look handsome," Lillian said when she finally reached him. Slipping her hands under his open coat, she wrapped her arms around his waist in a lingering hug. Her head rested comfortably on his shoulder, probably because she was wearing heels. He gave in to the temptation to bury his nose into her hair, trying to memorize the smell of freesia and flesh.

Jill cleared her throat. "When do I get to meet Beth?" she asked.

Lillian left her arm under his coat as though they were an old married couple who had attended a million black-tie functions together. Dave appreciated the opportunity to keep his hand on her hip, acutely aware that his thumb rested on the bare curve of her waist.

"She's home, sick, but sends her greetings." Dave pasted an unwelcome smile on his face when he answered Jill. He knew she didn't care about Beth; she wanted to remind him that he was married.

"Oh, poor Beth!" Lillian's mouth tucked down on one side. "You're feeling okay, though, right?" She put her cool hand on his forehead and then his cheek. When they were together she'd always check for a fever with a kiss, telling him that her lips were as accurate as a thermometer.

"It's not contagious, don't worry." He watched her face, tracing the familiar curve of her jawbone and the light wrinkles around her eyes that illustrated all too clearly when she was happy or sad. Today they spelled out happy and Dave felt relieved to find her so much improved from the day before.

"Good," Lillian said. She left her arm under his coat, one finger slung through a belt loop. Dave enjoyed her familiar body pressing against his side. What in the world was going on?

Jill seemed to be having similar concerns. "It was nice seeing you, Dave, but we'll have to meet up with you again later. The lady out front said Janice was waiting to see Lillian and I'm supposed to take her to the staging room right away."

"Oh, that's right," Lillian sighed, her hand dropping away. "I need to see Janice but I'm sure we'll sit by each other and maybe you can save me a dance?"

She took a step toward Jill, Dave's fingers reluctantly slipping off her slinky dress. "Of course!" he said, trying to keep his disappointment from showing. "Actually, I think it's a requirement. Janice wants us to open the dance together. It's a little old-fashioned but since we're the guests of honor . . . I thought it'd be okay."

"Okay? No, it sounds perfect." Lillian picked up the long trail of silver material pooling at her feet as Jill looped her pale, freckled arm through Lillian's. "See you in a few minutes."

Dave didn't see Lillian again until dinner and even then they were seated on opposite sides of the table with the CEO of Carlton, John Richard Carlton Jr., and his wife wedged between them. It was a night of unbearable small talk and answering the same three questions everyone always asked about the island: what did you eat, what did you drink, and where did you poop? Dave used to be amazed at how little tact people had but now he expected it.

When dinner concluded, a few toasts were made to Lillian and Dave and then they watched a video montage dedicated to Margaret, Theresa, and even Kent. Seeing Kent's ruddy face again made it hard for Dave to keep his food down. He couldn't help remembering what he looked like, dead, face swollen and cut after being dragged through the jungle.

Dave tried to peer around the middle-aged couple who separated him from Lillian. This had to be killing her. The wall of fleshy humanity between them had a tiny hole. Leaning forward in his chair he tried to see through. If he squinted, he could almost make out her profile. Occasionally, when a bright picture was projected on the screen, it reflected in her eyes. They were moist but serene, the exact opposite of what they looked like at the airport the night before.

The very last slide was black with white lettering. Dave almost didn't look but when whatever was on the screen made Lillian turn away, he couldn't stop himself.

In Memory of Paul Linden.

No picture. Just a name that wasn't his. A stabbing pain rushed from the hole that was still gaping in his heart, that space his son occupied before being ripped out when he died. He was the only lie Dave regretted.

The lights went on and Dave rushed to dry his face before turning to face the full banquet hall. This was the most extravagant event he'd ever seen Carlton throw, complete with news crews, live music, prime rib, and champagne. To Dave it felt a lot like they were trying to get some extra publicity off the castaways' miraculous return. Hey, if Dave had still been head of public relations, that's what he would've done.

During dinner the band had set up against one of the side walls, and when the lights came on the lead singer, wearing a cliché black leather jacket and scarf tied around his waist, grabbed a microphone. "Let's get this party started!" he shouted in a raspy voice.

The crowd erupted in a roar of applause before the band started a fast-paced, contemporary rock song. Dave didn't understand what all the fuss was about. Apparently this band was a one-hit wonder the previous summer, but he'd never heard of them. As the crowd cheered, the news cameras zoomed and Dave pretended to enjoy the song. When it was finally over, the sandpaper voice came over the sound system one more time.

"Please welcome the guests of honor—Lillian Linden and Dave Hall." A slow song pumped in the background as Dave descended from his elevated seat at the banquet table. Somehow Lillian beat him to the middle of the parquet dance floor, a spotlight glancing off her dress in a thousand tiny points of light that bounced over his dark tux and face.

The light also reflected off her full, dark pupils like the stars that canopied their old home, and the tiny sea pearls pinned into delicate curls piled on the top of her head seemed to wink at him in a private joke. His heart raced in that wonderfully uncomfortable way it had the first time they met, the first time he noticed how beautiful she was in her cutoff jeans and old T-shirt.

As the melody started, Lillian extended her hand, which Dave took instantly. He pulled her in close, enfolding her hand in his and wrapping his arm around her naked waist. They swayed wordlessly in impeccable unity and Dave had to force himself to not kiss the top of her head. She tipped her face up.

"You're so beautiful tonight," Dave whispered. "I didn't get to tell you earlier."

"Janice sent over a stylist for me and Jill. I've never felt this fancy in my life."

Dave swore she giggled. He twirled her around in a half circle. "You are . . . different tonight."

"You really can't remember me like this? This is me happy, David." She spun herself out and under his arm before he yanked her in with a flick of his wrist.

"It looks good on you." He was tempted to flirt but stopped himself, still aware of the eyes watching them, not to mention the cameras. "What brought this on?"

"I think I'm just excited about tomorrow." The dance floor was filling up and Lillian put her face against Dave's to whisper in his ear.

"So you aren't having second thoughts?" he said, trying to keep his lips from moving as he spoke.

"Beth will never know, right?"

"Not if you don't want her to."

"I'll never tell Jerry and you never tell Beth." Her breath tickled his neck and brought back memories he'd worked very hard to erase.

"Deal." He checked on Jill, still sitting at the banquet table, watching them dance and scowling. "How are you going to get away from your guard dog over there?"

"Don't worry about Jill. I told her I have an interview tomorrow and I've ordered a taxi."

"I wish I could pick you up but I know I can't." The song was starting to trail off and the couples surrounding them slowed to a stop. He kept his arms stubbornly around her and murmured, "I *will* meet you there at ten sharp?"

"I look forward to it," she breathed into his ear, then stepped away, thanking him with a deep curtsy that made him laugh.

They didn't dance again. Both spent the night trading off different partners; at one point Dave may have danced with a senator and possibly someone he'd seen in a movie once. He didn't notice. He could dance with the Queen of Sheba for all he cared because tomorrow could be one of the most important days in his life.

Only a few days compared. The day they crashed, the day of Kent's death, the day of their rescue, and, most of all, the day Paul was born. There used to be other days, like his wedding day and the day his father passed and his graduation day, but now it was hard to see those through the haze left behind by that small private jet that crashed into the ocean.

◆ ◆ ◆

Genevieve Randall's eager face chased away any bit of fog that still hung around Dave. She'd scooted forward in her seat, not only ready but excited for the current series of questions.

"So you're telling me Lillian was pregnant before the crash but didn't know it, and didn't discover it for *months* after you landed on the island? Then she spent the rest of her pregnancy on the island before giving birth to a completely healthy baby boy who lived only three months?"

"Yes, the poor woman, she did." Dave had to pretend he was talking about someone else, not his Lily and his little boy, Paul.

"Who delivered the baby when the time came? Was it Kent, or 'Scout,' as you called him?"

Dave's voice stuck in his throat and he coughed trying to dislodge it. This was the one thing he'd told Lillian he wouldn't lie about. "No, it was me. I delivered Paul."

CHAPTER 28
DAVID-DAY 465

The Island

I'm in love. I never thought I could love something or someone in this all-consuming, get-tears-in-my-eyes-just-thinking-about-it kind of way. I've been in love before, with Beth and Lily, but this love is different. He does nothing but lie in my arms, and squirm and nurse and defecate, but I'm convinced he's the most spectacular and brilliant human being that's ever existed on the planet.

It helps that he looks a lot like Lily. Right now his eyes are baby blue but Lily says they'll change in the next few weeks and settle into their own personalized color, which I'm convinced will be emerald green. His hair is thick and black with wispy curls at the end, which she says he gets from me. But his tiny pink cupid's-bow lips belong to his mother.

Lily's taking a much-needed nap. I never knew what hard work labor was, and after watching her give birth I think she should get to nap for weeks. The end of Lily's pregnancy was torture, physically for her and emotionally for me. She shrunk away to almost nothing and I saw bones poking out on her that I didn't know existed in the human body. It was hard to watch. I felt absolutely incompetent. I couldn't catch enough fish or pick enough fruit or pluck enough snails to keep weight on her.

The whole time she claimed to feel fine, but then she'd sit by the fire at night and fall asleep upright. I don't think it was only lack of calories that exhausted her; all those sweet little kicks and nudges reminded her of the two times she'd been pregnant before. She put on a brave face, but as much as she loves our baby, she'll always miss the other two sons she'll never see again.

Then this morning her water broke. About an hour later contractions started, fast and hard. She handled them well at first, breathing and lying on her side, but soon she became restless and tired of lying down.

She walked the beach, stopping to lean against a tree or me as each contraction hit. It was such a strange experience. In between contractions she could talk like normal, converse as though it were just another day, but when the pains started again, she was overcome. She'd close her eyes and she was gone away from me. Sometimes she'd let me rub her back or give her sips of water but mostly she followed some kind of instinct Mother Nature herself must've implanted in her.

I don't know how long that went on. It was nearly lunchtime, the sun high in the sky, when she felt the urge to push. I pulled out the supplies we'd been collecting since Lily realized she was pregnant four months ago: string to cut the cord, a clean mat to give birth on. Margaret's coat, washed in the freshwater pool, would be the baby's receiving blanket. Of course my knife, washed and sharpened, to cut the tied-off umbilical cord. I placed it near the fire to sterilize.

"By the fishing log," she gasped in the seconds before her next contraction. I left her leaning by our calendar tree to prep the birthing area. The woven mat filled the space in front of the log precisely, close enough to the water that afterward the cleanup would be very simple. I lay out my supplies on the log and then retrieved my Lily.

We stopped four times, Lily moaning through the pains, before we reached the mat. She still clung to me and would semi-squat through what seemed like never-ending agony. When I could tell she was bearing down hard, I helped her to the ground and readied myself to meet my child.

It took three pushes, that was all. Lily was spectacular. She didn't scream like women in movies, she held her breath till her face turned red and her eyes bugged out and she pushed. With the first push, I saw the top of his head, the second, his head was out, and by the third, I knew I had a son. A son. A beautiful baby boy.

Lily sat up, propped up on her elbows, and laughed when the boy cried. The tiny blood vessels that had broken on her face while pushing made it look like she was blushing. With her instruction, I passed him off to her waiting arms, the umbilical cord stretching far enough for him to rest on her chest comfortably.

"So," she asked, "Paul James?" Once she lay down, I took a quick second to place the dingy coat over the pair before tying off the slippery umbilical cord in two places and cutting. It was tough, like cartilage, and slick in my hands.

"I think it's great." Paul was her grandfather's name and James was my father's.

"Paul James Hall. Paul Hall? Is that a wise name selection?" she laughed, and the loose skin on her belly jiggled.

"How did we not see that problem before?"

"We could name him James Paul? James Paul Hall? That's not much better is it?" Her face flinched as an after-contraction hit. She made that humming sound she'd used during labor.

"Are you all right?" As over-the-moon happy as I was that we made it through labor, I knew we were not out of the woods yet. I'm guessing these first weeks after childbirth will be the most dangerous, fighting off infection and keeping an eye out for hemorrhaging. The birth was awe-inspiring but it was also so frightening.

"I'm fine, this is normal," she panted out as the discomfort faded. "I've never felt these contractions before. Remember? The miracle of modern medicine included epidurals." Her cheeks had a rosy glow, even under the broken blood vessels, so I knew she wasn't bleeding to death—yet.

"I like Paul better than James." I kept talking, trying not to obsess over the horrible maybes I'd been throwing around in my head for the past few weeks. "We don't have to worry about mean kids teasing him or family opinions. Let's name him what we want—Paul." When I said his name, the baby began to stir, as though he recognized it as his own already.

His wrinkled little eyelids squinted against the midday sun. Lifting his head a few inches off Lily's chest, he seemed to stare at her. "Well, hi there, buddy," she crooned. "Yes, I'm that lady you've been listening to all this time."

In all my years of wanting a baby, and in the months I'd desired this one's birth, I had no idea, none, how instantly I'd adore Paul. "Is it just me or is he the cutest baby that's ever existed?" His head bobbed up and down, like holding up his head was the hardest thing anyone had ever done.

"No, I agree. Cutest infant on the planet, for sure." Lily laughed and kissed the top of Paul's mushy, wet hair before closing her eyes, pain flickering over her face. "I think we're almost done here."

Only a few minutes later she was resting comfortably in the shelter while I cleaned up. I wasn't prepared for the massive amounts of bodily fluids, but after all my experience with fish guts and body disposal, I managed not to be grossed out. I buried the placenta deep in the sand by our fishing log after getting her comfortable. She seemed relieved when Paul nursed immediately after they settled in and then fell into a deep, tranquil sleep. Lily soon followed.

After all the cleaning and tidying was completed, I extracted his scrawny naked body from her arms and lay him on my bare chest where he's been resting for three hours now. His warmth and my warmth have mingled together under Margaret's coat and I can't stop kissing him.

Lily stirs and an odd feeling comes over me; this morning we were two and this afternoon we're three. I don't think I understood the reality of what was making all those wiggles and nudges the past few months. It was a whole person. I was once a tiny baby in my father's arms and he counted my fingers and toes and guessed at what I'd look like when I grew up. I wish my father were here. I wonder if he's watching from . . . somewhere? I pull Paul in tighter to my chest.

"How are my boys?" Lily's groggy voice interrupts my thoughts. She flinches, turning on her side.

"Good. This snuggling a newborn thing is amazing. I think they should offer it as a treatment for depression." I wrap his little fingers around one of mine. "Just looking at these tiny fingernails makes me smile."

"You're such a first-time parent." Lily chuckles but I can read the adoration in her eyes when she watches Paul. She sees how special he is too.

"How are you feeling? Are you hungry? I have some mango and coconut all ready for you." I assess her as though I could determine internal bleeding or bacterial infection with a quick sweep of my eyes.

"I'm starving. Thank you for thinking of it, hon." She smiles up at me, her hands out to grab Paul. "Anyway, I need to hold this little boy some more. I could eat him up, he's so sweet." She nuzzles the sleeping infant into her chest, kissing little pecks along his face and neck.

Running, I scoop up the fruit medley I prepared earlier and offer it to Lily. She takes it, whispering a little "thank you." I have to kiss her, I can't wait any longer.

Lying beside her, I sneak in tight and first kiss Paul, who has a sweet smell to his feather-soft hair. Then, I lower my face to hers until our lips are barely centimeters apart.

"I love you, Lily." Her breath is warm against my lips. I want to breathe her in and let her fill me.

"I love you so much, David. So much," she gasps, and I hope she means it. I can't hold off anymore, self-control is so overrated. Closing the gap, our lips merge, but when her tongue sweeps across my lower lip and the sharp ridge of my teeth, I have to pull away.

"Where are you going, sailor?"

"You just had a baby, ma'am. I think there are rules about these things." My cheeks are warm. I can't believe I still blush around her.

"Not about kissing, silly."

"Well, I'd rather be safe than sorry. I saw what that kid did to you and, lemme tell you, it was a little violent. You and that little boy have one job for the next few weeks and that's to relax."

She tips her head from side to side. "There's no way I can stay cooped up in here for more than a day or two, plus, you know I don't like you fishing alone."

"I'll be fine." I try to chase away her concern, pretending I haven't said the same words to her before. "Anyway, I want to work on the SOS sign and the fire shelter."

"The SOS sign?" Paul starts to wiggle on her shoulder and she shifts him to the other side. "I thought we decided the sign was a waste of time?"

I put my hand on Paul's back. My fingers would almost meet if I tried to wrap them around his torso. How can a human being be so minuscule?

"I want to take him home."

"Home?" Lily blows a curl out of her eye. "This is his home, David. He was conceived here and he'll live here for the foreseeable future. Plus, we haven't seen one plane or boat or submarine, for that matter, in over a year. I don't think we have much of a chance of seeing one now, even if our SOS was highlighted in neon lights."

Paul's hair is dry now and frizzing up in the humidity. I caress it, probing the quarter-size soft spot on the top of his skull before responding. "I don't *want* him to grow up here, Lil. I want to take him home and lay him down to sleep in a crib in his own nursery and buy ridiculously expensive diapers and, one day, teach him how to ride a bike and throw a ball."

"*This* is Paul's island. We should be planning ways to help him adapt to life here, not dreaming about diapers and trikes."

"I agree, but I refuse to give up. I'm his dad and it's an evolutionary requirement that I want what's best for him."

"Of course I want Paul to have the best life possible," she says. "But I can't live in some fantasy world anymore, David."

Oh crap, I've made her cry, and not good, happy tears like when Paul was born but mad tears that rush down her cheeks.

"No, no . . . Oh, sweetie, I'm so sorry." I rush to wash away the wet trails on her face. Her cheeks feel a little warm and that alone sends panic through me. "Let me get you some water. You're hot." I left the water bottle down by the fishing log, darn it, but before I can sprint down to retrieve it, Lily puts her blazing hand in mine.

"Never mind me, I'm being hormonal. You work on that sign if it makes you feel better. I'm guessing they won't be parachuting to our beach anytime soon. Thank God." Her laugh trills in an odd, high-pitched way and I inspect her closer. She's sweating profusely, her hair soaked nearly through, like she'd recently been swimming. What's going on?

"Lily," I speak methodically, worried and frustrated at the same time, "why does that make you so relieved?"

Her smile drops and she frees one of her hands from under the baby to wipe at her dripping brow. "It doesn't make me happy, you know that. I want to go home more than almost anything but," she coughs, leaving me wishing for that bottle of water again, "it does make things a little less complicated."

"Complicated?" I scoff. Isn't this whole thing complicated? Hasn't it been complicated from the day we walked onto that plane? She's trying not to look at me and she bites the tip of her tongue. "You mean me and Paul, right? We're your complications."

All the air sucks out of my lungs. She doesn't love me like I love her. I've been making a fool of myself.

"That's not what I meant, you know it." She attempts to sit up a little, pushing through whatever pain she must be feeling. "I love you both, but what would I tell Jerry and the boys?"

"You tell them we fell in love and we helped each other survive. Then you tell them Paul's your son too and you don't regret him, because I'd like to believe you don't. Please tell me I'm right."

"You forget that in the real world we're married, and not to each other. Most of the time I do forget, but when you're setting up signal fires and SOS signs, it makes me remember." She swallows hard like she's trying to force down a half-chewed piece of meat. "Please don't make me remember, David. Not today." She clears her throat and swallows again before lowering herself onto the floor, her breathing shallow.

"Lil, you okay?" Something's wrong. Lily is pale as her sun-stained skin allows and her grip on Paul has gone lax. "Wake up, Lily! Wake up!" I scoop up the baby and place him in the small nest-like bed we made in the corner of the shelter in preparation for his arrival. He stays asleep like a champ.

Then, scampering on my hands and knees, I lean over Lily's listless body and pick up her limp wrist. A pulse. I don't take the time to count. It's so hot in here; her clothes are soaked through with sweat. Quickly, I put an arm under her shoulder and another under her legs and lift her up. I try not to notice how light she is, how frail she's become after growing our son.

Reaching the shade by the fishing log, I put her down on the cool sand, propping her up on the weatherworn wood. I grab the half-full bottle of water and press it to her lips.

"Drink, Lily, drink," I urge. Her eyes roll around behind her lids like she's trying to get them to open. Tipping the bottle up, I drizzle a little of the liquid into her partially open mouth. Her tongue runs over her teeth and lips like she's a baby wanting a bottle. I lift it again and this time she swallows as it trickles down her throat.

"Lily? Can you hear me?" I can barely see her though the tears swimming in my eyes. "Please, please wake up." Pulling her into my arms, I cradle her like I held Paul minutes ago. I force-feed her more mouthfuls of water until her eyelids flutter and her breathing slows.

"I feel funny," she stutters. "I'm so thirsty and tired. Why am I so tired?"

I wish I had an answer. The only thing I can think is that she's lost too much blood but I don't know how to help if that's true. In movies they'd rig up some kind of tubing and needle to do a transfusion, but I'm not sure if I remember my blood type correctly, much less what types of blood kill other people and what types save lives. For now, water will have to do.

"You could be dehydrated. You worked super-hard today and your body's very tired. Let's keep drinking and eating. I'll take care of you." I kiss her wet hair, the salty sweat stinging my cracked lips.

She pats my face, her hand as weak as a kitten's paw. "I know you will, David. You take care of me." I pull her arm down and place it across her body, refusing to let her expend any energy on me. She continues talking in a hushed whisper. "I'm sorry about before. You can work on your sign. You can do whatever you want. I do want to go home. Will you take me home, David?"

Sliding out from under her long eyelashes, tears fall down her face and land on her collarbone. I glare at them. She doesn't have any spare liquid to lose right now.

"I'll try, baby, I'll try. Shhh. No more talking until you feel better."

She nods. In the distance I hear a small cry, like a frightened kitten. Paul's awake. I pull off my shirt and ball it up. Then, as carefully as I can, I settle Lily down into the sand on her side, shirt under her head, face free of any obstructions.

I run up the beach and retrieve my son to find that he's soiled one of the makeshift diapers we fashioned out of leaves and coconut husks before he was born. They're huge on him, since apparently neither of us remembered how impossibly tiny newborn babies are. It hasn't done much to keep the mustardy goop from leaking out all over his back and scrawny, wrinkled legs.

I wash him quickly in the waves and slip on another diaper, adjusting it as best I can. Luckily, Margaret's coat remains clean and I wrap him up tightly in it before carrying him and a bowl of coconut milk down the beach to his mother. She hugs him tight before offering her breast to nurse.

I sit close by, in case she passes out again and I need to catch the baby. It's hard to sit still, leaving me too much time to think about this day, about my new responsibilities and fears. I think about all the *stuff* I have at home that I used to think was so important—my car, my house, my flat-screen TV, my iPod, my iPad. Then I look around here. I own nothing.

I think I'd rather have nothing. Possessions are so temporary, they can go up in flames like our plane, or sink to the bottom of the ocean like our luggage. All I have of importance here are Lily and Paul, and I wouldn't trade them for a million cars or houses or planes. But I guess important doesn't mean permanent, by any means.

Watching as Lily fights off sleep to feed our tiny newborn, I realize he may never go to a doctor or have real clothes or diapers. He'll be cold and hungry more than any father would want his son to be. And Lily will have to rest and pray that Mother Nature will heal her like she's supposed to, because there's nothing I can do. Nothing.

Suddenly they seem more fragile, more temporary, than one single pane of glass in my house or headlight in my car or piece of crystal in my china cabinet. Possessions are breakable, that's for sure, but they're also replaceable. People, people you love, are not.

I forget whatever chore I was going to work on and settle my arm around the pair. Lily lays her head on my shoulder and slips into a deep, drug-like sleep. I put my hand under Paul to make sure he doesn't fall, his tiny heart racing hard against the palm of my hand.

I'm glad Lily agrees with me—we need to take our little family home.

CHAPTER 29

LILLIAN

Present

"My recovery was very difficult after Paul was born. It took me a good six weeks before I could help Dave and Kent around camp again. I don't think I ever fully recovered until receiving proper medical treatment at home." Lillian paused thoughtfully and added, "Like I mentioned earlier, it was soon after Paul's birth that Kent drowned."

"How did Paul fit into your daily life? Was it hard to adapt to tending to an infant's needs in such primitive conditions?" Genevieve sat on the edge of her seat. She was enjoying this. Is this why the reporter had picked Lillian's story? Was it because of Paul?

"He was such a good baby. He was very laid-back and loved to sleep in our arms. He'd sleep snuggled in between all of us at night so we could keep him warm. I was able to nurse him, so food was no problem as long as I ate and drank enough. We were very lucky."

Lillian was surprised at how easy it was to talk about Paul's birth and his time on the island. In the past she'd tear up just saying his name. She took it as a good sign, that she was healing.

She'd always wondered why it was so hard to talk about him. She loved Paul as much as her other children. Having him grow inside of her and then live in her arms and grow from the milk she fed him was one of the most rewarding things she'd ever done. It shouldn't be hard to talk about having him. It should only be hard to talk about losing him.

"Describe him to us, Lillian." Genevieve's voice was creamy and soothing. Lillian could almost believe she cared and decided to pretend she did. After checking Jerry, who'd been meticulously cleaning his fingernails for the past twenty minutes, she closed her eyes, trying to remember that face she saw only in her dreams.

"He was very small. I don't know if he was smaller than my other kids or if he seemed small after not seeing babies for so long, but he felt like a feather in my arms." A sad smile flitted across her face when she opened her eyes. "He had lots of black hair, thick and curly just like his brothers. His eyes were very blue. The gray in them slowly disappeared after about a month and they were a brilliant blue, like the ocean. He'd just started to smile the day before he . . ." Her voice stopped like a motorcycle hitting a brick wall.

"I can tell this is difficult for you to talk about," Genevieve said, stating the obvious.

"Quite hard." She didn't like to think about that day and did anything in her power to keep her mind away from it, including taking those small white sleeping pills to chase her nightmares away.

"Before we talk about his last day, I have a different question for you."

A question? Shocker. Lillian set her teeth, hoping it looked like a smile and not a dog ready to snap.

"Okay, I'll try to answer it." She rubbed her fingertips together, cracking her knuckles in quick succession, praying she could stay Zen now that they were talking about Paul's passing.

"Why are you lying to me, Lillian?" Genevieve asked, keeping her nice "I understand you" voice on.

"What? I . . . what are you talking about?" Lillian stuttered, her stomach sinking like she'd swallowed a boulder. Her brain was on overdrive, quickly reviewing the whole interview. Where did she mess up and give it all away?

"This is what I'm thinking," the reporter said, making Lillian's mouth go dry and sticky. She'd give anything for a Diet Coke. She wasn't ready for this. "Something's off about this Paul story. At first I thought perhaps you and Dave made him up to make your story more interesting, but then I watched interviews with the two of you. Do you know what I realized?"

"What?" Lillian responded reflexively, feeling like an idiot as soon as the word left her mouth.

"You didn't arrive on that island pregnant, did you, Lillian?"

Terror hit in a giant deluge. She glanced at the door. If she left the heels behind, how long would it take to get over to Jill's house, hug her kids, and give in to this nagging desire to call Dave? She could take a flight out tonight, get a hotel room. He's the only one that understood.

Taking a deep breath through her nose, Lillian let the oxygen bring her back to sanity. Running would make her seem guilty, she told herself, and running wasn't an option. She had to figure out how to lie—better. Over Genevieve Randall's shoulder, Jerry was suddenly focused and aware of what was going on. As Lillian opened her mouth to counter, Jerry cleared his throat loudly.

"I think that's enough," Jerry projected. He stood up, buttoning his suit coat in a very lawyerly way that made Lillian remember the eager young law student she married twelve years ago.

"Excuse me, Mr. Linden, but I thought you didn't want to be involved in this interview." Genevieve kept her frigid gaze on Lillian. Jerry's heavy footsteps echoed off of the oak floor.

"I'm not speaking as Lillian's husband. I'm speaking as her lawyer. You'll cease this line of questioning or Mrs. Linden will be forced to end this interview prematurely." He spoke with a little more force this time, standing directly beside the reporter.

Cocking her head from side to side like a prize boxer before a match, Genevieve rolled the Sharpie she was holding in between her hands, squinting up at Jerry with silent resolution. Even Lillian saw the fury in Jerry's black eyes from where she was sitting. She bit the tip of her tongue thoughtfully. She liked this protective side of her husband, and if he told her to stop the interview, she would.

"Fine." Genevieve spat the word out like poison. "I'll change my 'line of questioning' if you insist, counselor."

"I do insist. I also insist that if one word of those defamatory statements are broadcast, you *will* have a libel suit on your hands."

Genevieve shuffled through her cards in a frenzy. Clearly, this had been her endgame—outing Lillian about Paul. What she knew, how much she knew, Lillian would probably never find out. And Jerry, of all people, saved her.

Dizzy with relief, Lillian smiled unabashedly at her husband, who was returning to his seat after staring down the furious Genevieve Randall. Once at his chair, Jerry unbuttoned his coat before sitting. Folding himself in the chair, Jerry placed his elbows on his knees and his face into his hands, rubbing his eyes like a tired toddler. When he finished, his lawyer face had disappeared and a new one replaced it. She'd only seen this look once before in their life together. It was fear.

The last time she saw that face was six and half months earlier, the day after the Carlton Yogurt gala. She and Dave had spent the whole day together, leaving Jill behind in the hotel room working on teacher reviews. Jill had no idea they'd been together. Of course, she wouldn't approve.

Jill had spent most of the limo ride back to their hotel, the walk to their room, and the twenty minutes it took to remove the heavy gown, scrub her face with cold cream and soap, and slip into pajamas, lecturing Lillian about her behavior at the gala. Lillian tried to be indignant or offended but she couldn't muster the energy, not when she knew what she was planning with Dave the next day. She grinned and patted her friend's sharp hair before climbing into bed, aware she only had a few short hours to rest before her important day.

"You're sure it's okay if I walk you all the way to your room?" Dave asked, still holding Lillian's hand as they walked down the red-carpeted hallway.

"Jill texted me this morning, she's visiting her cousin in Santa Monica and won't be back till late. We're safe." Butterflies tickled her rib cage thinking about the empty room. As natural as it felt, she promised herself she would *not* invite him in.

"I can't believe it's over. I've been looking forward to this day since we said good-bye in Guam. Now I have to say good-bye again." The firm pressure of his fingertips made Lillian think maybe he couldn't let go, or wouldn't. She didn't know if she liked that or if it scared her to death.

"I'll miss you too but at least we can talk on the phone. I got a new cell number under a different name so we can text." Lillian pointed to door 223, second to last in the hall. "Here we are." Her feet shuffled to a stop right before the door. She turned to face him, counting the pearly blue buttons on the front of his shirt.

"I have to leave you now, don't I?" he asked, taking a step closer to her, looping a chunk of hair behind her ear. Even the brush of his fingers on her earlobe made her shiver. How could he still make her feel this way?

"We might be getting a little greedy." She laughed, trying to make the butterflies disappear so she could walk away without doing something she'd regret. "Let me know how things are going with Beth. If you need me again, I might just happen to have another 'interview' in LA in a month or two."

Lillian flipped her free hand to accentuate her joke but she could tell Dave wasn't listening. He was watching her lips like a cat with a canary. A hot blush flooded her cheeks; clearly he was done being good. He took a bold step toward her, their torsos nearly touching.

She was frozen in place watching his black eyelashes as he traced the lines of her face like he was memorizing it. Nearly drunk on his scent, she needed every ounce of self-control not to cross that invisible line, the one she drew when she told him they had to lie. But she wanted to, she really, really wanted to.

Putting her hand on his chest, she tried to push him away but as soon as they connected, she knew it was a mistake. A current coursed between them, as if electricity was running through her arm to his chest. His gaze flew to hers; he could feel it too. She wanted to tell him "no," or at least back away, but she also wanted to taste him again. She leaned in ever so slightly, when the door opened behind her.

A whoosh of air sucked out the vacuum of tension hovering between them. Lillian yanked her hand away, wishing she could force her pulse to slow down. Jill would read it in her eyes, she was sure of it.

Dave jumped at least a foot backward, hands shoved in his pockets, when the door jerked open at full speed. Even Lillian thought his attempt at indifference came off as guilt.

"Lillian, there you are," a deep, familiar voice boomed in the silent hallway. Spinning on one foot, she found herself face-to-face with Jerry. Lines of worry carved his face, a five o'clock shadow growing on his normally clean-shaven chin. He was wearing a rumpled pair of gray dress pants and what looked like a brand-new white dress shirt with the fold lines still pressed in.

"Jerry! What in the . . . ? I had no idea you were coming." Lillian forced herself to smile.

"That's usually the point of a surprise," he said, slightly hostile. "I tried to surprise you at your interview this morning but imagine *my* surprise when they told me you weren't scheduled for an interview today."

"Oh yeah. I ended up calling those in. It was a long night." Lillian bluffed the best she could. She couldn't tell him she'd never intended to go to those interviews, that they were just a cover so she could be with Dave.

"Yes," Jerry talked through gritted teeth. "So I heard."

Jill has such a big mouth, Lillian thought.

"Where's Jill?" Lillian asked aloud.

"She went home, to her family." Jerry tipped his head around the doorframe. "She said you two had a nice talk, isn't that right, Dave? Or should I call you David?"

"It's nice to see you again, Jerry. I've heard so much about you." Dave didn't move, just gave Jerry a sidelong glance before continuing. "And please, call me Dave." Dave folded his arms across his chest, the veins in his forearms bulging like he was lifting fifty-pound weights.

When Jerry spoke again, the skin on his jaw was so tight Lillian was afraid it'd burst. "Lillian, I'd love to know where you've been all day?"

"We called in our interviews and then Dave showed me around LA." She was thinking on her feet. What would sound like the most benign outing for two old friends? "He showed me his dad's old floral shop and then we went out to lunch at Ricardo's. Ricardo, the owner, is his dad's oldest friend and then . . ."

"You can stop lying, Lillian. I can see it all over your face."

"I'm not lying, Jerry. Why would I lie?" Lillian panicked, her calm persona fading fast.

Dave must've seen it, or sensed it. He leaned his head against the hall's textured wall like this was a huge imposition and sighed. "You're embarrassing yourself, Jerry."

Jerry's head whipped to the left. He was angry, angrier than Lillian had ever seen him. His lips blanched white and he was breathing heavily. She had a sudden desire to put herself in between the two men.

"*I'm* embarrassing myself, *David*? You've got to be kidding me." Jerry growled, fists clenching and unclenching by his side like he wanted to punch something. As far as she knew, Jerry'd never been in a fight before, not a physical one at least. He was always the even-tempered one, the one to consider things logically and analytically. He was nowhere close to calm at that moment. Dave wasn't helping matters.

"This isn't what you're making it out to be," Dave said, sounding bored. "You have no idea what's going on here, do you?" He shoved his hands deeper into the pockets of his jeans and stood up straight, giving Jerry a blazingly condescending look.

"Do you think I'm stupid, *David,* or just gullible?" Jerry took a step toward Dave, crossing the threshold of the hotel room for the first time. "I've seen all your phone calls. I know how many, what time, how long. I know you must wait until your wife's asleep to call *my* wife. After talking to Jill, I also know you aren't even apologetic for it. So what is it? Stupid or gullible?"

"I pick . . . incompetent." Dave's hands came out of his pockets and hung at his sides as though he knew he was asking for trouble. Jerry tipped back on his heels like a long jumper at the Olympics. Lillian needed to do something.

"Dave! Jerry! Stop!" Her voice echoed through the empty hallway. Both men looked at her as though they'd forgotten she was there. Sliding her body between them, hand on each man's bicep, she glanced up at both sets of glaring eyes, one black as night, the other blue as the island's lagoon. "Let's not make a scene. If you want to talk, Jerry, let's go inside and talk like adults."

Jerry grabbed her hand from his arm and wrapped his fingers around her wrist. "I'm not inviting that man anywhere."

"Excuse me, sir, but I'd take my hand off her if I were you." Dave leaned over her, pushing against her flat, firm palm.

"David," she said, slipping back to her nickname for him. Today he looked like a biblical David, his brow set with determination and righteous indignation. She knew that if it were up to him, they'd tell Jerry the truth and see where the chips fell. But not Lillian. She wasn't ready. "I can handle this. I promise. Give us one second, please."

His heart was beating so fast she couldn't keep count, and those eyes, wet with a touch of desperation. "Are you sure, Lily? Don't let him bully you."

"Bully her? You have some nerve." Jerry shook his head but didn't advance.

"I'm fine," she said.

Ignoring Jerry's existence, Dave took her hand in his, as though trying to take her with him. She tilted her head to the side, staring into his smooth face, trying not to remember.

But she did. All the happy times she'd tried to forget galloped through her memory like a thoroughbred at full speed. His arms, his lips, his skin, his courage, his determination, his loyalty. The way he held her all night and laughed with her all day and how he loved their son with every bit of his heart. Worst of all, she saw Paul in his face and when he moved away from her hand, it was hard to let him go.

She turned nervously to face Jerry. When she found the nerve to check his face, she was surprised at how the anger had drained out of it. He was pale with dark bags sagging under his eyes.

"I can't do this anymore, Lil," he exhaled. "First, I thought you were dead and I was devastated." He traced the high arch of Lillian's cheekbones with his fingertips. "I finally get you home and now I'm losing you again. To him." He cocked his head to the side, pointing with his raised eyebrows.

"To Dave?" she asked, knowing the answer already. "Dave's my friend, Jer. I care about him deeply, but we're not together."

"You say that but then you spend half your time on the phone with him, talking about who knows what. Then you fly across the country and lie about interviews just so you can see him." He lowered his voice. "You won't sleep in the same bed with me. How am I supposed to feel about that?"

Lillian checked to see if Dave was listening. He was sprawled against the wall in his defensive stance, but she could tell he was listening to every word.

"What else can I say, Jerry? Dave and I aren't having an affair. Simple as that. Dave and Beth are working on their marriage, going to a counselor." She took a step toward him. "Maybe we could try it too."

"I'll bet he doesn't tell his counselor that he spends hours talking to another woman on the phone at night." Jerry raised his voice, aiming it at Dave, who shifted his weight from one foot to the other like he was itching to respond to Jerry's barbs.

"It's not romantic," Lillian explained. "I need him because he is the only person who knows what I've been through."

That made Jerry shake his head. "That's so not fair, Lillian. How can I know what you've been through if you won't even talk to me about it?"

"Talk to you? You've never shown any interest in listening. Anytime I bring up Paul you tune me out or change the subject. And Dave *was with* Paul. He has memories of him, alive. I need someone else to remember that my baby Paul existed and that he died, in my arms." Lillian bit the inside of her cheeks till the taste of blood touched her tongue. She wouldn't cry for him again, not in front of Dave who wasn't allowed tears for his own son.

Jerry shook his head, mournfully. "I'll make this simple, Lillian: *David* or me? I don't mean me and the boys—I mean just me. Am I enough for you? No more midnight phone calls or clandestine meetings. It ends now, or"—his voice caught and he cleared it—"or we're done."

He stared at her, fear stamped on his face, like he was already certain of her reply. If Jerry cried, Lillian didn't know what she'd do.

The world froze in a misty haze around Lillian, like time slowed down but she was still at full speed. So she had to choose. Jerry, who she'd been married to for twelve years, the father of her children, who knew what she needed better than she knew herself? Or, Dave, who she was drawn to as though she were trapped in the kind of invisible force field from Josh's sci-fi movies, with whom she'd scrambled to survive, had a child against all odds, and witnessed death—the one person in the world she knew would always protect her, no matter what came her way?

This was so unfair. If it had been three months ago or even two, Lillian may have faltered, remembering that vision she had in the hospital after their rescue, those images of her life with Dave. But after today? No. Dave was with Beth and she was with Jerry.

Lillian dared check on Dave one more time before giving her final answer. He was squinting at the ceiling lights and it wasn't fear or even hope she saw there, it was resignation—and what also looked like shame. Jerry was worried she'd pick Dave but clearly Dave already knew who she'd go home with.

She looked back at her husband and whispered, "I choose you."

CHAPTER 30
LILY-DAY 589

The Island

The sand is so hot it burns my cheek, but I can't feel it. That's not true, I *do* feel it but I also deserve it. I press my face farther into the superheated granules, wishing I could hear his little squealy seagull cry one more time if I just dug deep enough.

Even after a month I can't stand how quiet it is with just David and me. I don't know why it's so hard to get used to. Paul was only here three months, a blink of an eye in the context of my whole life, but once he was here, it felt like he'd always been here. Now he's gone; I feel like I'm dead too.

I can't sleep in the shelter anymore. That's where it happened, where he took his last breath. I wasn't even awake to see it. My baby slept in my arms as he had every night since he was born. But at some point in the night he stopped breathing, and by the time I noticed, my breasts were engorged with milk and my tiny son was cold and blue in my arms.

My scream woke David. To see a man who found such fulfillment in fatherhood lose his reason for being, it was almost like I saw two people die that day. David says he doesn't blame me but I don't believe him. *I* blame me so how could he not? What kind of mother sleeps through the death of her child? Even if there was nothing I could do, which I'm not completely certain of, I wish I could've been there, to look into his eyes one more time and kiss his face while it was still pink and warm.

Instead, the memory of his stiffening, discolored body haunts me. I almost can't remember what he looked like before. I want to ask David. I want him to remind me of his rich black hair that was soft as cashmere and smelled more beautiful than any flower on our island. I want him to tell me about Paul's crooked smile that we had to work so hard to see but gave us more entertainment than any movie or television show ever could. I remember telling David, with all the sage advice of a seasoned mother, "Don't worry—soon he'll be smiling all the time." God, I hate being wrong.

If I could've switched places with Paul right at that moment, I would've. I've begged God for that exact thing thousands of times. It hasn't happened yet and I'm starting to think it won't. I don't get what I ask for. I certainly didn't ask for any of this.

I was living quietly as a Missouri housewife, clipping coupons, running the kids to and from sports practices, and perhaps participating in some yoga in my spare time. Occasionally I hoped that one day, when the kids were older, I'd go back to teaching like Jill was always begging me. Every day was a lot like the next, a blissful blur of family, chores, and homework. I used to think it was boring, that I was boring. But now I want it back. I'd rather live in a blur than live here.

Instead, I'm perpetually stuck here on a beach I hate, staring into a sky I can't stand and washing in water I despise. On top of it all, I've turned into a person I don't even recognize; I'm a murderer, an adulteress, an abusive parent. If I could hang those labels in signs around my neck I'd feel better, not worse. I don't know what that wuss Hester Prynne was complaining about.

The sand has grown cool under my cheek. Even sand lets me down. A loud grumble protests from my empty stomach. I'm used to the hunger by now but I still hate that sound.

Eating's always been a chore on this island, so now I've decided to forego it as much as possible. It's easier to feel the pain of hunger than the pain of losing Paul. I guess that's why I push David away too. I shouldn't be happy and comforted in his arms while my infant son is dead.

I've considered a few solutions to ending my pain, one in particular that appeals to me, especially when David's close, his hand on my leg or our fingers touching when we clean out the fire pit. I don't think he'd help me, though. I could trick him into it. He wouldn't know until it was too late.

"Lily! Time for dinner!"

It's David. He's still pretending I eat food. We do this every day and it's becoming a tidy little routine. I burn my pain out on the sand above our son's grave and he throws himself into work so he can pretend he's not devastatingly heartbroken that he lost his only child.

Then he whips up some sort of gourmet island dinner I pretend to eat as he counts my nibbles. We load more wood on the fire and then sit by it in silence until I fall asleep and he crawls over to his side of the shelter, as if I'd ever put a foot back in there.

"Lily!" he shouts again. He's growing impatient. If I wait too long he'll come out here and that never turns out well.

"Good night, Paul," I whisper into the sand. It ripples away from me on the breeze before I reluctantly pull my body up, my old scar tight with sunburn.

Trudging up the berm toward the fire circle, I notice the tangled mess of hair has fallen over my face. I'm hoping I won't have to make eye contact. He thinks he hides the pain and worry well but he doesn't.

We barely talk anymore and I haven't heard him laugh since the day before I woke him with my screams.

"Come here, Lil, sit by me." He signals me over as though we were in a packed high school cafeteria instead of the only two people in the middle of nowhere.

"I'm not super-hungry right now," I lie. My mouth's watering at the smell of cooked fish. *Crap, I used to hate fish. Why does it have to smell so good?*

"I know, I know. Just like you weren't hungry for breakfast, or lunch, right?" He pats the spot next to him on the weatherworn tree trunk. "Keep me company and maybe you'll remember your appetite."

"Fine." I flop down next to him like a spoiled teen. "I'll eat when it's pizza."

"Promise? You know I'll find a way to make fish pizza, right?" David shoves a full coconut bowl of chopped up chunks of food into my hands.

"Good luck with that one. Pizza isn't pizza without cheese." I put the brimming shell down on the other side of me as fast as I can, avoiding temptation and finding a tiny bit of enjoyment from the protests of my empty stomach.

"You burned your face again." His worried eyes are working me over again, that line developing between his eyebrows. He touches my scorched cheekbone and even the light pressure of his fingertips makes me flinch.

"It's a first-degree burn. I'll be fine."

His face gets hard and I can tell he's grinding his teeth. He always does that when he's trying not to fight. We never used to fight. Now we have the same argument every day.

"I'm gonna say it even though I know you don't want me to." He speaks slowly, seemingly unworried about his food getting cold. "You're the only thing I have left I remotely care about. I need you to stop hurting yourself. If you won't stop for you, stop for me." He slides his hand into that special place at the base of my skull where his fingers belonged.

The tiny caress makes my pulse race in that embarrassing way it always has when David touches me. I don't want to think about David and me and our whole island history. I want to think about anything else, the way my empty stomach churns hungrily against itself, or the sting of my burned skin. If we talk about this we'll talk about Paul and everything else we've lost because of this damned island.

"I can't stop. I can't be happy. I don't deserve it," I mumble, but my body betrays me, responding automatically to his touch. I lean into his hand, rubbing my sand-burned face against his warm skin.

"I don't expect you to forget him but it's okay to be happy sometimes. After my dad died I had a hard time getting out of bed in the morning and remembering that the only person who ever truly cared for me was gone. I felt guilty laughing at a TV show or having a good time with my friends. It took me a while to realize he wouldn't want me to go into hibernation. He loved me. He'd be glad to know I was happy."

As I listen, in some ways I know he's right. These are the same reasons I didn't feel bad about my relationship with David. I knew that if I couldn't be with them, my family would want me to be happy without them. And as much as it hurts, I hope Jerry will eventually find someone to love with welcoming arms and a big heart who'll give my boys the attention and care I can't. But this is different.

"Paul was an infant. All he wanted was to be taken care of and clearly I didn't do that well enough."

"It wasn't your fault. He died. He just died. It could've happened in his crib in an air-conditioned nursery in Missouri. Sometimes babies die. I hate it. But what're you going to do, punish yourself forever?" He lets his hands slip to my shoulders where they rise up and down as I shrug.

"I don't know. I've never felt this way before. I don't know how long it lasts." My voice quivers. I have to stop talking or I'll cry. If I cry now, I may never stop.

He pulls me into his arms and I press my face against his bare shoulder. His skin is almost as hot as the sand but it burns in a totally different way. This passionate connection between us reminds me of my idea, the one that might make the pain go away, if I can get him to agree. I'm fairly certain he won't, but I can try.

Rolling my head toward his face I brush my lips against his collarbone, letting the thrill of touching his flawless brown skin flash though my body like lightning. His arms tense ever so slightly, which brings me closer to him. I don't hold back. Leaving a trail of kisses behind me, I follow the line of his neck and jaw before pulling him into a fierce, needy kiss.

If he hesitates I can't tell because he takes me in, hungry, and when we're touching, pulling, grasping at each other, I feel nothing but a pumped-up sensual high. It's amazing. This might work.

I'd almost forgotten how good we are together. His hands know exactly where I need them to go. He moves down my neck, and shoulder, toward my breasts. His breathing's heavy and I can tell he's missed me as much as I've missed him.

When his mouth returns to mine I slide my hands down his taut back until I reach the loose waistband of his khakis. He's tied them with a piece of material he salvaged when he cut off the bottom half of his pant legs. Following the crude belt around to the front, I fumble with the square knot that keeps the pants in place, finding it difficult without looking. It only takes a moment of distraction for him to notice. His rough hand wraps around mine like a vise.

"What are you doing, Lily?"

"What does it look like I'm doing?" I ask, trying to remember how to flirt.

He tosses my hand away and stands up as if he's going to run. "Sorry, Lil, I'm not up for that today."

"Don't you miss us being together, David? You can't tell me you didn't enjoy it. Don't you want me anymore?"

"It's not about what I *want* now, it's about what's right and what's safe. I can't put my physical desires above your safety ever again. I won't risk your life with another pregnancy." He pulls the loops on his belt with a snap, tugging the loosened knot back into place.

"Would it be that bad, David?" I snap back, suddenly energized by the idea. "Another baby? I know it wouldn't be Paul but we were so happy when we had a baby to love together. As for the pregnancy, I did it before, so I know I could do it again and if something went wrong . . . at least I'd be off this island."

He freezes. "You didn't just say that. Please, don't tell me you came over here to seduce me so I could knock you up?"

"You *said* you want me to be happy. I've been thinking about it a lot. This would make me happy." Hearing the words out loud I realize I sound insane, totally bonkers, but I want the emptiness to go away. I don't know if this will work, but I want it to.

He thinks I'm crazy too; disgust and pity show on his face. I cover my eyes. I don't want to see. If David hates me I've lost everything. Everything.

"It won't be the same, Lillian." The sound of my old name shocks me and even makes me feel gross.

"I know," I mumble into my palms. And it hits me. My baby's gone. Forever. I can't make a new one as though he's a toy I can order online when a piece breaks. He's never ever coming back and it'll always hurt. Always. A pathetic sob stutters out and the shame of what I've become nearly chokes me.

It takes all the energy I have left not to collapse on the ground and cry like a toddler having a temper tantrum. I want to kick my feet and scream at the top of my lungs, *It's not FAIR!* because it's not.

What I need right now is David. He's my medicine, the one person who's been through everything I have, and more. I need his arms and his sweet words. He's always here for me, and without realizing it I'm waiting for him to hold me. I drop my hands and look around. The sun is setting and the fire's reaching up toward the sky. David's gone. If I squint I can see him, far out in the water, his head bobbing up and down, swimming. Congratulations, Lillian, you make the only person who still loves you disappear. I'll make this up to him one day, losing his baby, going totally crazy, making him become my perpetual caregiver. But not today. I'm not strong enough yet.

My stomach growls angrily and it hurts this time. There's the bowl of food beside me; cold fish has never looked so good. I pick it up, my hand shaking so badly the lumps of fish jiggle around in the shell. Hesitating, I snatch one piece of charred flesh and toss it in my mouth. The delicate salty sweet flake nearly dissolves on my tongue and my mouth floods with saliva at the taste of real food. What would it be like to have a stomach full of food again?

Then the shelter catches my eye. The mat is still there, covering the spot where I used to sleep with Paul, David snuggled up beside us. My fingers dig into the thin coconut shell. If I wasn't half starved it might've broken in my hand. Instead I take it and throw it in the fire, the precious food taking a moment to catch and turn black.

Who am I kidding? David's better off without me. The sun's ready to sink beyond the horizon, off to shine on my family on the other side of the world. David crawls out of the ocean, water dripping off his cutoffs. At least he's remembered that this is when the sharks come out.

I need to be gone before he comes to dry off by the fire. I can't look at him after his rejection. I toss another log on the fire and double-check that all evidence is burned to a crisp. Then I throw on Margaret's old coat, which still smells like Paul, and head down the beach and the peninsula. The sand will be cold now, and after tasting dinner I'm hungrier than I've been in days, but I deserve this ceaseless hunger.

CHAPTER 31

DAVE

Present

"Looking back on this whole thing, Dave, what's your biggest regret? What's the one thing you wish you could change?" Genevieve placed a bony knuckle under her chin. It'd been a long day and the stress was starting to make Dave loopy.

"I'd say . . . that the plane wouldn't have crashed, Ms. Randall." Dave snickered along with half of the crew. Even Beth was smiling smugly, sitting literally on the edge of her seat waiting for the interview to conclude. One look at Genevieve Randall pulled the smile off Dave's face. She didn't get the joke, or if she did, she didn't find it funny—at all.

"Yes, indeed." Her attempt at a smile was painful and brief before she gave her question one last shot. "Would you change it, Dave, or do you think this is something that had to happen?"

He opened his mouth to answer but nothing came out. Would he change it if he could? He'd discovered what it was like to love and be loved, he'd become a father, and even when he came home he found his lessons followed him. After some work and rough spots, he and Beth were making things work. His little son would be born in a few months, in a hospital, with a doctor. Would he change that? No. But could he ever admit that, out loud, to Genevieve Randall?

"If I could go back in time and cancel the Dream Trip promotion, I would. Margaret, Theresa, Kent, Paul, they'd all be alive. Period."

Genevieve Randall nodded and rolled through her cards one last time. Tapping them into a neat pile, she shoved them under her thigh and crossed her hands in her lap. "Thank you, Dave, for the interview. It was very enlightening." Sighing deeply she put on a stiff smile. "I hope you enjoy watching the final product in a few months."

Dave's eyebrows shot up, shocked and relieved. It was over. "Thank you, Ms. Randall. I look forward to it."

He'd done it. Gotten through the interview. And though Genevieve Randall had been aggressive and a thin film of cynicism coated almost every question, his secrets were still safe. He didn't care how much he'd loved Lillian or what they did together in LA when she'd visited, he was never doing another interview in his whole life.

There must've been some secret signal he didn't see but within seconds the room dimmed as the extra lighting was removed and cameras and cables packed up. A sound guy retrieved Dave's mic. When he stood up from the couch free of wires, he felt like he'd been released from prison.

Stretching his arms up above his head, he twisted his tight torso and searched for Beth. She was across the room talking to intern Ralph, probably making small talk and counting the seconds till all the people would get out of her house. Dave was about to take a step toward the pair when the lean, severe-looking reporter intercepted him.

"Well, David, you did it. Congratulations. It's over and you've kept all your little secrets." She glowered at him with unconcealed hatred. He'd seen plenty of Genevieve Randall faces through their interview but never this one.

"Uhhhhh, I'm not sure what you're referring to, Ms. Randall," Dave said.

"I mean, you did have some help." She sniffed and rubbed her nose, her fingers stained yellow from nicotine. "You have to give them credit too. Mr. and Mrs. Linden. Or should I say Counselor Linden and his little injunction?"

"I'm completely lost." Dave's head spun. "I haven't spoken to either of the Lindens in months."

She dug one shiny manicured nail into his shoulder, huffing. "This could've been Emmy-winning television, can't you see? If you'd just been honest. Now, it'll be just another fluff piece." She took a step closer to Dave, her stale cigarette breath puffing in his face. "What I don't get is why they keep covering for you."

"The cameras are off. I don't want to talk to you anymore. Please let me go to my wife." He eyed Beth longingly, silently begging her to look at him. But Beth kept talking, her hair bobbing with every friendly laugh. Man, that Ralph kid was getting on his nerves.

Genevieve Randall wasn't about to release him. "I'll let you go if you can admit it. It's so easy to see. And I think I've laid enough ground-work that even with the injunction, most semi-intelligent people will see through your lies. They're written all over your face." She clicked and unclicked the cap on the Sharpie in her hand over and over again, the sound getting in his head, each click echoing, *she knows, she knows.*

"Okay, you've got my attention," Dave said, no longer glancing around the room, his eyes locked on Genevieve's face. "I know you want to say it out loud, so please, go ahead." Dave went from want-ing Beth to be by his side to hoping she'd stay away until the reporter finished her confrontation. Genevieve took a deep breath, and Dave shoved his hands in his pockets, ready for the worst.

"I honestly can't believe you've gotten away with it this long. I can see it any time you say her name. You fell in love with her, didn't you? I don't know how long it took for it to happen but I know it did. Did she ever love you back, I wonder?" She searched his face as though she could find the answers there. "I can't read her as easily as I can read you."

Dave's short list of people he hated, the one that contained Kent, had grown by one person—Genevieve Randall. What a power-hungry, fame-seeking wretch. "This isn't a conversation. I'll listen but I won't be answering any questions. Not one."

"You already have, David." She said his name vengefully as though it were a nasty swear word. "I've figured it out. Like I said, you fell in love with Lillian and then she went and fell in love with Kent."

His lips twitched when he tried to hold them in a straight line as she continued, her face alight with more animation than she'd shown over the whole long interview session.

"You should've seen the way she cried in her interview when she talked about losing Kent. Sobbed, really." Genevieve Randall grinned like a satisfied cat, looking for a reaction. "And you . . . in our interviews you couldn't contain your hatred of Kent. It's clear you were eaten up with jealousy and when she had his child, you took matters into your own hands and murdered him in cold blood and then disposed of his body. Lillian, afraid of your temper and in desperate need of a caregiver once Kent was gone, agreed to go along with your lies. That's why you don't want Paul's body removed from the island and that's why you and Lillian are estranged though you put on a pretty good act in public at the Carlton Ball. You killed the man she loved and she can never forgive you."

She stared at him. The furious clicking had stopped and Dave thought she was trembling in anger. So this was what she'd been hinting at all day? This was the story she'd been dying to break and it was wrong . . . so wrong.

"That's a very interesting theory, Ms. Randall." Dave coughed to cover a laugh. "I'm sure you feel better now that you got that off your mind." He smiled politely, feeling like he could do a little dance. "Now if you'd please excuse me, I'd like to get started on my resolution to never speak to you again, ever."

Genevieve Randall gathered up her cards and her papers and her briefcase and left in a huff, sputtering about "the truth" and "fighting them in court." Dave shook his head. The infamous Ms. Randall, hard-edged investigative reporter, had been different than he expected. Smart? Yes. Ruthless? Yes. Correct? Not even close.

As he watched the hanging light fixture swing from the force of her exit, a horrible realization swept over him. If a journalist who'd met two sitting presidents, won a Peabody award and three Emmys, and interviewed terrorists, rapists, and murderers for a living could get his secrets so wrong, what did Beth think of his story?

Beth was finishing up with Ralph. Dave strode quickly across the room where he wrapped his arms around his stunned wife.

"I've wanted to do this all day," he said into her strawberry scented curls.

"I've wanted you to do this all day," she laughed, slipping her arms around his waist, her tiny belly pushing against him as if their whole family was in on the hug. Her head didn't even reach Dave's shoulder.

He searched for any remnants of suspicion or pain or anger, but found none. "I'm so done with that. If I live my whole life without speaking to another reporter, I'll be happy."

Beth scrunched her nose and smiled. "Sorry, I may have signed you up for one last interview."

"What?" Was that what she was talking to Ralph about?

"I invited them back after the baby's born."

Dave knew he had to be careful. He couldn't let on that he was hiding something but he also couldn't stand the thought of spending one more second in the same room with Genevieve Randall. Who knows what kind of accusations she'd have spinning in her head by then?

Beth seemed to notice something was off. "It's not a real interview, I promise. They asked to come and take some shots of us, with the baby. You know, to show how happy we are now."

"Ah, so no questions?"

She shook her head. "Nope, just you, me, and our baby. That sounds okay, right?"

"Pictures with you and the baby? I'd love it."

CHAPTER 32

LILLIAN

Six Months Later

Why she'd thought it was a good idea to invite people over to watch the *Headline News* premiere of their story, Lillian would never know. They'd titled it *Nightmare in Paradise*, which she found a tad melodramatic. But it fit with the tone of the whole piece, a big ol' mess of melodrama.

It'd been a full six months since Genevieve Randall had come to their house but it felt like years. The program was supposed to run in June, the one-year anniversary of the rescue, but because of the ongoing lawsuit it had been pushed back to the end of the summer.

In the end, *Headline News* gave up the battle. Jerry said the news program probably would have won on freedom of speech. But, Lillian guessed that her little story wasn't worth hundreds of thousands of dollars in legal fees. Or, maybe they realized the story had plenty of sensationalism already and the parts Ms. Randall wanted to extrapolate were actually unnecessary?

Whatever it was, it felt like they'd never see the completed program, so when Ralph called last week, explaining that they were scheduled to air, Lillian could hardly believe it. News spread fast in their little subdivision and everyone wanted to talk about the premiere. So instead of dealing with a hundred different questions, they decided to make a party out of it. Dashing off a quick e-mail, Lillian invited a few family members and neighbors.

That night, they let Josh and Daniel stay up a little late and join all the people gathered in their basement rec room. Once the show started, everything went by in fast-forward. The montage talking about the crash, the summary of events, and the stunningly boring interviews with the survivors were a blur. Every time they zoomed in on her face on that seventy-inch flat-screen monstrosity Jerry got when he'd been a widower, every line and pore were magnified. By the end of the night she'd decided HD wasn't her friend, but HD made the island look like paradise. In one segment they'd done a special zoom effect where the camera backed out farther and farther into the sky until her island disappeared among the vast ocean surrounding it. It felt like the same thing was happening in her life. The more time she spent off of the island, the more it blurred into the years before and after it. Some days she forgot about that part of her life entirely. But not today. Today she could remember every detail, the red-veined plants that surrounded camp, the itchy bites of the tiny brown sand fleas that snacked on her ankles, the smell of smoldering bamboo. Every kiss, every cut, every tear. She forced herself to watch anyway.

Dave looked amazingly normal in his interviews. His skin was a rich golden brown, close to the toasty caramel he'd been on the island, and his straight teeth shone like polished marble. Even if she'd never been in love with him, it was clear that he was gorgeous. At the same time, he didn't look like *her* David. Her David had more facial hair than Blackbeard. Even jittery and somewhat annoying Dave Hall from the plane had a nervous, insecure soft center that you'd never believe from looking at the self-assured, devastatingly handsome man on the screen.

Seeing Dave was surreal. If she squinted she could make out the remnants of the man she'd lived with. His rich baritone brought tears to her eyes and she had to turn away and pretend she'd forgotten something in the kitchen to keep everyone from noticing her reaction. It was that voice that brought her comfort through her worst trials, the voice that laughed and cried with her. Sometimes she wanted to hear it again, like wanting to listen to your favorite song over and over after not hearing it for a long time.

It'd been ten months since the ultimatum in the hotel hallway when she'd walked away and promised Jerry never to speak to him again. So many times her fingers had punched in the numbers, thumb hovering over the green Talk button, but every time she'd caught herself. Lying about a past that seemed increasingly surreal was one thing, but lying about real life? She was tired of being a liar.

The show was over fast, just an hour long, and between the commercials and snack breaks, Lillian felt like she did an above-average job keeping things under control. Even when they showed that final shot of Dave snuggling a dark-haired baby boy and Beth cooing at him in his father's arms, she let out an "Awww" with the rest of the group. They seemed very happy. It gave Lillian a conflicting rush of jealousy and relief; she didn't know which one was real.

Thankfully, everyone started to leave as soon as the credits rolled. Lillian's working theory was Jill had threatened them with physical harm if they dillydallied. Jill knew how to push her way into other people's business, but this time Lillian was glad for it.

After giving her last hug, she closed the door with a loud click and walked upstairs, intercepting Jerry as he was leaving the boys' room after putting Josh down in the bed beside his already-sleeping brother.

"Swear to me that we won't touch that mess until at least ten o'clock tomorrow morning," she whispered, wrapping her arms around his firm torso.

Jerry chuckled, kissing her on the nose. "As long as you promise you'll let me help. It's a big job for one person, learned that the hard way."

"Oh, don't worry," she said, pushing open the door to their bedroom, "it's going to be a whole family thing, and whether they like it or not, the boys are going to help too. Time's flying by. They'll be out of the house, living on their own, before we know it."

"Oh yes," Jerry joked, following her in. "Yale called, Josh is in. Full ride and everything."

"Great news!" Lillian laughed, flopping down on the bed, kicking off her tight heels. "But he'd better wait till he hears back from Harvard before he makes his final decision."

Jerry pulled off his belt and set it on the top of the dresser, then did the same with his watch. Untucking his blue polo from the top of his jeans, he sat down beside her to untie his Nikes. The bed squeaked and sunk just far enough that their shoulders touched. She let her head settle onto his shoulder.

"You did great tonight," he said, dropping his shoe to the floor with a thump.

"Everyone had a good time, didn't they?"

"You know that's not what I mean," Jerry whispered, bumping the top of her head with his. "Seeing Dave must've been rough."

She bit her lip. Why did they have to talk about Dave right now? They hadn't talked about him in a long time and it had been a good thing. This night was hard enough without being reminded of all the half-truths and bold-faced lies she told every day. She always had to lie about Dave, so even hearing his name made a pit of nervous guilt fill her midsection.

"It wasn't great but it's getting easier," she sighed. It was true; it was much easier to think about him now. Plus she hoped Jerry would drop it if she showed she was over *him*.

His hand crawled over the sage-and-white flowered bedspread to claim her hand. Her wedding ring, a plain shiny band just waiting for all those beautiful unavoidable scratches, dug into the top of her finger when he gave it a squeeze. Something about his silence was unfamiliar.

"That baby was cute, right?" Jerry asked, the subject suddenly changing.

Dave and Beth's baby. Of course, that's what this was about. Was he going to offer to have another baby, like he did every few months? Or perhaps he was playing the game of human lie detector, testing for some underlying jealousy hidden inside of her.

"He was beautiful," she answered, as blandly as she could, making sure her hand neither gripped his too hard nor loosened too much.

"Um," he stalled again, staring at a marinara stain on her jeans that had started to peel up. "Did he look like his brother?"

"Brother?" Had Jerry lost his memory that easily? "Dave and Beth don't have any other children, you know that."

He nodded. "I was talking about Paul."

The name sent a thrill through her but hearing the way Jerry said it made her instantly afraid. "What're you talking about?"

"You know what I'm talking about, don't you?" He didn't break eye contact.

She'd been lying about Paul so long it took half a second to understand what Jerry was saying.

"Oh my goodness . . ." she managed to say, her mouth opened in shock, ". . . you know."

She should've played it cool. She should've repeated the lie, but the way he said it made her realize Jerry would no longer believe her lies. This scared her so much she wanted to run.

"How?" she said, surprised he was still holding her hand. "How did you find out?"

"I've known the whole time." He almost smiled. "They told me in the hospital, while you were unconscious. I was your next of kin. I made all your medical decisions. When they told me you'd recently had a baby, I told them they were mistaken. Then"—he looked down as he relived this memory—"I saw the way Dave asked about you and spent every moment by your side. It was easy to put together what the doctors were saying and what I witnessed."

This was the moment she'd been dreading, someone finding out the truth about her and Dave, about Paul. It haunted her nights so she couldn't sleep and sat on her shoulders during the day so she couldn't be happy, she couldn't be normal, because someone might get close enough to find out.

"Oh, Jerry, I'm so sorry. Please forgive me," she pleaded, pulling his hand to her chest, against her heart.

He nodded, the corner of his mouth pulling up a millimeter. "I forgave you a long time ago."

"You should've told me you knew, Jerry. Why didn't you tell me? Do you know how badly I wanted to tell you? But I thought I'd lose you and the boys. I thought you'd hate me."

Jerry shook his head. "I don't hate you. I didn't even hate you back then. I kept waiting for you to tell me. When you didn't, I couldn't bring myself to say anything. I was too afraid you'd run off with Dave." That angry vein in his head started to swell. That meant his blood pressure was on the rise.

Lillian traced her cool fingers along the pounding vein. Under her touch, it started to slow. "If you forgave me," she asked gently, "why did you wait so long to say anything?"

"Because once we came home and all those news shows and reporters started to hound us, I finally saw why the lie was so important. If you told them about Dave and the baby, if we had to listen to it being talked about and judged on the screens of millions of viewers throughout the world, it would've killed our family." He kissed her palm before she reached around his neck, rubbing the short delicate hair that tapered off before the top of his collar. "You knew that, didn't you?"

"I had a very long time to think about it."

"You could've told me," Jerry said.

"I'm glad you know," she said before pulling him the last few inches to where their lips could meet in a short but tender kiss before Jerry held her away, his hands on either shoulder.

"You can't lie to me anymore. Promise," he pleaded.

"Never again." When the words left her mouth it was like a giant weight lifting.

Jerry put space between himself and Lillian, leaning against one of the bedposts. "Then I think you have something to tell me, don't you?" When he crossed his arms, Lillian was confused.

What further confession could he want? She had a lot of details to fill in but it seemed he had the gist. She'd had an affair with another man and had his child. She'd lied about this fact. The only other secret of any great significance was . . .

"How did you find out I killed Kent?" The words tripped out. If someone besides Dave told Jerry the truth, that meant her lies could no longer keep her safe.

"You did what?" he asked.

"Killed Kent, stabbed him, whatever. Who else knows?" She jumped to her feet . . . She had to call Dave. He'd be in as much trouble as she was.

"Lillian, I don't know what in the world you're talking about."

"You can't represent me, can you?" She crossed to her closet and pulled an empty suitcase from the top shelf. "You know someone good. Right, Jer? Or I could leave the country for a while." Throwing it on the bed she ran to her underwear drawer and started tossing every last bra inside.

He was by her side instantly, grabbing her elbow, shaking her just enough to break through her panic. "What're you doing, Lillian? I didn't say you killed *anyone*."

"But you said you wanted to know my other secret."

"I was talking about you visiting Dave in LA," he said, her overreaction scaring away the harshness. "*You* killed Kent?" Jerry took a step back. Now she'd done it.

"He was insane, Jerry, totally bonkers. He was always touching me, trying to do things. He found me alone once and tried to . . . He was going to . . ."

"Wait. He tried to rape you?" He was almost yelling. Lillian was afraid he'd wake the kids. "Why the HELL didn't you tell me?"

"I couldn't, Jerry. I *killed* him. I didn't want to make you an accomplice after the fact or whatever that was. You'd go to jail too. You could get disbarred."

"It sounds to me like it was self-defense." His lawyer brain was working.

"I don't know, Jerry. Dave tried to stop him and Kent was going to kill him so I . . . I stabbed him in the back." She bit her lip, waiting for the disgust she knew was coming. "I'm a murderer."

"That's not murder." Jerry touched her lips with his fingertip, compassion written in the wrinkles on his forehead. "Does anyone else know? Besides Dave?"

Lillian was surprised at the softness in his voice. "No. We lied, remember?"

"Good." He stared at her, silent for a moment. "What about the rape? Did he hurt you?"

She blew out a shaky breath. "He hurt me but he didn't rape me, if that's what you're asking. Hey, Jer." She took his hand. "I'm okay. We can talk about this later but right now I want to know what you meant about Dave and me in LA."

"Oh, that." He shoved the suitcase off the bed and placed her down as though she were a fragile piece of china that might shatter. "Dave. LA."

Lillian glimpsed herself in the mirror on the other side of the room. Her hair was growing, finally, and almost touched her shoulders; dark lines of mascara-stained tears snaked down her face. She wiped them with her fingers before grabbing the edge of the bedspread. Dave in LA. Easier than Kent but not by much.

"Before you start, that visit wasn't what you think it was," she said with a giant sniff, aware that she sounded like an incoherent idiot. She wiped her face, beyond caring that the blobs of mascara soaked into the white fabric. How she ever thought white a good color for anything in a house with kids, she'd never know.

"I know it wasn't." He climbed on the bed in front of her. He wasn't horrified, even though he'd just found out his wife was a murderer. "I had you followed."

"Followed?" Her mouth fell open. "Like by a detective?"

"I think they call themselves private investigators, but yeah, whatever you call them it means the same thing. I paid a man to follow you in LA and tell me what happened." He rubbed his forehead thoughtfully. "That sounds totally crazy when I say it out loud. You have to understand, I was insane with jealousy and certain that you were going to leave me any second. You'd think it'd be easier to accept that fact after living without you so long, but that made it harder." His hand rested on her knee and she covered it with her own. "I'll always love you."

"I love you too, Jerry." She let herself squeeze his hand affectionately before pleading. "I promised I wouldn't tell. He's kept his promises to me, I can't break mine."

Jerry didn't want to hear it. He slapped at the duvet cover. "Stop, Lillian. Would you listen? You don't have to tell, I figured it out, I have to admit"—he rubbed the angry vein on his forehead—"I was confused when the private investigator told me you two went to a fertility clinic. I couldn't figure it out. I thought that meant you were planning on being together, having a family. That's why I confronted you at the hotel."

"But I picked you," Lillian interrupted, leaning toward him till she could smell his cologne.

"I know. That threw me off. But I got this funny feeling when I talked to Beth and she told me how happy she and Dave were and how they were trying to start a family, and a strange thought stuck in my mind. Then, when I saw that baby tonight, it all made sense." He tapped his temple. "That baby they were holding, that's *your* baby, isn't it?" His look was hard and sharp.

"He's not my baby; he's Dave and Beth's baby." He put two fingers on her lips.

"You promised no more lies, Lillian. The truth."

She couldn't find any other way out. "The truth?" she asked, slowly.

"Yes. Genetically he's my son."

As soon as she handed over her last secret, she felt . . . free. She hadn't realized the weight of her lies had been holding her down so hard she could barely move, and even with Jerry sitting in front of her, angry and judgmental, she felt like singing.

"And that doesn't bother you?" Jerry asked.

"No, Jerry, it doesn't bother me. Beth's sterile so it had to be a donor. They were going to use a donor egg from a stranger and the thought of that killed me. Dave was a wonderful father to Paul and he said Beth had changed. If he's willing to forgive her, it must be true. I wanted to be the one to give them the chance to have some of the happiness we have with *our* boys. Plus, it helps me with missing Paul. I feel like a piece of him is living out there."

"Does she know?"

Lillian shook her head. "She doesn't know the identity of the donor."

He cocked his head to one side. "Don't you think she has the right to know?"

"The only reason Dave didn't tell her is because I asked him not to." She shrugged. "I thought it didn't matter since the donor was going to be anonymous anyway."

He seemed to consider her words for a second, looking small and too much like Josh for her to stay mad at him. She crawled across the bed and put her arms around him.

"I don't know what to think about this whole baby thing." He paused. "But I want you to know up front that, if it's okay with Dave and Beth, you can see him, Lillian. I won't keep you from your baby. I promise," Jerry whispered into the crease of her neck. She rubbed his back. "You must think I'm a monster if you thought you had to hide all this from me."

"I thought I was protecting you, but I was wrong, wasn't I?"

He nodded into her shoulder and then kissed it before holding her face in his hands; a little sniffle and some red around the eyes were the only sign he'd been emotional.

"We have a long night ahead. I want the whole story. The real one." He grabbed her iPhone off the bureau to his right. "And I think it's time that you call Dave and Beth."

"I can call Dave? Are you sure?" Lillian was stunned. She didn't know what changed inside her husband but she felt guilty she'd never thought him possible of it.

"Positive." He kissed her mouth before walking away, punching a few buttons on his phone to call the takeout place he still had on speed dial from his single-dad days. "Kung pao chicken?"

"Sounds great," she said. Watching him order their food, cross-legged on the bed, a growing warmth filled Lillian, multiplying exponentially by the second. In three years she'd lost her mother-in-law, her son, her integrity, and, most of all, her innocence. Running away from the truth hadn't worked super-well, maybe running toward it could.

Would the truth erase the past, leaving nothing more than a scar on her shoulder and some fading memories? Surely not, but telling it did seem to be bringing her back to being fully present in the life of her family better than any rescue helicopter or airplane. Finally.

She held the phone and looked at it a long while, the screen scratched up from when she let the boys play their apps. Then she knew she was ready. Tapping at the phone icon, she punched in the number she still knew by heart. It rang three times.

"Hello?" Dave answered. For a second her mouth felt full of marshmallows.

"Hi there," she responded, barely above a whisper.

"Lillian? Is that you?"

"Yup. I know it's been a while." Is that really all she could think of to say? Like they were old friends from high school who hadn't chatted since graduation? "We just watched *Headline News*."

He didn't respond. Lillian wasn't surprised. Why should he want to talk to her? She'd been so unfair to him. In the background, a woman's voice called her name. Beth.

"Dave! Is that Lillian? It is? Well, give me the phone, silly!" Lillian listened to the rustling before Beth's voice echoed through the receiver.

"Listen, I know I'm not supposed to know this but I've been dying to thank you for what you did for us." A little baby squealed close to the phone.

"He told you?" Lillian asked. Jerry was still ordering but held up an okay sign to check in. She nodded even though she wasn't sure if she was okay. Beth knew, Jerry knew. That had seemed "worst-case scenario" for so long that the knowledge was throwing her out of balance.

"I'm sorry, I know you wanted it anonymous but I made him tell me. It's a funny story actually . . ." The baby squawked, cutting Beth off. "Well, I'll have to tell you some other time. We'd love to visit eventually. I think it's great your boys and our son are half-brothers."

Beth wanted Lillian to know her son. She wanted Josh and Daniel to be a part of his life. "I'd love that." Lillian smiled.

"I tried to send you flowers after he was born but Dave wouldn't let me. I *told* him you'd love to know he was healthy." Relief cooled the drops of nervous perspiration on the back of her neck. He was healthy. Her son was safe. "You'll have to scold him for me, Lillian, all right?"

"Of course."

In the corner, Jerry hit the red End button and grabbed a sweat-shirt off the paisley armchair in the corner of the room. "Back in an hour," he mouthed, before slipping out the bedroom door. Did this mean he trusted her again?

Through the phone, the baby's cries went from annoyed to angry and Beth twittered nervously like the new mom she was. "Oh my, this boy is hungry. I'm going to have to pass you off to Dave." She paused and it sounded like she might be crying. "Lillian, really, thank you. I had no idea what it meant to be a mom. Don't worry, I promise I'll take care of him."

"I'm not worried, not one bit."

"Hey." Dave was back and his voice sounded different. "I'm sorry I broke my promise. After that horrible investigative reporter came to our house, I decided I had to tell Beth."

"So"—Lillian tried to speak calmly in case Beth was close enough to hear their conversation— "does she know *everything*?"

"No, only about you being the donor," he mumbled so no one could hear.

"Jerry knows it all," Lillian blurted out, feeling better after releas-ing the pressure.

Dave made a tsking sound followed by a deep sigh. "Just a second, I have to move into another room." He said something to Beth that Lillian couldn't make out, before returning to the phone, his breathing unsteady. "I know what I said in the hospital, about you coming to me when things didn't work out with Jerry, but . . . but I have to take it back, Lily. I'm happy with Beth and our baby. I can be your friend but I won't leave her."

Lillian laughed, pulling her legs up under her on the bed. "That sure is a little presumptuous of you, Mr. Hall. Who says I'd still want you anyway?"

"Wha . . . Oh crap. I did it again, didn't I? Why am I so good at embarrassing myself when I'm with you?"

"I don't know. I think it's a talent. Part of me wonders if you do it on purpose, just to make me smile." She'd missed this. In all the drama and the lying, Lillian had almost forgotten that before being lovers, she and Dave had been friends.

"Yes!" he said. "That's it! Totally on purpose."

"Good, because I'm not calling to ask you to leave your wife." She couldn't hold back one last chuckle. "I'm calling because I told Jerry, or more like—Jerry figured it all out. We're okay. It was his idea I call you. He was thinking eventually I'd want to meet the baby."

"That's great, Lily, so great." Dave let out a long breath, as if he'd been holding it. "Let's plan to get together over the holidays? Beth knows the schedule better than I do, so she'll probably be calling in a few days."

"I'll be looking forward to it." Awkward pause. "Well, enjoy the broadcast. It was . . . underwhelming. But the picture of you and Beth and the baby at the end—adorable."

"Thanks. They sent a professional photographer, so I'm sure that helped."

"You guys are a good-looking family; I don't think you need much help." Call waiting beeped. It must be Jerry, checking in. "I'd better let you get going so you don't miss it. Oh, wait! I forgot to ask you one thing." The phone beeped again but Lillian ignored it. "What did you name him?"

"His name is Solomon," he laughed, "like 'Solomon the Wise,' the king."

"Perfect," she said as old memories of a conversation on a beach flitted through her memory, the wisdom they both had gained from their life on the island. In that moment it did feel . . . perfect.

ACKNOWLEDGMENTS

To my friend Jeny Wasilewski, the first person to set eyes on this story, thank you for encouraging me to stop writing about a Southern belle and to keep writing about secrets, a plane crash, and sharks.

Thank you to Natalie Middleton, who forced me to share my secret novel with her and was always up for a reread. Without your encouragement I may never have had the courage to share *Wreckage* with the world.

To fellow author Lauri Fairbanks, you are the best writing buddy a girl could ask for. Thank you for putting up with texts day and night and inspiring me in more ways than I can list. I'll be forever grateful to pee-wee football and a Lego birthday party for bringing us together.

I'm also incredibly indebted to my critique partners and beta readers for their time, insights, and virtual therapy: Pete Meister, Mallory Crowe, Revo Boulanger, Samantha Newman, Elizabeth Owens and Michelle A. Barry. And to the writers on AQC, writing can be a lonely profession but I could never be lonely with all of you on my side.

Thank you to my wonderful agent, Marlene Stringer, for believing in me. Your experience and guidance is invaluable. Two of the most exciting days of my life also happened to be days I received phone calls from you.

Thank you to the hardworking team at Lake Union Publishing, including my visionary editor, Danielle Marshall. Thanks as well to Gabriella Van den Heuvel, Shannon Mitchell, and Thom Kephart. All the time, effort, and enthusiasm you put into making this book the best it could be is humbling and I've enjoyed every minute of it. Go Team!

Thank you to my family and friends for being more excited about this novel than I could've ever hoped for. You guys have no idea how much your exuberance means to me.

Thank you to my parents for always encouraging me and to my sister, Elizabeth Renda, for pushing me, pulling me, and loving me. I'm so lucky to have a little sister like you!

Thanks to my kids for understanding that their mother is a day-dreamer and that a computer on my lap is code for "I'm writing," and for calling me a writer long before I let myself say it out loud.

Most of all, thank you to my husband, Joe, for giving me a computer for Christmas two years ago and for telling me, "This is to help you to write your novel." You know my hopes and dreams better than anyone. Your confidence in me has opened my eyes to so many opportunities I never would've considered otherwise. I love you!

ABOUT THE AUTHOR

Photo © 2014 Angel Clark Photography

Emily Bleeker, a former educator, discovered a passion for writing after introducing Writer's Workshop to her students. She soon had a whole world of characters and stories living inside of her mind. It took a battle with a rare form of cancer to give her the courage to share that amazing world with others.

Emily lives in suburban Chicago with her husband and four kids. Between writing and being a mom she attempts to learn guitar, sings along to the radio (loudly), and embraces her newfound addiction to running. Connect with her or request a Skype visit with your book club at emilybleeker.wordpress.com.